Simply Sweet

Elaina Kellogg

Dedication

To my mom, who has encouraged me in all of life's adventures. From culinary school to writing, I wouldn't be where I am without you. Thanks for always being my first reader. My first cheerleader.

To my Dad, for your dry humor and tenacity. Your loyalty and unending support. For your easy way of simplifying the complexities that my brain can't sort out. You're always my rock in the storms of life.

Mere words can't express the gratitude and love I have for you both.

Contents

Acknowledgements

I need to give huge thanks and acknowledgement to Chelsea M. Brown, who made this book possible. Thank you for all your support, the mad dash critiques, and for being all around the best person. I don't know what I'd do without our weekly meet-ups.

As always, thank you to my husband and son for having Boys Night to give me writing time. You two are my world, and I am so lucky to have you. Love you forever and ever.

Mom, you already got the dedication, so I'll keep this short. Thank you!

And lastly, I've started doing something recently for myself that may seem a little odd to others, but it's been a big help with my mental health. I've started thanking past me for getting things done, and oddly, it's helped motivate me to keep moving forward. So, thank you past me for not giving up.

My dear, sweet reader,

Welcome to Fauna, Mississippi! Where the weather is hot and sticky, and so are the... pecan rolls! Come on now. What did you think I was going to say?

The first time I ever set foot in Mississippi was when my husband and I traveled there to look for a house. He'd just accepted a new job in Hattiesburg, and I was so nervous moving somewhere I'd never been. I'd always had this image of Mississippi in my mind that must have come from some ancient history textbook showing life during the Great Depression. When we arrived, it was nothing like I'd imagined. The landscape was gorgeous. It is full of beautiful cotton fields and tall, tall trees. They don't call it the Pine Belt for nothing!

After we'd lived there for a while, we took a weekend trip to Natchez, toured some of the plantation homes, and learned some of the local history. Something about the land right next to the great Mississippi River spoke to my soul.

The idea for Simply Sweet was born from a combination of my time working as a pastry chef and my joy at this new part of the country I was discovering. This story had been rolling around in my head for almost a decade before I decided to get it out onto the page.

I absolutely love small-town stories where you get to fall in love with a whole host of characters, and everyone is so interconnected that you couldn't have one person without the rest. The whole idea of people looking out for each other, as well as getting all up in each other's business, is so appealing to me. Why? Probably because I happen to be overly caring and nosy myself.

Kidding... about the nosy part.

What started as one story idea has morphed into the whole Flora & Fauna series. Simply Sweet is just the beginning for Fauna, Mississippi. I hope you fall in love with this magical little town as much as I have, because there's a lot more to come!

So, sit back. Grab some sweet tea and a cupcake, and enjoy.

Pastry Glossery

Croquembouche-
French for 'Crack in Mouth.' A tower of cream puffs, held together with carmelized sugar.

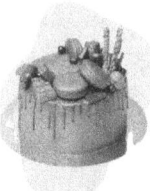

Ganache-
A smooth, creamy chocolate spread made by melting chocolate in hot cream and mixing until smooth.

Macaron-
A meringue based sandwich cookie made with almond flour. Can be filled with frostings or jams.

Pate a Choux-
A type of dough cooked on the stove-top, piped in desired shapes, and baked until hallow. Used for cream puffs, eclairs, etc.

Pavlova-
Named after the Russian ballerina Anna Pavlova, this is a meringue dessert. It is often called a cake and topped with whipped cream and fruit.

Petit Four-
A small dessert meant to be eaten in one or two bites. Often made of thin layers of cake and frosting or jam.

Spun Sugar-
Caramelized sugar, drizzled into thin strings. Used as decoration for desserts like croquembouche.

Chapter 1

T he Darlin' Diner was exactly as it had been almost twenty
years ago. The late summer sun glinted off its aluminum
siding, momentarily blinding Lexi as she staggered out of the
car. She felt all thirteen-hundred miles she'd driven over the
past two days as she stretched and rolled her shoulders.

The Mississippi air was heavy with humidity and the scent
of plants and earth. No other place smelled like this, smelled
so green. Lexi took a deep breath and smoothed her skirt
before heading toward the entrance. The neon red and blue
'Open' sign flashed in the front window as she pulled open the
door.

Lexi paused after she stepped through the doorway. The
drastic change between the steamy outside and the air-condi-
tioned inside was shocking. She debated turning back to grab
a sweater, but excitement pushed her in further.

She slid into the first booth on the right, just like she'd done
as a little girl. The cherry-red vinyl seat had faded slightly from
years of sun pouring through the windows. Her fingers ca-
ressed the tear down the center of the bench, a smile tugging
at her lips. Excitement and nervousness wrestled inside her,
twisting her stomach into knots.

"Can I help you?"

Lexi looked up at the waitress in her polka-dot uniform and apron, its cut very similar to her own vintage-inspired dress.

"Yes, Rosita," Lexi read her nametag, "I'd like a grilled cheese, please."

"Just a grilled cheese?"

"Do you still do Free Fry-day?" Lexi said in a low voice, looking around, not wanting to share the secret, but the diner was practically empty since she'd arrived in those odd hours between breakfast and lunch.

"Free Fry-day?" Rosita looked confused. "Um, no."

"Ok. Well, I'll get fries too." Lexi was disappointed for a second before perking up again. "Oh, and a pop. Sprite, please."

"Pop? I knew I hadn't seen you before, but now I really know you aren't from around here."

"Nope. But I will be soon." Lexi wiggled her shoulders in excitement. "I'm moving here. Today actually."

"Well, congratulations. And welcome to Fauna."

Rosita turned to go, scribbling the order in her small notepad, but turned back when Lexi cleared her throat.

"Um," Lexi held up a finger. "I know this is a long shot, but does a Silvia still work here?"

"Silvia, yeah." Rosita's eyes narrowed. "Why?"

"Oh, I was just curious. She was our server last time."

"Sheesh. When was that?" Rosita shook her head, her long, dark ponytail swishing over her shoulders. "Mama hasn't been a server since I was a kid."

"Silvia is your mom?" Lexi asked.

"Yeah. She's in the back office." Rosita nodded her head toward the door behind the counter. "I'll let her know you're here..."

"Lexi." She reached out and shook Rosita's hand a little more vigorously than needed. "Lexi Caehill."

"Right. I'll let her know you're here." Rosita gave a small smile before disappearing behind the swinging door.

Lexi had waited so long for this day; she couldn't believe it was finally here. Nervous energy poured out of her as she crossed and uncrossed her ankles, then drummed her fingers on the spotted tabletop. When her toes began tapping along with the Elvis song crooning from the jukebox in the corner, she started to annoy herself. She knit her fingers together and shoved them in her lap, pressing down on her legs as if that would keep her toes rooted to the floor.

She stared down at her hands clenched on top of her skirt and remembered the hours her mother made her sit like this as a child. "It's not ladylike to fidget," she'd say as a wooden spoon smacked down over Lexi's knuckles. As if being lady-like was the height of their concerns. Eventually, she'd started sitting with her hands clasped in her lap all the time to avoid her mother's attention.

Lexi quickly pulled them apart, hating that, even at twenty-eight and from halfway across the country, she still feared her mother's judgment and wanted her approval.

"It's always a good idea to start a meal with prayer," said a voice over Lexi's shoulder. "That is what you're doing, isn't it?"

Lexi looked up and smiled. Even after so many years, she recognized the woman who'd offered her so much kindness as a child.

"I wish, Miss Silvia."

The older woman set her sandwich and a heaping plate of French fries on the table and slid into the booth across from Lexi. Her dark, wavy hair had streaks of gray now, but her face hadn't been changed by time. Only the crinkles at the corners of her eyes hinted at the happy years she'd lived.

"I'm not sure if you remember me, but..." Lexi choked off the sentence, not sure what to say now that the moment had arrived.

"Of course, I remember you. As soon as Rosita told me there was a girl..." Silvia tilted her head and really looked at Lexi, "... young woman asking about Free Fry-day, I knew it must be you or your sister."

"I can't believe you remember that after all these years." Lexi's chest felt tight.

"How could I forget? Jeb Thompson heard me tell your mom about Free Fry-days, and I've had to feed him free french fries every week for the last sixteen or seventeen years."

"Wait, so Free Fry-days wasn't really a thing?"

"Eh," Silvia waved a hand at her, "you and your sister were so scrawny. And those parents of yours not wanting to get you proper food. No one leaves my diner hungry."

As Lexi had grown older, she'd often wondered if Free Fry-day was something Silvia had made up to feed two hungry kids and not insult their prideful parents. It made her even more grateful to her.

"I can't even tell you how much your kindness meant to me. I've wanted to come back so many times to thank you."

"Oh, niña," Silvia stopped and placed her hand over Lexi's, "it was just a couple plates of fries."

Lexi felt tears well in the corners of her eyes. She wanted to tell Silvia it was so much more than just plates of fries. It was the gesture. The pure, simple kindness that left its mark on her. It was the fact that she'd noticed her. But the words just wouldn't come.

This wasn't going at all how she'd planned. She wanted to show Silvia how far she'd come from those days of being dragged from one state to another, hopping from one couch to the next. She did not want to revert to the small, scared child she'd been the last time she sat here in this booth. But sometimes, going back to places of your childhood brought that part of yourself to the surface, and Lexi couldn't fight the tears that spilled down her cheeks. She grasped Silvia's hand tightly, savoring the warmth of the touch.

"Child," Silvia leaned in and whispered, as if she'd read Lexi's mind, "you aren't that little girl anymore. Let it go and be happy."

"You're right." Lexi sniffled and wiped the tears away, smudging her eyeliner. "I pictured this going so differently."

"Things happen as they are meant to." Silvia squeezed Lexi's hand before letting go and leaning back. "Maybe those tears have been waiting for just the right moment to leave you, which means you have been carrying them for a long time. Uncried tears are a heavy, heavy burden."

Lexi straightened in her seat, feeling the weight of each of those tears leaving her. She smiled at Silvia and popped a fry into her mouth.

"Mmm. You seriously make the best french fries I've ever had. And trust me, I've eaten a lot of them." Lexi stopped to squirt ketchup onto her plate. "French fries are not something they teach in culinary school, which is a real shame. What beats a delicious plate of fries? Nothing. That's what."

"Culinary school? Is that what you've done with yourself?"

"Yes, ma'am." Lexi beamed. "Not for fries, though. I'm a pastry chef."

"I'm proud of you, Niña. That is a big accomplishment. And your sister? Did she better herself as you have?"

"Uh, not really." Lexi set down her perfectly grilled cheese sandwich. "She hops from one job to another. One couch to another with my folks."

"Well, then what you have achieved is even more of an accomplishment. It is not easy to rise above what people expect of you."

The door jingled behind them, and Lexi watched as Silvia's face lit up. She heard heavy footsteps beside her before the newcomer bent over to hug Silvia. Lexi swallowed hard as the most perfect man's backside she'd ever seen graced her vision.

As the man stood, Lexi tried to avert her eyes and not stare, but her brain was stuck in ogle mode. A thin blue shirt fit snugly over broad shoulders and muscular arms. Worn jeans hugged those perfect hips like a buttery pie crust wrapped around her favorite filling.

"Ay, mi Corazon. What are you doing here?" Silvia beamed as she placed a hand on her chest. "I thought you were working out of town this week. You've been working so hard. I know you want to save that house, but a man must rest, must eat."

"I came back early. Just to get some of your shrimp and grits." His voice was deep and flowed like honey over Lexi. The slight Southern accent literally made her swoon. Silvia looked over at her, a knowing look in her eyes.

"A man must also live." Silvia shook her head and patted his arm before turning her attention back to Lexi. "I'd like to introduce you to C.D. Walker."

"Just Chaz." He smiled and reached out a hand. "Only Silvia here calls me C.D. and gets away with it."

"I'm Lexi," she chuckled and shook his hand. For the second time since she'd arrived, she relished the warmth of a hand in hers. He gave a firm shake and tilted his head to look at her.

"Pleasure to meet you. You've got a little something..." He reached up with his free hand and brushed under his eye to show her.

"Huh?" Lexi muttered, her brain still moving like molasses as her hand rested in his.

"Um, here." He leaned in, grabbed a napkin, and pressed it below her eye. His pinky brushed below the edge of the paper along her cheek. It was rough and warm but feather-light against her skin. "There. You just have a little something."

The damn eyeliner. She'd totally forgotten about it. And now the most gorgeous man she'd ever laid eyes on was rubbing a napkin to her cheek. Which maybe wasn't such a horrible thing.

"Thank you. I, um, should probably go take care of that."

Chaz stepped to the side with a smile, giving her room to get out of the booth. Her heels clicked on the checkered linoleum floor as she rushed to the bathroom. At least she'd opted to wear a nice dress today instead of the comfy travel pants she'd worn the day before.

"Oh, Lord," she muttered when she looked in the mirror.

Her adorable cat eye had turned into an owl eye, black rimming both and streaking down one cheek. The one Chaz had rubbed. She flushed pink at the thought.

Grabbing several paper towels, she furiously rubbed under her eyes, making them turn red as the black came off.

"Great. Now I look like I've got pinkeye."

She ran another paper towel under cool water and pressed it gently to her face. The coolness helped slightly, but not enough to fully make the pink go away.

"Well, you're just going to have to rock the contagious disease look," she told her reflection and squared her shoulders before turning to head back out to her booth.

Chaz was still talking with Silvia, casually leaning against the table. He glanced up as she approached and ran a hand through his dark hair. It fell in waves over his ears, and Lexi felt another sigh of appreciation trying to escape her throat.

"So, Lexi, what brings you to Fauna?" Chaz asked, stepping aside to let her back into her seat.

"I'm moving here, actually." She slid in as gracefully as she could, which wasn't as graceful as she'd hoped, and plopped into her spot.

"Really?" Silvia sounded slightly surprised. "Well, that's fantastic, Lexi. Fauna will be lucky to have you."

"You'll love it here." Chaz gave her a lopsided grin, creating a single dimple that softened his sharp features.

"I already do," Lexi said breathily. Realizing how that sounded, she cleared her throat. "I mean, I was here once as a kid, and it's kind of been my life goal to move here someday."

"Ha!" Chaz laughed. "Apparently, we made a good impression then."

"Oh, yes," Lexi smiled. "Everyone here was so nice, and everything was so clean. The day we spent here was the best day of my childhood."

"Well, nice and clean are definitely things Fauna does well," Chaz said. "I'd better let you ladies get back to chatting and eat my lunch before my boss gets impatient."

Lexi jumped when Silvia let out a booming laugh from across the table. Her molasses mind had practically forgotten she was there. She looked questioningly from Silvia to Chaz, feeling like she had missed something.

"He owns his own company," Silvia croaked out after laughing. "He's his own boss."

"Oh," Lexi smiled and laughed at the joke. "What do you do?"

"I'm a contractor. So, if you need any work done wherever you end up moving, just let me know."

"Thanks." Lexi took the card he offered, glancing at it to see that his phone number was indeed on it. Did small-town Mississippi men flirt like the ones in New York? Was he just giving her his business card, or was he trying to give her his number in a way that wasn't so obvious?

"You ladies enjoy your lunch." Chaz tipped his head and slid into a booth down the opposite side of the diner.

"So, you're moving here?" Silvia cut into her musings. "What are you planning on doing, Cariña?"

"Cariña?" Lexi raised an eyebrow.

"Sweetie. Like candy. Since you are a pastry chef, yes?"

"Oh, yes. I like that," Lexi smiled at the term of endearment. "Um. I'm planning on opening a bakery. My grandmother passed away not too long ago and left me a little money. Figured this would be my opportunity to get away and make my dream come true."

"I'm sorry to hear about your grandmother."

"It's okay. We weren't that close." Lexi nibbled on a cooled fry. "We were actually leaving her house when I stopped here as a kid. She kicked us out. Well, she kicked my parents out. She said Liv and I could stay, but my parents wouldn't hear of that. Leave their kids in a stable environment with someone who kind of cared about them and could provide them a good life? I think not."

"So, you were maybe close to your grandmother at one time?"

"Not really. She kept us all at arm's length. But I suppose she cared in her own way." Lexi let out a laugh she hoped didn't sound too bitter. "I'm the only one she left anything. Except for her cat. She left 98% of her fortune to her cat, 1% to her church, and 1% to me."

"That must be one special cat."

"It's fat and ugly."

They both dissolved into giggles before Silvia pushed her way out of the booth.

"You need to eat that lunch. And I'm going to get you something else to try. You can give me your professional opinion."

Lexi ate her few remaining fries and the last of her grilled cheese before Silvia returned with a small plate. She placed it on the table, and Lexi was glad to see a slice of pecan pie. Her palate for sweets was finely tuned, but if Silvia had brought out a hamburger, she wouldn't have been able to tell the difference between it and one she'd picked up in a drive-through on her way here.

"Taste," Silvia laid down a fork.

Instead of grabbing it, Lexi picked up the plate, turning it from side to side. She examined the color of the crust, which was evenly golden brown. The layer of pecans on top looked nicely caramelized, meaning the baker had made the filling ahead of time to let the flavors meld. Finally, she took the fork, slid it through the slice of pie, and pulled it away. The filling held firm and wasn't sticky. In her mouth, the flavors melted, perfectly balanced on her tongue.

"You're an exceptional baker. This is one of the best pecan pies I've ever tasted."

"Oh, I didn't make it. I have them made locally and brought in." She shrugged. "I was just curious how our pies stacked up against the big city."

"Well, it's excellent. You can tell whoever makes them, I'd be happy to hire them once my bakery is open."

Silvia snorted and shook her head.

"I don't think you'd want that, Cariña. She would be more of a headache than it would be worth."

"I will remember that." Lexi slid out of her booth and pulled out her billfold, but Silvia pushed her hand back into her purse.

"I have thought about you over the years. Seeing you and easing my curious mind is payment enough."

Lexi hesitated for a moment and then leaned down to wrap the tiny woman in a brief hug. Silvia squeezed her back, holding on longer than Lexi had. In the short time that she'd been in Fauna, she'd felt more warmth from other people than in all the years she'd lived in New York.

"Thank you, Miss Silvia. I will come back. A lot."

"Tia Silvia, Cariña. In Fauna, we are all family."

Chapter 2

L exi left the diner feeling brighter than a lemon tart on a summer day. Their meeting might not have gone as she'd hoped, but just like Tia Silvia said, it went the way it was supposed to.

And if the other men in Fauna looked anything like the eye candy currently sitting in the diner, then she was in for a treat. A sweet, sweet treat.

Lexi took a breath of the heavy outside air and decided to leave her car. A quick walk to the realtor's office would give her time to check out the town center. Tia Silvia had told her it was directly opposite the diner. As she strolled down the sidewalk, she saw the courthouse in the center of the square. Its large white columns and red brick walls set off in stark contrast to the giant moss-covered oaks surrounding its curving front lane. The buildings that ran along the outside of the square were all different sizes and colors, but they were pristinely kept. No chipped paint or faded signs. Every door had a pot of blooming flowers next to it. Just like she'd told Silvia and Chaz, Fauna was so nice and clean.

Lexi spotted the sign for R.W. Realty and pushed open the door. She ran a finger over the intricately carved casing and stopped just inside to let her eyes adjust. After a moment, she looked around at the warm, cinnamon-brown walls and dark leather chairs in the waiting area. The only things missing to make it a total boys' club were a bottle of scotch and a box of cigars on the sideboard.

She waited a few minutes, her foot tapping impatiently, before venturing down the hallway towards the back.

"Hello?" she called out. "Is anyone here?"

Faint music played from behind the door at the end of the hall in front of her. It opened onto a courtyard where music blared, and four shirtless men beat on punching bags while another barked orders at them through a headset. All five men stopped mid-punch and stared at Lexi as her mouth hung open in surprise.

"I...I'm so sorry." She looked back through the office, wondering if she'd gone in the wrong door. "I thought this was the real estate office. Maybe I'm in the wrong place?"

"You're in the right place." The man with the headset smiled at her and turned off the thudding techno music. "I just teach boxing classes every Friday over lunch."

"Ah. Okay." Lexi tried to avert her eyes from all the sweaty torsos and chiseled abs in front of her. "I must have missed the sign or something."

"There's no sign," he chuckled and ran a hand over his dark, slicked-back hair. "Everybody just knows."

"Well, not everyone, apparently." Lexi shot back.

"You're right." He held up his hands in surrender. "Only the locals know. I will get a sign put up in the window for the odd occasion when someone new visits my office."

He walked over to a bench and pulled on a t-shirt, then turned back to the other four men. After barking a few orders over the headset, they all jumped back into formation, pummeling the punching bags.

"I'm Rhys, realtor and boxing instructor extraordinaire. What can I do for you today?"

"I'm looking to buy a commercial space here in Fauna."

"Oh...kay." His eyes widened in surprise. "Why don't you take a seat in my office while I get changed, and we can discuss what you're looking for."

He ushered Lexi through the first door off of the waiting room. A massive wooden desk took up most of the space. Two chairs and a small refrigerator were crammed around it.

"I didn't get your name." Rhys pulled out a chair for her to sit in.

"Lexi Caehill."

"Well, Miss Lexi, can I get you a water while you wait? I'll only be a moment."

"Yes, thanks."

He pulled a bottle from the fridge and disappeared out the door. Lexi drank all the water quickly. The heat was more than she was used to. If she had to spend much more time outside, she'd look like a melted bonbon in no time.

"So, you said you're looking for a commercial property?" Rhys had changed into a sharp blue suit and was still straightening his tie as he walked in.

He lifted her water bottle off his desk and slid a coaster under it before moving to the other side, continuing to adjust his tie even though it looked perfectly straight to her.

"Yes, I'm hoping to find a space that can be commercial downstairs with an apartment upstairs. I know that might be asking a lot, and I'd be willing to look at two separate spaces if need be, but that would make my finances pretty tight."

"What kind of shop?" Rhys asked. "That might help me narrow down the search."

"A bakery. I'm a pastry chef."

"Ohhhhh..." Rhys stopped fiddling with his tie and looked up at her for the first time.

"Is that a problem?" Lexi folded her hands in her lap before quickly clenching them into separate fists.

"Nope. No problem." Rhys said hurriedly. "Let me just look at our inventory and see what might fit."

He turned to his computer, his fingers flying over the keys. Lexi studied him for a moment. He was lean and cut and belonged in the tailored suit he wore. His expression outside had been serious while he shouted orders, and it stayed the same here in his office. There was nothing calm or relaxed about him.

He wrote a couple of addresses and then stopped, his pen hovering over the page. After glancing between Lexi and the computer several times, he wrote one last address and set down the pen. Only three options, but in a town this small, that was more than she'd expected.

"I've got several choices for business locations. Two of them would be strictly commercial. The third could be both commercial and residential."

"Perfect. That's more than I expected. Let's take a look."

Rhys quickly printed off several sheets of paper and handed them to Lexi. The first building was very large and had a matching price tag, which would wipe out her bank account. The second was a small space in a strip mall on the highway that wouldn't have enough room for a kitchen and dining area, and she'd really hoped for something inside city limits. The third looked like it could be just what she needed, and the added bonus of the residential space upstairs meant she wouldn't need to find a house as well. So, her list quickly dwindled to one real possibility.

"That one." She slid the sheet across the desk.

"That one's nice, but..." Rhys's face twisted.

"But what?" Lexi leaned forward in her chair.

"The owner could be pretty prickly." Rhys locked his eyes with hers. "Very prickly. Like a cactus, but worse."

"I'm from New York. I can handle prickly. No problem."

"If you say so. You're the boss." Rhys stood and led her out to the waiting area. "If you'd like to ride together, I can drive."

"That would be great." Lexi followed him out to a small car at the curb. "I left my car at the diner."

Lexi opened the passenger door of the car, and heat rolled out across her legs. Rhys put the keys in, and the air started blowing, but it was just as hot as outside. She could feel the heat all the way down into her lungs. She knew the melted bonbon look would happen sooner rather than later.

They drove to the corner of the square and turned down one side. Lexi leaned back, watching the courthouse slide past. She closed her eyes, praying she didn't melt into a puddle right there in the seat of Rhys's car. He seemed like the type who would throw a fit if a wrapper got left on the floor of his immaculate interior. A melted city girl would probably send him over the edge.

He turned at the corner again and pulled to a stop.

"We're here." He said cheerfully and climbed out.

Lexi sighed and peeled herself out of the low seat. She knew sweat had soaked through the back of her dress. And she didn't even want to know what her hair looked like. She'd styled it in adorable pin curls, fastening the top half back with a beaded comb. That morning she would have done Grace Kelly proud, but now her auburn hair probably looked as graceless and frizzy as a sheepdog.

Her reflection in the car mirror showed her exactly what she expected. She had passed the sheepdog stage and run right into finger-in-the-light-socket. With a sigh, she ran a hand through her thick hair and walked around the car.

"I've just messaged the owner in case you decide to look inside," Rhys said as he slid his phone into his pocket. "But here's the property. Perfect location to open a business since it's right on the square. You'd get a lot of foot traffic here."

Lexi turned to see an old Victorian home on the corner across from them. A porch wrapped around the front and one side. The other side was accented with a small turret. Empty planter boxes lined the railing. The yellow paint was slightly faded, setting it apart from the rest of the immaculate shops on the square, but Lexi could see its potential.

"Oh, my." Lexi couldn't find any more words.

She could picture customers sitting on the porch, dining on her pastries, and sipping sweet tea with large fans overhead, stirring the air to keep them comfortable. The turret would be her reading nook. She'd always wanted a reading nook. She could imagine sleek modern railings on the porch, simple landscaping out front. A perfect mix of old and new, which is just what she hoped to bring to Fauna with her baking.

"It's perfect."

"Well, just wait until you see the inside." Rhys guided her across the brick street. "There's hand-carved spindles on the staircases, real wood chair rails in the dining and living rooms."

"Well, all that will probably have to go. I want something a little more modern to match my baking style." Lexi's mind was already planning colors for the exterior as they approached the porch. "When can we go inside? I'm dying to see it."

"Here's the owner now." Rhys pointed to the white truck pulling in behind his car.

Lexi couldn't believe her eyes when Chaz climbed out and walked towards them. Not only would she get to do the remodeling with him, but she'd get to go through the buying process, too? She was already imagining meetings over coffee with her fresh-baked biscotti.

"Chaz. I'd like you to meet..."

"Lexi?" Chaz looked up at her, recognizing her for the first time.

"You already know each other?" Rhys seemed confused. "I thought you just got into town."

"I did." Lexi smiled up at Chaz's silhouette, shading her eyes from the sun behind his back. "We met at the diner earlier today."

"Wonderful." Rhys clapped his hands together. "You want to unlock the door so we can show her the inside? I was just telling her about all the handmade touches."

"Nope." Chaz stepped out of the sun so Lexi could see him.

The smile fell from her face, and she took an involuntary step back as he crossed his arms. The sweet, easy-going Southern gentleman she'd met earlier was gone. Instead, she saw a steely-eyed, immovable wall of muscle.

"Show her something else, Rhys." Chaz's jaw ticked as he clenched his teeth. "I don't actually want to sell Meemaw's house to anybody, but especially not to her."

"What?" Lexi and Rhys said at the same time.

"You heard me," Chaz said as he turned on his heel and stomped down the steps. "Show her something else."

"Excuse me for a moment." Rhys raced after Chaz, grabbing his elbow to slow his march down the walkway.

"What do you mean, 'show her something else?' This property is exactly what she's looking for." Rhys lowered his voice, thinking Lexi couldn't hear. "She already said it's perfect. This could be an easy sale."

"Not happening, Rhys."

"And why not?" Lexi had heard enough. She marched down the stairs, right up to both of them. "The property is for sale, right?"

"The home might be for sale." Chaz emphasized the word 'home' as he responded.

"So, then what's the issue?" Lexi threw her hands up.

"You." Chaz turned to walk away again.

"Me?" Lexi sputtered. "You don't even know me."

"Chaz, you're being unreasonable. Lexi's opening a business that could be really good for Fauna."

Chaz's steps halted, and he turned. He narrowed his eyes at Rhys and pursed his lips, thinking. Lexi's blood was pumping hard and fast, but even in her anger, her brain registered how firm his lips looked, how his hard eyes shot sparks, and how she wished different kinds of sparks were flying.

"What kind of business?" he asked slowly.

"A bakery." Lexi jumped in. "I'm a pastry chef. And I could definitely help the town with jobs and sourcing local produc ts..."

Before she could get through her pitch, Chaz threw his hands in the air and laughed.

"A bakery?" He turned on Rhys. "Are you kidding me? Chris Anntha would murder us. Literally murder us. And you're wanting to sell her Meemaw's house? What were you thinking?"

"Who is this Chris Ann person?" Lexi practically shouted. "And what in the world is a Meemaw?"

"Who was Meemaw?" Chaz said through his teeth. "She was our grandmother, and this was her home."

"Your grandmother?" Lexi looked between the two men, finally noticing the dark hair and chiseled features they both shared. "You're brothers."

"Yep. And we have a lot of really fond memories in that home. And I'm not selling it to some big-city girl who can't appreciate its history."

"That's what this is about?" Lexi wasn't sure whether to be insulted by the city-girl comment or touched by his nostalgia. "Why put it on the market at all then? Doesn't sound like anyone would be good enough to move into it."

"You're right." Chaz looked from her to Rhys. "Thanks for your interest, but as of this moment, the home is off the market."

"Chaz, this is ridiculous. You're being ridiculous." Rhys crossed his arms, finally losing his cool. "Do I need to call Mama?"

"Don't you dare bring Mama into this." Chaz thrust a finger at Rhys. "And I'm being ridiculous? I'm not the one trying to palm off our memories to make a few bucks."

"Chaz," Rhys's voice softened, "the memories will always be there. But look at Meemaw's home. It needs someone to love it again. And what better way to honor the best baker we ever knew than by putting a bakery in her old house? It's like her legacy will live on."

"Then it can live on through Chris Anntha. Not some uppity outsider who'd probably tear out all the details that make it a home."

Lexi couldn't even believe what she was hearing. Uppity? Never in her life had she been pegged so wrong. In all the years of being thought of as less-than and people saying she'd never amount to anything. She'd proven them all wrong, and she'd do that here too.

"Excuse me, sir. But I am not 'uppity', and I may be an outsider, but I don't want to be. I've wanted to live in Fauna my whole life. I'm risking everything to move here, so don't think I'm making these decisions lightly. This is my life's dream."

"The dream you made after spending a few hours here when you were a kid?" Chaz sighed.

"Everyone needs a dream." Lexi cleared her throat. "And what's so wrong with holding on to a happy memory? Isn't that exactly what you're doing?"

Lexi felt her throat tighten as a wave of emotion ran through her. She glanced between the two men in front of her. Rhys wouldn't even make eye contact and found an invisible scuff on his shoe to obsess over. Chaz, on the other hand, stared directly at her, his dark eyes narrowed, obviously unaffected by her emotional plea. Her heart fell like a poorly mixed souffle.

"I hope that trying to crush my dreams makes you happy." She pulled back her shoulders but could feel tears prickling the corners of her eyes. "You can add this to your list of fond memories at your Meemaw's house."

Lexi pushed past them both and stormed down the walk-way. A sob threatened to escape her throat, but she wasn't about to let these two see her cry. She rushed out into the street, not remembering it was brick, and fell to her knees as her heel caught in a crack. She heard her dress rip and felt gravel dig into her knees.

A hand grabbed her elbow, helping her to stand. She shrugged it off, not bothering to look and see who it was. She reached down to pry her shoe out of the road and hobbled to the other side before taking off the other one. Without a single glance back, she rushed to the diner parking lot and threw herself into her oven of a car.

Was she delusional? Was this dream of hers crazy? What if the Fauna she visited years ago and built up in her mind didn't actually exist? What if she'd be an outsider here, just like she had been everywhere else?

All these questions rolled through her mind as she rolled the ripped seam of her dress between her fingers. She'd been so sure of this decision. So positive that life would fall into place here. She'd never once questioned what she'd do if it didn't work. If this wasn't where she was meant to be.

Her head hurt. She needed to clean up the scrapes on her knees and take a nap. That's exactly what she needed. A reset. Tomorrow would be a new, better day. She'd ask Rhys to show her the other two properties, and one of them would work out just fine. They wouldn't be perfect like Meemaw's house, but they'd be just fine. And she'd make them successful if it was the last thing she did.

The a/c kicked in almost instantly, making her thankful she'd spent some of her inheritance on a new car. She pulled out and headed towards the B&B she'd booked online. As she drove past R.W. Realty, she held her head high and didn't even glance at the little black car or white pickup parked outside its front door.

Past the square, homes lined the street. Azalea bushes were in full bloom, their pink flowers weighing down the branches. Lexi slowed down and turned into the driveway of the Sleepy Time Inn. The name couldn't have fit her current mood any better. She barely registered the woman who checked her in and hurried upstairs to her room.

The violet walls and flowered bedspread helped to calm her, but sinking into the warm, bubbly water in a claw-foot tub finally helped her relax. She soaked until the water turned cold, then hurried under the covers, curled up into a warm ball, and fell into a restless sleep, full of anxious dreams.

Chapter 3

Lexi awoke to the smell of something delicious. Her head hurt and her mind felt foggy, but her stomach rumbled, driving her out of bed. Her torn dress lay in a sad pile next to the tub, so she pulled on a soft pair of black capris and a cute lacy shirt. After running her fingers through her matted curls, she padded down the stairs, following her nose to a large dining room where other guests were serving themselves from the small buffet along the back wall. Lexi kept her head down as she piled her plate with pot roast, green beans, and mashed potatoes.

A small table sat under a window at the front of the house. She pulled out a chair and enjoyed the view overlooking the porch. The warm food hit her tongue with a burst of savory flavor that had her sighing in contentment, but that warm feeling quickly vanished as a pair of familiar boots walked up next to her.

"Do you mind if I join you?" Chaz asked, his brow furrowed. He stood next to Lexi's table with a dinner plate in one hand and the other shoved deep into the pocket of his snug jeans.

Lexi's left eyebrow rose a good inch. Her sister, Liv, always told her she could give The Rock a run for his money in the eyebrow department. What could Chaz possibly want?

"If you must." Lexi nailed the cool, dismissive tone she'd been shooting for and cheered internally.

The table was so small, meant for tea rather than dinner, that their plates and knees touched as he slid into the chair opposite her. Lexi did her best to keep her eyes on the window and take small bites of her dinner. But she could feel his cool gaze on her, bringing heat to her cheeks.

"Ok." Her fork hit her plate as she dropped it to the table. "Seriously. What are you doing here? Are you following me or something? Because, let me tell you something, Buster," she thrust her finger across the table at him, "I'm from New York. I know how to handle creepy men."

"I rent the carriage house out back. Lived here for a few years. So, if either of us is being creepy, it's you."

He leaned back in his chair and crossed his arms. As he slid back, his legs pushed further under the table, bumping into her scraped and bandaged knees. She sucked a breath in through her teeth and jerked back in surprise. Nothing like anger and annoyance to make you forget a silly thing like skinned knees. Chaz pulled back but looked at her questioningly.

"Skinned knees." Lexi's cheeks flushed. She felt like a kid complaining after a fall at recess.

Chaz was out of his chair and by her side in a heartbeat. His questioning look had turned into one of apology, the corners of his mouth downturned and his eyebrows pinched together.

"Aw, geez. I'm sorry. I just can't seem to do anything right around you." He shook his head.

The smell of sawdust tickled her nose as she blinked at his nearness. He was close enough to see the dusting of dark stubble along his jawline.

"Let me get you some ice."

Lexi's hand shot out as he turned to leave. For the briefest moment, they both stopped and stared at her hand on his arm. Slowly, she pulled it back.

"It's nothing. Really." She said hurriedly. "The knee, I mean. I think I was more startled than anything."

"Are you sure?" He looked down at her with concern in his eyes. "Mrs. Miller won't mind."

"No. No." Lexi shook her head and tucked her legs back under the table. "Just sit down. I'm fine."

Chaz hesitated a moment before returning to his seat. He slowly tucked his long legs under the tiny table, careful to avoid her knees. They both stared at their plates and ate a few bites in silence.

"Listen," Chaz took a deep breath, "I just wanted to apologize for my behavior earlier. My mama always says I get too attached to stuff, but that's no excuse for me saying the things I said."

"Thank you. I appreciate that. I'm sorry, too."

"For what?"

"You know. The dream-crushing thing." Lexi finally looked up from her plate. "You don't seem like the kind of man to go around crushing people's dreams for the fun of it, but then again, I don't really know you. Do I?"

Lexi was rewarded with an amused grunt and the faintest hint of a smile, which she would take as proof the man had at least a hint of a sense of humor. They both returned to eating, but the silence wasn't nearly as heavy. Only slightly awkward.

"Oh, good." A sing-songy voice approached their table. "Chaz is finally stepping up and playing host for once."

Lexi turned to see the woman who'd checked her in earlier. She was a large woman with beautiful white-grey hair tucked up in a bun and a neon green apron covered in strawberries. Just the sight of her brought a smile to Lexi's face.

"Mrs. Miller. You know I never slack on my duties." Chaz turned in his seat to face her. "But where in my rental agreement does it say I need to be the tour guide and chauffeur for all your guests?"

"Nowhere. Thanks for pointing that out. I'll be adding it in when it comes time for you to renew your lease at the end of the year."

"Oh, Lord," Chaz muttered, his face falling into his hands.

"Now, dear," she turned to Lexi, "I hope everything is to your liking. If you need anything, or if he gets annoying, you let me know. I've got a rolling pin that's dented the heads of a few presumptuous young men before."

Lexi laughed as Chaz sank even lower in his seat, still keeping his knees away from hers. His cheeks turned the exact shade of the pink lemonade cupcakes she was known for. Her mouth watered, and not just from the sudden sweets craving.

"I also have a large rolling pin, but can't say it's dented any heads," Lexi chuckled. "Although I'm not completely opposed to the idea."

"You and I are going to get on just fine, dear." Mrs. Miller patted her shoulder and hustled over to another table.

Lexi watched as she talked with the other guests, her whole body animated with excitement.

"You can tell she really loves this." Lexi couldn't help but smile.

"Yep. The Sleepy Time Inn has been around longer than I have, so she's been doing this for quite a while."

"It's so admirable, you know?" Lexi turned back to Chaz. "Watching someone in their element. And to stay with one thing for so long? Wow."

"Don't you feel that way about your baking?"

"Well, yeah," Lexi said around a mouthful of potatoes. "Just not something you see very often."

"Maybe not in New York, but around here, people stick with things. Even when... especially when things get tough."

Lexi felt a subtle shift in their conversation. They weren't talking about Mrs. Miller anymore. This felt like a test, a gentle prodding. But what was he trying to get at?

"I love being a pastry chef and can't imagine doing anything else." Lexi's eyes narrowed. "I'm damn good at it, and I've worked my ass off to get to where I am."

Chaz nodded and turned back to his plate, meticulously scooping a small portion of potatoes, one green bean, and a slice of pot roast in each bite. Apparently, she passed the test because there were no further questions.

"Well then," Chaz swallowed, "I suppose if you don't mind talking business over dinner, I've got a proposition for you."

Lexi slowly laid her fork on her plate and clasped her hands in her lap. They were clammy, and she could feel her heart kick up a notch. The clinking of forks, Mrs. Miller's laughter, everything faded into the background.

"I don't mind. What are you thinking?"

"My brother and I had a long talk after you... left." Chaz leaned forward and rubbed his fingers on his forehead as if trying to rub away a headache. "He's pretty stuck on having a bakery in Meemaw's house as an honor to her memory."

"Okay." Lexi held her breath.

"And he's right."

Chaz looked at her long and hard. Lexi didn't dare look away or shrink under his gaze. She could see the emotion rolling through him. His shoulders tightened. His hands thrust into his pockets. Everything about him was curling inward to protect the part of him that was struggling and hurting. His heart.

"I'll sell you the house..." his voice raw, "on one condition."

"Name it."

Lexi was instantly imagining how her bakery would look. Bright, white, and open. She hadn't seen the inside of the house yet, but she imagined some walls would need to be taken out to open the space for a large dining area with several sleek display cases. With any luck, she could get a crew in there and have the work done within the month and get her business started.

"I do all the remodeling." The sadness left his voice, replaced by fierce passion. "My hands are the only ones that work on that house. You hear me?"

"I do." Lexi resisted the urge to reach across and touch him to offer some kind of comfort as she debated the ramifications of that offer. "I think your grandma would really like that. Putting your love into the house again."

"Please don't act like this is anything more than a business transaction for you." Chaz pushed away from the table. "You didn't know her. And, as you said, you don't know me."

The next morning, Lexi stretched out in bed as warm light poured through the window. Normally, she was up before the sun and heading to work. Lying in that big, fluffy bed after 7 a.m. felt like the most luxurious thing she'd done in years. She wrapped herself around a pillow and snuggled further down into the sheets until her phone went off. Repeatedly.

Only two people had her new phone number. One was Mrs. Miller downstairs, and Lexi did not remember wake-up calls being offered. The other was Rhys at the real estate office. At that thought, her conversation with Chaz the night before rushed into her mind.

"My hands are the only ones that work on that house. You hear me?"

Lexi thought briefly about his hands working on other things, then shook her head to dislodge that train of thought. Rhys had said Chaz was prickly, but that wasn't quite right. Chaz was more like the weather in the mid-west. Cold, then hot. Sunny, then stormy. There was no telling which way the wind would blow with that man.

Lexi grabbed her phone. Multiple texts from Rhys pinged through as she was trying to check her voicemail. He had perfect grammar and punctuation, even in text messages. Very professional.

> *R.W.-Great news! Chaz has agreed to sell.*

> *R.W.- He wants to meet in the office at 8 to discuss paperwork.*

> *R.W.- I suggest you arrive early so he can't change his mind again.*

> *See u soon.*

Lexi added several excited emojis and slid out of bed. She rushed through a shower, slid on one of her favorite dresses, and hurried downstairs to grab some breakfast for the road. With a muffin in hand, she set out toward the town square. Even though the humidity was already like a wet blanket on her skin, she decided to walk the two blocks to the realty office. She'd have to get used to the weather at some point.

Lexi hurried across the brick street, navigating the heels of her shoes around the cracks in the road. Small magnolia trees dotted the edge of the sidewalk. Their large white blooms were barely opening. Lexi gently grasped a bud between her fingers and leaned in to smell the faint citrusy scent. With the sun shining on her back, she closed her eyes to savor the perfect moment.

"If you really want to smell the magnolias, you should come back in a week." A young woman holding a large camera stepped out from behind the tree Lexi had been admiring. "The air will be so thick with the smell of them you'll almost choke to death."

"Oh. Well, that sounds lovely."

"Sure does, doesn't it?" The woman let her camera rest on its neck strap and reached out a hand to Lexi. "I'm Lotus. Lotus Johnson. Named after the car, not the flower. You may have seen some of my work in the *Fauna Gazette*."

"I'm sorry. I haven't read the paper. I've just arrived." Lexi shook Lotus's hand and tried to follow everything rushing out of her mouth. "I'm Lexi Caehill. So, you're a reporter?"

"Not yet. Still working as a photographer. One of these days, Bill has got to give me a shot at writing an article." Lotus stopped talking for a moment and looked Lexi up and down. "So, what brings you to Fauna, Lexi? Something newsworthy?"

"Uh, well, I hope it will be newsworthy," Lexi said. "I'll be opening a bakery here soon."

"Hot dogs! A new business coming to Fauna? Bill will have to run my article when he hears about this. Stand right there." Lotus swung Lexi around in front of the magnolia tree and began snapping photos. "Tuck in your chin. Stand a little straighter. Oh, maybe I should run and grab a whisk or spatula or something for you to hold. No time! I do not want Bill to get the scoop on you before I've got my article in hand. Can you tuck that curl back? Nope, other side. There. Now smile. Perfect!"

"I really don't think I'm camera ready. I mean, I just drove into town. Could we maybe do this another day? When I'm a little more settled?"

"Don't you worry. My photos could make a dead fish look amazing."

"Ummm...."

"Oh geez. There goes my mouth again. You are not a dead fish. I just meant that I take pretty good pictures."

"It's fine." Lexi laughed and waved her hands. "After the couple of days I've had, mostly in the car, I don't feel like much more than a dead fish."

"Whooo..." Lotus whistled. "Days in the car? Where did you come from?"

"New York."

"Wow. I knew you must be big city from your clothes."

"My clothes? Is there something wrong with my dress?" Lexi asked, smoothing her hands down the soft fabric. Steel grey was on the darker side for Lexi's taste, but she'd wanted to look professional for her meeting with Chaz and Rhys.

"Oh no, fashion just takes a while to travel here, ya know? You just look like you stepped straight out of a magazine or something."

"I don't know about that." Lexi blushed. "My clothes are all vintage, so I am definitely not the height of fashion. Trust me. My taste has never been that mainstream."

Lexi took in Lotus's baggy jeans with rips in both knees and her flowy top tied off in a knot on the side. The bright red shirt set off her beautiful dark skin, and the jeweled headband nestled in her hair glinted in the bright July sunshine.

"Honestly," Lexi sighed, "you'd fit in better in New York than I ever did."

"Really? Please tell me more." Lotus slid her arm through Lexi's and began dragging her down the sidewalk. "Where are you headed, by the way? I need to know where I'm taking you. We could be strolling in the completely wrong direction. And you don't want to stroll in the wrong direction for too long in the summer. It is way too hot for that."

"The reality office." Lexi was stunned. "You'd take the time to walk with me? Aren't you busy taking photos?"

"Lexi." Lotus laid her hand on Lexi's shoulder. "Newsflash. This is Fauna, Mississippi. I hate to break it to you, but there really isn't much happening here. I mean, unless you count church socials and family dinners as front-page stories. Which we do sometimes. You are going to be the biggest news here for a long time."

The biggest news? Lexi stopped to think about that for a minute. She'd grown up keeping her head down and shuffling along with the masses. Being center stage sounded a little terrifying. And yet, exciting too. If it would help her business, then she would welcome it with open arms.

"Here we are. R.W. Realty." Lotus stopped in front of the big front window with the office's name in curvy gold lettering. "I sure am glad I bumped into you today, Lexi Caehill. But please keep your head down. I don't want Bill hearing about you until I have time to do a proper interview first."

"Ok. Well, I'm not planning on doing much, so that shouldn't be a problem."

"Don't do anything. Even doing 'not much' in Fauna can be a lot." Lotus wrapped her hands around Lexi's arms in mock alarm. "I'm serious. Do. Nothing."

"Ok. Ok. I will do nothing." Lexi laughed as Lotus smiled at her and turned down the sidewalk.

"And keep your eyes out for Chris Anntha. She isn't going to be happy you're here."

"What? Who?"

"Oh, you'll find out sooner rather than later." Lotus waved over her shoulder and kept walking.

Lexi watched her for a moment. Lotus strolled down the street, hand brushing the potted plants by every shop door as she went. She walked with such simple grace as if she were completely in her element. And Lexi supposed this was her element. She had a feeling that if anyone understood Fauna; it was Lotus.

"Oh," Lotus called from down the sidewalk. "Dinner tonight at the diner? 7 p.m. I need that interview."

Lexi gave her a thumbs-up and turned to the door with a smile.

Could it really be that easy to meet people in Fauna? They just popped out from behind the magnolia trees, started telling you their life stories, and invited you to dinner?

Chapter 4

After grimacing at her reflection in the large front window, Lexi was thinking her curls and the Mississippi humidity would constantly be at odds. She patted her hair and smoothed her dress before pulling open the realty office's door with a sigh.

She headed straight for the front office, where she'd sat down with Rhys the day before, but stopped when she heard voices coming from out back. Was Rhys teaching another class he'd failed to mention? She continued past the front office, noticing the three cups of steaming coffee sitting perfectly on coasters, and made her way to the back door.

Her hand reached out, but something about the voices on the other side made her pause. They sounded annoyed. Harsh. Not something Lexi had any desire to walk into. But not wanting to be part of the conversation did not mean she didn't want to hear it. She pressed her ear to the door, careful not to actually touch it, and held her breath.

"We should just be thankful she's out of town for the next month or so." Chaz's slow drawl reached her ear. "But when she gets back, I can guarantee we'll both be up for a whoopin' if we go through with this."

"Chaz, I think you're overreacting. She'll totally understand." Rhys's response was clipped, quick. "She knows how rare sales are in this town. She couldn't hold that against us."

"You wanna bet?"

Lexi could hear Chaz's boots striking the patio, each step a hollow thud. Over to one side, then back to the other.

"She still holds it against you that you didn't get her a Valentine in the fourth grade," Chaz continued. "And you don't think she's going to have an issue with this?"

Were they talking about a girlfriend? Fauna seemed like the kind of town where people started dating in fourth grade and stayed together forever. Partly because it had those small-town stick-to-it values, but also because the dating pool was pretty tiny.

What did that have to do with her, though? Was this other girl the jealous type and couldn't stand another woman on her turf? If that was the case, Lexi had a few things to say about women supporting other women and not tearing them down.

"We'll just explain it to her. She'll see our side," Rhys paused and continued quietly, "eventually."

Lexi leaned in to hear the last word and stumbled forward a step. Her cute little peep-toe kitten heel snagged on the threshold, and she fell through the door with a thud. It should have ended there, but either the knob wasn't fully latched, or it was old and didn't do its job anymore because the door swung open with Lexi leaning on it.

She lurched outside, trying to keep her balance as the sunlight hit her face. All she could see were the brick steps at her feet as her momentum carried her forward. She stumbled to a halt at the edge of the top step, her arms windmilled for balance, but she knew she was going down. There was no stopping this. Apparently, the karma for eavesdropping that morning was going to be swift and merciless.

Her body teetered forward, even as she arched back, her body contorting like a confused ballerina in the battle for balance. Her eyes clenched shut as she lost the battle and plummeted off the steps. She tensed for a painful impact but was pleasantly surprised by the warm embrace she received instead.

"Whoa there." Chaz's voice rumbled through her, his breath tickling her cheek.

She cracked an eye open and found herself face to face with her rescuer. This close, she could see that the deep brown of his eyes softened to a warm honey at the center. His sun-kissed skin was freshly shaven and moisturized. Who could pass up a man with a solid skincare routine? As she took in all of his delectable features, a faint smile touched his lips.

Lexi jerked out of his arms, pushing against his hard chest to get back to her own feet. She was there on business, not canoodling. After clearing her throat and straightening her dress, she finally looked up at the two men in front of her. Chaz stood with his thumbs tucked into the belt loops of his jeans, watching her every move. Rhys stood rigidly in his dark suit with his arms crossed, his eyebrows pulled together in worry. Aside from the dark hair and prominent cheekbones that gave them away as brothers, they could not appear any more different.

"Phew. Sorry about that," she stammered. "I thought I heard you guys out here, but I guess my shoe caught on the door."

"Uh-huh," Chaz smirked.

"Yes. Well, maybe you should get that knob fixed so that doesn't happen to anyone else." She turned to face Rhys so she wouldn't have to meet Chaz's knowing gaze. "I mean, you have a contractor in the family, so should be a simple job, right?"

"True. Could you fix it?" Rhys turned to Chaz.

"What?" The smile left Chaz's face instantly. "I did not come here for building maintenance."

"Oh, come on. It will take you like two seconds." Rhys reached out to usher Lexi back inside. "We'll just be waiting in the office."

"You've got to be kidding me," Chaz grumbled behind them as they walked inside. That was followed by a few spicy words that Lexi was sure a true Southern gentleman would never utter in front of a lady.

They walked into the front office to take their seats as Chaz stomped past them towards the front door. A few moments later, he stomped back with a small toolbox. Lexi and Rhys sat in silence, listening to the clink of tools and Chaz's mumbling, sharing small smiles across the desk.

After a few moments, Rhys picked up his cup of coffee and leaned back. Lexi took the cue and did the same. The coffee was perfectly warm, and as it slid down her throat, she could feel the caffeine soaking into her cells.

"Mmm..." she sighed. "You make a great cup of coffee."

"I wish I could take credit, but that's all Silvia from the diner." Rhys raised his cup in salute. "She definitely knows her way around a kitchen."

"She sure does." Lexi raised her glass as well. A warm feeling spread through her at knowing Tia Silvia. Like maybe that made her actually belong there. She straightened in her chair with a smile, ready for business. "So, what do we need to do this morning?"

"Right." Rhys set his cup down and opened a manila folder. "I figured we could start some paperwork, run your credit to get preapproval from the local mortgage lender."

"Oh, I won't need that. I'll be paying cash."

Rhys stopped flipping through the pages in the folder and looked up at her. He slowly blinked once, like his brain was recalculating how to proceed.

"Well, that changes things," he finally said. "We can get this deal finalized much faster."

"Door's fixed." Chaz slid into the seat next to Lexi with a sigh. "What's happening faster?"

"Lexi doesn't need to apply and wait for financing," Rhys said. "She'll be paying cash for the sale."

"Cash?" Chaz raised an eyebrow in Lexi's direction. "You have that kind of money sitting around?"

"Um, I don't think you're allowed to ask that." Rhys sighed.

"I think I have every damn right to ask that." Chaz scooted forward to the edge of his seat and turned fully towards Lexi. "I need to know what kind of person wants to live in Meemaw's house."

"That's fair." Lexi held her hand up to Rhys, who was looking a little frazzled at losing control over his meeting. "I got the money by donating my eggs. I figured, why not? I'm not using them. And I participated in a couple of pharmaceutical trials. Nothing too serious, just some antifungals and STD treatments."

"Seriously?" Chaz stared at her, slack-jawed.

"No!" Lexi threw her hands in the air. "I inherited a little money when my grandma passed away last year and figured I could either waste it on insanely high rent in New York City or make my dream come true and open my own shop here."

"Oh," Chaz snapped his mouth shut. "I'm sorry about your grandmother. We lost Meemaw last year, too."

"I'm sorry. It seems like you were a lot closer to your grandma than I was to mine."

Lexi wondered, not for the first time, what it would have been like to have a closer relationship with her grandma. Wondered what that kind of support could have changed for her throughout the years. But there was no point in pondering an impossibility.

"So, now that you know I'm not a pill-popper or drug dealer, what's next?"

Lexi looked up at the beautiful little Victorian house on the corner of the town square, where she would soon open her own bakery. Where she would live. Where she would build her new life in Fauna. Where her lifelong dream would finally come true.

As long as the hotheaded hunk next to her didn't change his mind.

Lexi watched Chaz out of the corner of her eye. He sighed heavily as his eyes moved over the old house. She knew he was noticing the faded paint and empty window boxes. It was far from dilapidated, but she could tell its current condition bothered him. Which raised a few questions.

"So, just for conversation's sake," Lexi spoke softly because she knew she was walking into dangerous territory, "if you own the house and don't want to sell it, why aren't you living in it? Fixing it up? Making it your home?"

"That is not a conversation I'm plannin' on havin' this morning." Chaz shot her a hard look, his eyes glinting like spun sugar in the light. Then his shoulders drooped, and he scuffed a boot on the sidewalk as his eyes darted away. "That's a family matter."

"Hey, I get it." Lexi nodded. "I have quite a few family matters that I don't plan on discussing this morning either. Or any morning, for that matter."

"But that's not my family." Chaz signed. "At least not how we used to be."

Lexi's heart sputtered. She knew the pain of family tensions too well. Her family didn't even know she'd left New York. And they certainly didn't know that Grandma had left her an inheritance. If they had, they'd have guilted it out of her, and it would have been gone within weeks, squandered on frivolous indulgences instead of being invested into a business. A dream.

"Sounds like you've had a lot of changes lately." Lexi turned to him as they made their way up the front walk.

"Yeah. It's been a rough year." Chaz scrubbed a hand over his face before running his fingers through his dark hair that curled slightly over his ears. "But we aren't here to talk about that. Let's look at the veranda and see what work needs to be done, then we'll head on inside."

"Ohhhh... the veranda." Lexi wiggled her shoulders and eyebrows in unison. "That sounds fancy. I love it."

"As opposed to what?" Chaz stopped on the top step and looked at her like she'd sprouted a unicorn horn.

"Um, the porch?"

"All you Northerners think anything on the outside of a house is a porch." He air-quoted the word and rolled his eyes. "Since this extends along the full front and around the side of the house, is covered with a roof, and is enclosed with a railing, it is, technically speakin', a veranda."

"Okay, Mr. Contractor, sir." Lexi smiled and saluted. "Glad to see you know your stuff."

"Trust me, darlin', I know my stuff."

For a moment they stood glued to the top step, eyes locked. Even if the morning hadn't been so hot already, she probably would have melted into a puddle right there. His rich, warm eyes never wavered from her icy blue ones. She blinked slowly, breaking the spell, and her mind sputtered back to life.

Flirting with a business partner was so not a good idea. Even if he was a yummy glass of sweet tea on a hot summer's day. Maybe especially because he was so yummy.

"Okay, let's not do the 'darling' thing again." Lexi patted his chest twice as she walked past him onto the veranda. "I was thinking we could add a couple of big fans out here for some outdoor seating. Add a fresh coat of paint, some flowers in the planters, and I think the outside would be fine. Unless..."

Lexi tilted her head, staring at the railing. The spindles were all intricately carved, which fit perfectly for an old-school, Victorian feel, but Lexi wanted to bring a little of New York to Fauna. In her mind, she saw sleek, black metal railings. Clean lines. A sharp contrast to white paint. No, not all white. Pale lavender on the house. White on the trim. She smiled as she pictured it.

"Unless what?" Chaz walked over; his voice tinged with worry.

"Picture it." She ran a hand along the railing as she explained her idea. She spun around, gesturing to where the large fans would go. Touched the side of the house where fresh paint would bring the vision to life. "Think high contrast. Sleek. Modern. A little piece of New York City right here in Fauna."

She felt rather breathless as she turned back to Chaz. He leaned against the railing with one hip and had his arms crossed over his chest. Lexi wasn't sure what he was thinking, but he had a small smirk on his lips, so she figured her impassioned speech must have moved him.

"Well, it's nice to see the passion come out of ya," he nodded and walked down to the other end of the veranda, "but you lost me when you said you wanted to paint my Meemaw's house purple."

"I said a nice shade of lavender," Lexi sputtered.

"And these railings were hand-carved right here in Fauna almost a hundred years ago. And you want to rip them out to put in metal?"

"Yes. Yes, I do." It was Lexi's turn to cross her arms over her chest.

"Let me show you somethin'," Chaz gestured for her to come closer and pointed to a specific portion of the railing. "Right here is where my brother got his head stuck between the spindles. My dad had to cut him out with a handsaw. And these two spindles right here?"

He knelt down and ran a hand over the wood. The two he pointed at didn't quite match the others; the cuts weren't as steady, leaving the curves slightly wavy.

"These were the first woodworking projects I ever did on my own," he continued. "Are they perfect? Nope. But these spindles right here are what showed me what I wanted to do with my life."

"Chaz," Lexi sighed, "I get that you have a ton of memories here. But who knows if you sell it to someone else that they wouldn't want to change out the railing too? If you're going to sell, you're going to have to make some compromises. This will be *my* bakery."

"You're right." Chaz stood and dusted off his knees. "We'll come back to it. I think if you give it some time, this railing will grow on you."

"Are you going to assume I'm going to forget or cave on everything? Cause let me tell you right now, that's not going to happen. I can be pretty persuasive too, buster."

"Persuading me is already gonna be a tall order. But it's not just me you have to worry about."

"What do you mean, not just you?" Lexi's eyes narrowed.

"Any changes to a building on the town square have to be approved by the town council." Chaz shrugged. "To make sure everyone is holdin' up our town's image and all."

"Oh, you have got to be kidding me."

"If you get all passionate and dreamy-eyed like you did here, I bet you'll sway a few of 'em at least." Chaz patted her on the shoulder as he walked past toward the front door. "Shall we take a look inside?"

Lexi wiped at her shoulder, hating that his warmth lingered. She spun on her heel and stomped into the house as Chaz held the door open.

Passionate and dreamy-eyed? Oh, she'd show him. When it came to her business, she could sell her cookies to a Girl Scout. Lexi knew Chaz was confident the town would side with him, but she was also confident. This was her dream.

And she'd show them all.

Chapter 5

L exi let her eyes adjust inside the house. Her thoughts and emotions were still churning from Chaz's dreamy-eyed comment and the news that she'd have to submit plans to the city council. His boots thudded across the floor behind her, followed by the swish of curtains sliding along a rod. Warm sunlight filtered in through the windows, and she got her first look at what would be her new bakery.

Warm mahogany wood dominated the foyer and adjacent dining room. The walls above the chair rail were painted a buttery yellow. She walked through the doorway and was surprised to see a large, open living space with a substantial stone fireplace on one side and a full wall-length mirror on the other.

"Beautiful, right?" Chaz stopped next to her and rocked back on his heels. His voice felt loud in the empty space.

"It's like the cover of all the Southern Living magazines." Lexi spun in a slow circle. "Minus the furniture and floral arrangements."

"Floral arrangements?" Chaz chuckled.

"From my research about Southern life," Lexi fidgeted with the hem of her sleeve and avoided looking at him, "floral arrangements are a key element."

"Lexi, please don't tell me your whole basis of Southern life comes from that magazine."

Lexi didn't need to turn around. Some things could just be heard in people's tone of voice. He was shaking his head at her. Maybe rolling his dark eyes at her ignorance.

Goddamn it, she wanted to belong here. Make a home. And if he kept picking holes in her piddly bit of confidence, she'd never make it. Everyone would see that she was just some city girl coming to live a Southern Living centerfold dream. A Southern sham.

Lexi stopped that train of thought and glanced around her at the beautiful woodwork, soaking in its warmth. She squared her shoulders and took a deep breath. She didn't learn to be a pastry chef in a day. That took years of schooling and grueling hours at work. Making a life here would be the same. She might not belong in Fauna just yet, but she'd learn. And she sure as heck wasn't giving up because Mr. Honeybuns over there wanted her out.

She turned on him, expecting the haughty stance and smirk. Hot words were cocked and loaded on her lips but cooled instantly at the sight of his face.

Chaz looked more relaxed than she'd ever seen him. His hands rested in his front pockets as he stared up at the coffered ceiling. They stood silently for a moment before he finally looked at her with a smile. It melted her heart faster than cotton candy on the tongue.

"Now, I'm not sayin' Southerners don't like things like sweet tea, red velvet cake, whiskey, and floral arrangements, just like the magazines say. Because most of us do. But let me show you what it really means to be from the South."

Chaz walked to the fireplace and placed a hand on the stone. When Lexi didn't move, he gestured for her to come closer. When she did, he gently took her hand and pressed it to the stone next to the one he'd touched. The contrast between the searing heat of his fingertips and the cold rock beneath her palm made her mind a little swimmy.

"My Pop built this fireplace back before havin' big, grand fireplaces was a thing. Why? Because my Meemaw wanted one. Her feet got cold and ached, and Pop wanted only the best for her." Chaz's voice was soft, almost wistful. "So, he asked the men in town to help him gather these huge rocks from down by the river and cart them up here. It took them three days of backbreaking work. And for what? It wasn't an emergency, just a luxury for his wife. But they still helped Pop and Meemaw because they knew when they needed someone, the favor would be returned."

"That's a lovely story, Chaz." Lexi pulled her hand down, giving the chunky rocks a quick once-over and stepping back. "But this really doesn't mesh with my vision."

"Hold on." Chaz held up a finger and started walking towards a hallway. "I'm not done yet."

He showed her the guest room where his daddy was born after the local doctor rushed back from a wedding in Jackson. He showed her the pedestal sink in the bathroom where his brother'd slipped and knocked out his front teeth, which were reattached after a house call from the town dentist. He walked her back to the dining room and told her about the colorful quilts created across the dining table by his Meemaw and her church group to pass out to families less fortunate than themselves.

"And finally, the most important room in any Southern home," Chaz pointed towards the only doorway they hadn't made it through yet. "The kitchen."

All of Chaz's stories were touching, but they didn't hold the same emotional weight for Lexi. Her family never stayed in one place long enough to form special memories with anyone or anything. And after living that way, she'd learned that if something needed to be done, she had to do it herself. Relying on others was too risky. They always let you down, one way or another. But if she could just get in to see the kitchen, she could start making out a plan for the first floor of the house to submit to the town council. Something modern and sleek. Simple, so the food was the star of the show.

"I can't wait to see it." She rubbed her hands together in anticipation as she walked through the door.

The kitchen was massive, with a center island and a large bay window at the opposite end that let in plenty of natural light. The cupboards were simple Shaker style, painted sage green, with a white countertop and backsplash. It felt fresh and springy. Lexi instantly loved it.

"Oh, my," she whispered.

"This is where the magic happened." Chaz slid past her. "Collard greens. Red beans and rice. Shrimp n' grits. Best fried okra in ten counties. My Meemaw ruled this kitchen like the queen she was."

"I think I would have liked your Meemaw," Lexi smiled.

"Everyone liked my Meemaw." Chaz leaned back against the counter. "She cooked for more than just our family here. She made bread for the soup kitchen every week. She canned jelly for the whole neighborhood. She taught more of the ladies in this town to cook than I can even count."

They stood silently for several minutes. Lexi had mixed feelings about her plans for a commercial kitchen in the space. This kitchen was so perfect as it was. She loved every detail of it, down to the magnolias painted on the tiles over the stovetop. But it wouldn't work for a business. A single oven couldn't keep up with a bustling bakery. It would have to go, and this was the first room where making changes didn't quite sit well with her.

"Do you see what I've been gettin' at, Lexi?" Chaz stepped away from the counter and moved towards her, his eyes searching. "What it really means to be from the South?"

"I mean, you've told me a lot about your family. And you really have a lot of memories here. But you do realize some things will have to change if I'm going to turn this into a business? I'm not trying to take those memories away from you. It's just the way it has to be."

"No one can take memories away. That's the joy of family. They'll always be there to remind ya if you happen to forget."

"Yeah, if you have fond memories to begin with." Lexi snorted.

"You can't tell me you don't have any good memories with your family?" Chaz took a step closer, looking puzzled.

"I bounced from one couch to another for my entire childhood. My parents took any opportunity they could get to be away from my sister and me." Lexi clasped her hands together in front of her. "So, no. Not everyone had the magnificent childhood you had. Some of us had to fend for ourselves."

"Well, if you want to live in Fauna, really belong here," Chaz closed the gap between them, resting his hands on top of her clenched ones, "that's the first thing you're gonna have to let go of. No one fends for themselves here. And that is something you can take to the bank, Lexi Caehill."

Tears sprang to the corners of her eyes. She took a step back to wipe them away before they could streak her mascara again. She was not rocking the pink eye look a second time. Chaz's nearness gave her both comfort and set her nerves on edge, like an open oven at your back.

"Mississippi has a heavy history, but Fauna is a special place. We all take care of one another." Chaz didn't move to step away, but let his hands fall to his sides. "Being a true Southerner isn't just about floral arrangements. It's about the people."

Chaz and Lexi spent the rest of the afternoon going through the upstairs and discussing what changes would need to be made to make it livable for Lexi once the bakery was complete downstairs. It would definitely need a bathroom and a small kitchen. She couldn't see herself sneaking down to use the commercial kitchen to cook herself dinner every night.

When they sat down to go over plans for the bakery, Chaz listened to all of Lexi's ideas. He wrote them down and drew them out on a blueprint. He didn't say a word as she talked about clean lines and white walls. He didn't even blink when she quietly mentioned gutting the kitchen to put in stainless steel, commercial-grade appliances and countertops. He drew in the simple metal railings she wanted to use on the porch without protest.

Then he pulled out a second piece of paper. He began writing, and Lexi looked over his shoulder to see what he was adding to her plans. But he wasn't adding anything. He was making a set of his own. The list of changes was much, much shorter, not taking into account any of the modernization she wanted.

"Seriously, Chaz?" Her rage bubbled just beneath the surface.

"I'm just tryin' to be prepared for the town hall meeting tomorrow." His tone was a little oversweet. "We need to have a backup plan in case they don't approve all these big changes."

"I don't think that's it at all." Lexi's tone was anything but sweet. "I think you just want to make a plan that's yours, that doesn't have any of the changes that you don't want. And you're going to push that one instead of mine so you can keep all your little memory spots in this house."

"I know this town, Lex." Chaz didn't even bother looking up from the plan he was making. "Nobody wants big-city style here. We want down-home comfort."

The fact that he'd used a nickname for her didn't escape her attention. It made her belly feel warm, like eating a bowl of butternut squash soup. But she couldn't focus on that; she had a point to get across.

"What, and down-home comfort requires chair rails and spindles?" Lexi threw her hands in the air.

"Yeah. Those are literally included in the definition of down-home comfort." He finally turned to face her.

Lexi could see a determination in his eyes that matched her own, but she wasn't one to back down. She'd spent a lifetime fighting for what she wanted.

"How do you know everyone in town wouldn't like a bit of big-city style?" She closed the space between them, eyes narrowed. "I think it's just you who wouldn't like something different because you're too afraid to let anything go."

"Oh, is that right?" He took a step in as well. "And you know this from your extensive knowledge of the town, right? Cause you've spent, what? A total of two days here now?"

Lexi closed the small space that remained between them and shoved a finger into Chaz's chest. She could feel the heat radiating off him down the whole front of her body through the fabric of her dress.

"Listen here, Buster. You might have scared me off yesterday with the 'you don't belong here' tactic. But that isn't working anymore." She twisted her finger against his chest to drive the point home. "I will make a life here. A damn good one, too. With or without your help."

Chaz opened his mouth to respond, but before the words could come out, the front door banged open and light footsteps came from the foyer. They both turned their heads just as Lotus walked into the living room. She stopped dead in her tracks at the sight of them pressed so closely together, and her eyebrows rose about an inch. Lexi's cheeks heated, and she took a hurried step backward.

"Can we help you, Lotus?" Chaz's voice sounded clipped, not at all like his typical sweet, Southern honey drawl. "It's pretty customary to knock before bargin' in."

"Hello to you too, Chaz Walker." Lotus just smiled. "I did knock, several times. Then I heard loud voices and figured you couldn't hear me."

"Oh." Chaz's tone softened. "What can we help you with?"

"Help me? I don't need any help. Lexi and I have a dinner date at the diner. I was a little early and Rhys happened to stop in and said the two of you were here, so I thought I'd come on over and get Lexi so she doesn't get lost or anything, bein' new here and all."

"That's very sweet," Lexi glanced around them, suddenly aware the sun was setting outside the windows. "Is it really 7 o'clock already?"

"On the nose." Lotus glanced down at the phone in her hand. "Time flies when you're having fun."

The day had been anything but fun. And Lexi was glad for it to be over. She grabbed her purse off the floor and walked over to Lotus.

"We can finish the plans tomorrow." She turned back to Chaz, who now looked as chill as a popsicle.

"Yes, ma'am."

Lotus threaded her arm through Lexi's, and they marched out the front door. Outside, the sky was a warm orange, and the air was sticky. But it felt fresh after being inside all day long. They walked down the front path and turned down the street toward the diner. Its lights were bright and spilled onto the walk of the town square ahead.

"Well, well, well," Lotus chuckled. "Getting settled and cozy with one of the Walker boys already, I see."

"What? No way." Lexi shook her head vigorously.

"Looked pretty cozy to me."

"That was the opposite of cozy."

"Passionate? Even better."

"Ugh. Lord, no. That man is infuriating. He battles my choices at every turn. He can't let anything go. And he is way too obsessed with the past and his family."

"What's wrong with being family-oriented?" Lotus looked perplexed. "Isn't that something people always want in a mate?"

"Mate? What is this, a shifter romance novel?" Lexi laughed. "No, being family-oriented is fine. He just has this way of bragging up his family that makes me feel bad about mine because it's different."

"Ah."

"Like, so what if my family moved around a lot and doesn't have a house that's been ours for multiple generations?" They turned at the corner toward the diner. "I could never be with a man who makes me feel bad about where I come from."

"Hear, hear!"

"Besides, I am so not in the place to start a relationship." Lexi paused outside the diner's door. "I have my bakery to open."

"Yes, you do, girl. And I want to hear all about it."

They both walked into the diner and slid into a booth. After ordering from Rosita, they settled in, and Lotus pulled a small notepad out of her purse.

"So, I want to know everything." Lotus tapped her pen against her lip, thinking. "What's the plan for the bakery? What's your baking history? But first, let's start with the big question. Why Fauna?"

"Well, that actually started right here in this diner..."

Lexi told her about visiting as a kid and the comforting feeling she had. And as she traveled down memory lane, taking her back to culinary school and the bakeries she'd worked at in New York, all thoughts of Chaz Walker slipped from her mind.

Almost.

Images of rich brown eyes and a tall, lean frame kept floating into her thoughts, bringing a slight frown to her face, but a flutter to her heart.

Chapter 6

After staying out way too late talking and laughing with Lotus at the diner, Lexi silenced all three of her alarms and snuggled further under her sheets until the sun was glaring through the window. When she finally reached for her phone, it shocked her to see that it was after 10 a.m. It'd been years since she'd slept so late, so long that she didn't even think she was capable of it anymore. But after the stress of the last week or so, she must have been more tired than she'd realized.

She rolled out of bed and padded over to the bathroom. While the shower water warmed up, she took a moment to evaluate herself. In the mirror, she saw her dark curls fanning wildly around her round face. Her hair was always out of control in the mornings, but that wildness didn't reach her eyes like usual. She always worried that the stress, pollution, and fast-paced city life would give her premature wrinkles, but that pinched, anxious look was gone and for the first time, her reflection looked serene. Almost happy.

"I guess there is something to this small-town life after all."

Lexi smiled and jumped into the shower, where she stayed until her fingers looked like prunes and her skin was rosy. She took time to twist her hair back and apply her favorite coppery eyeshadow. The shade reminded her of caramel, which made her think of a certain pair of dark, brooding eyes. Her stomach fluttered at the thought of Chaz Walker.

The clothing options in her suitcase weren't extensive, but she wanted to wear something impressive. Not only was she meeting with Chaz and Rhys to finalize the sale, but the city council meeting was that night, and she wanted to make a good impression. Last night, Lotus begged her not to attend the council meeting. She wanted more time to write a killer article that would get her published, but Lexi told her she couldn't delay the renovations until another council meeting. Lotus said they'd gladly call an emergency meeting because people lived for that kind of drama in Fauna, but Lexi didn't think that would make the best first impression and doubted Chaz would go for that idea anyway.

She settled on her favorite jewel-toned maxi dress. The top was a royal blue that made her eyes pop, and the skirt was covered in swirls of purples and greens. Lexi loved the feel of the fabric swishing around her legs as she hurried down the steps to find Mrs. Miller. She had a big favor to ask of the innkeeper.

"My, my, my. Aren't you a vision?" Mrs. Miller tutted from the hallway. "Give me a spin."

Lexi giggled and did as the older woman asked. She felt a little silly, but the attention also felt kind of good.

"You are going to have those Walker boys eating out of your hand, my dear." Mrs. Miller chuckled and went back to dusting the side table.

"I highly doubt that, but speaking of eating...I had a favor to ask." Lexi smiled nervously.

"Anything you need. Mi casa es su casa, as they say. I am in the business of hospitality, after all."

"I'm so glad you said that." Lexi linked her arm through Mrs. Miller's and started walking them both towards the kitchen. "I was hoping to bake a little something to take to the city council meeting tonight. You know, maybe butter them up a little. Both literally and figuratively."

"Ha. A little pastry chef humor?" Mrs. Miller pushed open the kitchen door and made a sweeping gesture with her arm. "The room is yours. Hope you don't mind if I watch. I'd love to see a master at work."

"Not at all!" Lexi exclaimed, clapping with excitement as she glanced around the large room. "You could even be my sous chef if you'd like."

"I would love that."

Mrs. Miller pulled two frilly aprons from hooks on the back of the door. She gave Lexi a brief tour of the kitchen and showed her the impressively stocked pantry.

"What do you want to make, dear?" Mrs. Miller's eyes sparkled.

"I'd hoped to make mini fruit tarts, but I wasn't sure if you'd have the correct pans. And I'll need to leave a few hours before the meeting to visit the real estate office. It's too hot here for those not to be refrigerated." Lexi pursed her lips to the side, thinking of other options that wouldn't need to stay cold.

"Didn't think I'd have the right pans..." Mrs. Miller muttered as she pulled several mini tart pans out of a cupboard. "Just leave them in the fridge here, and I'll bring them along with me when I head over tonight."

"You're going to the city council meeting too?" Lexi wasn't sure why she was so surprised.

"Of course." Mrs. Miller swatted her arm. "Don't let this old lady façade fool you. Every business owner goes to the meetings. Whether we're on the council or not, we all get a say."

"All business owners?" Lexi's eyes widened. "How long do these meetings last?"

"Oh, don't fret, dear. There aren't as many of us as you'd think." Mrs. Miller began pulling out tubs of flour and sugar. "Now, tell me all about your plans. I want to know ahead of time so I can start swaying the other council members to your side."

"You'd do that for me?" Lexi stopped opening the flour and looked at Mrs. Miller.

"I know a good egg when I see one." Mrs. Miller smiled at her, her gray eyes twinkling. "Besides, I'm not sure he knows it yet or not, but Chaz sees it too. No way he'd be selling that house to you otherwise."

"Oh." Lexi could feel her cheeks warming.

"In the few years he's been staying out in my carriage house, he's never sat down to eat with another guest." Mrs. Miller sighed, and Lexi could really see her age for the first time as her shoulders sagged. "That boy hasn't been right since Poppy passed. Mmm. A great woman, she was. One of my best friends. But that boy has been so stuck in the past, it's good to see him making some plans for the future."

"What?" Lexi sputtered. "You think those plans are with me?"

"Well, you're working together, aren't you?"

"Oh, yeah. I suppose we are." Lexi stared down at the flour again. "I thought you meant..."

"Oh, I did." Mrs. Miller bustled back from the fridge with butter and little baskets of fresh fruit. "We all know what happens when you're working in close quarters with someone you're attracted to."

"We are not attracted..."

"Oh, honey, that ship has sailed." Mrs. Miller threw her hands up with a full, bellowing laugh. "That match has been struck, and that spark is lit."

"Okay, geez. Is he attractive? Yes."

"Fine is more like it."

"Mrs. Miller!"

"What? I may be old, but I'm not dead."

"I'm here to start a business. Not a relationship." Lexi tried not to laugh as the old woman stared her down. "And if I were to get into a relationship, which I'm not, it wouldn't be with that stubborn, condescending, close-minded..."

"Hunk?" Mrs. Miller finished her sentence as she sliced strawberries.

"I'm not winning this argument, am I?" Lexi sighed.

"No, ma'am. Like I said, I know what I see. Now, tell me about these plans while you mix the dough. I need to know everything, baking secrets and remodel plans."

As Lexi gently mixed the cold butter into the dry ingredients, she told Mrs. Miller all about her vision for the bakery. She hoped that between the treats and Mrs. Miller's help, she could win over the council.

If it wasn't enough, and she was stuck with Chaz's 'backup plan' for her bakery, she didn't know what she'd do. How was someone supposed to handle their lifelong dream being denied and hijacked by a controlling contractor? As she prepared to roll out the tart dough, she guessed it could involve the head-knocking rolling pin she currently wielded. Lexi's knuckles tightened on the handles.

"I know what you're thinking, dear." Mrs. Miller said. "Sometimes people deserve a good whoopin', but sometimes you gotta sweeten them up. That whole 'you catch more flies with honey than vinegar' thing."

That gave Lexi pause. Growing up with zero control over anything in life left her with the philosophy to not take any guff from anyone. Most people would not describe her as 'sweet,' regardless of her profession. But maybe it was time to change that. Maybe changing her approach wouldn't hurt. New town, new start, and all.

As she rolled out the dough, her body fell into a rhythm. Her movements became fluid as she relaxed into the comforting task of making pastry cream, whisking the custard on the stovetop before putting it in the fridge to cool. She chatted with Mrs. Miller all while her mind rolled over possibilities. Could she be sweet enough to sway people to her side? Would that be better than stepping up and demanding what she wanted and deserved?

She couldn't make any decisions on the vinegar versus sugar dilemma because she didn't know the people she'd be dealing with. What she could do was make a backup plan of her own. Just in case. She just hoped she wouldn't need to use it.

Lexi paced back and forth outside the real estate office. It was time to close on the house, and her feet were colder than the liquid nitrogen she used to make ice cream. She knew the bakery could be exactly what she wanted, but she wasn't sure Chaz would let that happen. Or the city council. Especially since Chaz was kind enough to supply them with a backup plan that fell right in line with everything else already in Fauna.

Would being like everything else be so bad? She wanted to fit in after all. But could she do that if it meant not being true to herself?

Lexi sighed and leaned back against the shop window. The afternoon sun reflected off the glass at her back, making her already clammy skin damp with sweat. With the uncertainty of the council meeting that night, she wished they could put off this closing meeting until the next day. But Rhys had been adamant about closing as soon as possible so Chaz wouldn't have the option to change his mind and back out.

But closing before the council meeting didn't leave the option to change *her* mind or back out. Whatever they decided tonight was what she'd be stuck with. Was that something she wanted to risk? Or would it be better to close after the council meeting, but risk Chaz changing his mind and backing out? There was risk either way, and Lexi didn't like that.

She realized how naïve she'd been moving down here. She'd expected all rainbows and butterflies. To be welcomed with open arms and fit right in. Instead, she'd been saddled with a house that might or might not be her dream bakery and a snarky contractor who may or may not make that dream come true.

Lexi sighed deeply and let her head fall back onto the glass

"You doing alright out here?" Rhys asked from the doorway.

"Sure." Lexi plastered on a fake smile that crumbled almost instantly. "Maybe? No."

"That's a whole lot of options." Rhys chuckled.

He moved to lean against the glass next to her. Lexi eyed his suit, wondering how he looked so pristine and dry. How did anyone stay dry on a Mississippi afternoon? And it was only May. How much worse was it going to be at the height of summer? Rhys tugged at the sleeve of his wrinkle-free suit coat, picking at a flaw Lexi couldn't even see.

"I think maybe I just have cold feet." Lexi clasped her hands in front of her, clenching them over and over and watching as her knuckles turned from red to white and back again.

"That's totally normal." Rhys nodded. "Buying a property is a big decision. One of the biggest in most people's lives. Do you have any questions I can answer for you?"

"Yeah, can you get your brother to back off and chill out?" Lexi snapped. Her hand flew to her mouth as she realized what she'd just said out loud. So much for taking the sugar route. She was vinegar all the way through.

"Ha. Straight to the point. I like that." Rhys shook his head and smiled. "If anyone could figure out how to make Chaz chill, it would have saved a lot of people a lot of headaches. My brother is a lot of things, but 'chill' is not one of them."

"Maybe I should look at the other properties?" Lexi chewed her lip. She'd toyed with the idea all night, wondering if it would save her a lot of headaches down the road. "They don't have the space for me to live in, and that would drain most of my resources, but if they didn't need a lot of remodeling, I could probably swing it."

"Lexi, can I be straight with you?" Rhys turned to her.

His intense gaze held hers. His eyes were darker than Chaz's, the color of a rich ganache, and much more serious, making her wonder if he ever cut loose or relaxed.

"Always."

"None of those other options are going to give you the foot traffic and presence like a house right on the town square. You want what's best for your business? You're going to have to deal with Chaz." Rhys pushed off the wall. He paused and shuddered. "And that is not a task I would put on someone lightly. But, from what I've seen and heard, I think you, more than anyone, can handle it."

Seen and heard? Lexi's mind latched onto that one phrase and couldn't move past it.

"Heard? What exactly have you heard, Rhys?" Lexi wet her lips with her tongue, eager for the answer.

"I'm not going there. I will not be the middleman in this relationship." Rhys smiled and opened the office door. "But I'll tell you this, Chaz is out back pacing and fretting, same as you. I know for you this is business, but this is his heart. So, tread lightly. Please." Rhys stepped inside, out of the sun. "He may be pigheaded and sassy as a schoolgirl, but he's still my brother. And this last year has been hard on him."

"Can I ask you one more thing?" Lexi looked down at her shoes, wishing she'd gone with flats. Even a kitten heel was dangerous when the bottoms of your feet were sweating.

"Shoot."

"Why did he take your Meemaw's death so hard? Were they super close?"

Lexi waited a beat. Then two. Rhys stood unmoving in the doorway. His dark suit melded into the darkness of the interior, leaving only his hand on the knob visible in the sunlight. Lexi was beginning to think she'd crossed a line. Maybe some Southern thing she was ignorant of. But then Rhys let out a heavy sigh.

"There's a lot there I can't tell ya, 'cause it's not my place."

His normally precise speech was suddenly tinged with a hint of a drawl. A faint resemblance to Chaz. Lexi knew that was the emotion seeping into his words. She wasn't talking to her realtor now; she was talking to a brother and grandson.

"When Meemaw passed, Chaz took it on himself to try to hold this family together. But sometimes when you hold on too tight, you start to strangle the thing you love most." He suddenly stepped out into the light and clasped her hands in his own. "I think sellin' that house could be the healing balm our family needs. Chaz knows it too, just won't admit it. So, please don't let him scare you off. Our family needs this."

Rhys dropped her hands and quickly turned inside. Lexi began pacing outside the door again. That was a lot more information than she'd hoped to get, even if it wasn't anything specific. After that plea from Rhys, there was no way she could back out. And she realized she didn't want to.

Would fighting with Chaz over every detail be obnoxious? Yep. But if she was being honest with herself, a small part of her was looking forward to it. She liked the way his eyes deepened from honey to gingerbread when he was upset. And how his drawl got stronger as he argued. So, yes, the remodel with Chaz Walker would be annoying. But it would also be exciting. And Lexi knew she couldn't walk away from that.

Chapter 7

L exi finally stopped pacing and went inside the real estate office. She was worried she'd leave a trail of dripping sweat if she stayed outside any longer. The lobby was empty and blissfully cool. Lexi wasn't sure how anyone handled living in the South before the invention of air conditioners. If they didn't exist, her life dreams would have been very different, and she'd probably be living in Canada somewhere.

After Rhys told her about their family and Chaz's struggles since Meemaw died, Lexi felt a shift in her attitude. Yes, she wanted this bakery. Yes, she wanted to live here. And yes, she wanted to help Chaz through this. Even though they'd just met, she couldn't help feeling a connection with him. And not just because of his perfect backside, which definitely didn't hurt.

"That does not mean we have 'a relationship'." Lexi quietly repeated Rhys's words and scoffed. "No way. No how. Not going there. I mean, friends are great. I could definitely use some friends here. And they take *way* less time than a boyfriend. So, he'll just be a boy who's a friend. A friend with a gorgeous backside. I've had those before, right?"

Lexi tried to think, but she was one hundred percent certain she'd remember a backside like Chaz's. New York City didn't grow men like Chaz Walker. He came from a lifetime of physical work, like digging fence posts and rustling cattle. Lexi stopped when she realized her mind had veered off into some Western cowboy fantasy.

"Just because he wears boots and a hat does not make him a cowboy," Lexi muttered to herself and stopped pacing behind a plush leather armchair. "Leave the cattle rustling to the novels."

"You know that's illegal, right?" Someone cleared their throat behind her.

Lexi slowly spun on her heel to see Chaz leaning against the doorframe to Rhys's office. He twisted his worn hat between his fingers.

"How much of that did you hear?" Lexi's voice croaked. The thought of him hearing her mutterings about his backside turned her cheeks as red as maraschino cherries.

"Just you mutterin' about cattle rustling." His eyes narrowed. "That'll get you locked up faster 'en green grass through a goose."

"Huh?"

"Stealing cattle..." He slowly leaned off the wall and took a step towards her with each word, "...is illegal."

"Hold up." Lexi raised a hand. "Rustling is stealing?"

"Yeah." Chaz stopped his advance and looked at her like a cricket just climbed out of her nose. "What did you think it was?"

"I dunno. Wrangling them?" Lexi floundered for words. "Gathering them into a group...a herd?"

"Lord have mercy," Chaz muttered and shook his head. "You mean round up."

"Oh. Roundup. I'm going to have to go back and re-read a few books. This adds a whole new level of danger that I totally missed." Lexi smiled as she brushed past a befuddled Chaz on her way to Rhys's office.

"What kind of books are you readin'?" Chaz spun after her.

"The steamy variety."

"Steam? And cattle? What are you doin'? Roundin' 'em up to take to the day spa?"

Lexi stopped, looked at the seriously confused look on Chaz's face, and doubled over with laughter. Rhys stood up from his desk and looked between the two of them as Lexi's vision blurred with tears.

"Everything okay?" Rhys sounded both confused and like he wanted in on the joke.

"She's out there mutterin' about cattle rustling and doesn't know the difference between felony theft and a spring roundup." Chaz looked between Lexi and Rhys and threw his hands in the air. "If that's how you were plannin' to bankroll this purchase, the deal's off."

Lexi started laughing even harder. The image of her, in her vintage dresses and cat-eye makeup, on horseback, steeling cows was too much, and she toppled into one of the chairs in front of Rhys's desk.

"I've checked out her finances, and I assure you, Chaz, she doesn't need to resort to stealing cattle to pay for the bakery." Rhys plopped into his seat with a snicker.

"Then what the heck is she talkin' about steam and cattle in books for?"

Rhys gestured for Chaz to come closer and whispered in his ear. Lexi stopped laughing as Chaz leaned over the desk, giving her a perfect view. She tried not to stare and instead dabbed at the tears in the corners of her eyes.

"They do what now?" Chaz sounded shocked as he turned toward Lexi and raised an eyebrow. "I assure you, when you're rounding up a couple hundred head of cattle, there isn't time for 'steamy' romance."

"Oh, I assure *you*, they make time." Lexi glanced at Rhys and pressed her lips together to keep herself from laughing again. "It's just a little extra ride time."

"Or maybe some roping practice?" Rhys said, and they both started laughing as Chaz leaned back and crossed his arms.

"Well, this is definitely not how I expected this meeting to go," Chaz sighed. "I'm sure Meemaw is lookin' down, shakin' her head at this."

"Oh, please," Rhys smoothed his suit coat back into place. "She'd be throwing out more jokes than either of us and laughing even harder."

"For a contractor and realtor, you seem to know a lot about cattle." Lexi cleared her throat and slid her hands over her legs. "Is that something people around here just know?"

"Partly, I s'pose," Chaz said. "Other part is because our family's been workin' on a ranch for generations."

"Yep. Most of the family is still there." Rhys straightened his coat sleeves and leaned back slightly. "It's right outside of town if you ever want to see what cattle are actually like."

"I think I'll stick to baking and leave the rustling," she held her hands up in apology when Chaz glared at her, "sorry, round-ups, to the books."

"Can we just get a move on?" Chaz turned to stare at the wall. "I need to get everything ready for the council meeting tonight."

"I want to help with that." Lexi sat forward in her chair, leaning her head in to get Chaz to look at her. "Well, with my plan. You can leave yours at home."

"I just did that as a backup. In case the council doesn't want a slice of New York City here in Fauna."

"I think it's more because you don't want a slice of New York City here in Fauna."

"You're right. I don't." Chaz pressed his palms into the desk and stared at Lexi. "Why is it that big-city folks always come to small towns and think we want to be just like them? Ever consider that we live here because we don't want the big city life? That maybe we like our small, little slice of heaven?"

"Okay, I think we're getting a little off track," Rhys said.

Lexi raised a hand to Rhys and stared Chaz straight in the eye. Their beautiful honey color glinted at her like antique brass, hard and cold. Chaz wanted her to back down. To have a reason to walk away from the sale. Lexi hadn't forgotten what Rhys said. His family needed this. Lexi didn't know why, but she wasn't going to walk away. Not today.

"It's important for a town to have varied businesses to suit every taste. It's what creates a strong and prosperous market."

Lexi cheered internally when Chaz leaned back in his seat and eyed her suspiciously. He'd probably expected her to take the bait and get emotional, not pull out the business owner tactics. With a small smirk, she followed his lead and leaned back in her chair.

"What's next, Rhys?" She turned to him with a calm smile.

"I just need you both to sign a couple of papers and set up the wire transfer for the purchase funds."

"Okay," she pulled herself closer to the desk as Rhys slid a pile of paperwork across to her, "let's do this."

Lexi signed where Rhys indicated and then passed the paperwork over to Chaz, who still had yet to utter a sound. From the corner of her eye, she watched as he scrawled his signature on the page. His writing was tall and sharp, a lot like the man himself.

When they were finally done, Lexi and Rhys both turned to Chaz, wondering what his next move would be. The papers were signed. As soon as the wire transfer went through, the house would legally be hers.

She'd expected a fight. An emotional plea. Bargaining. But the silent resignation as he reached into his pocket and pulled out a set of keys tugged at her heart more than any of those other options could have.

He stared at the keys in his hand. The metal was worn and dirty, with specks of the original gold only remaining in the deepest grooves. They were both on a wooden keychain carved into a cluster of poppies and painted red. Lexi had a pretty good idea who made it.

He hesitated for a brief second before dumping the keys on the desk. Then, he stood without a word and walked briskly from the room, the sound of his boots ringing out across the lobby. Lexi spun to watch him go, wishing she could ease the tense lines of his shoulders and the deep creases between his eyes. The door slammed behind him, and the silence that followed was absolute.

She'd just bought a bakery.

Her dreams were falling into place.

So, why did her stomach feel like she'd just eaten an entire tub of lemon sherbet? Why did her heart ache and demand that she run after him?

She turned slowly; her dress swooshing softly against the leather of the seat. The red poppy keychain lay directly in front of her, but she made no move to grab it.

"Well, congratulations?" Rhys offered, pushing the keys closer to her with the end of his pen.

"Thanks," she sighed and reached out to touch the wood, feeling its smooth surface beneath her fingertips. Lexi wrapped her fingers around the keys and pushed back from the desk. They felt heavy in her hand, like years of memories and expectations. But she knew she could shoulder the weight. It's nothing she hadn't done before, proving herself time and time again.

"How are you going to celebrate?" Rhys leaned back, trying to act cool and salvage the moment.

"Um. Well," Lexi thought for a moment, "by going to this council meeting and winning them over to see my dream."

Lexi walked back into the early afternoon heat, the bakery keys jiggling in her hand. She almost wished Chaz had fought her on the sale. Had yelled. Cried. Anything but the quiet.

Her eyes darted one way down the street, then the other. She wanted nothing more than to go back to the cool, cozy B&B to rest so she could go to the city council meeting feeling refreshed, but she knew she couldn't. Her foot slid off the sidewalk onto the brick street, heading in the direction of the bakery. Her bakery. Her home.

Chaz said he needed to work on the plans, so she hoped that meant he'd actually be there. Her heart and her mind were both in agreement that she needed to see him, but their reasons were very different.

Her heart said that she needed to ease his pain somehow. There had to be a way to show him that his Meemaw's house was safe in her hands. Did she understand his emotional attachment to a house? No, because she'd never had a place to call her own, but that didn't mean she couldn't see what it meant to him.

Her mind, the selfish one, knew she couldn't go into the council meeting without Chaz on her side. As much as she hated to admit it, she needed him. And according to Rhys, Chaz needed her. She didn't need to know why the Walker family needed to get rid of Meemaw's house, but it did make her wonder. Did Meemaw leave them in debt? Was the upkeep of the house too much of a financial burden? At the diner, Tia Sylvia said Chaz had been working extra lately. Was that all for the house? Lexi tried to think of a reason other than finances that would require them to sell a home Chaz so obviously loved, but couldn't come up with anything. If money was the cause, she hoped the inheritance her grandmother left her would not only make her dreams come true but help solve the Walkers' issues as well.

As she strolled down the Magnolia tree-lined square, that final thought made her feel better. Buying the bakery was good for them both. She took a deep breath and felt some of the tension leave her shoulders. The keys in her hand didn't feel like as much of a burden, but more like, well, keys. To a new door that opened to a happier, easier life here in Fauna.

Lexi nodded at several ladies exiting a small shop on her way across the town square. She noticed a few raised eyebrows but didn't bother to stop for introductions. As she passed them, she smiled, remembering Lotus telling her to lie low. Although the little secret of her arrival would be blown out of the water at the city council meeting, she could at least try to keep a low profile until then. The idea of stopping to exchange pleasantries when she was in a hurry to get to the bakery sounded awful anyway.

Her step faltered as she hesitated. Was that just the New Yorker in her coming out? Wouldn't the polite, Southern thing be to stop and chat? Didn't time move more slowly down here? Or was that just the people? Lexi shook those questions from her mind and pushed forward. There would be plenty of time to confront her big-city behaviors in the future. Right now, she needed to guarantee her bakery even had a future. At least one that she wanted.

Chaz's truck sat outside the bakery. The man himself sat on the porch swing, rocking it gently back and forth. As Lexi climbed the steps, she could hear the rhythmic sound of his boots scraping against the wood. She stopped in front of the swing, leaning a hip against the railing. After watching him for a moment, she turned to stare out at the small yard where his eyes were glued. Together, they stared at the grass and watched heatwaves roll off the road.

"I figured you'd come here straight off," Chaz cleared his throat and slid the phone he'd been holding into his pocket. "Wantin' to see your new house and all."

"I came here to see you, actually."

"Me?" Chaz scooted over on the swing, and Lexi took the unspoken invitation to slide up next to him.

"To make sure you're okay." She looked down at the keys in her hand and then up at Chaz. "With all of this."

Chaz's eyes had never left the yard, and Lexi quietly watched his profile. His jaw ticked as he pressed his lips together before letting out a deep sigh. The tension rolled off him like water down the side of a glass of iced tea in the sunshine. He turned to her, looking more like the man she had met at the diner than any time she'd met him previously.

"Yeah. I'm okay," he said and smiled.

Actually smiled. With teeth and everything. Lexi gaped for a moment before remembering to snap her mouth shut. It was her turn to stare straight ahead, although hers was more from embarrassment than long, pensive thought.

"Really," he chuckled, the sound low, decadent, and causing butterflies to erupt in Lexi's stomach. "I'm okay."

"Seriously?" She dared a side glance at him through her lashes.

"Yep. Cowboy's honor."

"What the hell?" Lexi smacked his shoulder with the back of her hand a little harder than necessary.

"Ouch." Chaz turned to her, rubbing his arm. "What was that for?"

"After everything over the last few days, you just come and sit on the porch for a bit and everything is hunky-dory?" Her eyes narrowed as she turned to face him. Their knees collided on the small swing. At least her scrapes from their first meeting had healed enough that she didn't jerk back, but held her ground. "If I knew all you needed was a five-minute timeout, I would have done this the first day I met you."

"You think you could put me in time out?"

"You think I couldn't?" Lexi raised her eyebrows and crossed her arms over her chest.

"Honestly? I don't know, but I'd kind of like to see you try." Chaz waggled his eyebrows at her and stood so abruptly the swing lurched forward. "Now, how about we get inside and finish those plans of yours for the city council tonight?"

Lexi held on as the swing settled. What in the world was going on? Was this man bipolar? Was he more in touch with his feelings than any other man on the planet and able to work through them at lightning speed? Maybe he wasn't of this planet. Maybe he was from a more evolved race of extraterrestrial beings where they could turn their feelings on and off, or look at things with the logical mind instead of the sensitive heart? How else could she describe this abrupt shift in his behavior?

Lexi tilted her head, thinking for a moment, and decided she didn't care what caused this change in behavior. She would just take it as a blessing and run with it. But what she did know for certain was that Chaz was either mentally unstable or an alien. She hoped for the latter. She'd read a few sci-fi romances. And she definitely preferred them over the self-help and psychological genres.

She stood up from the swing, following Chaz to the front door. Her worries about the city council meeting were gone since Chaz seemed to be firmly on her side. She was slightly concerned for her own sanity as she gave Chaz a thorough once-over, looking for antennae, gills, or anything else that pointed to an alien life form. She didn't see any of that, but as they went inside, she did have to admit that his backside was definitely out of this world.

Chapter 8

The evening sun turned the small, white church the color of whipped butter as Lexi slid out of Chaz's truck. They'd spent the day at the house, finalizing her plan. Chaz had written down everything, drawn it on the diagrams, and hadn't argued even once. Not even over his hand-carved spindles on the front porch.

Lexi felt so close to her dream. So close to it actually coming true. She clasped her hands tightly in front of her as she stared up at the bell in the steeple. Everything in Fauna was like something from a storybook. And her very own Prince Charming was coming around to the passenger side to close the door behind her. He offered his hand as she lifted her skirt to step up onto the sidewalk. His warm fingers held hers firmly as their eyes met.

Lexi hoped she wasn't imagining the disappointment that flashed in his golden eyes as he slowly released her hand and cleared his throat. She wanted to ask him about his change in attitude over selling the house. Did he finally realize he wouldn't be financially burdened anymore? Was he ok with her specifically owning something that he loved? And if that was the case, what did that mean? If he loved that house, and everything pointed to him seriously loving it, and he was suddenly fine with her owning it, did that mean he accepted her? Maybe more than accepted her? Lexi couldn't even wrap her head around that idea.

"Hey, looks like you two have made up since this morning." Rhys hopped up onto the sidewalk next to them.

"What? I mean... We're fine. Right?" Lexi looked at Chaz, whose lips were pulled to one side in a smirk. "We're fine."

"What she said." Chaz placed his hand on the small of her back, urging her toward the church doors.

"Mom said you called Mason." Rhys stepped up to walk alongside Chaz.

"Geez. You guys have a calling circle set up or what?" Chaz picked up the pace, applying more pressure to Lexi's back.

"Something like that." Rhys matched Chaz step for step and leaned forward to smile at Lexi. "Good luck tonight."

"Um, thank you." She sounded like she had a mouth stuffed with marshmallows as Chaz's fingers on her back were doing crazy things to her brain. Lexi quickened her step to get some distance between herself and Chaz. She needed to have her head on straight for the city council meeting.

They all walked up the front steps, and Rhys pulled open one of the massive wooden doors and ushered her through. Inside, it was dark and cool. She could hear voices off in the distance somewhere and followed the Walker brothers down a side hallway to a set of stairs.

As the voices grew louder, so did the doubts inside her mind. What was she doing walking down a dark basement hallway in a tiny Mississippi town, placing her life's dream at the feet of people she'd never met for their approval? She clutched her hands into a ball in front of her, squeezing her fingers tightly together.

Just before walking through a set of double doors, thrown open and spilling light into the hall, both men turned to her and paused. Chaz looked magnificent standing on the border between light and dark. The shadows accentuated his sharp cheekbones, and seeing him like that was almost enough to take her mind off the upcoming meeting. Almost.

The smile slowly slid from Chaz's face as Lexi waited in the hallway. He whispered something to Rhys, who gave her a quick second glance, then turned and walked through the doors. She could feel her breath coming faster and prayed she wouldn't have a panic attack. Not now. Not in front of him. She clenched her hands together tighter, her nails biting into her palms.

"Hey." Chaz walked back to her side and rested a hand on her shoulder. "You alright?"

"No." Lexi croaked, thankful Rhys wasn't also here to see this. "What am I doing?"

"Currently, standing in the middle of a dark hallway." Chaz stepped in front of her to get a better look at her face. He smiled at her, but when she didn't smile back, he sighed. "What are you doing? Okay. You're following your dream. Right? That's what you said?"

"Yeah."

"Okay." He hesitated a moment, determining whether she was ready to head inside. When she didn't move, he continued, "You followed that dream all the way here to Fauna. You found the perfect place to make that dream come true. And now you're gonna go in there and make all of them see that dream. See you. Because it's beautiful—"

"Me or my dream?" Lexi interrupted.

"What?"

"What's beautiful? Me or my dream?"

Lexi could hardly believe the words coming out of her mouth, but her mind, and, let's face it, her body, were desperate for a distraction from the panic dripping into her veins like a melting ice cream cone. The cold, sticky feeling was quickly replaced by a warmth spreading outward from her center. She knew it was selfish to flirt with Chaz as a simple distraction, but she couldn't stop herself. It all felt so easy and natural with him.

"Does it have to be an either-or kind of thing? Or can we just say both?"

"I will accept that answer." Lexi could feel her heart beating faster, and not because of the anxiety this time.

"Now, you've gone and interrupted my grand speech." Chaz took a small step closer. "Where was I?"

"Currently? In a dark hallway." Lexi leaned closer, only an inch or so, but it was enough.

Chaz's eyes slid down to her lips, and she smiled slowly. He snapped his gaze back to hers. They both stood, frozen, for the briefest second before Chaz shook his head.

"Lexi, I'd be a foolish man not to want to kiss those lips of yours right now, but we happen to be standin' in the house of God, and that just doesn't sit right with me."

"People kiss at weddings all the time."

"This is not a wedding. And even couples at weddings only give each other a quick peck because kissin' in church is just weird."

"I mean, technically, we're beneath a church. Does the 'hallowed ground' thing go down into the earth? Or is it, like, a surface-level thing?"

"Are we really havin' this debate right now?" Chaz's hands slid from her shoulders down her arms and rested at her elbows.

"Yes. I believe we are." Lexi cocked her head and pursed her lips. "Do we get cell service down here? I can Google that and have an answer in half a second."

Lexi reached for her purse, but Chaz reached out to grab her hand.

"Lexi. I don't want to google whether we can have our first kiss. It will happen when it's supposed to."

"Is that a promise?"

"I sure to God hope so."

"Oop. We're in his house," Lexi pointed up, "remember?"

Chaz stepped back and rolled his eyes. "What in the world am I gettin' myself into with you, Lexi Caehill?"

"A lot of work. On the bakery, not me. And probably a lot of baked goods."

"Well, I happen to really enjoy my job and pastries. So, sounds like a win-win to me." Chaz let his hands fall from hers. "I never did finish my speech. Do you still need it?"

"Nope." Lexi straightened her shoulders and stepped towards the open doors. Out of the shadows and into the light. "You, sir, are an excellent distraction."

Lexi stared at the table of food set at the back of the large conference room. Cornbread. Peach cobbler. Biscuits with butter and honey. It was a smorgasbord of Southern delights.

"Can't have a meeting in Mississippi without at least thirty side dishes," Chaz whispered while popping a few fried okra into his mouth.

"Wish I had known that before making fruit tarts this morning," Lexi muttered, but didn't see them on the crowded table.

"Just save them for the presentation. Give them a real taste of who you are."

"That's a good plan," Lexi nodded, assuming they were with Mrs. Miller, and turned to the rest of the room.

Their near-kiss had been an excellent distraction in the hallway, but now that she was in the room, Lexi wished for something else to take her mind off the doubts resurfacing in her mind.

About thirty people milled around the room, most chatting in clusters at the small tables scattered in front of a large rectangular one. She craned her neck to scan the crowd, but didn't see Mrs. Miller anywhere. Hopefully, the fruit tarts weren't too much for her. Baked goods could be deceptively heavy. She had the arm muscles to prove it.

"Come on," Chaz said around a mouthful of something, "I'll introduce you."

"Hopefully, you'll finish chewing first." Lexi scolded, then hastily wiped crumbs from Chaz's shirt.

"Thank ya, ma'am." Chaz tipped his imaginary hat, then took her by the elbow and slowly guided her to a group of men standing at one of the back tables. "These are the farmers, ranchers, and livestock folk. They aren't gonna care much about what your store looks like, but if you want fresh milk, eggs, flour, and the like, these are your guys."

The thought of fresh, locally sourced ingredients perked Lexi right up, and she easily slipped into business mode. She shook hands, laughed at cow jokes (who knew there could be so many?), and exchanged contact information with several of them.

"Sure was a pleasure meetin' you, Lexi," one of them said. "We look forward to workin' with you."

"As do I," Lexi said. "Trust me, I'll be milking these relationships for all they're worth."

She let it sink in for a moment before smiling. Then she turned and walked away to riotous laughter.

"Who taught you how to win over ranchers?" Chaz guided her toward another group at a different table.

"Just matching their energy." Lexi shrugged.

"Well, I'd highly suggest not doing that with this crowd," Chaz raised his eyebrows and widened his eyes before turning back to the new group with a plastered-on smile. "Hello, ladies. How are you all doing this evening?"

"Oh, Chaz, darling. How are you?"

"You've been working so hard lately."

"Are you eating enough?"

"Yes, ladies," Chaz laughed as the old ladies clucked over him. "I'm fine. I'm eating. Everything is good. In fact, I want y'all to meet someone."

Lexi stepped around Chaz and gave the group a small wave. The women went from grandmotherly fawning to prim and proper in a split second. Their backs straightened and their feet tucked under their seats, neatly crossed at the ankles. A couple smiled at her, but most looked at her with bored, almost hostile glares.

"Ladies, this is Lexi Caehill. She's just purchased my Meemaw's house and will be opening a bakery right here on the town square."

There was a collective sharp intake of breath.

"Lexi," Chaz ignored their shock, "I'd like to introduce you to the ladies of the Garden Society, one of the most prominent clubs in town."

"We are not a club, dear," a lady sitting at the center of the group spoke up. Lexi could tell she was the ringleader by the way all the other ladies nodded a little too eagerly in response. "What do we look like? A group of boys gathering to guzzle whiskey and smoke cigars?"

"Of course not, Lady Carmichael."

"We are a society here to preserve the history and atmosphere of Fauna." She swiveled in her chair toward Lexi. "Something I seriously hope you'll be taking into consideration, young lady."

"Of course, ma'am." Lexi clasped her hands together in front of her.

"We saw your name on the evening's schedule. We were discussing if you belonged to the Caehill's in Vicksburg, but," she paused and Lexi could physically feel the woman's eyes rake up and down her body, "you obviously are not from our great state. So, tell me. Where do you hail from?"

Where Chaz's drawl was all warm honey and soothing to her ears, Lady Carmichael's was like undercooked marmalade. Should have been sweet but came out bitter.

"Well, most recently from New York," Lexi wrung her fingers, "but before that, a little bit of everywhere."

"A little bit of everywhere?" Lady Carmichael mimicked her, "No. Where did y'all grow up? A child has to have a home."

"As I said," Lexi could feel heat rising to her cheeks, "we moved around a lot."

"Well, that is a shame. Everyone needs roots. Otherwise, you end up weak. Stunted."

"I'm sorry," Lexi took a step forward, "did you just--?"

"Ack-hum. Hello." Someone cleared their throat into the microphone at the front of the room. "If everyone will take their seat, we are ready to begin."

Chaz latched onto Lexi's elbow and pulled her away. He led them to an empty table at the side of the room and plunked her into a seat. Lexi looked back at the Garden Society. All the women sat perfectly straight with their hands crossed in their laps, but she could see the slight smirk on Lady Carmichael's face.

"Did she seriously call me stunted?" Lexi hissed into Chaz's ear.

"That's almost a compliment from her." Chaz sighed. "Don't take it personally. They just don't handle change well. I mean, the whole purpose of their 'society' is to keep this town from ever changin.'"

"You couldn't have given me a head's up?"

"There is no preparin' for the Garden Society. You just take what you get and move along." Chaz turned from looking at the speaker in the front to look her square in the eye. "Trust me on this one, Lexi. You do *not* want to get on their bad side. They will ruin you before you even open in this town."

"So, everyone just lets them act like that? No consequences?" Lexi said in a hushed whisper as the speaker in front began his welcome speech.

"They aren't all bad. They do a lot of good for Fauna. Raise a lot for charity."

"That's like saying Hitler was a good guy because he preserved all the artwork he looted."

Chaz barked out a laugh before covering his mouth. Lexi felt the tension ease out of her shoulders as she dissolved into silent giggles next to him. Half the room stared at them as they huddled together beside the table, shaking with semi-silent laughter.

"Well, since they already have our attention, I guess now is a good time to give them the floor," the old man presiding over the meeting spoke into the microphone. "Lexi Caehill and Chaz Walker, please come up and present your business plan to the committee."

Chapter 9

The laughter between Lexi and Chaz died instantly. She could feel everyone watching them as she stood. Her eyes darted around the room as she slowly skirted between the tables. She felt a small amount of tension ease when she saw Mrs. Miller standing across the way, holding the box of fruit tarts. Lexi gave her a small wave, which was returned so enthusiastically that the bakery box teetered in the old woman's arms. Lexi breathed a sigh of relief when she set the box down safely on a table.

At the podium, Chaz laid down his notebook containing their remodeling plans for the bakery. They'd agreed that he would talk first since he was a known, and according to him, trusted face in town. He would give her a brief introduction, then let her sell her dream.

"I'm going to hand out the fruit tarts while you get started," Lexi whispered and veered off without stopping.

The less time she stood at that podium, the better. While she wasn't exactly scared of public speaking, she abhorred being the center of attention. And usually, when one spoke in front of a group, they tended to attract all that unwanted attention.

"Hey, Mrs. Miller," Lexi spoke in a low voice and placed a hand on her shoulder. "Want to help me pass those out?"

"Oh, I can manage this, dear. Serving is part of my job, after all." Mrs. Miller opened the box, and the smell of sweet tart crust and strawberries wafted out. "You go join your man up there."

Lexi's head whipped back from counting tables. "My man?"

"He works for you, doesn't he, dear?" Mrs. Miller smiled coyly.

"I'm onto you, Mrs. Miller." Lexi squinted at the smiling woman. "You sure you got this?"

"Yes, yes." Mrs. Miller waved her off and began hustling to the next table with fresh tarts in hand.

Lexi cleared her throat and turned back to Chaz, who was still setting out their paperwork precisely on a small table. Her breath caught in her throat, and the moment hit her like a chocolate overload cake with too much ganache. Too heavy, like the weight of what she needed to do. Right now. It was no longer a pipe dream. No longer 'down the road.'

It was now.

As she passed the last few tables, Lexi plastered on a smile she knew could rival any beauty queen— far too big for the occasion and obviously fake. Once she was in front of all the tables, past their prying eyes, she swallowed hard and leaned in towards Chaz.

"How many papers exactly do we need for this?" she asked through clenched teeth, forcing the smile back into place for the council sitting in front of them.

"Well, I have the necessary permits," he pointed to the first stack, then continued down the line, "then there are the drawings of your remodel, printouts for the council, and—"

"Are we about ready, Chaz?" the old man from the front cleared his throat and looked at them with a rather bored expression before Chaz could get to the final stack of papers. "I'd like to get home in time for the evening news."

"Of course, Mr. Mayor. Just making sure I've got everything in order so this will be as quick and painless as possible."

The people behind them chuckled, and Chaz threw them a smile over his shoulder. Lexi stopped chewing her lip and marveled at how easily he spoke to everyone. There wasn't an ounce of tension in his broad shoulders, and his smile, unlike hers, looked completely natural. Lexi took a deep breath and reminded herself that she was in his capable hands.

At the thought, her eyes drifted to his hands. Tanned and calloused, with scars sprinkled across his knuckles. She marveled as he stepped around the podium and began speaking, and he gestured to her and then his stack of papers on the small table. She could still feel the warmth of his hands trailing down her arms from their moment in the hallway. Her lips fell from the overstretched smile into an actual grin.

Always a good distraction, she thought, thanking Chaz silently as he continued the introduction.

"In the short time I've known Lexi Caehill, I've seen the dedication to her business." Chaz's eyes locked with hers, and he slid his hands into his front pockets. "I think she'll be an asset to Fauna by addin' permanent jobs, purchasin' local ingredients, and, as y'all are tastin', providin' us with some top-notch pastries. And whose world isn't better with pastries, am I right?"

Lexi broke eye contact with him and glanced around the room to see the townsfolk nibbling on her tarts and nodding. Mrs. Miller gave her a double thumbs-up from the back of the room. Lexi let out a breath and relaxed. If she knew anything in this crazy world, it was baking. She could always rely on that to carry her through.

"I trust her and her vision enough that this morning we finalized the sale of my Meemaw's house on the town square." Chaz cleared his throat and looked up at the ceiling. Lexi reached out and squeezed his arm briefly as murmurs surrounded them. "I think y'all will agree after hearing from her."

Chaz motioned for her to step forward. He gave her a slow, lopsided smile that set her stomach on tilt. Lexi stepped up to the podium and let her eyes meet those of each council member. There were six in all, each waiting to hear what she had to say.

"Thank you, Chaz, for that marvelous introduction." She busted out her best Bette Midler impression, but got no reaction. "No Hocus Pocus fans here, then? Ok..."

What in the world was she doing, starting her speech with a movie quote? She'd rehearsed this moment hundreds of times and not once did she start it out with an impersonation of any kind, especially not from a Halloween movie.

"...well, I am not a witch. That I can guarantee." She stammered.

Lexi could feel the heat rushing to her cheeks. How could she be so stupid? Pretty sure the first thing they taught in public speaking class was not to open with ridiculous quotes. And if that wasn't the first thing they taught, it should have been.

She glanced at Chaz, who was looking at her like she had sprouted a couple of croquembouche horns, but waved his hands, urging her to continue. She turned back to the council and closed her eyes briefly. People shuffled their feet behind her; chairs scraped against the linoleum floor.

'*Pull yourself together, woman,*' Lexi thought.

"Um, a witch I am not," she repeated, clearing her throat. "But I do know how to whip up some magic in the kitchen."

That garnered her a few whoops from the audience at least. She smiled and stepped out from behind the podium. It was time to shine, so shine she would.

"Ladies and gentlemen of the city council, I stand before you with a dream. A dream that you," she pointed at the mayor, "can make come true."

She stopped for a breath. And to add suspense. She wanted them hanging on the edge of their seats, which wasn't really happening. In reality, their attention was hanging on by a thread.

"I came here with my family as a kid, and I was sold. Sold on this small-town lifestyle. Sold on the picturesque atmosphere. Sold on Fauna." She walked to one end of the council table as she spoke. "I was only seven at the time, but I wanted this life. In this town."

She walked the length of the table, meeting their curious gazes with a smile. Business Lexi was fully engaged.

"As I grew up, moving from one city to another, Fauna never left my dreams. I knew I'd return here one day. And here I stand, ready to make that dream come true."

She stopped in front of the podium. Making her stand.

"In the couple of days I've been here in Fauna, I've received more kindness than in most of my years in New York City. A large part of that is thanks to Chaz," she turned and gave him a small smile, "and his brother, Rhys, who found me the perfect location. Their beautiful Meemaw's home on the town square will be the future location of my bakery."

Lexi looked back at Chaz and gave him a quick nod. He reached down, picked up the first two stacks of papers, and approached the council's table, where he quickly handed them out.

"As you can see, we have all the permit applications in place for the remodeling we plan to do, as well as a detailed drawing and description of the project." Lexi met Chaz's eyes and smiled at the thrill of sharing their plans. "I plan to use the top floor of the house as my residence, and most of the remodel work will be to modernize the ground floor to use as the business location. It will contain a commercial kitchen, a tasting room for private parties, and the main area will hold display cases and tables for people to enjoy their treats in a minimalistic and modern setting. I really want the food to be the star here, so we plan to keep the colors neutral, with sleek, simple lines to the furniture and decor."

Several of the council members began whispering to each other, pointing to the plans on the handouts. The people at the tables behind her rustled in their seats, probably curious to see the plans. Why hadn't they thought to bring copies for the audience as well?

"We will carry that same look to the outside of the home, replacing the wooden railing with a simple metal one. We'll install large fans and provide outside seating for customers to enjoy when the weather is pleasant." Lexi could see it all so clearly in her mind. "It will truly be a little taste of New York City right here in Fauna, Mississippi."

Lexi took a step back behind the podium and clasped her hands together. She hoped her well-rehearsed speech made up for her introduction blunder. Chaz stepped up next to her and bumped her shoulder lightly. Together, they watched as the council flipped through the plans and squinted at the drawings.

"A little slice of New York City, you say?" The mayor looked at her over the top of his glasses as he continued to read through the plans.

"Yes, sir, Mr. Mayor, sir," Lexi said. "I spent most of my working years in some of the high-end restaurants around New York and love the modern techniques used in the desserts. I believe mirroring that simplicity in the décor will give customers a thoroughly big-city experience without having to leave Fauna."

"Well, that makes me curious," the mayor took off his glasses and rubbed the bridge of his nose. "You begin by telling us you're sold on our small-town living, but then want to change that by bringing in the big city?"

"Um, well. Yes?" Lexi's brow creased. This was not the response she'd expected. "Every business market is stronger through diversity. I think that having something unique could bring in people from neighboring towns. Which would bring more customers to all businesses here in Fauna."

"The last thing we need is a bunch of those rednecks from Greenston coming to our town." Someone from the audience called out behind her.

As the smile slid from her face, she began to really look at the council members. What she'd thought were curious whispers earlier now looked angry. The members stabbed at the plans with their fingers as they discussed them with their neighbors. Something Chaz said rang through her ears.

'Nobody wants big-city style here. We want down-home comfort.'

Maybe she'd made a mistake. Maybe she should have focused on just wanting a minimalistic style, and not a modern, big-city style. She looked at Chaz with wide eyes as the room around them erupted.

"Now, hold on, folks," Chaz held up his hands.

'Oh, thank God. He'll talk them into it. He knows them. How to talk to them,' she thought.

Lexi relaxed, remembering she was in capable hands. She took a small step back and let Chaz approach the podium.

"I know the idea of somethin' big city sounds a little strange, maybe even a little scary," Chaz started.

'Yes. Now he tells them why it's not...' Lexi thought.

"That's why I made up a backup plan that keeps the house in a more...traditional style."

Lexi's vision blurred and burned red around the edges as Chaz picked up the last stack of papers. The only one he'd conveniently not mentioned to her. He'd gone behind her back. And rather than fight for her vision, he was just sneaking in with his own. Lexi's stomach sank, right along with her dreams.

Chapter 10

L exi collapsed into a chair, unable to listen to the betrayal spewing from Chaz's mouth. He stood there at complete ease, not even bothering to pretend to be apologetic or embarrassed. Through the red haze of her rage, she glimpsed the plans Chaz handed to the council. His backup plans. HIS plans. Keeping the wooden spindles on the porch, the chair rail and wainscoting inside. Nothing modern or minimalistic like she wanted in her bakery. In her dream.

How could he?

Lexi knew she shouldn't go down that train of thought. Anger would fuel her to get stuff done. And stuff definitely needed to happen. But as much as she tried to grab onto that flash of rage, it quickly burnt out and left behind a gaping hole of desperation. She'd been lost in those depths before and told herself she wouldn't go back, but the darkness was familiar, and she could feel herself falling.

The council members stood to take a break, apparently satisfied with Chaz's plan. Lexi remained in her seat, unable to decide what her next move should be. Confront Chaz? Chase after the council and beg them to reconsider her plan? Accept Chaz's plan and move forward? There were so many options, but which was the right one? She couldn't choose, so she did none of them.

"Lex?" Chaz's face appeared inches from hers. "Earth to Lexi?"

She slowly blinked, bringing his face into focus. His beautiful, smiling face.

A growl rumbled in her chest as she imagined wiping his smile right off. Maybe by breaking in her rolling pin. What was it Mrs. Miller had said about head-bashing?

"How...could...you?" Her teeth ground together as she forced out the words.

"How could I..." Chaz let the question trail off as his brow creased in concern.

"You just conveniently worked up that backup plan? Conveniently had the copies made up? Conveniently forgot to mention that to me?" She stood and stepped into his space, pushing closer with each question. "Do you think you could grab something for me?"

"Wait. What?" He looked at her, bewildered, as she turned from him.

"The knife you conveniently stabbed in my back." Lexi glared at him over her shoulder.

"You really need to keep your voice down," Chaz grabbed her shoulders and spun her back around. "You're makin' a scene."

"Oh, I plan to make a scene."

"Seriously, Lex?" Chaz stepped back and stuck his thumbs through his belt loops. "You want the whole town to see you raisin' a stink because I came prepared?"

"Excuse me? Prepared would have been coming with the agreed-upon plans and helping me get the support I need for them." She clenched her hands at her sides but lowered her voice to a harsh whisper. "What you did was...I don't even know, Chaz. It was wrong."

"Heeeeeyyy you two," Lotus said slowly as she appeared at Lexi's shoulder. "Everything okay here? People are staring. Tongues will be wagging tonight. Was that a heated lovers' spat? Or is there business trouble already? I can just hear my Mama-"

"Not now, Lotus." Chaz shook his head and sighed. "There's nothin' goin' on. We're just chatting about how our presentation went, right Lex?"

"That is most definitely not what we are discussing, and you know it."

"Alrighty then." Lotus rocked back on her heels and gently grabbed Lexi's arm. "How about we go get a piece of pie at the diner, and you can tell me all about it?"

"I don't want pie," Lexi turned to her friend like she'd lost her mind.

"You sure? You could tell me all about it," Lotus lowered her voice to a whisper, "away from the eyes and ears of the entire town."

Lexi paused for a moment and glanced up through her lashes at the crowd around them. Everyone within earshot was badly pretending not to hang on her every word. She pressed her lips together and looked back at Lotus.

"Remind me again real quick. Which one is stealing? Rustling or roundup?" Lexi asked softly.

"Rustling, obviously." Lotus didn't even blink at the shift in conversation.

Lexi turned back to Chaz, stiffening her spine and raising her chin as she did. She stared straight into his delectable honey-colored eyes, reminding her where that sweet, golden liquid came from. Bees. And bees could sting.

"You are nothing more than a dream stealer, Chaz Walker," Lexi took a step back. "A low-down, dirty dream rustler."

Lexi turned, with Lotus on her arm, and together they walked towards the door. Lexi imagined a grand exit, but that was hindered by all the tables and chairs they had to squeeze around, apologizing as everyone scooted out of their escape route. Lexi didn't slow down or look back. That piece of pie at the diner was the only thing on her mind. It had to be.

"Dang, girl," Lotus whistled and pulled her to a stop once they stepped outside the church. "You don't throw around the word 'rustler' in these parts. No, sir. Those are some serious accusations."

"Obviously I didn't mean he was stealing cows, Lotus." Lexi began pacing the small stoop outside the church door. "It was just something we talked about earlier, and it fit the mood. Okay? That was the vibe. We were stuck in a rustling vibe."

"I get it. What he did in there was dirty. No doubt about it." Lotus leaned against the railing and stuck her hands into her pockets. "But you've gotta keep it together. You can't let him make you look like a fool in front of the town. Sure, he left you standing there gaping like a fish out of water, but you've gotta be smarter than that."

"I know," Lexi groaned, and they started walking down the street toward the diner. "I let my anger get the best of me, and now no one is going to take me seriously."

"Oh, you don't have to worry about that. Everyone saw the surprise on your face when he pulled out those plans. Pretty sure people realized he pulled the wool over your eyes, and folks don't take kindly to that kind of behavior."

"Really? So, my plans might still have a chance?"

"Nope. Didn't say that." Lotus patted Lexi on the back. "But I guarantee every granny in town is gonna be tugging on his ear at church this weekend."

"Good. He deserves a talking to. Or ten."

Lexi smiled at the thought of Chaz getting lectured by all the old ladies in town. In fact, it made her quite giddy. She actually smiled as they slid into a booth at the Darling Diner.

"Two pieces of pie and two chocolate milks, stat," Lotus told Rosita, who looked at the goofy look on Lexi's face with concern.

As the first bite of lemon meringue melted on her tongue, Lexi relaxed. And with the relaxation came the guilt and the shame.

"I blew it tonight, didn't I?" Lexi slumped over her plate and slurped some chocolate milk through a bendy straw.

"Ehhhh," Lotus shrugged. "I've seen worse. One time the debate got so heated, Cal Rinkins dumped an entire pail of raw milk over Doug Jennings' head. Let's just say, the gathering hall had the stench of spoiled milk until the carpet was ripped out. And that kind of smell only reminds people of the sour feeling that went along with it. "

"Well, at least my meltdown won't leave a lingering stench." Lexi sighed. "I'll just carry my shame with me."

"Shame? What are you talking about?" Lotus leaned across the table and grabbed Lexi's hand. "You went toe to toe with one of Fauna's golden boys. And you held your own. Everyone saw that. You didn't back down. That takes some gumption." She squeezed Lexi's hand reassuringly and then leaned back in her seat. "I think good ol' Chaz might have finally met his match."

"Oh no. Not you, too." Lexi shook her head vigorously, sending her dark curls flying. "There will be no 'matching' with Chaz and I. That ship has sailed. After what he did tonight, I don't even want to see him."

"Well, this is Fauna. You have to see everyone. All the time. That's part of the small-town charm." Lotus smiled softly at Lexi. "I know you're not going to want to hear this, so don't chuck that chocolate milk at me or anything. What Chaz did tonight might feel like a low-down double-cross, but maybe try to look at it from a business standpoint. Chaz is nothing if not prepared and thorough."

"Are you defending him?" Lexi gasped in mock surprise and then relaxed into her booth, mirroring Lotus's relaxed posture. "I can see your point. Some plan is better than no plan. Logically, that makes sense. But emotionally, I want to rip his head off."

"Well, that should make for a fun and totally healthy work environment." Lotus laughed.

"Ugh, I know." Lexi crossed her arms on the table and flopped her head on top. "How am I supposed to see him tomorrow? We have the insurance inspection scheduled in the morning."

"Seems to me you've got two options," Lotus said. "Be mature, talk it out, and move on. Orrrrr...give in to your dark side and make him pay."

Lexi thought about those options, but neither of them seemed like her.

"How about option three?" Lexi sighed again, deeper this time because she could practically see what was coming. "I wallow, make passive-aggressive comments, and flip-flop between being civil and loathing him so much that he gets emotional whiplash? Then, after way too long, my brain will finally settle on a permanent reaction, usually without my consent, and I'll be stuck with that feeling for the rest of my life."

"Well, I mean, as long as you have a plan."

Lexi clomped down the stairs at the B&B. She'd tossed and turned all night, alternating between fiery hatred and cold despair.

Mrs. Miller was in the dining room, clearing away the breakfast dishes. She glanced over at Lexi and beamed.

"Good mornin', sunshine. I saved you a plate in the kitchen. Figured you might like a little quiet this morning." She patted Lexi's back as she slipped past her. "And that maybe you'd like to avoid a certain carriage house resident?"

"You are a lifesaver, Mrs. M." Lexi's eyes grew big and her stomach rumbled when she saw the heaping plate of waffles, sausages, and fresh fruit. "And a goddess on Earth. Yummmm."

Lexi popped a strawberry into her mouth and sank onto a stool at the island. She ate silently as Mrs. Miller scurried around her, bringing all the serving platters back to the sink while humming some old tune Lexi couldn't place.

"Now you're looking a little more chipper." Mrs. Miller tossed a dishtowel onto her shoulder and leaned a hip onto the counter. "Everything is easier on a full stomach."

"Usually, yeah. But not today. We have our insurance appraisal." Lexi wiped the last of the syrup off her plate with a finger and stuck it in her mouth. "Here's an idea. I'll stay here, work with you, and take over the B&B when you decide to retire."

"While I'd love your company, dear, I don't plan to retire until I'm dead." Mrs. Miller chuckled. "And while you may have what it takes to run this kitchen, I'm not so sure you've got the, um, personality for the rest."

"What?" Lexi threw her hands in the air. "I love people."

"Enough to be gracious when they're complaining about things you have no control over? Or treat you like their personal maid, chef, and butler rolled into one?"

"Um, well..."

"Exactly." Mrs. Miller walked around the island to stand next to Lexi. "Hospitality isn't for the faint of heart, as you well know."

"I know, but—"

"No buts, dear. Running a B&B isn't your dream. And it won't even get you away from you-know-who. He lives here in case you forgot." Mrs. Miller put her small arm around Lexi's shoulders and gave a quick squeeze. "Now get out of here and go make your actual dreams come true."

"But how? How can I do that? I might not have stayed for the end of the meeting, but it was pretty obvious the city council shot down my plans."

"You'll figure it out. You're smart, capable, and driven. And so is that contractor of yours, if you'd just get on the same page."

"I don't want him on my page," Lexi stood and carried her dishes to the sink to rinse, "or anywhere near my page."

"Oh, hogwash. You want that man all over your page and you know it."

"Not going to happen." Lexi grabbed her wallet and keys off the island and hurried out the door, calling over her shoulder.

"There will be no page sharing if I have anything to say about it."

Lexi shook her head and hurried outside. The sun hid behind a thin layer of clouds, making the heat slightly less shocking than usual. She tugged at the hem of her shirt, wondering if she should have gone with something a little more business-professional and less shabby chic. In an effort to look like she didn't care, she'd chosen a simple T-shirt, jean shorts, and tennis shoes.

But maybe I went too far the other way, *and now it's obvious that I do care by how hard I'm trying to look like I don't.*

But I don't care. Definitely don't care.

If anyone could hear her internal monologue, she knew they'd see through that charade in an instant. She did care. A lot. What Chaz had done left a gaping hole in her already fragile self-confidence, like a drop of water instantly dissolving a mound of cotton candy.

Lexi pulled into a space in front of the bakery and parked next to two big trucks. She closed her eyes and took a deep breath. She could do this. She could figure it out. She could still make her dream come true. Maybe she could steer the insurance appraisal that morning in a direction that would benefit her. Point out some loose porch railings, maybe some cracked plaster on the wall by the chair rail. Maybe the insurance company would come back and say these things needed to be replaced, and Lexi could have another opportunity to get her design plans in place.

Yes! Now I've got a game plan.

On that thought, she hopped out of her car and jogged right up the steps to the two men leaning against the porch columns.

"Morning, boys. Let's get started, shall we?" Lexi walked past them, straight to the front door.

"Just waitin' on you, ma'am."

Lexi unlocked the front door and held it open. Chaz looked at her, eyes drawn together in concern, as he slowly walked past. Lexi raised an eyebrow and turned away. She wasn't about to let him weasel his way back into her good graces after what he'd done. Instead, she plastered a huge smile on her face for the man behind him.

The insurance appraiser looked to be in his late twenties, the same as Chaz, but that's where the resemblance ended. He stood a full head taller and had broad shoulders that made him twice as wide as Chaz. He had reddish hair and a full beard. Lexi could totally picture him on the cover of a lumberjack magazine.

"Lexi, I'd like to introduce my pal, Harlan Moore. He's our local wood wizard and the only appraiser in three counties." Chaz smacked his friend on the chest, hard. "Harlan, this is Lexi Caehill."

"Pleasure to meet ya, ma'am." Harlan held out his hand.

"That's quite the introduction." Lexi's eyes widened as his massive palm wrapped around hers. "I might need some more details about being a wood wizard.'"

"I like to carve things."

"Ah. Okay." Lexi turned her back to Chaz, giving Harlan her full attention. "And being the only appraiser in three counties, that must keep you busy. I bet Fauna is glad to have you."

"I suppose so."

"Well, where would you like to begin?" Lexi's cheeks felt like they were about to crack from the force of her smile.

"I was thinkin' we could start at the back of the house, work our way to the front. Then move upstairs and finish outside," Chaz rocked back on his heels.

"I didn't ask you," Lexi spoke through clenched teeth. "Where would you like to start, Harlan? Since this is your job and all."

"Back's fine."

Harlan moved towards the back of the house, giant feet oddly silent on the hardwood floors. Lexi stared after him, wondering how to win over a man who barely spoke.

"Yeah. Harlan and I go way back." Chaz threw his arm around Lexi's shoulders. "He's probably been my best friend since, what, kindergarten?"

Chaz raised his voice so Harlan could hear him from the back bedroom. A loud grunt was the only response. Lexi glared and shrugged his arm off.

"We haven't seen each other in a couple weeks," Chaz continued. "We've got a lot of catchin' up to do."

"Somehow, I hardly believe that."

"Yep. Buckle-up sweetheart, you're in for a long day of huntin' tales and tool talk." He lowered his voice and leaned in with a smile. "I know what you're tryin' to do here, and it isn't gonna work."

Lexi narrowed her eyes at him. How could he know? There's no way he knew her that well.

He's bluffing. He has to be.

"So, this is a bromance?" She asked. "This thing you two have?"

"Maybe. You jealous?"

"Definitely not," she scoffed and turned toward the back of the house. "I hope you two are very happy together."

She tried to look confident as she walked away, but inside, she was shaken. The last thing she needed was the soft-spoken, giant best friend of her evil contractor to be the one person she needed to sway to her side.

Oh, biscuits.

Chapter 11

L exi, Chaz, and the insurance appraiser, Harlan, had made it through the back of the house, the front, the upstairs, and were now outside. Try as she might, Lexi couldn't get a word in. Chaz hadn't been joking when he'd said it would be a day of bro talk. Even though the actual talking was pretty one-sided. It seemed that Harlan's communication was a complicated mixture of grunts, shrugs, and, surprisingly, booming laughter.

While Chaz talked about some new method the ranchers were using to cut and bale hay, Lexi walked the perimeter of the porch searching for any loose railings to point out. She was trying to be as stealthy as possible, moving slowly, kneeling to tie her shoe, and secretly testing each one.

All day she'd looked for something wrong. Anything. She'd come up empty-handed inside, and outside wasn't looking promising either. Not a single spindle so much as wiggled in her hand. No floorboards were warped beneath her feet. There was literally nothing that a simple coat of paint wouldn't fix.

This never would have happened in any of her New York City apartments. There, you could walk into any room and find a handful of problems. Cracked walls. Ceiling stains. Leaking pipes. You name it, she'd lived with it. She should be thankful that she'd finally purchased such a well-kept and sturdy house. But she wasn't.

Damn it. *Curse Chaz and his stupid perfectionist work ethic.*

"That should do it." Harlan wrote a few last notes on his clipboard and then looked over to Lexi.

"You sure?" Lexi clasped her hands in front of her. "Do you need to check the attic, or maybe there's a crawl space or something?"

"Nope. Looks fine, ma'am," Harlan handed her some papers and his card.

"So, there's nothing?" Lexi's eyes darted over his notes on the paperwork.

"Clean as a whistle."

"As if you'd find anything less at a Walker house," Chaz patted Harlan's back.

"It's not a Walker house," Lexi whispered to herself, holding the papers up to shield her face. "It's a Caehill house."

"Since you're planning to do some work," Harlan cleared his throat, "I'll need to come back once you're done."

"Yep." Lexi sighed and sank onto the front step. "I'm sure you won't find anything then either."

"Prolly not." Harlan turned to Chaz and shook his hand, then walked down the steps and got into his truck.

"Great guy, that one." Chaz plopped onto the step next to Lexi. "But you're definitely not his type. So, don't get your hopes up."

"Not his type? Why would I care what his type is?" Lexi turned to Chaz, really looking at him for the first time that day. She'd avoided his eye contact because she knew those molten copper pools were his most lethal weapon against her defenses.

"Come on, you were flirting with him all day." Chaz raised his voice to a ridiculously high octave and flounced his arms around, pretending to mimic her, "Harlan, come look at this wall. Does it look crooked to you? Harlan come under the sink with me, let's check the pipes."

"Wha- I- That's..." Lexi sputtered and jumped to her feet. "That is not at all what I was doing."

"Oh, please. I could tell as soon as you got here this morning you were playin' at something." Chaz jumped up too. "And after you stormed out of the meetin' last night, I figured you'd have some scheme today."

"And your brain automatically went to the high school girl tactic of 'let's make him jealous?' Wow." Lexi yanked open the screen door and stormed inside. "You really don't know me at all, do you?"

"What the hell else am I supposed to think with you fawnin' all over my best friend all mornin'?" Chaz stormed in behind her and followed her to the kitchen.

"Hm, I dunno. Maybe give me a little more credit than a ninth grader." Lexi spun on him and narrowed her eyes. "If I have a problem with someone, I will just tell it to their face."

"Well, here it is." Chaz circled his hand around his head, then stood back with his arms crossed over his chest.

Lexi took a deep breath, ready to unleash her rage on him. But right as she opened her mouth, the flame of her anger guttered out, leaving nothing but a thin wisp of smoky betrayal in its place.

Her plan to win over the insurance appraiser had failed. Her hopes for this bakery had already failed. Lexi turned and leaned on the counter, pressing her palms onto the cool surface to ground herself. She could feel her mind spiraling in a dangerous direction.

If she couldn't even sway a few votes for a remodel, how could she win over a town with her baked goods? How could she run a business?

Failure. Failure. Failure.

Maybe her family was right. Maybe she never would amount to anything.

Take a deep breath. Count to ten.

Hot tears plopped onto the counter between her fingertips before she realized she was crying. She sniffed loudly and wiped her cheeks.

"Have you ever wanted something your whole life? A dream that helped get you through all the bad days and all the struggles?" Lexi's voice was quiet, her energy gone, dissolved with her rage. "Something that made all the hard work seem worth it because you were working towards something?"

"Course." Chaz shuffled his feet behind her.

"Have you ever gotten so close to finally having that dream, only to have it taken away from you by someone you thought you could trust?" Lexi finally turned to him, tears still running down her cheeks. "Someone you thought you had a connection with?"

"Lex," Chaz reached out to her, but she pulled away.

"You went to that meeting last night fully prepared to stab me in the back, all while you laughed and joked with me." She sniffed and wiped at her face again. "Talked about kissing me."

"Stab you in the back?" Chaz straightened, stiff as a board. "What are you even talkin' about?"

"That you miraculously happened to finish your backup plans and have just enough copies for the board." Lexi sighed and turned for the door. "Well, I fell for it, Chaz. I fell for the small-town good-guy routine. But you played me dirtier than anyone ever did in New York."

"That's not at all—" Chaz started walking after her.

Lexi held up her hand to stop him as she pushed through the kitchen door. She couldn't bear to see him anymore.

"At least in the big city, they don't hide who they are." Lexi pressed a hand to her chest. "They don't act like they care before they slip the blade between your ribs, so at least you know what to expect."

Lexi let the kitchen door swing behind her and walked out to her car. Chaz didn't follow her, which made her both relieved and angrier. It was only late afternoon, but her bed at the B&B sounded like the perfect place to treat her battered heart and ego.

"At least in the big city," Lexi said to herself as she drove, "they don't try to steal your heart and your dreams at the same time."

"You will submit, you heathen. I will tolerate nothing less than complete surrender and utter compliance," Lexi muttered as she forced her curls through the small hair tie, wishing she could tell a certain local golden boy the same thing.

Taking the previous afternoon to regroup after her confrontation with Chaz was exactly what she needed. After collapsing onto the cloud of a bed and sleeping for several hours, her mind was completely clear again. Apparently, all the IT techs were onto something when they said you should shut it off and turn it back on.

Then, until the wee hours of the morning, Lexi sat in the middle of the mattress, surrounded by lists. The first one being her gratitude list. She still had a lot to be thankful for, and she'd lost sight of that. The smoky wisps of betrayal and despair can do that to a person. She wrote everything on that paper, down to the pen in her hand and the air in her lungs. That long, long list was just what Lexi needed to show that she wasn't a failure if she had so much to be thankful for.

Then she moved on to making a list of all the things she could still control. Where she'd source her ingredients. How she'd design her desserts. What the sign on the outside of the bakery would say.

If she couldn't control what her bakery was going to look like, she could deal with that. *Having* a bakery was the dream. Having a modern slice of NYC in Fauna was just the icing on that dream cake. And after years of cake decorating, she could make any icing look good. Working in fast-paced, high-end restaurants taught her to roll with the punches. Chaz's backup plan might have knocked her down, but she wasn't out. Not by a long shot.

After gathering her mountain of lists and tapping them into a neat pile, she stuck them under her arm and trotted down the stairs. With a smile and a wave to Mrs. Miller, she grabbed a muffin and was out the door. The heat inside her car was suffocating, which was not something she could control, but she blasted the A/C for the few blocks it took to get to Meemaw's house.

"I am the master of my destiny. Cool winds shall blow at my back," Lexi said in a deep, raspy voice while chewing her muffin. The car's A/C finally kicked in and the vent blasted right on her. "Or in my face."

She shook a stray curl out of her eyes and pulled in next to Chaz's truck. She'd debated long and hard about how to handle what happened yesterday, and she decided it would be best to just move on. Clean slate.

Lexi made her way to the porch, where Chaz was waiting on the swing. He gripped his hat tightly in his lap.

Yesterday is in the past. Just don't talk about it.

"Mornin.'" Chaz nodded at her. "I was hoping we could talk about yesterday."

"Ugggggghhhh..." Lexi groaned.

Can't anything go my way?

"I'd really rather move forward." Lexi pulled out her pile of lists and wiggled them a bit. "I'd like to get started on some actual work."

"I appreciate your drive, Lexi, but we aren't gonna be workin' until we clear the air." Chaz patted the porch swing next to him and waited. Once Lexi flopped into the space with a groan, he continued. "My Mama raised me to make amends if I ever make a lady cry, so that's what I plan to do."

Chaz pulled a stack of papers of his own from underneath his hat and laid them on top of Lexi's. She picked them up and flipped through them quickly, her heart beating quicker with each page.

"I was able to pull a few strings." Chaz cleared his throat. "Not that it takes much. People in this town love the drama of an emergency council meetin'."

Lexi barely heard him as her head spun. She'd been so ready to throw out all of her previous plans for the bakery, but looking at the stamped and signed papers in her hands changed that.

"Did you...did you call an emergency meeting just because you made me cry yesterday?" Lexi clasped the papers in her lap and squeezed her eyes shut.

"Well, I sure as heck didn't mean to make you cry. Shoot, I didn't even understand what was wrong until I ran into Lotus and she explained it to me." Chaz chuckled softly. "That woman reamed me up one side and down the other for what I did."

"She did?" Lexi opened her eyes and smiled.

"Sure did. But here's the thing, Lex," Chaz turned to her in his seat, sending the swing rocking, "I didn't mean to hurt you. Part of my job is always having backups. And backups to my backups. I have to be prepared for anything. And I thought I was doing the right thing having those other plans there so we wouldn't have to wait a whole month to show another round of plans at the next meeting."

"So," Lexi turned to face him on the swing, "you just had those extra plans to be thorough? And save time?"

"Well, I know you're itchin' to get started here in Fauna, and delays in this industry are expensive. Time's money." Chaz looked down, wringing the brim of his hat in his hands. "So, I'm real sorry I made you cry. I should have explained myself better. I hope you can forgi—"

"Oh, Chaz. Thank you!" Lexi threw her hands around his neck. "I can't even tell you what this means to me."

"Well, now, here I went and made you cry again." Chaz squirmed an arm underneath hers to get to his shirt pocket and pulled out a handkerchief.

"Is this a real life, embroidered and everything, handker-chief?" Lexi took it from him and held it out between them. "What is this? The 1950s?"

"I'll have you know that my Mama made a set for me and all my brothers for Christmas last year," Chaz held his hand out, "and if you don't want it, you can just give it right back."

"No, no," Lexi gestured to the sundress and saddle shoes she was wearing, "you don't understand. I love the 50's."

"Well then, call me John Wayne and take me to the soda shop." Chaz set his boots on the floor, stopping the rocking of the swing. "But don't get too excited yet. I couldn't get them to agree to everything you were wantin'. They're pretty picky about making sure businesses on the square all fit a certain image."

"Okaaaay..." Lexi looked back at the papers in her lap, still with a big grin on her face.

"They wouldn't go for the metal railings, but I talked them into paintin' them a contrastin' color. Like brown or black, whatever you decide for your accent color." Chaz pointed to the first page of the plans, then flipped to another page.

"I can live with that." Lexi leaned down to see where he was pointing.

"And the lavender paint was a no-go, but they said white would be fine. Or a nice buttery yellow. Or a lovely chocolate brown."

Images of color pairings flitted through Lexi's mind. None of them would be the cool, modern vibe she'd initially wanted, but maybe this compromise would be even better. Her mind settled on something so warm and comforting, it reminded her of all the Christmas magazine clippings she kept as a kid.

"Warm brown paint, white accents and railings." Lexi closed her eyes, picturing the old Victorian with a fresh coat of paint. Her eyes popped open, and she bit her lip as she glanced at Chaz. "And call me crazy, but..."

"Lord have mercy," Chaz tipped his head back and took a deep breath, "what now?"

"I'm thinking a smoky blue door." Lexi tilted her head to the side, eyes still closed as she visualized it. "Oh. Nope. Sage green."

"That actually doesn't sound too bad."

Lexi cracked one eye open to look at him.

"Really?" she asked.

"Yep," Chaz stood and swiped his hat across his legs, "I take back being called John Wayne. They'll just call us Hansel and Gretel because we're building a legit gingerbread house now."

Lexi stayed on the swing as Chaz walked down the porch. She could see it. This little old house of hers. She could see it with bright flowers in the little front yard. She could see it wrapped in twinkling lights for Christmas. She could lean into adding new twists to the comfort foods everyone already loved. She could practically taste the cinnamon and ginger on her tongue; if she could, customers would too.

Lexi stood, ready to make this new dream a reality. This new plan, this compromise, felt so perfect. It was perfectly Fauna. It was perfectly Lexi. It was perfectly right. Why had she wanted something so modern when vintage was her whole vibe, anyway? What had started as a financial necessity had turned into her aesthetic of choice, and before leaving NYC, the ladies at the thrift stores knew her by name.

She could see the pictures on the front page, taken by Lotus, of her in her favorite polka-dot dress with her hair in perfect pin curls, standing in front of her Victorian bakery. And it made her heart stutter with anticipation.

Sometimes the best plans were the ones you never saw coming.

Lexi turned towards the front door, her mind a slideshow of images and possibilities. As she pulled it open, she turned to Chaz with a grin that made him pause mid-step, nervousness crossing his chiseled features.

"Now, about the inside..."

Chapter 12

Lexi spread all her papers on the kitchen counter, except for her gratitude list. It had a few too many mentions of a certain honey-eyed contractor that Lexi didn't think he needed to see. His ego was big enough already.

Lexi pulled out her list of appliances to purchase. She pulled out her list of possible suppliers. The list of desserts she planned to sell. The list of her marketing strategies. And finally, the list of what she wanted to include in her upstairs apartment.

Chaz gave a low whistle as he leafed through the piles of papers.

"And here I thought I liked bein' prepared," he said as he looked intently at the list of items for her apartment.

"These aren't all for you." Lexi snatched the papers from his hands and gave him the one listing the commercial kitchen appliances she needed. "This is the one I wanted you to see."

Chaz promptly put that list on the counter and snatched back the one Lexi had taken from him.

"I'm gonna need to see this one, too. And it seems a little more interestin'." Chaz waggled his eyebrows at her. "Shall we go up and take a look?"

Without waiting for her to respond, Chaz took off up the back stairs to look at what would be Lexi's apartment. She followed him with a growl.

"I'm a little more concerned about the commercial kitchen downstairs," she tried and failed to focus on anything other than the man's beautiful backside before her eyes. "I can stay at the B&B longer if I need to, but I really need to start taking orders and getting my name out there."

"We will, darlin', don't you worry." Chaz stopped at the top of the landing and looked around the large space. "Man, lots of memories up here."

Lexi stopped next to him and looked at the massive room as if those memories would make themselves known to her. But they didn't. All she saw was a large, open space that spanned the whole upper floor of the house. The walls were a light cream color, and the ceiling showcased beautiful rafters and beams. At the far end, the corner jutted out into the small turret, making a perfect little nook that was just calling for bookshelves and a cozy bench to curl up on.

"That's my reading nook," Lexi called out and rushed over to the small area.

"That's what my Meemaw used it for, too." Chaz followed her. "She had her favorite rocker and lamp in there, and she'd sit and watch out over all us kids while we played."

"That sounds really peaceful."

"Ha!" Chaz barked out a quick laugh. "Peaceful isn't something the Walker kids do. When you've got six boys and a—"

"I'm sorry," Lexi sputtered, "did you just say six boys?"

"Yep. My mama had her hands full." Chaz sighed, a sound full of longing. "That's why we opened up this whole space, took out the walls. Plenty of room to run and play."

"I can imagine."

"I suppose you'll want some walls, though?"

"At least for a bedroom and bathroom. The rest I don't mind being open. Kind of reminds me of the lofts I lived in back in New York. Only way, way bigger."

"I like that idea. Keeps a lot of the light from the front of the house flowin' through to the back where there aren't as many windows."

"Exactly." Lexi could feel her creative juices flowing already. "I can see an open kitchen in that corner," she pointed opposite where the stairs entered the space, "a dining table here in front of it, a living space here by the reading nook. Warmth. I want it to feel warm. And open."

Lexi paused and looked back at Chaz. He stood next to the turret nook, the early morning sunlight highlighting his high cheekbones and setting his eyes on fire. He stared at her for a moment before shaking his head.

"You sure you're in the right business, Lex? You might have missed your calling as an interior designer. Or some poor ol' contractor's assistant."

"Oh, no. Baking is where I belong. But thank you." Lexi smiled and wrapped her arms around herself, soaking in the compliment. "I guess creativity can flow in a lot of different directions when you let it."

"Yes, indeed." Chaz nodded and turned back to the only corner Lexi hadn't included in her plan. "Now, this would be the bedroom and bathroom, I suppose."

"Yep. Bathroom on the outside, so it's accessible to guests." Lexi held up her hands to section the spaces visually.

"And do you plan on having many guests?" Chaz asked.

"Um," Lexi started, pulled out of her design mode. "Well, I suppose I'd like to." She narrowed her eyes at him. "And why do you need to know?"

"Part of my job." Chaz shrugged. "The more I know about your plans for a space, the more I can help make it accommodate those plans. So, what kind of 'friends' are we talkin' about?" He air-quoted around friends and gave her a devilish grin.

"That, sir, is none of your business." Lexi could feel the heat rising in her cheeks and immediately tried to change the subject. "I didn't have many friends in New York. Too busy working. I hope that isn't the case here."

She cringed inwardly. Of all the things to say, why'd her brain land on that one? She didn't want to sound like a sad, pathetic loner to anyone, especially not to Chaz.

Chaz just grunted and nodded. He pulled a pencil out of his shirt pocket and started jotting notes on the back of her list.

"And the bathroom? Tub and shower combo? Separate?"

"What about moving that claw-foot tub up from downstairs? Guests at the bakery aren't going to need a bathtub. And it's so lovely, it'd be a shame to get rid of it."

"That's a great idea." Chaz nodded and began walking to the far corner where Lexi said she'd like the kitchen. "I've soaked in that tub plenty of times. Downright comfy."

Lexi gulped at the mental image of Chaz's bare backside in what would be her bathtub. She shook her head quickly to get rid of those images, but they were permanently imprinted in her brain now.

Must...change...subject...

"Um, as long as we're on the topic of moving things upstairs," Lexi rushed over behind him, trying to leave that dangerous train of thought behind her, "would it be possible to move the kitchen up here too?"

Chaz stopped his scribblings and pivoted towards her on his boot heel. He blinked several times before saying anything.

"You want my Meemaw's kitchen?" he asked slowly.

Lexi couldn't read the emotion on his face. Was it anger? Was it shock? She wasn't sure, but his silence set her nerves on edge.

"Well, it'd be a shame to waste...and it'd save time and money..." Lexi threw her hands up. "It's a beautiful kitchen, okay? I can feel the history in it. And I like that." She looked down at her black and white saddle shoes and continued softly, "It's something I've never had."

Chaz still didn't say anything, so Lexi dared a glance up at him through her lashes. He was still staring at her with that unreadable expression.

"If it's too weird, then don't do it. I'm not trying to steal your precious memories or anything." Lexi huffed. "It was just an idea."

Chaz cleared his throat and pivoted back to the corner of the room. He stared at the space for a moment and then went back to scribbling.

"It's a right fine idea, Lex. I think Meemaw would have loved it."

There was a slight hitch in his voice, and Lexi guessed that if she could see his face now, his eyes would be a little extra shiny. On the outside, Lexi looked up with a small smile. On the inside, she was jumping for joy. She'd finally done something right.

"Now, let's go take a look at your list of appliances. We're going to need to order those ASAP." Chaz finished one last note and slid his pencil back into his pocket. His voice was back to its usual Southern drawl. "Things can take their sweet time making their way here to Fauna."

"Ohhh..." Lexi hadn't thought of that.

"Don't worry. We can probably have you up and running in a few weeks."

"Oh." That wasn't so bad.

"So, tell me more about your plans for the bedroom." Chaz pulled his pencil out again, but Lexi whacked it out of his hands.

"You are incorrigible, Chaz Walker." Lexi rolled her eyes and stomped down the stairs.

"What? It's for the job," Chaz called after her, laughter lacing the edges of his words.

Lexi couldn't help but smile as she picked up the list of commercial appliances. It was going to be a long few weeks with that man, trying to keep her mind on opening her business when it just wanted to think about Chaz taking a bath. A beautiful man in a beautiful tub. What wasn't to like?

Pull yourself together. You're starting a business. Not settling down with some small-town golden boy.

Settling down? Just the day before, she'd been hoping to never see him again. Lexi knew the bakery had to come first. Whatever this was between them needed to chill.

But if you put out a flame right as it was beginning to smolder, would it ever relight? Or would it be extinguished for good?

The next week was spent in a blur of emails, phone calls, and vendor visits. She had sales associates showing her everything from industrial mixers to bulk ice cream cones. Chaz joined her for any meetings about equipment, wanting to make sure they had all the electrical needs met, as well as fitting everything into the kitchen layout.

"Bulk ice cream is never a bad idea," he whispered in her ear as he got up to leave a meeting with a vendor from Jackson, "specially in the summer."

Lexi smiled as the conversation shifted from equipment to food. She knew what she wanted, what a fair price was, and wouldn't settle for any inferior products. She'd been in charge of ordering at multiple jobs in New York, and knew how to play this game. Lexi walked out of each meeting with a grin as the vendors left, looking slightly bewildered by what had just happened. They weren't prepared for big-city wheeling and dealing.

"Dang, Lexi Girl. I thought you were going to make that one cry," Chaz chuckled as she walked into the kitchen. "All I have to say is I'm glad I'm buildin' walls and not slingin' chocolate."

"Eh," she shrugged. "All in a day's work." Lexi tilted her head from side to side, stretching her sore neck muscles. "And what a day it has been. I will be so glad when I can get back to just working in my kitchen and not having to talk to people *all* day long."

"I mean, isn't talking to people kinda part of the business?"

"Sure, about cakes and pastries. Which I could talk about all day. None of this haggling and mental chess with people who want to bleed me dry."

"Hate to burst your bubble," Chaz pulled air in through his teeth. "You just described almost every business interaction I've had since I started my business. The people of Fauna are nothin' if not shrewd. Or, as my Meemaw liked to say, behind closed doors, of course, we're all just a bunch of penny pinchers who'd wash and reuse our dental floss to save a buck."

"Ew." Lexi's lip curled. "You don't do that, do you?"

"Course not. That's just a sayin'. But we do wash baggies. Reuse foil." Chaz glanced at the ceiling as he ticked items off on his fingers. "Save wrappin' paper."

"I mean, environmental hippies do all those things too." Lexi laughed.

"You callin' us a bunch of tree huggers?"

"I mean, if the name fits?" Lexi grabbed her purse off the counter. "Now, if you'll excuse me, I've got a girls' night to attend."

"A what now?" Chaz pushed off the wall, suddenly very interested.

"A girls' night. That you, for obvious reasons, aren't invited to." Lexi jingled the keys and ushering Chaz towards the front door.

"Well, I'll be. I'm right proud of you, Lex." Chaz looked at her over his shoulder as she pushed him out the door.

"I know," Lexi shimmied her shoulders. "Look at me. Making friends and everything."

"Darn straight."

Chaz gave her a fist bump and smiled, his dimple sending little shivers of appreciation through her.

"Now who's all comin' to this girl's night?" Chaz tapped his chin. "No. Don't tell me. Acacia?"

Lexi's nose scrunched as she shook her head. "Who?"

"Has to be Lady Carmichael then. She is the social leader of this town, after all."

"If you must know, it's just myself, Lotus, and Mrs. Miller."

"The first two I understand, but help me out with Mrs. Miller." Chaz shook his head. "Are you taking her out on the town? You know her bedtime is like eight o'clock, right?"

"We are actually having a night in at the B&B," Lexi walked off the porch to her car. "And that is all I'm saying about it."

"Gettin' crazy at the B&B," Chaz nodded as he opened the door to his truck. "I like your style, Lex. But if there's loud music, I smell smoke, or hear too much gigglin', I'm gonna have to come put a stop to it."

"That is a very interesting list of intolerances." Lexi looked at him over the top of her car before sliding in.

"What can I say? Can't have you crazy girls keepin' me up all night." He hollered at her through her passenger window. "I've got to be at work in the morning, or my boss will have my hide. She's a bit of a taskmaster."

Lexi shook her head and grinned. With a wiggle of her fingers in his direction, she backed out and turned toward the B&B. She'd been looking forward to tonight all week, and now the thought of having Chaz's beautiful hide wouldn't leave her mind. Not in a creepy serial killer way. In the hands sliding over skin, getting goosebumps kind of way.

Lexi knew she needed an evening with a lot of wine and laughter to get those images out of her mind. Stat.

Lexi and Lotus sat at the kitchen island, wearing matching aprons and eager expressions. Before them, Mrs. Miller had laid out a vast assortment of ingredients and equipment.

"Tonight, as requested, we will be making some traditional Southern favorites." Mrs. Miller rubbed her hands together in excitement. "Buttermilk Biscuits. Jambalaya. And —"

"Peach cobbler." Lotus blurted out as she bounced on her stool. "Mmm."

"I can't thank you enough for showing us your secrets." Lexi smiled at Mrs. Miller.

"Psh. I can't claim these as secrets." Mrs. Miller waved her off and grabbed some milk from the fridge. "These are just Southern traditions. We all know them and love them. Right Lotus?"

"Well, with my mama passing when I was so young, I didn't get all the kitchen wisdom."

Lotus twirled the wineglass in front of her, staring at the countertop in deep thought. It was not Lotus' norm to have so little to say. Lexi reached over and placed a hand on her shoulder.

"She passed when I was four. I kind of remember watching her in the kitchen, but I was still too little to really get in there and help." She shrugged and squeezed Lexi's hand. "Since then, it's just been me, and Daddy, and Isaiah. Some aunties showed me a few things, but I've been floundering in the kitchen ever since. I'd rather take pictures of food than make it. But it'd be nice to know one solid recipe to make at home. I'm sure Daddy would appreciate something other than red beans or frozen meatloaf for once."

"I'm happy to teach anytime." Mrs. Miller wrapped her arms around Lotus' shoulders from behind, giving her a deep hug. "Now, let's get started so my guests aren't eating dinner at bedtime."

"Yes, ma'am." Lotus slid off her stool and practically ran to the pile of ingredients. "Come on, girl," she waved Lexi over, "we can't be the reason for hungry guests."

"Alright, alright," Lexi laughed. "So, what are we starting with?"

"Biscuits. Need time for the dough to chill," Mrs. Miller pulled on her own apron and looked at them both. "Now, what are the three trinities of biscuit making?"

Lexi shrugged her shoulders. She might be a baker, but she had no clue about the holy rules of Southern biscuits.

She glanced at Lotus, who wiggled her shoulders and smiled smugly.

"I know, but you go ahead, Mrs. Miller."

The older woman nodded and held up three fingers. She pointed to the first one and ticked them off as she spoke, "White Lily, cold butter, don't twist your cutter."

"That kind of rhymes." Lexi chuckled. "I might make that into a poster for my kitchen."

"Whatever you do, just don't forget them."

Mrs. Miller pulled a large bag of White Lily flour out of the ingredient pile and proceeded to show them how to measure and sift to make the biscuits extra fluffy. Then they each took their own bowls and followed along.

"So, what about your family, Lexi?" Mrs. Miller asked while sifting another batch of flour. "Any family recipes? Traditional foods?"

"Ha. Definitely not." Lexi shook her head. "My parents wouldn't know how to boil water for tea, I'm sure. And my grandmother had a private chef and probably never set foot inside her own kitchen."

"Oh. I'm so sorry, dear."

Lexi shrugged. "It is what it is."

"So, how'd you become a pastry chef?" Lotus asked.

"We were staying with this family friend one time. She was a little kooky, but sweet. She asked if I wanted cookies one day. Of course, I said yes. What kid wouldn't? I watched as she mixed all these seemingly random things together, and then out popped warm, delicious cookies. I couldn't wrap my head around it. And from then on, I was hooked."

"So, one batch of cookies set you on your life's journey." Mrs. Miller nodded as she mixed the butter in with her hands. "Isn't that just lovely?"

"Better than the alternative of being a lifelong grifter like the rest of my family." Lexi shuddered at the thought.

"You've mentioned a sister." Lotus said. "What does she do?"

"Same as my folks. My mom grew up wealthy because of my grandma. But then she married my dad, Grandma cut her off, and she still thinks she's above working an actual job."

"Still livin' the high life without the high funds, huh?" Lotus shook her head.

"It's a real shame when people can't move past what shoulda been and can't see what is." Mrs. Miller sighed. "But you turned out amazing in spite of all that. And that says a whole lot about you."

"For real. You got some spunk."

"Well, thank you, ladies." Lexi gave them each a slight bow, thankful this topic seemed to come to an end. She didn't like talking about her family. Her memories filled her with such a mix of emotions that it was hard to settle on just one. Anger. Shame. Pity. None of them were good and left her feeling burnt out and hollow if she sat with them for too long.

"So, tell me about more Southern foods. I want to experience them all."

"Oh, you have to try fried green tomatoes." Lotus smacked her lips.

"Fresh." Mrs. Miller pointed out.

"Of course."

By the time the dough was in the fridge, Lotus had covered the majority of the island and herself in flour, and they had covered so many delicious-sounding Southern foods that Lexi's stomach was growling.

"You were *not* joking about floundering in the kitchen, were you?" Lexi giggled as they cleaned up.

"Ha. Ha." Lotus stuck her finger into the flour and booped Lexi on the nose. "Not all of us can be kitchen wizards."

"Oh, I like that. Although, wouldn't a woman be a kitchen witch?" Lexi cocked her head and her lips to one side in thought. "I always get the magical names mixed up."

"Don't ask me." Mrs. Miller shook her head while she scrubbed a few utensils in the sink. "I live right here in the ordinary world, where I promise you there is no magic unless you count the miracles the Lord provides."

"Amen to that." Lotus raised one hand towards the sky. "My most recent miracle was this wonderful lady coming into my life on a warm early summer morning."

She threw her arm around Lexi's shoulder, leaving a flour handprint on her shoulder. Lexi couldn't help but beam at both of them.

"Man, I can't tell you both how much I needed this," she told them.

"Same girl, same," Lotus chimed in. "I'd like to propose a toast."

All three of them grabbed their wine glasses and leaned into the center of the island.

"To a Southern feast between friends," Lotus smiled and thrust her glass in.

"To new memories made and skills learned," Mrs. Miller added her glass.

They looked at her expectantly. Lexi clinked her glass against theirs.

"And to finding what makes your heart happy."

Chapter 13

Lexi glanced around her new kitchen with a sense of pride. It had taken a couple of weeks and a lot of elbow grease, but they had put in the finishing touches during the wee hours of the morning. Neither one of them wanted to leave until the job was complete.

"Mornin', Sunshine," Chaz sauntered in behind her, setting his toolbox on the floor. "How's she look without the haze of exhaustion?"

"She looks perfect." Lexi took a deep breath and smiled, looking around the kitchen again.

"Sure wish we could have found some newer appliances," Chaz ran his hand over one of the bigger dents in the side of the 30-quart Hobart mixer next to the door.

It wasn't the white-walled, sparkling stainless steel kind of kitchen she was used to working in. She couldn't afford all new appliances, so they'd found used ones . And while they weren't shiny and new, they were new to her, and that was good enough. She'd scrubbed each one as it came in on the delivery truck and got to know every ding and dent in each machine. As she looked around, she knew in her heart that they all belonged here. Brand new, shiny steel wouldn't have gone with this house. Something with a little wear, a few dents, now those fit in perfectly.

"Nah, these are just right." Lexi tilted her head and looked at it. "Shiny steel would look off in a house like this. They kind of add to the character and history, don't you think?"

"Hm. You may be right." Chaz leaned back on the counter and crossed his arms. "So, what's on the agenda today?"

"I'm going to take some flyers around to the other shops on the square and see if I can drum up some business."

Lexi's stomach fluttered at the thought. That was the dream. Finally, running her own business. Lexi stopped rubbing random appliances long enough to look at Chaz.

"What about you?"

"I'm going to start framin' in some walls upstairs." He pushed off from the counter and grabbed his toolbox. "Pretty soon you'll be workin' and sleepin' here. Then nothin' will stop ya."

Lexi shivered with excitement.

"What do you think of this?" She pulled out a flyer she'd printed at the B&B last night with Mrs. Miller's ancient computer. After that life-altering, or halting, experience, she moved purchasing a business computer to the top of her list. It would be necessary once she began taking orders, anyway. Invoices weren't going to make themselves.

"Looks darn good." Chaz held the paper, looking at all the details. "How many you got?"

"Just the one. If you knew how long it took me to print that in Mrs. Miller's 'business office' last night, you'd understand."

"Oh, trust me, I do. I had to use it when my laptop broke, and I was waitin' for a new one. Longest week of my life." Chaz shuddered. "I ended up taking half the week off to avoid havin' to print anything else."

"So, any idea where I can get some copies?" Lexi batted her eyes at him.

"Sure, there's a copy center at the post office on the highway."

"Thanks." Lexi snatched the flyer from him and grabbed her purse. "Have fun with the walls."

"Will do. I'll just be up there working on your bedroom all by my lonesome." Chaz stuck out his lower lip in a pout.

Temptations. Temptations. She shook her head. *Stay the course.*

"Okay." Lexi rushed out the swinging door. "Have fun. Don't do anything I wouldn't do."

"And what does that include?" Chaz called from the kitchen.

"I go on a case-by-case basis." She smirked as she made it out into the Mississippi morning.

The drive across town was uneventful, as Lexi assumed most drives in Fauna would be. Any kind of traffic jam or fender bender would probably make front-page news around here. She smiled at the thought of Lotus taking those interviews and photographs, trying to make a mountain out of a molehill.

The post office sat next to a single-pump gas station on the edge of town. Beyond the parking lot, tall grass led to a row of old oak trees growing along the riverbank. Spanish moss draped over their branches like lace doilies at a tea party. Lexi sat for a few minutes, marveling that this was her life now. She'd never expected to be excited about moss-covered trees, but here she was.

She rushed into the squat brick building, getting through the heat as quickly as possible. Random knick-knacks and home décor cluttered the front of the shop. Candles filled the shelves along the walls, making the air smell like a floral shop explosion. She held her breath and plowed toward the back where the copy center sign hung from the ceiling.

As she looked at the list of services provided, a tall woman bustled from the back room carrying a stack of boxes. Lexi smiled as the woman hummed and shimmied to the far wall, stacking the boxes on a shelf.

"Oh, Lord have mercy." The woman clutched her chest when she turned around and saw Lexi. "Honey. You about sent me to see my maker."

"Sorry," Lexi smiled awkwardly, "I just need some copies made."

"Of course, darlin'," the woman hurried over, her long legs crossing the shop in about four strides. "How many are you needing?"

"Oh, I was thinking twenty should do? Maybe twenty-five?"

"You tell me, Hun. We can do as many as you want. I think I've got about 20,000 sheets of paper ready to roll if you are."

"That'd be more than one per person for the whole town of Fauna."

"Probably." The woman smiled down at Lexi and stuck out her hand. "I'm Dhalia. Dhalia Bronson."

"Lexi Caehill." She took the woman's hand and shook it.

"Oh, I already know who you are, Sugar. Whole town does." Dhalia placed the flyer into the copy machine, but didn't press any buttons.

"Ugh." Lexi cringed. "Already?"

"After that Walker boy done you dirty at the council meeting, you bet your Sunday best that word got around." She pursed her lips and looked at Lexi. "You look like a woman who can take care of herself, but if you need some help with that boy, you come to any of us Nanas and we'll set him straight."

"That is unbelievably kind of you, Ms. Dhalia." Lexi gave herself an inward high-five for remembering to add the 'Ms.' like all polite, respectable Southern folks do to show respect. "But we got it sorted out. I haven't had to do any head-bashing yet, but I'm not opposed to it."

"Glad to hear it, darlin'. Now, what are we doing here?" Ms. Dhalia nodded towards the copy machine.

"Well, I'm going to hand these out to the other shops on the square." Lexi clasped her hands in front of her, wringing them together. "I'm hoping to get a few orders before the bakery actually opens."

"Hm." Ms. Dhalia pursed her lips again, but this time it wasn't in appraisal; this time was to keep something in. Something she wasn't saying.

Lexi watched her as she pushed the buttons on the copy machine, suddenly silent. Ms. Dhalia turned, busying herself with collecting each copy as it came out, and Lexi's palms began to sweat. When they were done, Lexi quickly paid, wondering all the while what she'd said to make the chatty woman close up like a hand pie; her mouth pinched and creased like the fork lines used to hold the crust together.

"Um. Would you mind displaying one here?" Lexi tried to sound confident, but there was a distinct warble in her voice.

"There on the bulletin board," Ms. Dhalia finally spoke, gesturing to a board cluttered with fliers next to the entry door.

"Thank you." Lexi gathered up her copies and turned to leave.

"Don't be thanking me yet," Ms. Dhalia took two giant steps towards the back room, muttering as she went, "Chris Anntha is gonna chap my hide when she sees that, Lord have mercy..."

Lexi couldn't make out the rest of what she said as the door closed behind her. This wasn't the first she'd heard of Chris Anntha, and she doubted it would be the last.

The next morning, Lexi shuffled into the bakery, her canvas bag dragging at her feet. Yesterday had been brutal. As she handed out flyers to the other businesses on the square, most took the paper from her with a smile and then hid it behind their counter. Some allowed her to put it up on already crowded bulletin boards, like Ms. Dhalia at the post office. And none seemed very excited about it.

Sighing, she made her way into the kitchen. Just seeing all her beautiful equipment ready to go made her heart a little lighter. She ran her fingers over the dough sheeter, envisioning all the croissants she'd soon be cranking out.

Once they see what I can do, they'll change their tune.

The sound of an electric saw buzzing upstairs grabbed her attention. Lexi hurried up the stairs, eager to see what progress Chaz had made.

Lexi stopped at the top of the stairs, looking into what would be her home. A thread of longing curled in her stomach, aching for something to call her own. Her brow creased at the unusual sensation. What had always been her safe space in the past was never a place, a home, or her family; it was her friends and her job.

Behind the pile of cupboards they'd moved upstairs from Meemaw's kitchen, her eyes settled on Chaz. She wondered if that strange new feeling came from this place or this person. Or maybe both.

Chaz ran his circular saw through a two-by-four, sawdust drifting into the air. It clung to his shirt and his jeans. Lexi took a deep breath. She lived for the scents of vanilla and cocoa, but there was something about the earthy smell of freshly cut wood that she could definitely appreciate. Especially on a man like Chaz.

Sunlight filtered in through her reading nook windows, turning Chaz's hair into molten caramel and highlighting the reddish stubble on his jaw. Lexi had read enough romance novels to know that noticing glistening facial hair was always a telltale sign that the heroine was developing certain feelings.

Lexi shook her head and groaned. She wasn't a heroine in some romance novel. She was just Lexi Caehill, pastry chef and budding entrepreneur. Sappy love stories would have to wait until her business was up and running. Then she'd welcome a romance with open arms. Right now, she just wanted to shoo it away.

"You comin' in or just standing there to admire the beauty?" Chaz's eyes hadn't left the wooden frame he was building, but Lexi could see one side of his grin. "Either way, don't let me stop ya."

"Very funny." Lexi rolled her eyes. "I just wanted to see if yesterday went any better for you than it did for me. And by the looks of it, it did."

"Sure. Truckin' right along up here." Chaz made a quick mark on the board and tucked the pencil behind his ear as he stood up. "Should have these walls framed out by the end of the day."

"That quickly?" Lexi smiled, excited at the prospect of moving into her new bedroom soon. "That's fantastic."

"Well, the framin' is the easy part. Then you've got to run electrical and plumbing, hang drywall, do the mudding, sanding, priming, and painting."

"Kind of like building a wedding cake, I guess." Lexi nodded in thought. "Everyone assumes it's just slapping some icing on a cake, but there's a lot that goes on inside to make the outside look good."

"See, what we do isn't so different," Chaz walked over and nudged her with his elbow. "Now, why was yesterday so bad for you? You were practically glowin' when you left."

"Ugh." Lexi sagged onto a cupboard, temporarily sitting in the middle of the dining area. "Everyone was so hesitant to help me out. Most of my flyers got shoved into drawers, probably never to be seen again. All because of—"

"Hello? Anybody home?"

Lexi and Chaz looked at each other at the sound of a woman's voice downstairs.

"Were you expecting someone?" Lexi whispered.

"Nope." Chaz shook his head and shooed her towards the stairs. "Looks like maybe those flyers worked after all."

Lexi gasped and rushed downstairs. She'd assumed it was a nosy neighbor, not a potential client. She smoothed her curls back into their ponytail and straightened her shirt as she hurried through the kitchen.

"Hello," the woman called again, just as Lexi rushed through the kitchen door.

"Hi. Hello." Lexi smiled, panting slightly. "How can I help you?"

"Ah. There you are. I'd like to place an order." The woman ran her fingers through her short, blonde bob. "I heard you were up and running...but that doesn't seem correct."

She raised an eyebrow, looking at the blank walls and empty rooms, and tapped her immaculately manicured nails together, waiting. Lexi could feel the judgment rolling off this woman in waves.

"You heard right." Lexi said, overly cheerful. "The kitchen is up and running, even though the bakery isn't yet. I am totally able to take orders."

"I suppose it's better than the alternative." The woman turned and wandered into the living room, her heels clicking on the wood floors. "My aunt, Lady Carmichael, whom I believe you met, is hosting a formal tea for the next Garden Society meeting and will need refreshments."

It took all of Lexi's willpower to keep her lip from curling in distaste as she pulled out her phone to take notes. That computer purchase needed to happen soon. Taking orders on her Notes app was both embarrassing and unprofessional.

"Oh, yes. Couldn't forget the lovely welcome your aunt gave me."

"So true. She really is the sweetest."

"What name can I put the order under?" Lexi asked.

"Oh, silly me. I'm just so used to everyone knowing everyone around here, but with you being new and all..." she shrugged. "I'm Acacia Carmichael."

She held her hand out primly and gently clasped Lexi's with the tips of her fingers, then dropped them without so much as a single shake. Just a tiny squeeze.

"It's a pleasure," Lexi said through clenched teeth.

"I'm sure it is. Now, we'll be having tea on the twenty-fourth in honor of International Self-Care Day. We all work so hard;

we deserve a little treat. We're expecting about twenty people. It's a formal tea, so make something appropriate." Acacia tapped the phone Lexi held in her hands with a single fingernail. "Are you going to take down notes?"

"Yes, ma'am."

Acacia leaned back with a haughty smile as Lexi stabbed at her phone. Chaz sauntered in through the kitchen door, and Acacia transformed into a whole different person.

"Oh, Chaz, darling, how are you?" Acacia gushed and fluttered over to him, kissing both his cheeks.

Lexi saw red as Acacia smiled up at Chaz warmly and rested her hand on his arm as if it had every right to be there.

Not that I have a say in whose hands touch Chaz's anything.

To his credit, Chaz stepped back and casually leaned against the wall. The red at the edges of her vision faded until Chaz looked at her with a quick wink before turning back to Acacia.

That cocky little...

"Nice to see ya, Acacia. How's your mama an' them?"

"They're doing great, so sweet of you to ask." Acacia bowed her head with a smile. "Mama's back is doing so much better since she started seeing that new chiropractor over in Jackson."

"That's real good to hear." Chaz nodded. "So, what brings you to Lexi's bakery?"

"I'm placing an order for this month's Society meeting in honor of International Self-Care Day. We work so hard for this town. It will be nice to have a day to relax and treat ourselves. And speaking of which, I gotta jet. I've got an appointment with Iris at the salon."

Acacia pulled a pair of sunglasses out of her large handbag, a Louis Vuitton if Lexi's time in high-end restaurants had taught her anything. A style from several years ago, but still ridiculously expensive.

"On the twenty-fourth, formal tea." Acacia pointed at Lexi's phone and raised a brow. "Don't forget."

"Got it." Lexi jiggled the phone in her direction.

"Perfect. We have very discerning tastes, so I hope you can handle it." Acacia turned to Chaz and waggled her fingers at him. "Bye, Chaz. So great running into you. Tell your mama hi."

"Will do." Chaz tipped his imaginary hat in her direction, sending her out the door with a giggle.

"Oh, my lands." Lexi sighed. "This town is like a real-life version of Mean Girls."

"Not sure what that is, but I get the gist," Chaz pushed off the wall and walked until he was straight in front of Lexi. "Let me tell you somethin'. Those women can make or break you. You gotta suck it up and hide that spitfire side of yourself."

"And just take their stuck-up, snotty crap? I don't think so, Chaz."

"Nope." Chaz shook his head. "Didn't say you had to take it. You just have to learn to play the game."

She wanted nothing to do with people who played mind games. There'd been enough of that from her family growing up. She didn't escape them, just to be thrown in with even smarter, better-equipped manipulators.

"What the hell even is a 'formal tea?' Is that common knowledge around here?" Lexi paced across the living room and back. "Oh, and the 'Sorry I forgot to introduce myself. We aren't used to outsiders.' Ha! She knew exactly what she was doing."

"Well, I won't be any help with the tea thing. Never been to one since men aren't invited." Chaz watched Lexi pace back and forth with a slight smile on his face. "But I do know these women. And I can verify that she 100% knew what she was doing."

"Ughhh," Lexi half groaned, half growled. "I hate manipulative people. Especially the kind who try to make other people feel worse. You want to manipulate people to get free stuff, you're just a freeloader and a cheat. But if you manipulate people's emotions to make them feel worse or yourself feel better, well you're nothing more than a —"

"Whoa there." Chaz walked over with his hands up. "I can see you're gettin' yourself worked up into a tizzy here and I'm gonna have to, kindly, tell you to knock it off."

"Excuse me?" Lexi sputtered.

"I don't know what kind of history you have with people like Acacia, but it obviously was not a good one by your reaction," Chaz placed his hands on her shoulders, gently, forcing her to meet his gaze.

"Damn straight, it wasn't good." Lexi crossed her arms over her chest and narrowed her eyes at him.

"But, darlin', you're playin' right into her game."

"Don't 'darlin'' me, Chaz Walker." Lexi pushed him away and turned towards the kitchen. "I have every right to feel what I feel."

"I'm no psychiatrist, or what have you, but do you think maybe some of your anger isn't really at her?" Chaz followed right on her heels. "Maybe just a little?"

Lexi growled low in her throat as she pushed open the door and closed her eyes to the warm sunshine flooding in.

"Fine," she said quickly. "Maybe a little."

"I figured as much. Cause, darn, what she did ain't even that bad. You should hear some of the things she's done to my—"

"I know. You're right." Lexi thunked her elbows down on the counter and rested her chin in her hands. "I've never been good at tamping down my reactions."

"That'll just make you more fun for them."

"I knowww...." Lexi whined. "But it's so hard. And they're so smug. And I just get so angry and then say things. And then I regret it."

"And you feel bad, and they move on like nothin' happened."

"Yep."

"Yep."

Chaz walked over and held his arms open wide. Lexi eyed him wearily, but when he wiggled his fingers to guide her in, she stepped into his embrace. As the smell of sawdust wrapped around her, she relaxed against him. After a few deep breaths, she raised her arms and hugged him back.

Being held by him felt good. And not just in a physical way, though she wasn't complaining about that. His warmth seeped into her and calmed every single one of her frazzled nerves. Like a hot bubble bath after a long day. Or a shot of top-shelf whiskey. Smooth, warm, and too much could lead to bad choices. Chaz, with his golden eyes and amber hair, had way too much in common with a nice bottle of whiskey.

And, damn, if it isn't my favorite drink, *too.*

"I've had my fair share of run-ins with the Garden Society women, Lex," Chaz's voice rumbled in his chest under her ear, "and the best way to deal with them is to not let them see you squirm. Don't give 'em the satisfaction."

"I know. It's something I've never been good at," Lexi mumbled into his shirt, "but I'll work on it."

"Atta girl."

Chaz rubbed small circles on her back, and Lexi closed her eyes, leaning into him even more. Neither said anything for a few minutes. When a contented sigh escaped her lips, Lexi's eyes flew open.

Yep. Too much like whiskey.

Lexi slowly let go and stepped away, instantly missing the warmth as the cool air came between them. Clasping her hands in front of her, she cleared her throat.

"Well, thank you for that," she quickly gestured between them. "I have a lunch date I need to get to."

"Oh, really?"

"Well, I mean... not a date."

"Don't let me keep you." Chaz stepped back and gestured for the door.

"I'm meeting Lotus," Lexi blurted. "It's just a girls' lunch."

"I didn't say anything."

"Oh, hush."

"Yes, ma'am."

Lexi snatched her purse and rushed out of the room while Chaz smirked.

The smell of burgers and fries inside the diner brought a smile to Lexi's face. Lotus waved to her from a booth at the end of the row. All the tables were full, and the air buzzed with chatter. People stopped and nodded in her direction as she passed, which she returned with a tight-lipped smile.

"People's kindness still freaking you out?" Lotus said in a loud whisper as Lexi slid into the booth.

"Not that, so much as actually being noticed." Lexi shivered at the thought. "No one gave me a second glance in New York."

"Well, like I said. You're front-page news around here."

Lotus pulled a newspaper out from under the booth and slapped it on the table. The picture Lotus took of Lexi standing by the magnolia trees graced the top page.

"Oh my gosh," Lexi gushed and reached to grab her friend's hand. "You got the front page?"

"First article in print," Lotus beamed. "All thanks to you."

"Not thanks to me. This is purely your talent, Lotus." Lexi grabbed the paper, her eyes darting over the words surrounding the picture. "And you were right. You made this dead fish look good."

"You are *so* not a dead fish." Lotus took a sip from her glass, then wiped the condensation off with a napkin.

"I sure felt like one. Man, I was tired."

Lexi smiled, remembering her first day in Fauna. It felt like a different lifetime, even though it had only been six weeks ago.

Rosita stopped by their table and took their orders. As she turned to leave, Lexi stopped her.

"I think today calls for milkshakes. Two of the largest, sweetest, highest calorie shakes you've got, please."

"You got it." Rosita scribbled in her notepad and hurried behind the counter.

"And what do we need these super fattening beverages for?" Lotus leaned on her elbows, rubbing her hands together in anticipation.

"To celebrate," Lexi answered. "Look at us now, both living the dream. You're writing articles. My kitchen is up and running."

"It is?" Lotus gasped. "Why didn't you tell me?"

"What do you think this lunch is for?" Lexi laughed.

"Oh, I don't know. To catch up with your bestie, whom you've been neglecting for the last few weeks, to polish kitchen equipment."

"I know. And I feel awful. But you can come and see it after lunch. And," Lexi leaned in with a sly grin, "I can tell you all about the first order I got today."

"What?" Lotus squawked. "Details. Now."

Lexi filled her in on handing out flyers and it being a bust. Then about Acacia's visit to the bakery. She left out the cuddle with Chaz afterward, not quite ready to unpack that yet.

"Ah, yes. Their annual 'Self-Care' tea party." Lotus rolled her eyes. "Those women take more care of themselves than the rest of the town combined. I'm pretty sure the 'society' single-handedly keeps the salon and dress shop in business."

"Well, let's see if we can add my bakery to that list." Lexi giggled. "I don't care how much of a pain in the butt they are, money is money."

"You say that now..." Lotus smirked and leaned further across the table to whisper, "They rent swans every year for this event."

"I'm sorry, what?" Lexi sputtered.

"Yeah. They rent them to just waddle around the lawn while they eat fancy food inside. Something about them symbolizing grace and purity, blah, blah, blah."

"What exactly does that have to do with self-care?" Lexi wondered out loud.

"Maybe they're hoping some of it will rub off on them?" Lotus shrugged. "Or maybe they're a sacrifice. Lady Carmichael doesn't seem to age..."

They both dissolved into giggles as their food arrived. Rosita plunked giant chocolate milkshakes covered in chocolate syrup, sprinkles, and whipped cream in front of each of them. They both took a drink and sighed.

"I'm going to need some help, you know," Lexi said between sips. "With the tea party."

"I'm not going into that viper's den." Lotus leaned back and shook her head.

"Please. You're the only one I trust." Lexi wrapped her hands together, begging. "It'll only be for serving. A couple of hours, tops. And I'll pay."

"Keep talking." Lotus narrowed her eyes.

"Add in all the pastries you can eat? Oh, and all the gossip you can overhear." Lexi waggled her eyebrows. "Wouldn't that help with your articles?"

"Of course it would. The question is, do I want it bad enough to deal with all that?"

"Please. Please. Please." Lexi widened her eyes and stuck out her bottom lip.

"Fine. But if a story comes up that I have to cover, I can't promise anything. That would take priority. Especially since I'm officially a journalist now."

"How often do articles come up?" Lexi asked innocently before taking a large bite of her burger.

"Oh, shut it." Lotus rolled her eyes again. "Fine. But I require an apron. A pink one. The frillier, the better."

"Deal. Eeekkk... this is going to be so fun. Lexi and Lotus. Dream team."

Now, all Lexi had to do was pray to the small-town gods that nothing else newsworthy happened that day, or she'd be left to her own devices with the venerable ladies of the Fauna Mississippi Garden Society.

Chapter 14

Lexi hummed and spun across her commercial kitchen with sheet pans of macrons piped and ready to rest in the speed racks. It'd been a week since Acacia had placed her order for the 'formal tea party' the Garden Society was having tomorrow and Lexi was in her happy space. Her to-do lists were made, and she was checking things off like the jolly man himself on Christmas Eve.

After Lotus told her they rented live swans to decorate Lady Carmichael's expansive lawn, Lexi'd run with that theme for the pastries. Lotus also told her that formal tea meant the guests would be arriving in ball gowns, and no expense was spared on their accessories. The nail salon would be booked solid for manicures, pedicures, and facials all week. The stylists at the beauty parlor would be booked for the morning of the tea party. And her mixer and stove were fired up and ready for some long hours at her bakery.

All this so some pampered Southern belles could claim a day of self-care.

Lexi had to chuckle. She didn't have the bone-deep dislike built up over years of snubs and mistreatment that Lotus felt towards these women. Lexi just knew she wouldn't like them.

She'd dealt with plenty of wealthy clients in New York who thought that money and reputation were solid replacements for manners and respect. She couldn't stand them there, and she couldn't imagine she'd like them here either.

Her mind drifted back to what Chaz had told her after Acacia left. 'Don't give them the satisfaction of seeing you squirm,' he'd said. Her emotions tended to burst out of her, whether she wanted them to or not. But she had every intention of following Chaz's advice. As best she could.

She'd even been practicing with Lotus, who would randomly hurl some entitled, manipulative BS her way just to get a reaction out of her. They'd ended up in a giggling heap multiple times, which Lexi was positive wouldn't happen at the tea party tomorrow.

The steady hum of sawing overhead stopped, and Lexi turned as Chaz's boots thudded down the back stairs. He walked into the kitchen, wiping his forehead with the back of his forearm.

"You're looking hot today," Lexi said with a small smile.

"Why, thank ya, ma'am. I'm workin' up a sweat in there." Chaz walked to the double-door refrigerator and stuck his head inside. "Ah. That's more like it."

"You better get your sweaty head and dirty hands out of my clean fridge." Lexi swatted at him with the towel she'd thrown over her shoulder. "I've got a business to run here. A sanitary one."

Chaz leaned around the open fridge door, waggling his eyebrows as he ran his fingers down the handle. Lexi narrowed her eyes at him and readied her towel for another swat, but he quickly stepped out from behind the door with a bottle of water.

"There's no need to accost the appliances if all you need is a drink," she rolled her eyes and turned back to her recipe book. She snapped it shut and pulled out the bags of Valrhona chocolate that had been delivered just the day before. The scent of 66% cacao hit her nose, and she closed her eyes. "Mmmm..."

"Somethin' over there must be pretty good to make those sounds come out of ya." Chaz peeked around her shoulder. "That's just a bag of big chocolate chips."

"Ha!" Lexi scoffed. "Chocolate chips? Please. Chocolate chips don't cost almost $100 a bag."

"I'm sorry, what now? You spent $100 on that itty bitty bag of chocolate?" Chaz fell against the counter, clutching his chest. "I can run down to the grocery and grab some bars for a dollar."

"That's not real chocolate."

"Like heck it isn't."

"Those chocolate bars are almost all sugar and flavorings. There's very little actual chocolate in them." Lexi shook her head. "This chocolate? This is the real stuff. Here," she grabbed a stool and pulled it in front of him, "sit."

Lexi placed three bags on the counter, carefully opening each and organizing them in order of cacao content. This had been one of her favorite parts of culinary school. Sampling the different chocolates until she could detect the flavor notes underneath the bitterness.

"We'll start on the lower end since you obviously aren't used to quality chocolate." Lexi pulled two pieces out of the bag. They were much larger than typical chocolate chips, thicker too. "Here. Try this."

Lexi handed him a piece. He tossed it into his mouth, chewed, and swallowed. He gagged and started scraping his tongue against the roof of his mouth, trying to get rid of the flavor. Lexi doubled over laughing.

"Yuck. That tastes like bitter dirt."

"You're not supposed to chew it. You suck on it. This is meant to be savored."

She tried to hand him another one, but he turned his head away.

"Nope. No, thank you. I'll stick to my grocery store chocolate."

"Just try it." Lexi grabbed his face in one hand and shoved the chocolate between his tightly clenched lips with the other.

He glared at her but didn't chew. She popped one into her mouth and closed her eyes as it melted on her tongue.

"This is a single-origin chocolate from the island of Madagascar." Lexi leaned back against the counter, rolling her tongue over the chocolate in her mouth. She kept her eyes closed, focusing on the flavor. "You can really pick up the acidity and fruity flavors in this one."

When the chocolate finished melting in her mouth, she finally opened her eyes and turned to Chaz, who'd been oddly silent. He still sat on his stool, with his elbow on the counter and his chin propped into his hand, staring at her with an expression she couldn't place.

"I don't know if I've ever seen you look so at peace," he finally said. "If I knew all it took was a chocolate chip to bring that rapturous look to your face, I would have bought you some a long time ago."

"Again, they aren't chocolate chips." Lexi sighed and dumped some of the chocolate into her tempering machine. "But yes. I have a bit of a thing for chocolate. The good stuff. You bring a grocery store chocolate bar in here, and I'm kicking you out."

"Well, don't tell my mama that her chocolate isn't good enough. She's won first place with her chocolate meringue pie three years running."

"I would never dream of telling your mother she's done anything wrong," she paused, looking up at the ceiling briefly, "except maybe raising such a scoundrel."

"A scoundrel? You wound me, fair lady." Chaz leaned around her, reaching for another one of the chocolate bags. "Hand me one of them."

Lexi swatted his hand away. She reached in and pulled out a single piece as she watched the blades on the tempering machine spin. She turned to face Chaz when he didn't take the chocolate from her hand and found him sitting with his mouth wide open.

"I'm sorry, do you expect me to feed you now, too?"

He nodded his head, golden eyes flashing with mischief. Lexi laughed and moved in front of him. His knees brushed her thighs, and alarm bells blared in her brain.

Don't do it. No distractions, remember?

She hesitated for a moment, her hand holding the chocolate hovering between them. Chaz must have sensed her hesitation because he wrapped his long fingers gently around her wrist and guided the chocolate the rest of the way to his mouth.

Lexi stood transfixed as his lips wrapped around the tips of her fingers. Warmth spread down her arm and up into her cheeks. Her gaze left his lips and locked onto his eyes. Those golden pools, currently tinged with a heat Lexi was sure mirrored in her own.

His lips slid from her fingertips, but he kept his hold on her wrist as if he were afraid she'd drift away. And she might have. The alarm bells were on full alert. The little people in her brain, like in that kids' movie, were running around flailing their arms above their heads in panic.

"Mmm," he sucked on the chocolate again. "There's a nuttiness to this one."

"There's certainly something nutty going on in here."

Lexi and Chaz's gazes flew to the kitchen door, where Lotus stood with her eyes wide, staring at the two of them. Lexi glanced down at herself, pulled between Chaz's knees, and knew how it must look to Lotus. She sprang back, yanking her wrist free of Chaz's soft grasp.

"Lotus. Hey. Wasn't expecting you until tomorrow."

"Obviously." Lotus's face broke into a huge grin before she straightened it into something much more serious. "And that's what I came to talk to you about."

"Okayyy..." Lexi didn't like the sound of that.

"Something's come up with the paper. They want me to head to Jackson." Lotus hesitated. "Tonight."

Lexi stared at her and blinked a few times, trying to process what she'd just been told.

"I know it's leaving you in a bind, and I feel absolutely terrible. But this is a huge opportunity to get my journalism career up and running, and, really, I did warn you when I agreed to this that it was a possibility. A slim one, but a possibility nonetheless. I am really sorry, Lexi. I wanted to see if there was anything I could do to help you today instead."

"No. No." Lexi rushed over to Lotus and wrapped her in a big hug. "I am so excited for you. Don't you worry about a thing here. I'll be just fine. You go get ready for your trip. This is huge."

"It really is, isn't it?" Lotus did a little shimmy. "An overnight stay. Hotel. Shoot, Bill's even giving me per diem for food."

"You're in the big time now." Lexi joined in on the shimmy-ing.

"Thanks for not being mad. I really do feel awful."

"Don't. You're doing exactly what you're supposed to be doing, and I couldn't be more happy for you." Lexi smiled at Lotus and began shoving her towards the door. "Now get on out of here so you can get on the road. And I expect to hear all about it when you get back."

"Okay. Thanks, Lexi." Lotus waved awkwardly over her shoulder as Lexi pushed her through the door. "Bye Chaz. Good seeing you both."

As the door swung shut, Lexi dropped her forehead on it with a thunk.

"Ugh. This is going to be a disaster," she mumbled, "unless..."

Lexi turned to Chaz, pursing her lips to the side.

"Why are you lookin' at me like that?" Chaz's eyes widened as he caught Lexi's drift. "Oh, no. I don't think so. You get that crazy idea out of your head right now."

"Come on, Chaz. You're the only other person I'd trust with something like this. There's no way I'm going to be able to get everything delivered, staged, and served on my own."

"I told you men aren't allowed at these tea things. It's like Southern law."

"You can stay back in the kitchen. No one even has to see you."

"No way, Lexi." Chaz shook his head, his hair curling onto his forehead. "That's never, ever going to happen. Not in a million years."

Lexi eased down the stairs at the B&B and out into the still early morning darkness. She hadn't been up this early since she'd moved to Fauna and didn't realize how much she'd missed the peace and solitude she felt when the rest of the world was asleep.

She drove the few blocks to the bakery, relishing the calm before what she knew was going to be a whirlwind of a day. All she had left to do this morning was prep work, since she finished the baking yesterday. She ran through her to-do list for the hundredth time as she unlocked the door. Box up the pastries. Dip the gold leaf. Fold the whipped cream into the pastry cream. Fill the cream puffs. Make the caramel. Spin the sugar. The list continued as she flicked on the kitchen lights and got to work.

Two hours went by in a blur of powdered sugar and piping bags. Lexi was loading up the last of her utensils when the front door opened with a bang. She rolled her eyes in annoyance.

If he isn't going to help today, the least he could do is stay out of the way.

She'd been in tougher situations before and knew she could pull through today. It was just going to be twice the amount of work for one person, and she'd be bone-tired once it was over.

The kitchen door creaked open, and Chaz slunk in, rubbing his eyes and yawning. Lexi instantly noticed the lack of stubble on his chin. And he'd traded in his long-sleeved tees and jeans for a white button-down shirt and black slacks.

Lexi stood frozen in place. His slacks hugged him in all the right places. And the top button of his shirt was undone, which was about to leave Lexi undone. That man was a sight to see in his everyday clothes, but it was something else altogether to see him freshly shaven in his Sunday best.

"You can close your mouth now," Chaz said, his voice still rough with sleep. "I couldn't get a wink of sleep last night thinkin' of you workin' yourself to the bone when I could've helped." He paused and cleared his throat. "Sorry for the way I left things last night."

He reached up and rubbed the back of his head, looking as sheepish as a schoolboy caught in the cookie jar. Lexi took his advice and snapped her mouth shut but couldn't find any words.

"So, what do you need me to do, boss?"

"I... ugh." Lexi quickly shook her head to clear her mind and pulled up her checklist. "Next thing up is to load everything into my car."

"Sure thing." Chaz moved to pick up the box of her utensils but stopped when Lexi placed her hand on his arm.

"Thanks for this," she said softly. "I really appreciate it."

"Hey, what are friends for?" Chaz smiled down at her and turned away with the box in hand.

Friends. Right. No distractions.

Lexi snorted at the absurdity of it though. Chaz was always a distraction, whether she liked it or not. And looking like he did today, she'd be lucky to keep her head in the game at all. C-H-A-Z may as well have been spelled T-R-O-U-B-L-E, and Lexi was a glutton for punishment.

She followed Chaz out, carrying a small cake box filled with pastries, and enjoying what those dress slacks did for his backside. She turned the car on and popped the trunk. Chaz slid his box all the way to the back of the massive space. Before moving to Fauna, she'd known delivery space was a requirement, and the trunk was the reason she'd bought this car. Somewhere down the line, she hoped she'd be able to invest in a delivery van, but until that day, this car would have to do.

Back inside, Chaz went to grab the next box. He slid his hands onto the sides.

"Whoa, whoa, whoa. The first rule of pastry club," Lexi jumped next to him and threw her hands out over the box.

"We don't talk about pastry club?" Chaz finished.

"No. We can discuss pastry club all you'd like." Lexi took his hands in hers, her fingers nestling between his, and slid them underneath the box. "Always carry from the bottom. Not the sides."

"Not that I'm questionin' you, boss," Chaz bent his knees and exaggerated every movement as he picked up the box from the bottom, "but why does that matter?"

"If a cake or pastry inside is close to the edge, you'll damage the decoration if you grab it from the sides," Lexi explained. "These boxes have a lot of flex, so you have to be careful."

Chaz nodded and headed out to the car. They made several trips back and forth, saving the refrigerated boxes for last. It was like a game of Tetris, fitting the boxes just right, until they were snug and wouldn't slide around on the drive over.

"Let me grab my chef's coat, and we can head out." Lexi turned to run back inside.

"Grab one for me, too. I'd hate to get chocolate or somethin' on my shirt." Chaz glanced down and rubbed at his buttons. "Lady Carmichael would throw a conniption if I tried to serve guests with so much as a crumb on me."

"Sign of a good chef is a pristine white coat," Lexi shrugged. "I only have one chef coat here, but I do have the apron I ordered for Lotus."

"That'll do." Chaz slid into the passenger seat.

"You say that now," Lexi muttered as she ran up the steps.

She threw the coat and apron into the back seat and backed out onto the road. The town came alive around them. The lights on the diner flashed on as they drove past, the smell of bacon wafting outside. Someone flipped over the open sign in the bookstore window. The sun just crested the tops of the buildings on the square, bathing everything in a hazy gold.

"Sure is beautiful," Lexi sighed.

"Sure is." Chaz nodded.

If anyone'd asked her six weeks ago if she'd be delivering her first order with her very own cowboy contractor at her side, she'd have laughed. Lexi glanced at him out of the corner of her eye. His lean body was folded into the passenger seat, but he was leaning back, relaxed, and right with the world. Her eyes moved up the length of him, from his polished boots, up his long legs that barely fit under her dash, over those strong, tan hands, and rested on the profile of his face as he watched the world pass by. She could smell a hint of spicy cologne that was new and enticing. Being in such a small space, just the two of them, left Lexi feeling slightly breathless.

"OK there, boss?" Chaz nodded towards her hands. "You're about to choke the life out'a that poor steerin' wheel."

"Oh," Lexi chuckled nervously. "Guess I'm a little more nervous about today than I thought."

Lies.

She hadn't been thinking about today's job at all. In fact, it had vacated her mind entirely, which was concerning. This man was too much and darned if he didn't know it. The lopsided smirk on his face told her he knew exactly what she'd been thinking.

"Well, I'm here to help you with whatever it is you have on your mind."

"I'm sure you are, but I need you on your best behavior today, so none of that."

"None of what?" he asked innocently. "Just offering my assistance."

"Don't think I can't see that smirk of yours, Chaz."

"Don't think I can't see those long glances of yours either, Lex."

Damn.

Her side-eye must not be as stealthy as she'd thought. That left her with two options. Play it off as his imagination. Or be direct.

"Ok. I admit. I was admiring your change in attire." She hesitated for a second and then continued quietly. "You look nice today."

"Well, thanks, Lex." Chaz straightened in his seat and reached over to tuck a wayward curl behind her ear. His fingertips lingered in that sensitive spot just at the edge of her jawline. "I really like what you did with your hair today."

"I put it in a bun," Lexi exclaimed, trying to focus on the road and not on the fingers brushing her skin. "That's hardly a seductive hairstyle."

"Oh, I beg to differ." His hand trailed down her neck, his fingertips barely brushing the exposed skin.

Lexi shivered and then swatted his hand away.

"As lovely as that is, we gotta focus today. So," she looked at him, still swatting her hand between them even though he'd already returned his hand to his lap, "no more of that."

"I'll try, but no promises."

"Thank you." Lexi leaned over the wheel, looking for the driveway the GPS was indicating.

"Don't use that one," Chaz pointed past the drive she'd slowed to turn into, "go to the next one."

"What's the difference?"

"The first one takes you to the front. The second takes you around back to the 'servants' entrance,' as the lady of the house likes to call it."

"You mean the service entrance."

"Nope. Not in an old plantation home."

"Seriously?"

"As the dirty side of a hurricane."

"I have no idea what that even means."

"Stay in the South long enough, and you will." Chaz pointed to a small driveway. "Turn here."

Lexi turned onto the narrow gravel road. To the left of the car was a wall of tall green bushes. To the right, a vast lawn covered in ancient oak trees. Lexi barely contained a gasp at the beauty. The lowest branches of the oaks hovered just above the ground, beckoning people to sit in their embrace, staring up through the dappled canopy. Moss hung in long curtains, swaying in the slightest breeze.

They rounded a bend in the road, and the house came into view. It sat at the top of a circular drive surrounding a small pond. The house was exactly the style Lexi had expected, but she was still shocked. Her lifelong obsession with anything Southern had led her to read about old plantation homes from all around the area, but she'd never seen this one. It could have graced the front of any magazine, with its two-story white columns, wrap-around porch, and upper balcony. Its red brick contrasted with the white wooden porch and black shutters.

"She's a looker, isn't she?" Chaz asked.

"Yeah. I've read all about plantation homes in the area, but I never saw this one."

"As old as this house may look, it's actually fairly new."

"What? How?"

"Lord Carmichael commissioned it as a gift for his new wife. He wasn't from around these parts, if you hadn't guessed by the 'Lord' and 'Lady' thing." Chaz motioned air quotes with his hands. "He moved over from England and was obsessed with the history here."

"So, you're telling me she's a legit 'Lady'?" Lexi couldn't believe it. "I thought that was just out of respect or something."

"Nope. She married herself a legit royal."

"Well, I'll be damned." Lexi shook her head as they drove past the front of the house and around the back. "So, they just built a house to look old?"

"Nope. They used all reclaimed building materials from other period homes in disrepair. I got to come out with my Pa once when I was real little. Wish I'd paid more attention; I'd die for that opportunity nowadays."

"So, it's all old stuff, just put together in a new way?"

"Sure, kind of like a historical jigsaw puzzle, but with modern conveniences like electricity and central heat and air."

"Best of both worlds." Lexi marveled at the idea. That must have cost a fortune, something only legit royalty could afford.

The tires crunched over gravel as they came to a stop by a large double door at the back of the house. Her hands gripped the steering wheel again.

Time to make this dream come true.

Chapter 15

"Well, bust out that chef's coat, and let's get this show on the road." Chaz rubbed his hands together and hopped out of the car.

Lexi left the engine running and grabbed her coat and the apron from the back seat. She joined Chaz on the other side of the car, but the view of the backyard was blocked by a privacy fence. It wouldn't do to have the guests see the delivery trucks while they were strolling through the backyard. She'd seen the same thing at a lot of the restaurants in New York if they had a back patio anywhere near the delivery door.

"Please don't hate me," Lexi cringed as she pulled on her chef coat and held out the apron.

"Oh, Lord. What now?" Chaz turned to her, and his eyes got wide.

"I had this made for Lotus. It's the only one I had."

She held up the apron, covered in frills of all different shades and prints in bright pink, just as Lotus had requested.

"Bless it," Chaz muttered as he snatched it from Lexi's hands and pulled it over his head. As he tied it around his waist, he did a little twirl and curtsey.

"Honest opinion?" Lexi tapped her chin with a finger. "Pink is a good color on you."

"Damn straight." Chaz straightened the apron and puffed out his chest. "Every color is a good color on me."

"Okay, Mr. Modest." Lexi motioned for him to spin around and retied the sad bow he'd created. "Why don't you get the door, see if you can prop it open, and I'll grab some boxes."

"On it." Chaz trotted towards the door, apron frills flapping.

Lexi popped the trunk and felt the refrigerated boxes to make sure they were still cool. She grabbed the largest one and joined Chaz at the door.

"It's locked," he said as he jiggled the handle. "I can run around..."

"No," Lexi handed him the box she was holding. "I'd like to make first contact since it's my business and they're my customers."

"Good point."

"Can you put that back in the car so it stays cool? I'll be right back."

Lexi hurried around the side of the house, thankful for the shade once she rounded the corner. She heard some commotion out front and cringed at the shrill voice of an older woman. Lexi could not believe her eyes when she saw the front yard.

"Control your animal, sir." Lady Carmichael huffed as she grabbed the strands of pearls at her throat.

"They're swans, ma'am. As I explained on the phone, they're not trained."

The older woman stood at the base of the front stairs in a pair of slacks and a flowing blouse. Her hair was pinned in an elaborate updo. The poor kid she was berating looked like he couldn't be more than fifteen or sixteen. Lady Carmichael noticed Lexi's arrival and nodded in her direction.

"If a cat can use a litter box, then a bird should be able to handle it. Don't you think so, Alexandra?"

"It's just Lexi. And I can't say I've ever heard of a litter-trained bird, ma'am." Lexi withered under the glare of the older woman's sharp grey eyes before backpedaling. "Not to say it can't be done, though."

"You see, young man. Nothing is impossible. Now clean up that offensive mess before my guests see it. Or worse, step in it."

The poor boy dug through his pockets, pulled out a used napkin, and slowly reached toward the greenish goop on the front walkway. He glanced up, hoping for some pity. But the look he received could have frozen a fresh cherry cobbler on a Mississippi summer day. With a gulp, he turned his head and scooped up the waste.

Lexi rushed toward the front steps, grateful Lady Carmichael's attention was focused on someone else. Better her annoyance be focused on a kid who'd probably never have to see her again, even though guilt ate at her for throwing him to the wolves. And Lady Carmichael was just that— a wolf.

Lotus had told Lexi over their milkshakes at the diner that the ladies of Fauna Mississippi had formed a pack decades ago, with Lady Carmichael as their leader. They dubbed themselves the Garden Society, not because they had anything to do with landscaping, but because each and every one of them was named after a different variety of Southern flora. Their love and loyalty were fierce, but if anyone threatened their town or ideals, they could take them down with one swipe of their immaculately manicured claws. Anyone who thought these gals got together to talk about dresses, décor, and other fripperies was sorely mistaken. They talked power plays over their biscuits and ran this town one tea party at a time.

Lexi couldn't help but admire them. She'd never stayed somewhere long enough to feel any kind of pride or protectiveness. But Fauna had a way of getting under your skin. Making you want to stay and put roots down into the hot, red earth.

"Sorry to intrude, Lady Carmichael, but the service entrance is locked."

"Through the door, all the way back, and to the left," Lady Carmichael waved her past. "And Alexandra, don't get used to using this entrance. It's for guests only."

"Of course, ma'am."

Lexi rolled her eyes as she hurried through the massive double doors. Her steps slowed in appreciation of the opulence of the main hall. The intricate moldings. The ornate spindles of the stair railings were carved into hundreds of magnolia blossoms. The lush brocade curtains that were probably imported from Paris. Underneath the scent of wood polish, Lexi could practically smell the history.

Through the main hall, she turned left in search of the kitchen. Warm air flowed lazily through the wall of floor-to-ceiling windows that ran the length of the house. Fans whispered softly overhead so that it felt comfortable, even without any hint of air conditioning.

Lexi glanced through several doors, seeing a sitting room and what looked like a small business office. She gently pushed open the last door, hoping it was the kitchen and praying she wasn't walking in on anyone while they worked. She sighed when she saw a massive refrigerator and dark wood cabinets. While the rest of the grounds and house may look like they came straight out of another lifetime, the kitchen was all granite and stainless steel.

Lexi rushed through the room towards the double doors at the back. With a click of the lock, she threw one open and rushed out into the sunlight. Chaz leaned against the car, possibly looking even more gorgeous because of the ridiculous apron. Not that Lexi had a thing for guys in aprons. She had a thing for confidence. And it took a very confident man to look as at ease in that hot pink monstrosity as Chaz did at that moment.

"All right, we're good to go in here. Do you mind bringing in the boxes?" Lexi grabbed a roll of paper towels off the counter. "There's something I need to do real quick."

"Sure thing, boss. It's all under control."

"Don't forget," Lexi called over her shoulder, "the first rule of pastry club."

Lady Carmichael's clipped reprimands reached her before she made it outside. The poor boy was waddling behind a swan, holding his crumpled napkin, just waiting for a flick of the tail or any other sign it might mess again. The look on his face was a sad combination of horror and revulsion.

Lexi carried the paper towels over to the swan wrangler and handed them to the young man.

"Just do what she asks. As silly as it may sound," Lexi whispered with her back to Lady Carmichael.

The boy just nodded.

"And if you can sneak away later, come around back. I'll have some juice and cookies waiting. As long as you wash your hands first. No swan poop allowed in my kitchen."

He smiled and wiped his hands on his trousers.

"What are you two whispering about?" Lady Carmichael stood with her hands on her hips.

"Just giving him some cleaning supplies, ma'am."

"That's very thoughtful of you." Lady Carmichael turned on her heel and stood waiting at the base of the steps. "Now, where is your helper? You aren't planning to do this alone, are you? Is that why you're running late? I was beginning to wonder if you were coming at all."

"I've got all your pastry ready to set out, and the party doesn't start for over an hour, so I should have plenty of time."

Lexi hurried over, assuming Lady Carmichael was waiting for her to accompany her up the steps. And she was right. As soon as she was at the older woman's elbow, Lady Carmichael started up the stairs.

"I don't want you scurrying around setting things up when my guests arrive. Everything needs to be in place. Can you imagine? Arriving at a party to see empty platters on the serving table? Disgraceful."

"Don't you worry, Lady Carmichael. I've got this down to a science." Lexi said as they passed through the front doors to stop at the bottom of a curving staircase.

"Don't let me down. This is a big opportunity for you. Now I need to get ready. Aster? Aster?" She turned her head impatiently, searching for someone. "Ah, there you are. Come help me with my gown."

Lexi watched as she swept up the stairs, leaving Aster to follow. Lexi heard that Lady Carmichael would turn eighty this fall, but you couldn't tell it from the way she flowed up the stairs like a ballerina in her twenties.

Lexi shook her head in amazement and rushed back to the kitchen. Chaz was just closing the large door at the back, and her boxes all sat on the counters.

"What was all that?" Chaz raised an eyebrow at her as he leaned on the island.

"There's a poor kid on goose grease patrol out front and only had the old napkin from his pocket. Poor thing," Lexi shuddered.

"Did you say goose grease?"

"Yeah, would you prefer something else? Poo? Doo?" Lexi started ticking off the words on her fingers. "Oh, droppings?"

"Doo?" Chaz lowered his head with a sigh. "And here I was gonna say there might be a little Southern in you after all."

"I'll still take the compliment," Lexi beamed. "Now, let's get to work. We've got a lot to do in a little amount of time. And I'm stuck doing this with a lowly trainee."

"Lowly, you say?"

"Yep. Going to have to start at ground zero with this one."

"Maybe, just maybe, he'll surprise you."

Lexi looked at Chaz, leaning against the island. His dark hair was falling over his forehead as he smiled over at her. Lexi's heart stuttered, as it had a tendency to do in his presence.

"I think he already has."

The parlor where the tea party would actually take place was through the swinging door at the end of the kitchen and down a small, undecorated hallway. As she walked down it for the first time, she really wanted to stick some gaudy poster or sign on the wall, just to make this hallway less bland and to leave her mark on this grand house. But she could never actually do it. Rather than making her feel a little rebellious, it made her feel like she would be tarnishing something in this grand house. Even though the odds of any guest using this tiny hallway to the kitchen were next to nothing. This bland, uninteresting hall was for workers only.

She trailed her fingers along the cool plaster walls and pushed open another silent, swinging door. Muted sunlight wafted through flowing white curtains, glinting off the rose gold serving set displayed on the table. Marble urns overflowed with pale pink blossoms, set off with large white feathers cascading down onto the floor like snow. The chairs were covered in rose-colored silk, edged in lace.

"It's more beautiful than I imagined." Lexi's hand pressed to her chest.

She walked into the room, noticing all the themed details. Golden eggs lined the mantel. Lilies floated in a water feature in the corner. White feathers trailed down the back of each chair, giving the illusion of spread wings. There wasn't an actual swan anywhere except out on the front lawn, but the theme was evident on every surface and in every corner of the room.

Lexi walked over plush rugs to the table. The rose gold serving set was nestled amongst fine white cloth, just waiting to be filled with her delicate pastries. She scanned the shapes and sizes of the platters, planning where each type of pastry would be placed. Her mind whirred through the many options, deciding on the best arrangement of color, flavor, and texture.

A low whistle of appreciation came from the door behind her. Chaz looked around the room, arms crossed over his chest. With all his long, stern angles, he looked so out of place in such a soft, feminine setting. With six brothers at home,

Lexi wondered how he'd handle all the women today and hoped it wasn't a mistake bringing him along.

"Aster sure has an eye for detail." Approval laced each word Chaz said.

"She did all this?" Lexi had assumed Lady Carmichael did the décor, but then realized how ridiculous that idea was. "I was going to ask about her."

They both made their way back through the simple hallway to the kitchen. Lexi grabbed a box and pointed to one for Chaz to grab too.

"She went to school to be a historian and asked Lady Carmichael if she could write her thesis on the buildin' of this home, tracin' all the reclaimed pieces back to their origins and such." Chaz filled her in as they made their way back to the parlor. "Somehow she got roped into bein' Lady Carmichael's assistant and hasn't left since."

"Is she being held prisoner?" Lexi whispered, glancing around the room.

"No one really knows what Lady Carmichael has on her. I just know Aster isn't talkin' about it and doesn't want anyone's help."

Lexi heard the bitterness in his words and wondered what the backstory was there, but there wasn't time now to delve into what was undoubtedly some sordid, small-town drama.

Later though. I need to know.

Lexi filed it away to ask Lotus and turned her attention to the table in front of her. She opened the box she'd brought out and started gently placing the pastries on the platters. On the central, tiered stand, she placed rows of alternating pistachio and honey-flavored macrons. As she emptied that box, another one appeared in its place. Lexi's head stayed in design mode, balancing the placement of flavors and colors on the table. Another platter was filled with feather-light lemon souffle dusted with powdered sugar. Lexi gently placed poached pears into golden, spun-sugar nests. She set out neat rows of rosewater petit fours and miniature ginger cupcakes topped with flaked coconut.

"Wow, Lex," Chaz placed a hand on her back, rubbing gently when she finally leaned back and stepped away to look at the table as a whole. "You were totally in your element there, huh?"

"Guess so," she arched her back into his touch, and he pressed harder, easing the tension that had built up as she'd leaned over the table.

She glanced at her watch and decided it was time to pull the tray from the refrigerator. She'd saved the largest platter at the front of the table for last.

"Ready for the last box?" Chaz asked like he could read her mind.

"Yeah, if you don't mind."

"Sure thing, boss," Chaz made a show of bowing out of the room. "I live to serve."

Lexi laughed and fiddled with arrangements until he returned. She glanced at her watch again.

"Do you mind consolidating all the extra pastries into a single box and moving all the empty ones out to the car?" Lexi's mind was already working through how she'd place the final pastry. "I'll finish this, and we should be right on time."

Chaz disappeared back to the kitchen, and Lexi got to work. Out of the box, she gingerly picked up pate choux swans, filled with a Bavarian cream. Each little beak had been covered in gold leaf. Once the swans were in place, she scattered individually molded chocolate feathers throughout the display, adding texture where it was needed. Satisfied, she stepped back to admire her work. The table looked perfect. And she was right on time.

Lexi clapped her hands quietly for herself and hurried back towards the kitchen. In the hall, she heard voices and stopped before entering the kitchen. The excitement drained from her body as the words sank in.

"... she's going to be back soon." A woman's voice said in a hushed tone. "I mean, you're basically cavorting with the enemy here."

"Lex isn't the enemy," Chaz said.

Lexi leaned in a little further, pressing her ear to the door.

"You know she isn't going to see it that way," the woman sighed. "I'm just trying to look out for you, Chaz. You don't want to get on the bad side of—"

Lexi's foot slid over the hill of the thick carpet where it transitioned into the kitchen tile, and the door creaked open. She stumbled into the kitchen and froze. Lady Carmichael's assistant stood close to Chaz, her hand resting on his forearm. Chaz hurried over to Lexi's side and offered his arm. Aster's eyes narrowed at his back.

"Oh, geez," Lexi tried to smile and brush it off. "Watch that transition there. Would hate to trip on that while we serve the tea." She approached Aster and cranked up her smile. "Hi, I'm Lexi. We haven't officially met."

Aster hesitated a moment, looking over Lexi's shoulder at Chaz before taking a deep breath and smiling. The look she gave Lexi seemed genuine, so Lexi didn't understand the tension, but decided it must have something to do with the backstory she was still missing.

"Hello, Lexi. It's nice to finally meet you. I've heard a lot about you."

"Oh, really?" Lexi pivoted to give Chaz a look. He just shrugged and stuffed his hands into his pockets.

"Oh, nothing bad. Just typical small-town gossip." Aster hurried over to the sink and ran water into several pots. Then she moved to the cupboard and pulled down several small glass canisters.

"What tea flavors would complement your pastries?" She looked over her shoulder and tucked her short, dark hair behind her ear. "Lemon ginger? Citrus mint?"

"Well, I've already got lemon and ginger flavors, and I'm not sure about the mint."

"Oh, I just got a new hibiscus in that I could mix with raspberry?"

"That sounds perfect."

Lexi watched as Aster took a pinch from one jar and a spoonful from another. On top of being a master designer and historian, apparently, Aster was also an astute tea mixologist.

Lexi moved to the sink to rinse a few spatulas. Chaz stood at the island, cool as a cucumber. He either had no shame or was the best actor in the world and deserved an Oscar.

Why would anyone consider Lexi their enemy? She'd just moved here. And while her welcome from the Garden Society hadn't been super warm, here she was in their leader's home serving them tea. She wouldn't consider that enemy territory, just hoity-toity behavior.

"Okay," Aster said slowly as she gave a pitcher of pale pink liquid a final flourish with a tea strainer spoon. She poured some into three cups on the counter. "How does this taste? It may need to steep more."

Lexi slowly took a cup, still a little unsure of how to read Aster. She held it to her lips, letting the floral, fruity steam fill her nose, then took a tentative sip.

"That is delightful," Lexi closed her eyes and sighed. "And you just threw this together?"

"I like tea," Aster shrugged and then swatted at Chaz, who'd drained his cup already. "Tea is for sipping, not guzzling."

"Sounds exactly like what I had to tell him about good chocolate," Lexi snickered.

"Ever since he was a little kid, he's never savored anything." Aster chuckled. "I'm not even sure he chews."

"Right?" Lexi gasped, deciding maybe she didn't have to dislike Aster after all. "And where does it all go?"

"Okay, I see where this is goin'." Chaz clunked his mug back on the counter. "It's gang up on Chaz time? I will not have it."

"Oh, calm down." Lexi patted his chest and turned back to Aster. "The tea was delicious. And I can vouch because I actually tasted it."

Chaz pushed at her shoulder gently. A look passed over Aster's face as she watched Lexi and Chaz together. With a small smile, she turned back to the other pots on the stove and started taking pinches from the little glass jars again.

The high-pitched tinkle of a bell came from the parlor.

"That's her sign," Aster said. "Lady Carmichael is ready for tea."

Chapter 16

Lexi clenched her hands in front of her, twinning her fingers together and squeezing them quickly before releasing a big breath and reaching for the trays on the counter. Aster pulled down three delicate glass teapots. Gilded magnolias bloomed from the handles and bone-white butterflies lifted off the glass where the spouts began to curve. The decorations stood out in beautiful contrast to the soft pink tea Aster poured inside.

"Is there a special way to pour tea?" Lexi suddenly realized she'd never poured from a teapot. Her tea always came from a spigot or the microwave. "Am I going to offend someone by pouring from their left side or something?"

"No special pours." Aster tried to hide her smile, pressing her lips together. "Just try not to spill."

"Spills definitely don't go over with this crowd," Chaz shuddered. "Not that I'm speakin' from personal experience or anything."

"Oh my God," Aster leaned onto the counter, fighting back laughter. "I'd almost forgotten about that."

Lexi looked between them as they both started snickering, waiting to be filled in, but the ding of another bell chime cut off any hopes of that story. They seemed to know a lot about each other, and Lexi wondered if that was typical, small-town behavior, or if there was more of a past there than just friendship.

Aster set the teapots onto the trays Lexi had spread out and covered with gauzy white fabric. She quickly placed cups and saucers around them, like a mama hen surrounded by her chicks.

"Ready?" Chaz asked, leaning in toward Lexi. His warm breath tickled her ear.

"No." Lexi clasped her hands in front of her again.

Chaz wrapped his long, warm fingers around hers as his gaudy apron brushed her knees. She looked up into his eyes, and he winked before giving her hands a quick squeeze.

"Come on, City Girl," he pulled away and grabbed a tea tray, "we'll show you how we do it here in Mississippi."

Aster led the way through the swinging door, with Chaz at her heels, both balancing the tea trays easily in front of them. Lexi grabbed the final one and rushed out behind them, cups clinking on their saucers with each step. Lexi took a deep breath. This was no different from the high-end parties she'd catered in New York.

No difference at all.

Except in the city, she'd never see those people again once the event was over. Here in Fauna, if she messed up, she'd never live it down. These women could destroy her. One simple decree from the Garden Society, and she'd be toast. Burnt, blackened toast.

Lexi took another deep breath. And another. She stared at the door, still swaying from Aster and Chaz making their way through. Another breath. And another.

Lexi shook her head, like an Etch-A-Sketch, to erase any negative thoughts and pushed through to the drab hallway. Chaz's back was just disappearing into the parlor. The sound of soft laughter and quiet conversation drifted through the open door, and Lexi straightened her spine. She'd handled women like this in the past, and she would handle these today as well.

"Humph," she dropped all the doubts right there in the hall and smirked as she pushed through to the parlor.

Lexi slowed her steps on the plush rugs, using a heel-toe roll to level out her stride. The teapot and cups sat silently on her tray as she made her way over to the cluster of small tables.

"Alexandra, a word."

Lexi pivoted toward the door, where Lady Carmichael stood ramrod straight, waiting for the final guests to arrive. She'd changed into a champagne-colored chiffon gown that set off her white-grey hair perfectly. A gold magnolia locket rested at her throat.

"Again, it's just Lexi. And you look lovely," she smiled at Lady Carmichael. "That's a great color on you."

"Yes, I know." Lady Carmichael said hurriedly. "Thank you. We will only need tea for twenty today. Iris is out of town, and Myrtle is home with a twisted ankle. I'll need you to package a small box to deliver to her this afternoon."

"Of course," Lexi made a mental note, hoping she wouldn't forget the names, and turned to leave.

"One more thing, Alexandra," Lady Carmichael's voice lowered. "We do not allow men in our midst. They are nothing more than a distraction from the business at hand."

Lexi glanced at Chaz, who was being fawned over by at least six women as he poured tea. They patted his arm, looking up at him with doe eyes. Or running their fingers over the frills on his apron. A hot jolt of jealousy ran through her. She watched as long, freshly manicured nails rested on his arm, and her vision tinged red. Turns out Chaz wasn't a distraction for just her.

"I apologize, ma'am," Lexi turned back, trying to get herself under control, "my sous chef got called away on important business."

"Important business?" Lady Carmichael sputtered, hands flopping at her sides. "What could possibly be more important than this?"

"Apparently some newsworthy event in Jackson," Lexi shrugged, enjoying the look of shock on the old woman's face so much she forgot about Chaz.

"Well, I'd suggest you find another, more suitable replacement. That man, in that apron, is making a mockery of our esteemed gathering."

"Of course, ma'am. It won't happen again."

Chaz would be glad to hear he'd been permanently banned from helping her. And she'd like to say that also made her happy, but it was a shame, really. He'd turned out to be an intuitive, careful assistant. And who was she kidding? She enjoyed his company, probably more than she should. Especially at a work function.

As she made her way over, Lexi took in the array of women before her. The variety of dresses and gowns was impressive, but so were the women themselves. There were young and old, some looking no older than teenagers, while others were hunched with age. After everything she'd heard about this group, she'd expected a predominantly white crowd, but the array of skin tones rivaled that of the dresses they wore. Lexi couldn't help but be shocked and impressed.

Maybe this group isn't as bad as I'd thought.

Then the questions started.

"Where'd you grow up?"

"Why would you leave New York for Fauna?"

"What about your family? Where are they?"

Some of them seemed innocent enough, just curious. And those women, she answered gladly. Other questions were rather intrusive, and she did her best to be polite but brief. And some were just thinly veiled attempts at making sure she knew her place.

"Fill my cup for me, won't you?" Acacia asked. She was wearing an off-the-shoulder periwinkle gown with lace and beads cascading down the bodice onto the flowing skirt. "Make sure it isn't too hot, like my last cup was."

"Of course, so sorry about that."

Lexi felt the side of her pot, not sure how else to test the temperature without sticking a finger straight into Acacia's teacup. It didn't feel overly warm, so she poured it slowly into Acacia's waiting cup.

"Oh," Acacia puckered after taking a sip. "That still won't do. I sure hope you're better with pastries than you are with tea."

Lexi pinched her lips together and straightened to her full height. If they wanted to be intrusive and rude about her personal life, that was one thing. But to bring her business into it was not acceptable. She jutted out a finger, ready to say just that.

"Ladies, I assure you Lexi's pastry skills are unmatched." Chaz slid in front of her, pushing her hand down behind his back. "Once you have a chance to check out the table and taste what she's made for y'all today, I'm sure you'll agree."

"Well, that's high praise coming from you, Chaz." Acacia adjusted her skirt and blinked up at him with a smile.

"I have been known to eat a treat or two." Chaz smiled at the bunch of women and ushered Lexi to stand beside him. "So, let's show Lex a little of that Southern hospitality we're famous for."

Acacia flinched at his shortened use of Lexi's name, but all the other women simply raised their teacups to them and went back to their conversations. Lady Carmichael made her way over with the final guest at her elbow; their long gowns gliding soundlessly over the carpet. She ceremoniously picked up a small gavel on the mantel and officially called their meeting to order. With their serving duties complete, Aster, Chaz, and Lexi all hurried toward the hallway.

"So, what do you think?" Aster asked once they were in the kitchen. "Not so bad, right?"

"Well, if they'd stop prodding into my life and focus on tea, it would have been great." Lexi flopped back against the counter and ran her hands over her hair, tucking any loose curls back into the bun.

"It's because you're the only one with anything left to prod into," Aster laughed while she placed the teapots in the sink and filled them with soapy water.

"We already know everythin' about everyone here." Chaz placed any unused cups back into the cupboard. "You're the only one with any mystery."

Lexi thought about that as she opened the pastry box on the counter and gently set the remaining pastries on a tray to replenish the serving platters in the parlor. She also made small plates for the swan wrangler and for the woman who couldn't make it, darned if Lexi could remember her name though. That little exchange with Lady Carmichael felt like eons ago.

"Oh, are those the extras for Myrtle?" Aster's shoulder bumped Lexi's as she reached to open the cupboard overhead. "I'm happy to swing them by her place this afternoon."

"Thanks, that'd be wonderful." Lexi smiled, enjoying the ease the three of them worked together in the kitchen. "I need to replenish the table; it was looking a little picked over."

"Means they liked it," Chaz snatched a macaron from the box and popped it into his mouth. "Damn, and I don't blame 'em."

"It's true," Aster added. "They usually just pick at stuff. They're actually eating yours."

"Oh, well! That's wonderful." Lexi perked up at the compliment.

"Just don't expect 'em to tell you they liked it," Chaz said around his mouthful of food.

"So, they won't say they liked it, even though they obviously did?" Lexi shook her head with a chuckle and tapped him under the chin to get him to close his mouth.

"Right," Chaz nodded.

"How does that make any sense?"

"The Garden Society doesn't have to make sense."

Chaz shrugged and planted himself next to the pastry box, eyeing each one before picking up a petit four. Lexi made her way to the fridge to grab a couple of the swans for the extra plates. On the bottom shelf, Lexi spotted an open bottle of champagne.

"What have we here?" She grabbed it and turned to Aster.

"Oh, that's just left over from dinner last night," Aster shrugged and went back to rummaging through the cupboard.

"So, it's not being used for anything?" Lexi smiled when Aster shook her head. She pulled out some orange juice with her other hand. "What do you say we make ourselves a drink?"

"Oh, I couldn't," Aster bit her lip, looking between Lexi and Chaz.

"Sounds peachy to me," Chaz opened a couple of cupboards before he found a set of Champaigne flutes and set them on the counter.

"Come on. One mimosa isn't going to hurt." Lexi waggled her eyebrows. "Might make the next couple hours of clean-up a little more bearable."

She poured equal amounts of juice and champagne into the flutes and topped them off with some fresh raspberries. Lexi set one next to Chaz, one by Aster, and pulled her own up to her nose. The sweet orange, mixed with the dry champagne, was the perfect combination as the bubbles popped in the glass.

"Hm, thanks." Aster took a small sip and closed her eyes. "Maybe just one won't hurt. That is rather refreshing."

"Atta girl." Chaz held his glass up. "A toast to a job well done, ladies."

"To warm Saturday afternoons and perfect pots of tea." Aster grinned, clinking her glass against Chaz's.

Lexi beamed as she added her glass as well. They may have gotten off to a rocky start, but it was turning out to be a really great day.

"To old traditions and new friends."

Lexi and Chaz were quiet on the car ride back to the bakery. It'd been a long day and Lexi was beyond tired. She chose to work in the back of the house for a reason. Dealing with people was draining in every way imaginable. And the people she'd had to deal with today had been on another level.

She wasn't sure why Chaz was silent, but she was guessing it had something to do with the twenty women all demanding his attention before he was allowed to leave. Just watching what they put him through made her tired. And when that red-hot jealousy reared its ugly head again, Lexi excused herself to the kitchen. She gave those countertops a very thorough, white-knuckled cleaning.

Jealousy wasn't a feeling she was used to. Granted, she'd never had a shot with anyone like Chaz before. She'd dated a few guys in the past, but nothing long-term. Her work hours pretty much made it impossible to date anyone outside the hospitality industry. After one exceptionally bad breakup with a co-worker, Lexi swore off dating anyone she worked with. Which had dropped her dating pool to zero. So, she buckled down and focused on getting better and better at her job. She knew she'd made the right choice when she received promotion after promotion, but it still stung when her friends fell in love, and she went home to an empty apartment every night.

And all those years alone were probably for the best. Would she have moved here if she'd been in a serious relationship in New York? Nope. She'd have never come to Fauna. Never followed her dream. Never opened her own bakery. And never met Chaz. It was crazy to think about being in a relationship, especially a serious one, with a man she'd only known for a few weeks. Crazy and scary. But also exciting. If she weas being honest, she couldn't blame the Garden Society women for flirting with Chaz. He was handsome, confident, and easy to talk to. All the good things.

She glanced at him out of the corner of her eye, hoping she was a little stealthier this time. His head leaned back on the headrest, and his eyes were closed. The image of him, looking just as peaceful with his head on a pillow as morning light streamed through the window, popped into Lexi's mind. He'd open his beautiful eyes, long dark lashes fluttering as he blinked away sleep. That slow, lazy grin of his would spread across his face when he saw her, and her heart would melt. Then he'd lean in and...

"What you thinkin' about over there, boss?" His voice was low and slow, making his accent thicker than usual.

"Just how much of a success today was." Which wasn't a total lie. It's what started her train of thought.

"If your job brings that kind of smile to your face," he adjusted in his seat and turned his head towards her, "then you're definitely in the right profession."

Lexi could feel heat rising up her neck to her cheeks, but kept her eyes on the road. She'd been direct with him on their earlier car ride, but she was not about to divulge the little fantasy she'd just been having.

So, deflection it is.

"All the ladies today really loved you," she said with a sly smile.

"They always do." Chaz shrugged. "Most of them knew my Meemaw."

"Most? Half that group is younger than me," Lexi glanced at him and caught his grin. "Which is honestly kind of admirable. The Garden Society wasn't quite what I expected."

"As obnoxious as they are, they aren't as bad as we make them out to be." Chaz sat up straight in his seat, tapping his hands on his knees. "They do a lot of good for Fauna and they take what they do very seriously."

"Obviously."

Lexi pulled into a parking space in front of the bakery and sighed. She sagged against her seat, relaxing for a moment before she had to unload and clean all her utensils.

"You really don't have to stay. I can take care of the clean-up myself."

"Nope. I'm not leavin' you when we're almost to the end zone." Chaz opened his door and hopped out with more energy than Lexi could possibly muster. "Let's get 'er done."

Lexi dragged herself out of the car and grabbed a few of the empty cake boxes from the trunk. Her feet felt like lead weights as they climbed the front steps and unlocked the door. The few weeks she'd been off work had made her soft. This kind of work in New York wouldn't have even fazed her. But the mental and emotional work here in Fauna had been heavy too. Everything here meant more, and she found herself second-guessing all her choices. Which was exhausting in itself.

"Thanks so much for your help today, Chaz," she sighed and slumped against the counter in the kitchen. The empty boxes could wait to be broken down until tomorrow. "I don't know if I could have gotten through it without you."

"I know you could have," Chaz leaned onto the counter next to her, their hips bumping. Neither of them moved. "It was really something else seeing you in your element. Here in the kitchen and at the tea party today."

"Oh, well, thanks." Lexi reached up to run a finger through her hair.

His body was so close to hers that she could feel the heat of him all down her side. She fought the urge to lean into him for about half a second and then gave in. She slid her shoulder over until it met his. Chaz didn't move for a moment, but then lifted his arm and wrapped it around her shoulder. Lexi melted into him. They stood looking out over the kitchen for what could have been a few seconds or a few years; Lexi had no idea.

But then Chaz shifted, taking his warmth with him. Lexi looked up into his face as he turned to her. This close, she could see the flecks of dark brown in the outer rims of his eyes. His arm slid off her shoulders, fingers tracing a line across her back.

"Lex," his voice was thick as honey.

"Chaz."

Lexi's heart thudded in her chest as the late afternoon sunshine filtered through the kitchen windows. Chaz's hand slid down her arm and rested on her hip. His other hand twined itself into the curls at the nape of her neck. There was no rush in his movements. His touch was so soft, so gentle.

Her eyes drifted over his face, from his liquid gold eyes to his sharp jawline, now dusted with dark stubble, and landed on his lips. She snapped her gaze back to his and wondered what it would be like to actually kiss those lips. To actually give in to the feelings they'd been avoiding for weeks. He must have been wondering the same thing as his eyes moved slowly to her lips too.

His fingers on her hip tightened slightly, and he tilted his head, a small smile tugging at the corner of his mouth. Her eyes fluttered closed as they both leaned in, inching closer. Chaz's fingers in her hair rubbed small circles at the base of her neck, sending happy little sensations down her spine. Chaz stopped, his lips just out of reach. Her eyes slid open, fixing on his gaze.

"Lex?" he asked, his breath warming her skin, and his intention warming her heart.

"Yes."

That was all the permission he needed. His eyes closed and his fingers curled into her skin. Lexi's breath stopped.

Finally.

"Lexi! Oh my God, you're not gonna believe this."

Lotus burst into the kitchen, arms open wide, panting with excitement. Lexi and Chaz froze, millimeters apart.

"Oh my God, *I* don't believe *this*," Lotus scurried out of the kitchen with a squeal.

Chaz and Lexi both released the breaths they'd been holding with deep sighs.

"We have got to start locking that door," Chaz growled.

"Her timing is perfect, as always," Lexi nibbled her lip, still admiring Chaz's face so close to hers.

Chaz turned back to Lexi, his gaze instantly softening. With a smile, he gently pressed his lips to the tip of her nose. Lexi closed her eyes, savoring the tenderness of the moment. It wasn't the kiss she'd hoped for, but it would have to do for now. The moment had passed. Their bubble had burst. Chaz took a step back, untangling his fingers from her hair.

"S'pose you better go see what's got her all riled up," Chaz scuffed his boot on the floor and tilted his head towards the backdoor. "My truck's out back, so I'll see ya tomorrow, Lexi Girl."

"Okay. Night," she gave him a feeble wave as he walked out the back door. Then, she turned towards the dining room and narrowed her eyes. "Girl," she called out, "you have got to work on your knocking."

"I know. I know," Lotus raised her hands in surrender when Lexi joined her in the dining room. "I'm so sorry. I thought you'd be alone, but you obviously weren't alone. Why didn't you lock the door if you were going to be canoodling in here?"

"The canoodling wasn't planned. It just happened." Lexi threw her hands up. "Who says 'canoodling' anyway?"

"What would you prefer? Necking? Making out?"

"Ew. Gross, no." Lexi's lip curled in distaste. "We were doing none of those things." She crossed her arms, pouting. "Thanks to you."

"You're really going for it, huh?" Lotus asked.

"Well, in that moment I had decided to."

"And now that you're out of the moment?"

"I'd still do it."

"Oh, dang. That looks like it was quite the realization for you. Need a milkshake to wash that down with? Cause I'm starved."

"Yeah." Lexi pushed her friend towards the door. "I need to hear all about your news article."

"And I need to hear about the tea party."

The two headed towards the Darlin' Diner, arm in arm, as evening set over the town square. She tried not to think about it, but Lexi's heart was still beating erratically. Maybe she could have it all. The bakery and the boy. Maybe it could all work out.

Just maybe...

Chapter 17

Over the last week, Lexi and Chaz had worked themselves to the point of exhaustion on the upstairs renovation projects. Chaz set a grueling schedule and wouldn't call it quits until every last thing was ticked off his list, which Lexi had to admire since she was a list checker, too. They were both so worn out at the end of each day; they slunk back to the B&B and crawled into bed. Their own beds, sadly.

Lexi was still thinking about that almost-kiss after the Garden Society's tea party and asking the universe why it couldn't have given them just a few more minutes to themselves. With deliveries of reclaimed wood, plumbing fixtures, drywall, and electrical wiring, they hadn't had more than a few minutes of peace. They could have had plenty of time, but Lexi was learning that the ways of Southern life included a lot of talking. About the family. About the farm. About the job. And everyone wanted Chaz's time as much as she did. He was always the perfect gentleman, giving them his undivided attention. In New York, you'd be lucky to get two glances before someone dismissed you entirely.

And that's probably why everything moves like molasses down here.

At the rate they were going, the entire renovation would be done before they got any time to themselves again. And then, Chaz would move on to another job, and she'd be busy with opening the bakery.

Lexi let out a deep sigh as she held a sheet of drywall in place. She despised drywall. The dust was unbearable. She'd given up on cute hairstyles and dresses and showed up every morning in a simple t-shirt and ponytail. This look had basically been her uniform back in the city, minus the chef's coat, so it was nothing new. But she'd hope to put a little more effort into her appearance here. Especially since all the women she ran into on the square always looked impeccable. Perfect makeup, crisp outfits, and sparkly accessories.

How? In this heat? How do they not melt?

And if Chaz was used to that level of effort, how would he feel about her lack of care? Did that matter to him? Or would he appreciate her simpler nature? Was she overthinking things? Probably. That was her way.

Lexi sighed again, falling deeper into her spiral of dark thoughts.

"You makin' it over there, Lexi Girl?" Chaz's head peeked around the framed wall they were working on encasing in drywall. "Those sighs sound like you're either love struck or contemplatin' somethin' darn heavy. I'm hopin' it's the former, but if it's the latter...lay it on me."

"Hm?" Lexi snapped out of her whirlwind of anxiety. "Oh, well..."

She wasn't quite sure what to say. Should she really complain that he wasn't trying to ravish her every chance they got, at the cost of both their businesses? He was being a perfect gentleman and not rushing her into anything she wasn't ready for, so why was she so annoyed?

"So deep, you're speechless, huh?" Chaz got up off the floor and dusted his hands on his knees. "I've been there."

"Haven't we all," she muttered as she pulled away from the freshly attached drywall. "Looking good. The wall, I mean."

Chaz chuckled as he dropped a few tools into the box on the floor. They'd just completed the wall separating her bedroom from the living area. The space was really coming together. The bathroom just needed tile, paint, and fixtures. The bedroom only needed paint on the walls. Lexi turned in a circle to take in the space around them. Most of the cabinets they'd moved up from downstairs still sat in the dining area, but they didn't need to worry about that project just yet. The bedroom and bathroom were the bare necessities she needed to move in. And as much as she loved staying at the B&B with Mrs. Miller and her fabulous cooking, it was starting to take a toll on her bank account. The sooner she was able to move in, the better.

"Did I ever tell you about the time my baby brother lost his tooth over there?"

"Uh, no?"

"Winston was wrestlin' with my Pa and his tooth got stuck in Pa's belly button and it flew right out." Chaz's eyes got a faraway look. "Took us all an hour to find that tiny little bugger. Wedged itself right under the baseboard. Took a pair of pliers to get it out. The Tooth Fairy left us all a little somethin' that night as a thank-you for helpin' find it."

"I'm sorry, his belly button?"

"God's truth." Chaz nodded and smiled.

"And that memory just assaulted you out of the blue?" Lexi started laughing.

"We were talkin' about somethin' deep," Chaz said as if that explained it. When Lexi looked at him even more confused, he continued with a triumphant grin. "No one, and I mean no one, had a deeper belly button than my Pa."

"Oh, Lord," Lexi doubled over laughing with her hands on her knees. "I don't think I ever even saw my Grandpa's belly button."

"Belly button knowledge is a marker of a close family," Chaz nodded.

"Which I don't have," Lexi's laughter stopped pretty quickly, and she straightened up.

"That's a real shame, Lexi Girl. Cause you deserve nothin' but the best, far as I'm concerned."

"Aw. Thanks, Chazy Boy."

They looked at each other, curled their lips, and shook their heads.

"Nope. That does not work." Lexi cringed at the attempted nickname. "I've gotta come up with something."

"It'll come. Don't force it. Then it gets weird." Chaz wiggled his fingers in her face and turned back to the wall they'd just built. "I'll get this taped and mudded this afternoon. Then I'll need to sand it and get a couple coats of primer up there. This bare drywall is thirsty."

"Uh huh." Lexi half-listened as she reached for her phone.

The text notification was a sound she hadn't heard very often. She got a new number when she moved, and only a select few had it, one of whom was in the room with her. When she saw a New York area code, her stomach dropped.

> Mia: Hey Sis. Long time no chat. Stewart said you left a couple months ago. It just slip your mind to let your dear family know?

Lexi wasn't surprised to hear from her sister. She wasn't sure how, but her family always found her. She was honestly shocked it took them this long. Must have been missing their bi-weekly 'loans' on her paydays.

Lexi closed her eyes and took a few breaths, then fought the urge to chuck her phone across the room and instead stomped in a circle. When she opened her eyes, Chaz was staring at her with his mouth still open.

"I'm sorry? Does primer offend you?" he asked.

"Of course not." She thrust her phone at him. Once he took it, she stomped over to the kitchen area and stared at the ceiling as she fumed.

"So, this is your actual sister?"

Lexi nodded.

"And you didn't tell your family you were movin' here?"

Lexi shook her head.

"And who is Stewart?"

Lexi startled at the hard hint of jealousy in Chaz's voice.

"He was my boss." She snatched her phone and stuffed it back into her pocket.

"Okayyy..." Chaz stood next to her, shoulder to shoulder, but didn't reach out to her. "You're gonna have to fill me in here, Lexi Girl. You haven't said a whole lot about your family."

"For a reason." Lexi snapped and instantly regretted it. Chaz wasn't the enemy here. He just wanted to understand. "You know, my childhood wasn't great." When he nodded, she continued. "My family... they still just drift around. They can never hold down jobs. The only reason they even talk to me is to ask me for money."

"Ouch."

"Yeah. And I didn't tell them about the money Grandma left me because I knew they'd suck me dry before I had a chance to say, 'Thanks Gram Gram.' Which would mean no moving to Fauna, no bakery, no dream come true."

"They'd do that to you? Take away your dream like that?"

"Without a second thought." Lexi sighed. "They already think I'm some hoity-toity for working a 'fancy' job. It doesn't matter that I worked seventy hours a week and put myself through culinary school. Oh, no. It just meant they had a steady source of income."

The shame and anger that settled on her were familiar companions, but these past few weeks in Fauna had been so peaceful that she'd almost forgotten the weight of carrying them. It had been just long enough since she'd heard from her family that she thought maybe she'd finally slipped through their greedy grasps.

Lexi hung her head, but before her chin hit her chest, she found herself wrapped in a warm embrace. Chaz held onto her like she was going to fall apart if he let go. She wound the back of his shirt in her fists, matching his fierce tenderness.

"I'm gonna tell you somethin', and I'll tell it to you as many times as you need to hear it." His voice was muffled as he spoke into her hair. "The label of 'family' only goes so far. If they don't fill that void for you, find the people who do. You are not them. They do not deserve you. Find the family you deserve. Cause from where I'm standin' you deserve a whole hell of a lot better, Lexi Girl. You hear me?"

"Says the man with the perfect family." Lexi knew she shouldn't be snarky when he was being so sweet, but her anger seeped into her words anyway.

"The Walker family has never been perfect." Chaz didn't move, didn't pull away at her words. "Even more so since Meemaw died."

"I'm sorry, Chaz. That was uncalled for."

"No, it wasn't. I know I talk about them a lot." Chaz sighed, shifting slightly, but not loosening his hold on her. "I think it's because I miss how we used to be."

"Well, I'm glad you have all the memories." Lexi turned her head to rest her cheek on his chest. "I enjoy hearing them."

"No, you don't." Chaz chuckled, the sound rumbling in his chest. "Don't lie."

"No lie. It annoyed me at the beginning because I thought you were just rubbing it in that you had this amazing childhood when I didn't. But now I can see the joy they bring you. And I get to know you a little better with each memory. So I will cherish them with you."

"Here I am tryin' to make you feel better, and instead you're pickin' up my pieces."

"That's what we do for each other, right?" Lexi didn't say, 'That's what friends do,' but she also couldn't label them as anything more than that, so they were simply 'we.'

"We sure do." Chaz gave her a final squeeze before stepping away. He brushed her hair back from the sides of her face and stared into her eyes. "Now, what are we going to do about that text? How would you normally handle it?"

"I'd apologize and make excuses so they won't get mad at me." Lexi cringed at how weak that made her sound, but Chaz just nodded and began pacing the small kitchen area.

"That doesn't really matter now that you're here, though, right?" Chaz continued pacing. "If you're here and they're there, why does it matter if they're mad at you?"

"I guess it doesn't." Lexi nodded along with him, feeling his confidence slowly seep into her.

"Do you even need to explain yourself to them?" Chaz stopped and looked at her.

"You know, I don't think I do," Lexi pulled out her phone again and looked at the message one more time before clicking 'block number' and deleting it. Better get rid of it while she was feeling confident so she couldn't go back to it in a moment of weakness.

Lexi beamed at Chaz as she put her phone away. She'd either made the biggest step toward independence from her manipulative family or the biggest mistake ever.

"I cannot believe the Garden Society tea party pushed my article off the front page." Lotus tossed the day's newspaper onto the counter in front of Lexi. "They have one of those every month. How is it that special?"

"Welll..." Lexi groaned, "that may be partially my fault."

"I'm sorry, what?" Lotus's hands went to her hips as she stared at Lexi. Hard.

"I may have told Lady Carmichael that my sous chef had to cancel on me last minute for something more newsworthy. She didn't take that very well."

"And Bill just caved when she came to him about it." Lotus lost her rigid stance and patted Lexi on the back. "It's not your fault, girl. It's my lovely editor's lack of a spine to blame here."

"I'm sorry, Lo. That really sucks." Lexi leaned her head onto her friend's arm and looked up at her with a sad smile. "If it makes you feel any better, Lady Carmichael floundered like a fish out of water when I told her you had something more important to do."

"That actually does make me feel better." Lotus's smile grew into a maniacal grin. "I can just picture it."

Lexi laughed and turned back to the stack of papers on the countertop before her. She'd taken several more orders over the last week, but they were all for several weeks out. She was just thankful a few orders were starting to trickle in. After the lackluster response she got when she handed out flyers, a small seed of doubt had planted itself in her stomach.

"So, what are you working on today?" Lotus pulled up the stool next to her and flipped through papers absentmindedly.

"Finding some kind of filing system to keep my orders and their details organized." Lexi rubbed her temples with her index fingers. The computer she ordered was supposed to be coming in a few days, but for the time being, she was trying to find a system for her paperwork.

"Why are you wasting FaFoFe day on paperwork?"

"I'm sorry, what now?" Lexi shook her head and put down the paper she'd been reading. "FeFerneFel day?"

"How have you been in this town for the last couple of months and not figured out FaFoFe day?" Lotus picked up a pen and started doodling a picture of a tree on Lexi's notebook. "It's literally on a banner across Main Street and has been for a week."

"Oh, I guess I missed it." Lexi shrugged. "I've been here before sunup and until dark every day. Guess I just didn't see."

"Girrrlll... you are killin' me," Lotus groaned.

"I'm sorry! I'm exhausted." Lexi turned to her friend. "So, are you going to tell me what Feffernuggen is or just leave me hangin?"

"Feffer what now?" Lotus shook her head. "No. Fa. Fo. Fe. Fauna Founders Festival."

"Ahhh. So, like the day the town was founded, kind of thing?"

"Yes, ma'am."

"That's cool."

"You bet your cookie makin' butt it's cool." Lotus slammed her hand onto the paper Lexi had turned back to.

"Hey!"

"Lexi." Lotus grabbed her arms and forced her to turn on her stool. They sat face to face. "FaFoFe is the biggest festival this town has outside of Christmas."

"Okayyy..." Lexi shrugged again. "And how does that affect me?"

"In every possible way!"

"You're going to have to elaborate."

"Why do you think you don't have any orders for this week or next?"

"Uhh...people were nice and ordered stuff in advance?"

"Ha. No." Lotus shook her head at the preposterous idea. "That will not happen in this town. People will come in the day before to order a wedding cake. That's how things work here."

"Well, that's awful." Lexi was starting to dread what her schedule would look like in the future if that were the case. It would be impossible to plan if people all waited until the last minute.

"It's because everyone is at home doing their own baking for the festival, duh."

"I'm still confused."

"It's like the biggest contest in the history of contests. Blue ribbon type seriousness. First place in pie, cake, or jelly will give the winner bragging rights for a full year."

"Well, why the hell didn't anyone tell me there was a baking contest?" Lexi jumped off her stool, ready to start rolling pie crust.

"You're not eligible; that's why."

"And why the heck not?"

"You're not a home baker, now are you?" Lotus crossed her arms over her chest. "Wouldn't really be fair to the rest of us if professional chefs were allowed to enter. We'd have people coming from all over to get their greedy little hands on our blue ribbons."

"I highly doubt that," Lexi muttered as she slid back onto her stool.

"Anyway, the kickoff is tonight. So, what are you going to wear?"

"What? Nothing."

"You can't come neck-ed, Lexi. It's not that kind of festival." Lotus snickered behind her hand.

"No, no. I wouldn't go naked. I mean, I'm not going."

Lexi turned back to her paperwork, focusing on the dates of orders to see if Lotus was onto something. Would this be a yearly occurrence that her shop would be dead for two weeks? If so, she could use that time to do a yearly deep clean.

While the idea of going to a festival sounded fun, Lexi had checked the schedule Chaz left pinned to the wall upstairs. Today was painting day, and she highly doubted she'd feel up for festival activities after a long day of slapping paint on walls. Lexi finally noticed the silence coming from the seat next to her and swiveled her head to find Lotus blinking at her with her mouth hanging open.

"What?"

"No. No. No. No. No." Lotus stood up and started pacing the kitchen. "That most definitely will not do. You don't skip the FaFoFe. No one does. Not even Myrtle with her twisted ankle. She's getting carted around in a special trailer behind Jeb Thompson's four-wheeler. So, no, Lexi. You will not be skipping it. Do you want the life Fauna has to offer you? Then you show up at the FaFoFe."

"Ok. Ok. Ok." Lexi laughed at the intensity of Lotus's speech. "I'll think about it."

The front door opened and slammed shut, followed by the clomp of boots across the dining room floor. The kitchen door swung open, and Chaz walked in just as Lotus decided to lay into Lexi.

"Did you not just hear my impassioned plea? You don't get to 'think about it.' That's not what we do in Fauna, Mississippi."

Lexi glanced at Chaz, who looked amused by the situation he'd walked into. Rather than make any kind of greeting, he leaned back against the counter to take in the drama unfolding before him.

"I'm sorry, did you just say the people of Fauna don't think about things?" Lexi couldn't help but laugh.

"That is not what I said, and you darn well know it, Lexi Caehill." Lotus huffed and stalked over to Lexi. "You will go to that festival. And you will like it. Back me up here, Chaz."

"I might actually be able to help ya on this one, Lotus." Chaz pushed off the counter and crossed the kitchen to stand in front of Lexi as well. "Mayor Bennett just sent me over to cordially invite you to be the tasting judge for the pie contest tonight."

Lotus gasped and spun to Chaz.

"No, he did not."

"I assure you, he did." Chaz nodded solemnly. "Apparently Chef Higgins from Jackson came down with a head cold and can't accurately taste sweets at the moment."

"A head cold?" Lotus snorted. "In August?"

Chaz just shrugged, and they both turned back to Lexi.

"So, what'll it be, Lexi Girl? Want to eat a bunch of pie and make a few enemies tonight?"

"Sounds like the perfect evening." Lexi gushed, clasping her hands under her chin and batting her eyelashes.

"You have no idea how big of an honor this is. Oh! You can even pick her up, since you'll both be at the B&B." Lotus smacked Chaz on the shoulder.

"Ouch." Chaz rubbed the spot. "Sure."

"Perfect." Lotus smiled at Lexi. "See you tonight."

"Yep. I'll pick you up at 5." Chaz turned back towards the door. "Lots to do. See you then."

"Yep." Lotus turned towards the door with him. They both began muttering as they walked out together. "Can you believe she wasn't going to come?"

"Wait, so we're not painting today?" Lexi called after them, looked around the now empty kitchen, and got no response. "What the hell just happened?"

One minute she was happily organizing her paperwork, the next she was roped into taste-testing who knew how many pies and probably making half, if not more, of the women in Fauna hate her.

"Hold up." Lexi slid off her stool, still talking to the empty room. "Did Chaz just get forced to ask me on a date? And did

I just get forced to accept?" Lexi started laughing. "Lotus, you sly fox."

Off to the FeeFurFush she would go, arm in arm with her beau.

Maybe? Maybe that's what just happened?

Whatever it was, it sounded a lot better than painting walls.

Chapter 18

W hat was she supposed to wear to a FeffelFrost Festival?
Lexi had no idea, so she went with something comfortable for the August heat. She wore one of her favorite vintage-inspired dresses in a nice shade of royal blue with white
polka dots. It had cute, capped sleeves, was tight through the
bust, and flared over her hips. Paired with cute white sandals,
and a large floppy hat for sun protection, she was ready for
whatever the evening had in store.

That wasn't true. Not even remotely.

She had no idea what to expect. Small-town festivals were
not something she had any experience with. And going with
Chaz? Finally, having time together? Oh, boy. The butterflies
were swirling in her stomach at the thought. She'd been so
anxious for some one-on-one time with him, but now that
it was here, she was just a bundle of nerves. Spontaneity is
what got her through romantic situations, not planned dates.
Planning ahead gave her brain too much time to stew on all
the possibilities, which usually left her a neurotic mess by
the time the guy showed up. Her first date success rate was
abysmal.

Calm. Down. It's just Chaz.

Just Chaz, her mind tells her. Just Chaz? There was no such thing as *just* Chaz. He was not a man to be minimized or brushed off in any way. He was thoughtful and caring. Driven. Hot as asphalt on a Mississippi summer day. And, for whatever reason, he seemed to be interested in her.

Lexi checked her curls one last time in the mirror and hurried downstairs. Chaz was waiting in the foyer with Mrs. Miller. At her approach, they both turned to stare. A smile split Mrs. Miller's face, but Lexi was focused on Chaz, who stared at her with an intensity she wasn't quite comfortable with. Licking her lips, she resisted the urge to fidget or tug at her dress.

"Lexi Girl, you sure are a sight," Chaz shook his head slowly. "Like a blueberry pie with a dollop of whipped cream." He reached out and tapped the brim of her large, white hat. "Which just so happens to be my favorite."

"Really?" Lexi sighed in relief. Food was always something she could talk about. "I'll keep that in mind."

"You two go have fun now," Mrs. Miller shooed them out the door. "And I don't want any favoritism towards my pie. I want to win, fair and square."

"What? You're in the contest?"

"Of course, I am." Mrs. Miller sounded shocked at the possibility of *not* entering.

"This is a blind taste test, right?" Lexi looked between the two of them in panic. "I mean, I'm not going to know whose pie is whose while I'm tasting it, am I?"

"Now, that's just silly," Mrs. Miller swatted at her. "This contest is as much about us getting to carry our pies up and present them to the judges as it is about the taste."

"You've got to be joking," Lexi deadpanned.

"Now, why would that be a joke?" Mrs. Miller crossed her arms, looking sterner than Lexi had ever seen her.

"How is the judging supposed to be impartial? How is it supposed to be about just the pie when it sounds like it's more pomp and circumstance?" Lexi's palms began to sweat. "People are going to think I'm just voting for people I like."

"That's usually why we have Chef Higgins come over from Jackson." Chaz placed his hand on her lower back. "We'd better get movin' if we're gonna make it in time. You better get a move on, too, Mrs. Miller. Wouldn't want to miss the entry deadline. You know how strict they are."

"I was one minute late. One!" Mrs. Miller spun on her heel and stalked back into the house.

Lexi stared after her, stunned. She'd gone from sweet, homey grandma to head-bashing old lady, and Lexi wasn't sure what to make of it. Apparently, the FlitFen Festival brought out the worst in some people.

"Shall we?" Chaz waved his arm, pointing down the front walk to where his truck sat waiting at the curb.

"Sure," Lexi hesitated and looked back towards the B&B when several loud bangs came from inside. "Should we?"

"Nope." Chaz turned her back toward the truck with gentle hands on her shoulders and ushered her down the walk. "Don't get involved on FaFoFe day unless you must. Getting sucked into the drama is a surefire way to ruin your night."

"But... but... you already drug me into the drama!" Lexi sputtered. "You told me to be the judge."

"That's a different drama." Chaz waved off her concern and opened the truck door for her. "That's power. I'm talking about the ladies who are all stressin' and snappin' at their husbands and kids as they load up their pies, or cakes, or jams."

"Sounds like you're speaking from personal experience," Lexi glanced at him as she slid past into the passenger seat.

"I never, and I mean *never*, saw my Mama as stressed out as she was on FaFoFe day." Chaz shuddered as he shut the door. "And that's sayin' somethin' when she had all us kids to deal with."

Lexi smiled and looked around as he eased the door shut. It smelled faintly of cleaner, which made sense because the dash was gleaming. The floor was missing its usual mixture of dirt and sawdust. The backseat was void of the customary toolboxes.

"Chaz Walker," Lexi exclaimed when he opened his door, "did you clean your truck?"

"Can't take a beautiful woman to a festival covered in work dust, now can I?"

"I suppose not." Lexi smiled and settled into her seat, resisting the urge to brush off the compliment.

The ride to the festival was quick. They drove down the highway, past the post office, and turned at the sign for the fairgrounds. There were more cars on the road than Lexi had ever seen in Fauna. If she squinted, she could make out license plates from all the surrounding counties.

"Dang. FlapForg Festival really is a big deal," she whistled.

"Flap what now?" Chaz shook his head. "Lexi Girl, if you're gonna be a judge, you at least have to say the name right?"

"Not sure I can. Too many vowels with not enough consonants."

"It's an acronym." Chaz sounded exasperated.

"No, it's not," Lexi shook her head and glanced away from the crowd outside the window to look at Chaz. "Acronyms are first letters only. So, it'd be FFF. Triple F. Now, that I can remember."

"You can *not* go in there calling this Triple F."

"Watch me. Next year, I'm making shirts. Tasty pies at Triple F."

"No." Chaz slid into a parking spot and popped the shifter into park.

"Triple F. Triple the fun."

Chaz rolled his eyes and got out of the truck. Lexi was still chuckling when he got to her door and offered her his hand. As soon as her fingers touched his, all silly thoughts left her mind. She slowly slid out of the truck, fully expecting Chaz to drop her hand once her feet hit the ground. But he didn't. Instead, he tucked her hand into the crook of his elbow and started strolling toward the collection of buildings and tents at the end of the parking lot.

"Um, if you just want to drop me off at the judging tent, I don't mind." Lexi cleared her throat as they strolled past several older couples who all perked up at the sight of them arm in arm. "That way you can go spend time with your family and friends."

"Nah, I'm good." Chaz looked down at her and slid his free hand over hers.

The late afternoon sunlight hit his hair, bringing out a hint of red Lexi didn't often see, but rather enjoyed. It matched the red tinge to his face scruff.

And let's be honest. Who doesn't love a little face scruff?

They made it to the main row of typical fair games, and the noise was intense. Bells were ringing. Music was playing. Game lights flashed as they passed.

"Are you sure?" Lexi practically yelled. "I really don't mind."

"It's fine..." Chaz hollered back, but the noise made it hard to hear. "My folks...the airport...picking up my..."

Lexi watched his mouth move, trying to fill in the blanks that were covered up by the loud banging sounds coming from the game they passed. She was able to get the gist that his parents were picking someone up from the airport. Lexi shrugged. The thought of meeting his parents already was a little intimidating, so not meeting them tonight didn't bother her in the slightest.

"Okay," she hollered with a smile.

They strolled through all the rides. Chaz waved to practically everyone, but otherwise, his attention was dedicated to her. He pointed out all his favorites from when he was younger, like the tilt-o-whirl that made Lexi feel like losing her cookies just watching it. They grabbed frozen lemonades to sip as they meandered up one row and down another. Lexi was shocked at the size of the fair. It was far bigger than she'd imagined.

"Ooff, what is that smell?" Lexi waved her lemonade-holding hand under her nose.

"That's the smell of money, honey," Chaz chuckled and walked her to the entrance of a massive warehouse building. "The ladies might be concerned with the baking, but the kids are all in here with their livestock."

"Did you say kids?" Lexi stopped at the doorway, pulling Chaz's arm before he walked inside.

"Course." Chaz stopped next to her. "Ever heard of FFA or 4-H? These kids are raisin' these animals from when they're tiny things."

"The kids or the animals?"

"Both." Chaz smiled at her and nodded towards the entrance. "Care to stroll through?"

"I'd rather not have that, um, odor affect my sense of smell before judging." Lexi cringed as she looked at the hay-strewn floor and then at her cute, strappy sandals. "Smell is directly linked to taste, you know. I'd rather not have any lingering scent while I'm trying to judge the pies."

"Nothin' like a little cow pie with your pecan pie," Chaz turned them towards a large tent set off in the back corner. "Those squirts really are talented. You should see 'em barrel race. They give the grown-ups a run for their money. Nothin' like being young with no inhibitions."

"Man, isn't that the truth." Lexi held up her lemonade glass, which was mostly empty now. "To being young and free."

"Or old and wise," Chaz clinked his plastic cup to hers. "And here we are, my lady."

Lexi looked around. They entered a large, open-sided tent filled with chairs. At the front sat several large tables. Women dressed in their Sunday best milled around, holding all sorts of food containers. Chaz walked her through the crowd, smiling and exchanging pleasantries as they went. Lexi kept staring at that front table, hoping and praying that she wasn't making a mistake. Pissing off the women in the town she was trying to build a life in was not the best foot forward.

"Here you are, Lexi Girl." Chaz stopped in front of the table and picked up a pin reading "Judge" in big black letters. "May I?"

Lexi gave him a small nod and looked around the tent. Everyone was staring at them as Chaz placed the pin just beneath her collarbone. She could hear the soft hiss of their whispers. Chaz's hands brushed against the soft fabric of her dress, bringing her attention back to him. They looked into each other's eyes as he straightened the pin on her chest.

As nervous as she was before coming, being with Chaz always felt just right. Like his favorite blueberry pie with a dollop of whipped cream. They just made each other better.

"So, who's in charge here?" Lexi squared her shoulders and looked at Chaz.

"Oh, Lord, Lex," Chaz sighed and scrubbed his hand over his face. "I know that voice. What exactly are you plannin' here?"

"Something that should have been done long ago." Lexi glanced around them at the growing crowd. "So, who is it?"

"Mayor Bennett," Chaz dropped his hand and gestured at the old man Lexi recognized from the city council meeting.

"Thank you." Lexi patted him on the chest and walked directly toward the mayor. "Mayor Bennett, may I have a word, please?"

"Oh, Lexi, dear, thank you so much for agreein' to help us out in such a pinch." He smiled up at her as he adjusted his grip on the cane he had resting against his knees. He looked like he'd stepped out of another time, with his linen suit and straw boater hat.

"Don't thank me just yet, Mayor," Lexi smiled at him. "Is there somewhere we can talk?"

"Oh, of course."

The old man pushed himself up from his seat and walked slowly over the uneven ground toward the back of the tent where curtains had been constructed around a metal frame. Lexi guessed they would be used as some kind of backdrop later on, but right now they made the perfect separator between them and the crowd she knew was straining to hear every word she uttered.

"Now, what can I do for you?" Mayor Bennett pulled a striped handkerchief from his front pocket and dabbed his forehead.

"It recently came to my attention that this is not a blind tasting." Lexi clasped her hands in front of her.

"Oh, yes, they do love to parade up their pies, you see." He smiled and chuckled.

"Well, that's not going to work for me."

"I'm sorry?" His laughter stopped abruptly, and he pushed his glasses higher on his nose to look at her through narrowed eyes.

"I'm in a bit of a precarious position, Mayor Bennett," she squeezed her hands together to keep from gesturing with every word, a nervous habit.

"Elaborate, please. And it's just Davis when we aren't conducting formal city business."

"Thank you, Davis. I appreciate that." Lexi unclenched her hands and relaxed slightly. "As you know, I'm in the process of opening my bakery here. I can imagine some of the entrants in this pie contest won't be too happy with me if they don't win, and that could be detrimental to my business."

"Hm. I s'pose I can see that." He shuffled, adjusting his cane again.

"I don't want anyone to claim that my judgement is based on anything other than the pies themselves."

"So, what are you suggestin', dear?"

"A true blind taste test. If we can get our hands on some notecards, we number them, set them out along the tables, and the contestants place their pies on top of a number. They hold on to the notecard as proof of which pie is theirs. I can taste in front of them, so they can see my reactions. But I will not know whose pie is whose."

"Hmmm..." He tapped his cane on the ground while Lexi waited. "You're takin' a risk here. This contest has been judged this way since we started FaFoFe. You may anger them more by changin' things than by just going with the flow."

"That's a risk I'm willing to take, Davis." Lexi took a deep breath. "At least this way I can be one hundred percent certain that judging is based on the pie and pie alone."

"Well, if that's what you want, we can give it a try." Mayor Bennett shrugged. "If it's a total flop, we'll just bring Chef Higgins back from Jackson next year."

"Wonderful." Lexi patted the old man's shoulder as they turned back to the judging area. "I appreciate it."

"I'll send my assistant to find some notecards, and we'll get started. And I'll leave the announcement about the changes to you, hmm?"

Lexi watched as he hobbled back to his table and whispered to a middle-aged man in a badly wrinkled suit. She made her way over to Chaz, who leaned against the judging table with his arms crossed over his chest.

Why is he always so darn chill?

Lexi wished she could embody that level of ease and confidence, but doubted she'd ever achieve such an unattainable level of existence.

"Causing chaos already, Lexi Girl?"

"Oh, ya know," she shrugged, "it just seems to follow me."

"It doesn't follow you. It *is* you."

"Yeah, yeah." She waved him off and leaned next to him.

They watched the milling masses as more and more people made their way into the tent. Seating was getting scarce, and Lexi's palms began to sweat. When the mayor's assistant finally returned, Lexi made her way over to get the notecards. Her eyes widened when they told her there were thirty-seven entrants. Good thing pie was her favorite food, because she'd be eating a lot.

She numbered the notecards and set them out in order on the tables. By the time she was done, the tent was buzzing with agitated whispers; a hive ready to swarm.

"I'll give you a brief introduction, then let you take it from there," Mayor Bennett whispered to her, tapped his hat, and then turned to face the crowd. "Welcome. Welcome, ladies and gentlemen, to one of the most anticipated events at FaFoFe. As many of you have heard, Chef Higgins wasn't able to make it this year due to an unexpected illness. Please send him some prayers for fast healing. In his place, we are lucky enough to have our own local pastry chef, Lexi Caehill—"

"Thank you, Mayor Bennett. I'm so happy to be here and able to lend my palate to what I'm sure will be a very delicious event."

She smiled at the crowd. The city council meeting she'd gone to had left her feeling like a bundle of nerves, but she'd been discussing remodel plans and construction permits. Today was about food. Her element. She didn't like speaking in front of crowds, but if she had to, at least it was about the one thing she was confident about. Her nerves stayed at a low simmer as she continued.

After a deep breath, Lexi explained the changes she'd made to the judging style. Then she told them why the changes were necessary.

"I hope you'll see why this method will help find the most delectable pie. Because I'm sure that's why we're all here, right? Pie judging isn't a popularity contest; it's a baking contest. So, I'll excuse myself and allow you all to place your pies on the tables. Take your numbers. And when everything is in place, I'll come and start the tasting."

Lexi hurried back behind the separator amid a mad dash to the tables. The commotion on the other side of the thin fabric was surprising. It sounded more like running with the bulls instead of people dressed in their finery carrying delicate pies. Why she'd expected them to slowly and calmly bring their pies to the front, especially after she saw Mrs. Miller's behavior, she didn't know. She just wished she could see the chaos. All those people rushing and shoving each other to get prime table positions would be a sight to see.

Finally, Chaz came behind the curtain and told her everything was ready. She walked over to the tables and began inspecting each pie. She picked up a notecard and started scoring them on appearance alone, listing them in order from best to worst. The audience, to their credit, sat silently in their seats.

"I'm ready for tasting." Lexi murmured.

To her surprise, Chaz stepped forward and took the knife next to the first pie and sliced through the crust. Lexi gave him a quizzical glance before turning all her attention to the crackle of the crust as it was cut. He expertly slid a single piece onto the waiting paper plate. Lexi grabbed a plastic fork, lifting the bottom up to inspect the crust.

"This pie has a beautifully cooked top crust," she explained to the audience what she was looking for. "The bottom is pretty well done but could have used another minute or two to really bake it through."

She took a bite of the caramel apple pie, letting the sweet and spicy flavors wash over her tongue.

"Excellent flavor. Apples are perfectly cooked. Homemade caramel is a nice touch. I would add a smidge less cinnamon to allow that caramel to shine through."

After taking a swig of water, she moved on to the next pie. Chaz used a new knife to slice into it and served a piece on a fresh paper plate, like he'd done this a thousand times. She walked the crowd through the same steps and hoped that her information was helpful. Some people always took feedback as criticism, no matter how kindly or well-intentioned it was. But if she was judging, she wanted them to know what they were being judged on. It also helped them know what to improve, and who wouldn't want better pie?

Lexi ate her way through apple pies, strawberry pies, pecan pies, blueberry pies, buttermilk pies, pumpkin and sweet potato pies, and one grasshopper pie that was so loaded down with crème de menthe she was surprised it even set up. All the while, as she walked down the tables with Chaz serving her pies, she took notes on her cards. Keeping track of who the frontrunners were. Finally, she made it to the thirty-seventh pie, and she was so glad she hadn't eaten dinner before judging. Thirty-seven individual bites of pie had to equal at least several slices altogether.

"Overall, I'm blown away with the quality of pies you've all made." Lexi dabbed at the corner of her mouth and took another drink of water. "You should all be really proud because these pies are as good, if not better than the pies that were served in the high-end restaurants I worked at in New York City."

A large round of applause rippled through the tent.

"I've picked out my top five pies and I'd like to have them brought to the center of the table for final tasting and judging." Lexi glanced at Chaz, who nodded and got his hands ready. "Numbers five, fifteen, seventeen, twenty-six, and thirty-one."

A loud 'woop' came from the crowd, but Lexi didn't look up as Chaz brought the front runners to the center of the table. She didn't want to see who was celebrating. It would throw off her unbiased opinion.

Chaz sliced one more piece from each pie and placed them on individual plates. The audience was completely silent as she examined each pie again, starting from the top with appearance, then moving into structure, then taste. She closed her eyes as she took a bite of each pie, letting the flavors melt in her mouth. She had a lemon cream pie with the perfect tartness and a crumbly graham cracker crust. A strawberry-rhubarb pie that balanced the sour and sweet perfectly. A pecan that rivaled the one she'd tasted with Tia Silvia her first day back in Fauna. A pumpkin full of warm spices and a splash of molasses. And an apple crumble pie with a perfectly baked bottom crust and filling that held up beautifully but still had texture.

How am I going to choose?

She glanced at Chaz out of the corner of her eye. He really seemed to know what he was doing with cutting and serving all these pies, which would lead her to believe he'd know what he was doing tasting them.

Well, if I've already pissed off most of Fauna, what's a little more fuel to that fire?

"I'd like to allow my co-judge to get his opinion of the finalists."

Lexi gestured to Chaz at the five pies sitting in front of them. His eyes grew big, and he turned his back to the crowd.

"I'm just here for slicin' and servin', not tastin'." He whispered.

"You got me into this mess," she said through her teeth as she smiled at the audience, "you can help get me out."

Chapter 19

Lexi held out a fork for Chaz, waving it in front of his cringing face. He turned back to the crowd, plastered on a fake smile, and gave a small wave. Had she ever seen him so flustered? She wasn't sure if she was enjoying it, or if seeing him so nervous meant she should be more nervous.

"Start with the pecan," Lexi said in a soft voice. She slid him a notecard and her pen. "Write down your thoughts. Then we'll discuss."

"Yes, boss," Chaz scooped up half the slice in one bite and shoved it in his mouth.

Lexi expected him to swallow without pausing to chew or savor, as he'd done with everything she'd ever seen him eat. But to her surprise, he closed his eyes. She could see his tongue rolling around in his mouth as his cheeks bulged, soaking in all the flavors.

"Mmm. Yep," Chaz opened his eyes and nodded. Then he scribbled a few notes on the notecard and took a swig of water. "Next."

Lexi slid the lemon in front of him, then the apple. She followed that with the strawberry rhubarb, alternating the sweet and the tart. Finally, he took a bite of the pumpkin, sighing as the custard hit his tongue.

Watching him eat and savor the flavors was a magical experience. He was a man who embodied his emotions fully, his whole body reacting in joy. The wiggle of his shoulders. A small stomp of the foot. Clenching the fork as he pressed his hands into the table's surface. Each bite of pie brought out a new response, and Lexi didn't want it to end. She wanted to learn all of his body's signals of joy.

But I want those reactions to my food.

As she watched him take the final bite, the pumpkin disappearing into his mouth with that small sigh of satisfaction; she wanted nothing more than to slide him a bite of something she'd baked. Something she'd poured her love into. Just for him.

I'm baking this man a blueberry pie.

Making food and eating could be such a sensual experience, one that too many people looked over or ignored. Lexi never did. In that split second, as Chaz swallowed the pumpkin pie, Lexi was stabbed with such intense longing that her breath caught in her chest. It was a moment of realization that literally left her breathless. Food was her love language, and she wanted desperately to share that. She wanted those moments and memories. Here, in Fauna. With friends.

With Chaz.

The world slowed to a crawl around her as she realized what this meant. The dream was always to start a bakery, wasn't it? Images flitted through her mind of all the times she'd thought about Fauna.

All the times she fantasized about living in Fauna, having her shop here, it hadn't just been about the business. It had been about finding a family. Creating a home.

The business was just the icing on the cake.

Everything snapped back into focus as Chaz turned to her with his notecard in hand. He gently spun her around so they could huddle with their backs to the audience.

"You okay there, Lexi Girl?"

"Um, yeah," Lexi shook her head. "Just really enjoyed watching you eat the pies."

"Oookkk..."

"No, not like that. Ok, I mean, maybe a little like that, but mostly not like that."

"As much as I want to continue this conversation, we do need to decide on a winner."

"Right, you're totally right."

"We will finish this conversation later, though."

"No, we won't."

"Oh, yes. We will," Chaz's low chuckle filled the small space between them. "So, pies?"

"Yes, pies." Lexi pulled her notecards up in front of her face to hide her flushed cheeks. "Your thoughts?"

"Strawberry Rhubarb, first. Apple, second. Pumpkin, third." His finger trailed down his notecard as he listed his favorites.

Lexi blinked in surprise.

"That's exactly what I was thinking."

"Great minds." Chaz tapped the pen to his temple with a massive smile. "Shall we?"

They turned back to the audience. The only sound was the creaking of chairs as people leaned forward in anticipation. Lexi cleared her throat.

"In a unanimous decision, we have our winners." She swallowed hard, not sure she was ready for the reactions they were about to get. How rowdy would these folks get? Was chaos going to erupt? Cringing slightly, she continued. "In fourth and fifth place we have our lemon cream and pecan. Numbers five and fifteen."

Two elderly ladies stood and walked forward to take their ribbons. Cameras flashed as Lexi and Chaz posed with their pies for photos. The taller of the two, the baker of the lemon pie, looked about as tart as the filling. Fourth place was obviously not what she'd hoped for, but she didn't say a word.

"In third place, we have our pumpkin pie. Number thirty-one."

Lexi held the pie up, scanning the crowd for the baker. It took a moment, but eventually, a man stood in the back row and edged his way out to the aisle. In a nervous action Lexi recognized he wrung his hands in front of him and slowly walked forward.

"Mr. Labota," Chaz exclaimed. "I had no idea you were a baker. Let alone such a skilled one."

"Oh, well, thank you, Chaz." Mr. Labota continued to wring his hands and look thoroughly uncomfortable. "I picked it up after my dear Sunny passed away. It makes me feel closer to her. That woman could certainly bake a pie."

"She certainly could." Chaz reached across the table to the small, trembling man. They clasped hands warmly and shook them longer than necessary. "You've done her proud."

Lexi was touched at the quiet conversation passing between them, quickly putting Mr. Labota at ease in front of the crowd. She gave him a big smile and handed him the third place ribbon.

"Your crust was flaky and cooked to perfection. Well done..."

"Greg. You can call me Greg." He reached out to take the ribbon.

"Greg, did I detect a hint of molasses?" Lexi whispered, not sure he wanted his secret ingredient shared with the audience.

"Maybe." he gave her a small smile.

"Let's give Mr. Labota a round of applause," Chaz said to the crowd, who clapped as pictures snapped.

"In second place, we have our delicious apple. Number twenty-six." Lexi looked out over the crowd again.

A woman Lexi recognized from the Garden Society meeting pumped her fist in the air as she stood and hurried to the front. She quickly grabbed her ribbon, turned, posed perfectly for pictures, and returned to her seat.

"Ok. I suppose you all know that means the strawberry-rhubarb is our first-place winner. Number seventeen. Come on up."

A girl, looking about seventeen years old, stood and walked toward the front. Lexi was shocked that someone so young could produce such a well-baked pie. But then again, she started baking at a young age, too. Baked goods always seemed to delight her parents and were, to this day, the only thing about Lexi that got a positive reaction. She wasn't sure what drove this young lady to bake, but she hoped it was a happier reason than her own.

"Hi. I'm Dandy. It's such a pleasure to meet you," the girl gushed as she walked towards Lexi. "As soon as I heard a real-life pastry chef had moved to Fauna, I just knew I needed to introduce myself."

"Well, this is quite the first impression." Lexi smiled. "It's nice to meet you, Dandy. I'm Lexi."

"Oh, I know who you are." The girl brushed her long blonde hair over her shoulder, eyes beaming up at Lexi. "I read the articles about you in the New York Post and Times. I mean. You're like, legit."

"Oh, wow. Well, thank you." Lexi's hand pressed to her chest in surprise.

"Do you think I could sit down with you sometime to discuss career options in the pastry field?"

Lexi blinked at the girl in front of her. Here she'd thought she was just judging a pie contest, not influencing the future generation of pastry chefs in America.

"Of course, I'd be happy to. Let's get you your ribbon and let these other folks go, then we can discuss it more."

"Oh, thank you." Dandy looked across the table at her with the biggest smile, then turned dramatically to the crowd, ribbon in hand, to pose for photos. After several poses, she finally seemed finished.

"Dandy, you make a right fine pie," Chaz told her.

"Thank you so much, Mr. Walker. That means a lot since you've probably eaten more baked goods than anyone else in Fauna. Well, except for Lexi, I'm sure."

"That is probably true," Chaz chuckled.

Lexi couldn't believe Chaz's insatiable sweet tooth was that well known throughout town. The man did know how to cut a pie, which was a bit of a lost art and took some skill. Wherever those skills came from, Lexi was thankful for them today.

"And thank you for instituting a fairer method of judging." Dandy turned back to Lexi. "I loved... loved... hearing your thoughts on all the pies. So informative. And I know Mr. Labota and I wouldn't have stood a chance with that other chef from Jackson. I mean, I almost didn't enter. But then, when I heard you were judging, I knew I had to throw something together. Fresh from my own garden, mind you."

"Impressive, Dandy." Lexi chuckled at the girl's enthusiasm. "Why don't you drop by the bakery some afternoon, and we can discuss your future plans?"

"Excellent. I'll be by on Monday if that's okay."

"Sounds perfect."

"I think someone has a superfan," Chaz whispered in her ear as Dandy walked away, waving her ribbon above her head and squealing.

"Apparently so. She seems sweet."

"Speakin' of sweet... that was a lot of pie. How are you doin'?" Chaz placed a hand on her lower back, leaning in to study her face.

"Honestly, I could use a big, greasy cheeseburger to counteract all that sugar."

"Done."

He slid her arm through his, and they slipped out the back of the tent, heading toward the midway. They stopped at a food cart advertising 'fried everything.' They didn't sample any of the fried options, but the burger was exactly what Lexi needed. She inhaled it, relishing the snap of the lettuce and the juicy tomato as the burger dripped juices onto the table.

"Oh man. This is glorious." Lexi said around the final bite she stuffed into her overfull mouth.

"I'll let Jim know you said so." Chaz chuckled, leaning back and watching her. "Seeings how it's already dark, I think the livestock will have to wait for another night. You up for round two tomorrow?"

"Oh, sure," Lexi wiped at her chin, hoping she didn't have grease or ketchup on her face. "That sounds great."

Holy cow pie. Did he just ask me on a second date?

While she didn't go out much in New York, the dating pools there were sometimes on the sketchy side, and that was putting it nicely. Walking through animal poo wouldn't even go down as the worst date she'd been on.

Lexi yawned and stretched. The dreaded sugar crash was threatening to hit at any moment.

"Let's get you home, Lexi Girl. Tomorrow's a new day," Chaz offered her his arm again. "One I'm sure will be full of old ladies askin' why their pies weren't good enough for ya."

"Ughhh…"

Lexi could still smell the livestock aroma in her hair as she washed it in the shower. She'd had a great time with Chaz the night before visiting the fair for the second time, learning all about the 4-H programs they had in Fauna, and seeing the students show their animals like pros.

Quite a few ladies had cornered her while they walked through the fairgrounds, but only a few complained about not winning the pie contest. The vast majority told her they appreciated the blind judging style, which surprised both her and Chaz, and that they thought her critiques were informative and helpful. One lady told her that she was "braver than the last piece of chocolate at a Weight Watchers meeting" for coming in and making such big changes, and Lexi decided that was her new favorite saying.

After she dried her curls, she threw on a t-shirt and leggings. Today was going to be painting day at the bakery. And Dandy, the first-place pie baker, had said she'd be stopping by in the afternoon to discuss a career in pastry. Both of those tasks left

Lexi feeling excitement bubbling in the pit of her stomach, like the light fizz of a good champagne.

That fizz quickly turned sour as she glanced down at her phone. Three missed calls from a New York number. She listened to the first few seconds of one of the voicemail messages, just long enough to hear her mother's clipped tone, and quickly hung up. Those three messages sat on her screen, slowly dragging her happy mood down like an anchor in turbulent waters.

She thought back to how she'd handled the text from her sister. But she hadn't really handled it on her own. Chaz had been there to help her.

What would Chaz do?

Probably one of two things.

One, delete them and move on with his day like nothing was amiss.

Or two, call her back and politely, but firmly, tell her mother to lose her number and not call again.

And I can't do either of those. Physically. Can. Not.

Lexi sighed and slid her phone into her purse, the messages still sitting there. Waiting. Lexi plodded down the stairs, feet thudding hollowly against the wood.

"Good morning, dear," Mrs. Miller was just placing out the platters for the breakfast buffet.

"Morning," Lexi grabbed a plate and took a whiff, instantly feeling lighter. "Mmm... nothing better than the smell of butter in the morning."

She snatched up a massive biscuit, still warm from the oven, and held it under her nose, all traces of her mother left behind as the warmth soaked into her fingers.

"Everything ok? You look a little... pinched." Mrs. Miller glanced at her as she buzzed around the dining room.

"Pinched? If by that you mean nervous, anxious, filled with dread. Then yes, I suppose so."

"It's a little early to be filled with dread, don't you think?"

"Tell that to my mother," Lexi broke open the biscuit, steam wafting up, and sat it on a plate to smother with sausage gravy.

"I mean, who calls someone this early in the morning? Let alone three times?"

"Ah," Mrs. Miller stopped at her side, offering a comforting smile. "I'd never presume to know what goes on in someone else's family, but by the sound of that, you don't want to talk to your mother?"

"The only reason she'd ever call is to see why I haven't dropped off the money they 'borrow' from each of my paychecks."

"Oh, my."

"Yeah. My folks are real pieces of work."

"I'm so sorry, dear." Mrs. Miller reached over and added another scoop of gravy as if the warm sauce could fill the void her family left in her heart. And the way she cooked, it probably could. "Is there anything I can do?"

"You already have. You're like the mother I never had."

"Oh, dear. You're going to make me cry." Mrs. Miller dabbed at her eyes with the corner of her apron. "And it's far too early for dread or tears. So, go eat some breakfast. Everything seems better with some food in your belly."

Lexi sat at the small table by the front window, looking out over the covered porch and front lawn, just as Chaz hurried up the front steps.

"Hey there, Lexi Girl," he sauntered over with a warm smile. He had on a sleeveless shirt, showing off his toned shoulders and arms.

"Bustin' out the big guns today, huh?" Lexi swallowed heavily.

"Paintin' day. It's always a hot one," Chaz quickly flexed his biceps and winked. "No use getting all tangled up in sleeves. Who needs 'em?"

"Not you. That's for sure." She took a sip of her coffee and leaned back to admire the man in front of her, briefly wondering when she'd become comfortable oogling him so openly.

Where is your shame, girl?

"Well, thank you for my mornin' confidence boost. I thought I'd drop off your bill for my services before I head over to pick up the paint. Unless you wanted to come?"

"Nah. I've got a mountain of biscuits and gravy to eat. And that is significantly more important to me than ensuring you pick out the paint color we've discussed every single day for the last couple of weeks."

"Mrs. Miller's biscuits'll have that effect on ya." Chaz nodded solemnly. "And if I pick the wrong color?"

"It will be totally worth it." Lexi stared lovingly at the bite on her fork before popping it into her mouth.

"I'll leave you to it then."

Chaz slid a thick envelope onto her table and sauntered out the front door, his shoulders pulled back a little straighter than when he'd walked in.

I did that.

She chuckled and opened the envelope Chaz had left on the table. He'd been working on the house for over a month, and this was the first bill she'd received, so she was expecting a fairly hefty total. Part of her hoped maybe he'd take a little off. Just a little. Maybe. As a sign to her. Since they were on such friendly terms. If the tables were reversed, she'd never dream of charging him for a cake. That's just not what friends did. And extra-friendly friends? Definitely not.

When her eyes settled on the total at the bottom, the biscuit in her mouth turned dry as ash.

"Holy... what the?" she sputtered.

Dread coiled back in her stomach, this time emboldened by the offerings of delicious biscuits. There was no pleasant fizzing feeling now.

"That man's going to break me." She shoved away from the table and snatched up her plate in her free hand, the biscuits having lost all their appeal. She muttered to herself on the way to the kitchen. "Not break me. More like broke me. Cause I'm gonna be broke sooner than later at this rate."

"Done already?" Mrs. Miller hummed at the stove.

"Yep. I've got a bone to pick with the most expensive contractor on the planet."

"Come on now. It can't be that bad," Mrs. Miller's brows creased as she peeked at the papers in Lexi's hand. "Oh. My. Well... that is a large sum."

"Right? Astronomical. Like, look at this line," Lexi pointed to the itemized list. "$9,700 for reclaimed wood? Doesn't reclaimed mean used? Why am I paying so much for already used wood? Is he building me a whole new house that I didn't know about?"

"I'm sure some of that can be returned." Mrs. Miller didn't look as confident as she sounded.

"Well, I'm going to go find out." Lexi scraped over half of her biscuit into the trash. "Sorry for wasting. I just lost my appetite. And over half of what's left in my savings."

At the bakery, she paced from the front door to the back of the kitchen and back again. She ran numbers over and over in her head. If this was just the first bill, there's no way she could afford to finish both the bakery and the upstairs. But she couldn't afford not to finish the upstairs. Living at the B&B was a large expense, even after Mrs. Miller gave her the full-timer discount.

When she finally heard Chaz's truck pull up outside, she rushed out the door and down the steps. She was breathing heavily when she reached the driver's door, more from the anger charging through her than the small sprint out of the house.

"Lex, I can practically see the flames explodin' from your eyeballs." Chaz rushed out of the truck and clasped both of her arms, concern etched across his face. "What's happened now?"

"You... You...—" She stepped back, waving the thick bill between them.

"Me?" Chaz looked at the papers she was holding and re-laxed. "You read the bill?"

"Yes!"

"And that's what this is about?"

"What do you think?"

"I think, in the South, we talk privately about things like money, not out in the middle of the town square." Chaz turned to grab a large bucket of paint from the back end. "So, let's head inside and figure this out."

Lexi narrowed her eyes at his back.

"In the South, we talk about money privately," she muttered, curling her lip as she slowly followed him back inside. "In the South, we don't do this. In the South...yadda yadda. Well, where I come from, friends don't blindside each other."

Lexi squared her shoulders, much like Chaz had done earlier. But instead of confidence, hers came from anger. She wasn't going to let him delay her dreams. As she stepped into the house, Lexi was ready for battle.

Chapter 20

"I don't really care what you do in the South," Lexi stormed into the dining room that would soon become her tasting room. "What I care about is getting my business up and running so I can start making a living here."

"Well, maybe instead of relying on your grandma's money," Chaz stopped on his way to the kitchen to set down the bucket of paint, and slowly pivoted on his heel towards her, "you should start earning some of your own."

"Excuse me? I am trying." Lexi clenched the paper bill in her hands, crumpling it as they fisted. "Not that I need to explain my business plans to you, but I assumed I'd get more orders after the Garden Party. But then there was the pie festival, and now, for whatever reason, the orders just haven't picked up yet." She paused, pinching the bridge of her nose. "It would help if I had a completed bakery people could walk into. And that's not going to happen if you keep giving me these ridiculous bills."

"Ridiculous? There's nothing ridiculous on there." Chaz leaned against the wall, always the image of cool, calm, collected. "I even left a few things off as a friendly gesture."

"What? Like a box of screws? Gee, thanks, Chaz."

"Nope, the screws are on there," he moved toward her and pointed to the itemized list at the top of the first page. "It's mostly my labor that I've left off."

"Oh. Well," Lexi felt her heart flutter in her chest as her anger started to cool, "I appreciate that."

"Didn't feel quite right calling it work when I was having so much fun."

So, I did get the friendly friend's discount.

The rest of her anger thawed like ice cream on a hot summer's day, leaving behind a sticky, uncomfortable feeling.

Here she went, overreacting again. What was he going to think of her? Flying off the handle at every offense, imagined or real.

"You make it really hard to be mad at you." She brushed her palms against her sides, trying to get rid of that sticky feeling of shame and guilt.

"I know."

"But seriously, we need to talk. I can't afford bills like this."

"They won't all be like that. Scout's honor." He held up three fingers in salute. "But let's go sit and we'll talk through each item."

"We're gonna have to." Lexi pushed past him towards the kitchen door. She wasn't quite ready to meet his eyes yet. "I have to know what to expect for budgeting."

"Course you do. You've got a business to run, same as me."

Chaz followed her to the stools at the kitchen counter. He slid onto the one next to her, his knee brushing hers. The contact was a reassurance she needed more than she wanted to admit.

"How do you stay so cool all the time?"

"I don't. Remember the first day we met?" Chaz raked his hand through his hair. "Definitely not cool."

"Ha. That's right." Lexi laughed. "That feels like so long ago."

"Could've been a whole other lifetime." Chaz smiled, then sobered quickly. "I guess I only let myself get riled up about things that really matter to me. Like *really* matter."

"Like your Meemaw's house." Lexi nodded, thumbing the corner of the papers in her hand.

"And for you, your dream bakery."

"Huh. Yeah. I guess what really matters to both of us is all intertwined now."

"Sure is. And that just means we're gonna butt heads about it sometimes."

"And we're not going to hold that against each other?" she asked hopefully. More so because of her behavior that morning than for any future offenses she was sure to commit.

"Course not." Chaz turned to face her, his knees resting on either side of her stool. "That's not how we do things in the South."

"Oh, please." She rolled her eyes. "I think the South is known as much for holding grudges as it is for its famous hospitality."

"You may have me there." Chaz chuckled, a low rumble that rolled through Lexi like hot tea with honey. "I'm gonna be straight with ya, Lex. I'm not going to cut corners or use cheap materials. This house... and you... deserve better than that. I will not compromise my work to save a few bucks, but let's see what we can do about this bill."

"I'm okay with that. To an extent." She tossed the bill onto the counter between them and smoothed it as best she could. "But ten grand on used wood? Come on now."

"Excuse me. That is to make the fireplace mantel that you yourself designed and signed off on."

Who knew I had such expensive taste?

"Well, I don't know how much something like that costs." Lexi threw her hands up halfheartedly. She couldn't really blame him for doing exactly what she'd asked him to do. "Next time tell me it's a ten-grand idea, and I'll dial it back."

They spent the next hour going over each item listed on the bill, whether there were more cost-effective alternatives, and whether those alternatives were up to Chaz's standards or not. They huddled closely over the counter, talking animatedly about the plans until Chaz's stomach rumbled.

"Kinda wishin' I hadn't skipped out on Mrs. Miller's biscuits and gravy this mornin'," he said as he leaned back and rubbed his belly.

"How about I run to the diner and grab some lunch, and you can get everything set up to bust out some painting this afternoon?" Lexi rolled her head from side to side, working out the kinks.

"Sounds perfect." He rubbed her shoulder quickly and stood to stretch as well. "Thanks, Lexi Girl."

"No problem. It's the least I can do, seeing as how you're basically working for free."

"I can add my labor back on if that'll make you feel better."

"Nope. That would definitely not." Lexi threw her purse over her shoulder. "We just got the bill down a tiny bit, so I'm going to leave before it goes back up."

Lexi hurried out the door and turned towards the diner. It was nearing the end of August, and she thought it would cool down a little with fall approaching. But the heat wasn't letting up one bit. She worked up a sweat in the short walk and was thankful for the blast of cool air as the door opened.

The diner was packed. Men in suits sat next to men in jeans and work boots. Ladies fanned themselves with menus as they chatted. Conversations drifted around her, some heavy with the drawl of rural Mississippi, some with just a slight trace of drawn-out vowels and missing final consonants. A few of the ranchers and farmers she'd spoken to at the city council meeting nodded at her as she walked towards the counter.

"Hola, Cariña. We've been missing you." Tia Silvia stood behind the counter, pouring coffee into several mugs. "It's been too long."

"I know. I've been so busy with the remodel." Lexi cringed. Silvia was the first person to really accept her in Fauna. She needed to make an effort to visit more often.

"And how is that coming?"

"Good, except..." Lexi stopped, remembering what Chaz said about discussing money.

"Except?"

"I was told it isn't polite to talk about money in public," Lexi leaned forward and whispered loudly over the noise behind them.

"Ahh," Tia Silvia nodded. "Come to my office, Cariña."

"Oh, it's okay. I don't want to take you away during the lunch rush. I can come back to chat later."

"No," Tia Silvia slung her apron over the hook next to the swinging door. "This is Mississippi, remember? Things move slower here. Come on."

Lexi cringed at making everyone else wait, but followed her back through the door and into a small office next to the kitchen. After decades of frying, the smell of grease permeated everything. The clang of pots and the hollering of kitchen staff felt like home to Lexi.

"So, you are having money trouble?" Tia Silvia sat heavily in the chair behind the desk.

"Not really. Not yet, anyway." Lexi slid into the only other chair in the room, clasping her hands in her lap. "Chaz is just a little pricier than I anticipated."

"That man won't compromise his work for anything." Tia Silvia smiled and shook her head. She propped her foot up on her knee and rubbed her calf. "Even the woman who has stolen his heart."

"Oh, I don't know about that." Lexi's cheeks burned.

"You may be the only one who doesn't, then, Cariña." Tia Silvia's booming laughter filled the small room. "I have a proposition for you."

"Oh." Lexi perked up at the abrupt change of tone. "Ok."

"My sweet Rosita is leaving for college soon."

"Oh, Silvia," Lexi reached across the desk and placed a hand on her arm. "That's exciting, but how are you doing?"

"Oh, I'll be okay." She waved off the concern. "But with her gone, I could use a little more help around here."

"And you mean me?" Lexi couldn't believe what she was hearing.

"If you're interested. I know you're busy."

"I mean, I do miss the bustle of working in a restaurant." Lexi thought wistfully of the time she had spent working in New York. The excitement. The energy.

"I think our 'bustle' may be a little less than you're used to." Tia Silvia shrugged. "But you could come over in the evening when you're done working at the bakery. It would just be for a short time until you're up and running. That would give me time to train someone new."

"Silvia," Lexi shook her head in disbelief, "this is such a generous offer."

"Not so much generous, but mutually beneficial."

Lexi smiled. The idea of working in the diner that she had dreamt about so often since childhood was like a dream come true.

"You've got yourself a deal," Lexi stood and held out her hand across the desk.

Tia Silvia stood, took her hands, and pulled them around to the end of the desk.

"Family doesn't shake on it. Hugs work much better."

Ten minutes later, Lexi left the diner with two lunch specials: meatloaf and mashed potatoes. Chaz's comment about earning some money of her own floated back into her mind.

"Won't he be surprised when I come back with lunch and a new job?"

Lexi had spent the last week shadowing Tia Silvia at the diner, and tonight was her first night working solo. She'd never worked as a server. Her happy place was the back of the house, in the kitchen. Where the only interaction she had to have was with other staff and not having to deal with pesky customers. Actually, having to wait on people was going to test her patience.

Which we all know I have very little of.

She tucked a rogue curl behind her ear and smoothed down her apron for the hundredth time. The downstairs bathroom at the bakery had become her staging area for cleaning up after long days working on painting, drywall, or whatever other torture Chaz cooked up for the day.

Since they talked about the bill, Lexi could feel a slight change in their relationship. It felt more formal and less care-free. Less flirty. More mechanical. Was she just looking for something wrong?

Chaz hadn't said anything. And they had agreed not to hold grudges where the bakery stuff was concerned. But saying and doing were two different things, and Lexi was afraid she'd crossed some invisible line. Had she insulted his work? Forced him to compromise on something just to save a buck? She didn't think so, but what did she know? Her knowledge of men and romance was pretty limited. Her father's example set the bar pretty low. Like, floor level. The few guys she'd dated in New York were nothing like Chaz, so she felt like she was stumbling through the dark, trying to say and do the right things, but more than likely flubbing it all up.

Lexi sighed and turned away from the mirror, forcing herself to focus on less frustrating and more imminent topics. Tia Silvia had given her a uniform that consisted of a 50s-inspired dress in a white and red checkered pattern and a white apron. She'd paired it with a black sweater and her own pair of saddle shoes. Her hair was twisted back into a vintage chignon at the nape of her neck, which was one of the simpler styles to pull back her mass of dark curls after an already long day of work at the bakery.

"Chaz," she called up the stairs, "I'm heading to the diner."

"My. My. My," Chaz tisked behind her. "Aren't you a sight?"

He stood in the kitchen doorway, wiping his hands on a towel. His warm eyes drifted over her hair and dress. His eyebrows quirked when they landed on her shoes. Lexi gave him a little curtsey, with a heel kick for flourish.

"If we weren't havin' a family dinner tonight, I'd head over to the diner right now to be your first customer," Chaz looked down at his work boots, "but my Mama would come, find me, and drag me out by the scruff of my neck if I even thought of missin' tonight."

"Family dinner sounds nice." Lexi hoped the tinge of longing in her voice wasn't too obvious.

"Well, I'll ask my Mama about bringin' you along to the next one. The whole family'd love to meet you."

"Really?" She didn't even try to hide her surprise.

"Course, Lex," Chaz laughed. "You're the talk of the town."

"Oh, well, that makes sense."

"And you bought Meemaw's house. That pretty much makes you family, anyway."

"Alright, bro." Lexi punched him softly on the shoulder. "Sounds good, bro."

"On second thought..." Chaz curled his lip in distaste and shook his head, "we'll call you family adjacent."

"Every girl's dream," Lexi clasped her hands together under her chin and batted her eyes at him, then dissolved into giggles. "Seriously, though, it's fine. I think my evenings will be pretty full for the time being. Speaking of which, I gotta run. Enjoy your dinner."

"Knock 'em dead, Lexi Girl," Chaz called to her as she hurried out the front door.

An invitation *to family dinner? Dang.*

She wasn't sure what to make of that. Was it because Chaz was more serious about her than she thought? Like, saw them as an actual couple? Sure, they spent every day together. But that was work. Outside the bakery, they didn't see much of each other. Granted, the only time they weren't at the bakery was when they were sleeping.

In our own separate beds. Away from each other.

But maybe it was like he said, and his family wanted to meet her because she was the new, exciting addition to Fauna. As far as she knew, she hadn't met any of Chaz's family aside from Rhys. And with a whole herd of them running around Fauna, that was fairly surprising. She forgot how many brothers Chaz said he had. Five? Six? It was hard for her to even imagine a family that large. And his poor mother, being the only woman in a house of Walker men?

Lexi shuddered.

Could she even handle a Walker family dinner? Did she even want to? That big of a family sounded like... a lot.

The cold blast of the diner's A/C blew all those thoughts away as Lexi turned her mind to work. She hustled to the back and stored her purse and sweater in a cubby.

"Cariña, there you are," Tia Silvia called from the back office.

"I'm not late, am I?" Lexi glanced around for a clock, but saw it was still a few minutes until four o'clock, when her shift started.

"No. No." Silvia laughed. "I've just been waiting to see your sweet face today."

"You are too sweet yourself." Lexi walked in and planted a kiss on the old woman's cheek.

They'd really gotten to know each other over the past week, and Lexi wouldn't trade that time for anything. Aching feet be damned. In all her years growing up and fantasizing about moving back to Fauna, Silvia had always been present. She played a vital role in Lexi's memories of the town and why she'd always wanted to come back.

"You seem tired." Lexi tilted her head, taking in Silvia's humped shoulders and slack face. "Everything ok? You could have called me in earlier."

"I'm fine. I'm fine." Silvia flapped her hands over the desk, batting away Lexi's concern. "We just have a large catering order for tonight. For a rather... particular... customer."

"Ah. I got ya. Fill me in and I can take it from here."

Tia Silvia gave Lexi the rundown on the order, which was much larger than Lexi had imagined. She left the office and got right to work, packaging all the food that was waiting. She'd just finished boxing the last of the lasagnas when the door chimed. Lexi looked at the monitor over the server's station. It was still early enough that the dinner crowd hadn't arrived, and one lone customer made her way to the front counter.

Lexi took a deep, calming breath and pushed out through the swinging door.

"Hello, Acacia. I just finished packing up your order. I'll get it bagged up and brought out for you."

Lexi hadn't seen Lady Carmichael's niece since the tea party, and that wasn't nearly long enough.

"Lexi. What on earth are you doing here?" Acacia grinned and tapped at her chin with a pristine purple nail.

Claw is more like it.

"As I'm sure you know, Silvia's daughter, Rosita, left for college last weekend. So, I'm helping out until she can get someone trained for the position."

"That is so terribly sweet of you. Bless your heart."

Lexi might not have been from the South, but she knew exactly what that phrase meant, and it was the opposite of what a blessing sounded like.

"I thought for a second seeing you working here meant your bakery didn't take off after all," Acacia leaned her hip against one of the spinning chairs and set her giant Chanel bag on the counter, its metal chain-link strap clinking against the surface.

"No. I'm still finishing the remodel. With Chaz." Lexi paused, savoring the purse of Acacia's lips. "It should be open soon. Within the next few months."

"Oh, thank goodness. I thought maybe Chris Anntha got more people to sign her petition."

Lexi stopped bagging napkins and pivoted towards Acacia, who just blinked at her innocently.

"A petition?" Lexi's stomach clenched. "A petition for what, exactly?"

"Oh, you haven't heard?" Acacia's voice was sickly sweet as she clutched at her necklace. "I thought for sure Chaz would mention it. Seeings you're so close and all."

"He hasn't mentioned a petition." Lexi's eyebrows pulled down together. "Or this Chris Anntha. Who is she exactly?"

"Oh. Oh." Acacia sputtered, dropping her innocent act. "If he hasn't mentioned Chris Anntha, you are definitely not as close as you'd like to think."

"My relationship with Chaz doesn't concern you," Lexi said through clenched teeth.

"Hey, don't shoot the messenger." Acacia slipped back into the slippery, sweet act.

"So, what about this petition?"

"Sweetie, I think you should ask Chaz about that." Acacia's smile sent a chill down Lexi's spine. "He'd have a lot more information than little ol' me, anyway."

Lexi rushed back to the kitchen, mind whirling like a storm. Was Chaz keeping something from her? Or was Acacia just stirring up trouble? Lexi grabbed the bags of food and plastered a smile back on her face. She could play nice for a few hours, but when her shift ended, Chaz was going to see a different side of her. And she was going to get some answers.

Chapter 21

L exi's first solo shift at the diner went by in a blur of burgers and banter. Being a server was going to force her to meet a lot of new people, which she had mixed feelings about. On one hand, she wanted to belong in Fauna, and that involved knowing everyone. But the city side of her still cringed at small talk.

Everyone she saw had questions about her life and the plans for her bakery. But whenever she said anything about looking forward to seeing them in her shop, their eyes would get shifty, and they'd make some noncommittal grunt.

After Acacia's visit, she knew this had something to do with Chris Anntha's petition.

Who the heck is Chris Anntha? And what did I ever do to them?

As far as she knew, she'd never met Chris Anntha, but maybe she was one of the ladies at the Garden Society's tea party? Had she accidentally wronged her in some Southern offense Lexi had no idea existed? Did she just hate outsiders? Lexi didn't know, but she was determined to find out. Which meant she needed to talk to a specific someone Acacia so giddily threw under the gossip train.

Chaz.

From Acacia's gleefully uninformative chat, it didn't sound like Chris Anntha or her petition were anything good for Lexi. Chaz wouldn't be involved in something that went against her and the bakery. Would he? Lexi couldn't believe he'd betray her while simultaneously taking her life savings to finish the remodel.

And taking my heart.

Lexi helped lock up at closing time, but her mind was a whirlwind of questions. Her feet ached as she slid into her car and sent Chaz a text to meet her in the kitchen at the B&B. Mrs. Miller would be asleep by now, and the kitchen, any kitchen, was Lexi's safe space. If all else failed and Chaz was indeed a double-crossing low life, she knew what drawer the head-bashing rolling pin was kept in and already had Mrs. Miller's express permission to use it as necessary.

In a blink, she was at the B&B. She parked her car around back in the gravel lot for long-term residents, which currently totaled three vehicles. Mrs. Miller's sedan was in its usual place next to Lexi's, but Chaz's truck was absent.

Lexi glanced at her phone as she quietly shut the car door and walked up the back steps. No response yet.

How long do family dinners last? Geez.

She quietly made her way through the back door and dropped her purse on the counter. After rummaging through the fridge and freezer, she pulled out a tub of fudge ripple ice cream and was scooping herself a bowl when the backdoor opened again.

Lexi licked a drop of melting ice cream off her thumb and pushed the tub down the counter toward Chaz. He stepped up next to her, smelling like wood smoke and freshly cut hay. His shoulder brushed hers as he reached for a bowl, and she closed her eyes for a moment, wishing desperately that he wasn't a backstabbing scumbag. Thinking of life in Fauna without Chaz's slow drawl and honey eyes was like banana bread without the walnuts. It would be fine, but nothing exciting and pretty bland.

Lexi's mind wanted to make a joke about life needing nuts but instead grabbed her ice cream and hurried to the other side of the large island. Thinking about nuts of any kind wasn't going to help her get the information she needed. The thought of Chaz betraying her, with another woman no less, brought her anger to a simmer just beneath her skin.

Don't jump to conclusions.

"So," Lexi's voice seemed too loud in the silent house, so she continued in a whisper, "How was the family dinner?"

"It was all right." Chaz's voice sounded clipped and hard, nothing like when he typically talked about his family.

"That doesn't sound 'all right,'" Lexi loud-whispered across the island.

Chaz sighed and rubbed his hand over his face, scraping over his stubble. With his back still to her, Lexi watched his shoulders tense, bunching beneath his thin t-shirt as he finished scooping out some ice cream.

"You're right." He finally turned to her, a tortured look on his face. "Lexi Girl, there's some stuff I gotta tell ya, and I know you're not gonna like it."

"Ok." Lexi gulped. "I had some questions for you as well."

"Ladies first."

She knew that wasn't just an attempt at stalling. Chaz was always a gentleman, even if it pained him to be one at that moment.

"Acacia came into the diner today." Lexi stuck her spoon in her mouth, not even registering the flavors on her tongue.

Chaz's head fell back as he groaned. He pulled his head back to look at her, but didn't say a word. His gaze never wavered from hers, even though she could see the battle of emotions happening inside him.

"She told me people are signing a petition. Something to do with Chris Anntha. And that I should ask you about it." Lexi paused, but Chaz still made no move to talk. "She made it sound like it had something to do with my bakery, Chaz. If you know something about this petition or Chris Anntha, you have to tell me."

"That's what I was wantin' to talk to you about, too," Chaz's voice rang with the sad tone of resignation.

"Ok."

Lexi couldn't remember being this nervous for a talk since learning about the birds and the bees from her parents. That had been an utter disaster, filled with inaccuracies and innuendos she had no hope of ever deciphering. She said a silent prayer that this conversation went better as Chaz slowly walked around the island. His jaw ticked as he slid onto the other stool and took her hands in his. This close, she could see the lines of worry creasing his forehead. He rubbed his thumb over her knuckles as her heart beat erratically in her chest.

She'd never seen him so worried.

And that makes me very, very worried.

"Now, I promise I didn't know anything about what Chris Anntha was pullin' until dinner tonight," Chaz shook his head as he spoke, "and once I found out, I did everything I could to put a stop to it."

"Um. Thanks, but I still don't know what exactly *it* is."

"Chris Anntha was havin' folks sign a petition to not shop at your bakery."

"What?" Lexi yelped. "Why?"

"Because she's done all the baking in Fauna for years."

"Ohhh."

Lexi remembered back to the pie she ate her first day back in Fauna and Tia Silvia's laughter when she said she'd hire the baker. And Lotus's comments about meeting Chris Anntha. It all made sense now.

"Why didn't anyone tell me? If this is just about competition, I can handle that." Lexi pulled her hands from Chaz's and leaned back, the tension in her shoulders evaporating. "Now, if she'd been some crazy ex-girlfriend," Lexi tilted her head and pursed her lips, "I don't know about that. I mean, I can usually handle city craziness. But I'm not sure about small-town crazy. I feel like that might be a lot more intense."

Lexi laughed until she saw Chaz's face.

"Lex, what are you talking about?"

"Um, I'd just worried that Chris Anntha might be a psycho ex of yours."

"Mother of all that's holy." Chaz whispered as his face fell into his hands and he looked out at her over his fingertips. "How do you not know who Chris Anntha is? I know I've talked about her."

"Uh, nope."

"At the fair the other night. I told you my folks were picking her up from the airport."

"Oh! That's who that was."

"What about all the times I told you about the memories in Meemaw's house?"

"You told me about your herd of brothers," Lexi's mind was trying to keep up, trying to piece together what Chaz wasn't saying. "I think I'd remember you mentioning a crazy name like Chris Anntha. What kind of name is that anyway? British? Is it a family name?"

"It's short for Chrysanthemum. My Ma's favorite flower." Chaz raised an eyebrow at her.

"Your mom's..." Lexi's smile fell away as the realization hit her.

"Chris Anntha's my sister, Lex. I swore you knew that."

"She's your..." Lexi pushed back on the stool, stumbling away from Chaz. "Let me get this straight. Your sister is the one trying to ruin my business. And you didn't think to mention that to me?"

"I told ya, I didn't know about it until dinner tonight." Chaz stood too, turning towards the other side of the island. "I should've figured she'd pull somethin' though. Typical Chris Anntha."

"Oh, yeah. Typical." Lexi laughed, slightly hysterical at this point. "So, the guy I like...am seeing?" Her eyes darted to his face, but it was too dark to see from across the room. "I'm flirting with, yeah, we'll just leave it at that for now, has a sister who, let me see if I got this straight, is having people in town sign a petition to not shop at the bakery I will be opening in her grandmother's house. Do I have that right?"

"That's the gist of it."

"And you didn't know about it until your family dinner tonight, where she was, because she's your sister."

"Lex, I swear if I'd known—"

"So, this is why you didn't want me to buy MeeMaw's house in the first place, isn't it? It wasn't some obsession with memories; it was because I'd be competition for your sister."

"Well, yeah, that was part of it. If you knew Chris Anntha, you'd understand. You do not want to be on her bad—"

"Well, I don't know Chris Anntha," Lexi snapped, still trying to keep her voice down because the thought of Mrs. Miller stumbling down into their 'discussion' in her pajamas was just too much.

"We can change that," Chaz rushed around the island and clasped her hands. "How about we set up a meetin'? Probably be good for both of you to get a few things off your chest."

"I am not going to have some little 'share session' with your sister." Lexi pulled her hands from his. "You said you discussed it tonight. I assume that means it's taken care of?"

"Well, not exactly," Chaz scratched at his neck, "the family is a bit... divided on this issue."

"Divided?" Lexi shook her head. "Of course they are. And what about you?"

"I told her what she was doin' wasn't right. I've seen you in the kitchen. I know how talented and passionate you are."

"Then why do I sense a 'but' coming?" Lexi's eyes narrowed, knowing she wasn't going to like what he said next.

"But she's my sister. And this is family." Chaz fell back onto a stool as Lexi's heart shattered.

Never good enough for my own family. Now, not for his either.

Lexi bit her lip to hold back the wave of disappointment and shame. When would she ever find someone who put her first? She'd been a fool to think Chaz would choose her over his family. After all the times he'd talked about his memories and how important they were to him. Part of her knew, but the rest of her just hoped she'd been wrong.

"We just need some time to sort this out," Chaz continued. "As a family."

"I see." Something inside Lexi snapped. Whether it broke or snapped into place, she couldn't tell. But something changed.

I won't take second place anymore. For me or for my business.

Her mind was empty and silent as she straightened her shoulders and lifted her chin. "I'm going to give you until tomorrow to clear your tools out of *my* business. I'll be finding another contractor to finish my remodel."

"What?" Chaz looked at her, bewilderment written all over his face. "You can't be serious."

"I've put you in a tough spot for long enough. I can't have someone working for me that's feeling 'divided' over the success of my bakery."

"Lex, we have a deal," Chaz's voice was dark and sharp. "No one works on that house but me."

"We had a verbal agreement, nothing more." Lexi walked towards the door, stopping to rest a hand on its cool surface before pushing through into the dark hallway. "You aren't willing to compromise your work. Neither am I, Chaz. I'm not going to compromise on my dream any longer. You have twenty-four hours."

"Lexi, come on. You have to come out of there sometime."

Lexi groaned when the pounding began again and pulled the blanket over her head. She cracked one eye and peeked at the clock. 11:20. Was that A.M? P.M? She didn't know, and she didn't care. She just wanted a day or so to wallow and give her heart a rest.

And give Chaz time to move his tools out of my house.

The thought popped into her mind, forcing her back under the covers with a deep sigh.

"That's it. I've called in reinforcements."

Lexi heard the jingle of keys and knew Lotus had finally brought Mrs. Miller to her door. Why were they making such a big deal about this? So she wanted to hide in a dark room and lick her wounds. Was that such a bad thing? It's not like she planned to stay there forever. She did have a bakery to open after all.

"We're coming in, dear." The key turned in the lock. "We're not breaking and entering or anything. Just concerned about you. Please make sure you aren't indecent."

"Or dead." Lotus quipped as the hallway light poured into her dark room and across her bed.

"It'll take a lot more than a deceitful man to take me out." Lexi rolled towards them and lowered the blanket to her shoulders. "I promise you that."

"She lives!" Lotus rushed into the room and flopped herself onto the bed, where she crinkled her nose. "She also stinks."

"Yeah, yeah." Lexi shoved her shoulder and sat up.

"We're pretty worried about you, Lexi." Mrs. Miller's forehead was creased with concern, like layers of puff pastry rolled one on top of the other. "Chaz mentioned what happened. And then, when you didn't show up at the bakery today, he was really worried."

"He doesn't get to be worried. Traitor." Lexi muttered the last word under her breath as she crossed her arms. She realized she was acting like an overdramatic teenager, but she didn't care.

"Well, what about us? And Tia Silvia?" Lotus snapped in front of Lexi's face, anger lacing her words. "We've been worried, too. I sent you like five bazillion text messages. You could have just responded to one."

"Sorry, I turned my phone off. Didn't want to hear from... *him*."

"Now, I am not defending him, so don't take this the wrong way, but what exactly did he do?"

"What didn't he do is more like it." Lexi's hands fisted in her lap, crinkling the comforter between her fingers. "He lied; he omitted the truth."

Chose his family's side over mine. Even though they are obviously wrong.

"Ok. Get to the part worth all these dramatics." Lotus motioned with her hands to keep going.

"He chose them over me. Ok?" Lexi felt a sob in her throat at the admission, but she cleared it away, not wanting to cry. "He made it very apparent that this stupid petition Chris Anntha is having people sign against *my* business is a 'family matter' that I get no say in. My business. And I get no say?"

"The Walker family is pretty close-knit, Lex," Lotus shrugged. "Not sayin' he's right, but I can see why he said it."

"Well," Lexi sputtered, "all that's after finding out he had a sister. And that sister was trying to sabotage my life's dream."

"Hold up, you didn't know Chris Anntha was his sister?" Lotus raised an eyebrow.

"He swears he mentioned her. I can remember he has six brothers, don't you think I could remember one measly sister?"

"Phew." Mrs. Miller shook her head. "We're all a little at fault for that one, I guess. We are so used to everyone knowing everyone, we just assumed you knew."

"Nope. See the issue now?"

"Well," Lotus stretched out the word like taffy. "I mean, maybe this is how you handle all your drama? I guess we don't know, but I assumed you'd just keep kickin' ass and takin' names like usual."

"This is not how I handle 'drama.' This is different." When both Lotus and Mrs. Miller continued to stare, Lexi added, "This is how I deal with a broken heart. Just give me a day to sulk, and then I'll be fine. I just need to feel these feelings and be done with them."

Lotus and Mrs. Miller exchanged a look that Lexi couldn't decipher, but then each woman grabbed one of her arms and dragged her towards her bathroom. When they finally had her in front of the shower, Mrs. Miller turned the water on steaming hot. Lotus grabbed a shower steamer out of the basket on the counter and tossed it in.

"Now, no more of this heartbreak talk." Mrs. Miller patted her shoulder. "Things with the Walkers are far from over."

Oh, yes they are.

"Yep. You can't let one little misunderstanding ruin something special." Lotus edged towards the door. "What is this, some romance novel?"

"That's what I keep asking myself." Lexi realized her mistake too late.

"See. Your story isn't finished yet." Mrs. Miller walked out. "Now, take a shower. Get some life back into those bones and join us downstairs for brunch mimosas."

"Is this what having friends is always like?" Lexi peeled off her socks and tossed them at the closing door.

"Eh, only if you're lucky."

Well, at least I'm lucky in that department, but I'm not getting my hopes up again for romance. No matter whether they think this story is over or not.

Chapter 22

I t had been one week. One week of avoiding Chaz. One week of working from the B&B. One week of avoiding the home and business she rightfully owned. One week of swinging from jaw-clenching anger to sorrow over losing something she wasn't sure she ever had to begin with.

Lexi had picked up extra shifts at the Darlin' Diner to fill her daytime hours. Something about the hustle of restaurant work always took her mind off everything else. Besides, Silvia needed the help. Last weekend, Rosita had moved into her dorm at Southern Mississippi University in Hattiesburg, and Silvia seemed off-kilter without her daughter.

"Hey," Lexi peeked into the office before she stowed her purse in her cubby. "How are you doing this morning?"

Lexi took in the slumped shoulders and dark circles under Silvia's eyes. She hated seeing her like this but knew there wasn't much she could do. Some things just took time.

"Oh, a little better today, I suppose." Silvia scrubbed her hands over her face. "The house is just so... quiet. I don't like it."

"Well, I can come over and play some of Rosi's favorite music on high, dirty up some dishes, and throw some clothes on the floor if that would make you feel better."

"Actually," Silvia huffed a half-hearted laugh, "that might help."

"I'll pop over after my shift then." Lexi smiled and turned to put her purse away.

The sun hadn't quite risen yet, leaving the sky a combination of purples and pinks, and the diner was just starting to come alive. The line cook, Chuck, was busy in the kitchen turning on all the griddles, fryers, and most importantly, the coffee machines. People would be coming in soon looking for the morning hit of caffeine, and Lexi did not want to be the person to tell them they had to wait.

"Lexi."

She turned at the sound of Silvia's voice in the doorway.

"Yeah?"

"Thank you."

"Of course." Lexi rushed over to Silvia and wrapped her in a tight hug.

"Having you here has made all this a little easier," Silvia said into her shoulder, then pulled back to look up into Lexi's face.

"I'm happy to help, you know that."

"Oh, I don't mean you helping here at the diner. Although that really is a huge help."

Silvia reached up and patted Lexi's cheek. "I just mean you. Being here. You have been such a blessing on this old woman's heart."

"I could say the same about you," Lexi pulled back, blinking furiously. "Now, don't make me cry first thing in the morning. People don't want to see this blubbery mess to start their day."

"Ok. Ok." Silvia patted her arm and turned back to her office. "But I do know there's a certain contractor who would like to see that face in the morning, blubbery or otherwise."

Lexi's breath caught.

"What?" She hurried behind Silvia into the office, closing the door behind them. "What did you hear? Did he say something? I mean, not that I care or anything. It'd just be nice to know what people are saying about me. That's all."

Her words tapered off as she slumped into a chair, knowing just how sad and needy she sounded. She'd been the one to kick him out and end their business relationship. Just business. And yet, here she was, hoping he'd still be thinking about her and talking about her.

Did she even have a right to want him to miss her? So, they'd flirted a bit. That didn't mean she'd actually meant something to him. For all she knew, he could flirt with all the new girls who came to Fauna, however few and far between those may be. Maybe he just liked the challenge or needed some novelty in his life.

But even as Lexi thought it, she knew it wasn't true.

Even though he'd left a few massive details out of their conversations, she still knew he was one of the most genuine and honest men she'd ever met.

Damn, those cowboy ethics.

"I know you miss him, Cariña. And he misses you," Silvia said softly. "So why not just fix what happened between you?"

"I don't know if this one is fixable." Lexi sighed.

"Anything is fixable if you want it to be."

"That's the thing." Lexi straightened in her chair, the anger rising in her again. "I've spent my whole life being the last choice, or no one's choice. My whole life never feeling like, hands down, someone had my back. Like I *really* meant something to them."

Lexi's breath came out in a hard rush. How many times had these thoughts circled through her mind, like a tornado hellbent on causing chaos and leaving nothing but rubble in its wake?

"I can't do that anymore. I won't." Lexi stood and looked at Silvia with sorrow etched across her face. "As much as I'd like to, I can't be with Chaz knowing that I would always play second fiddle to his family. That's not fair of me to expect it from him. And it's not fair to myself to accept less than what I know I deserve."

"I respect that, my dear." Even though she said she understood, Silvia shook her head. "But maybe you should stop
looking at it as picking sides and more like incorporating new
ingredients. Sometimes it takes a few tries to figure out how
to mix something new into the fold."

"So, what? I'm just the weird nut he's trying to add into his
already smooth and creamy ganache of a family?"

"I never called you a nut. Your words, not mine." Silvia
laughed. "And maybe they aren't a ganache. Maybe they are
brownies. And everyone knows brownies are better with a few
nuts."

"Silvia, I appreciate the thought. And I definitely appreciate
the baking metaphors." Lexi took a deep breath and turned
toward the door. The people of Fauna needed their breakfast,
and she needed to serve it to them. "But I can't be with Chaz
as long as he's so obsessed with his family."

"You see the solution there, don't you?" Silvia called out as
Lexi grabbed her apron from her cubby. "You have to become
part of his family so he'll be just as obsessed with you."

Become part of his family?

Lexi didn't even know if she knew what family really meant,
let alone how to be part of one.

No. This was for the best. She had diner shifts to work and
her bakery to open, and that was enough. Just like she wasn't
the nut for his ganache, he didn't fit into her plan either. Some
ingredients just weren't meant to go together.

The morning disappeared in a rush of pancakes, omelets, and
small talk. Since she'd started at the diner, people seemed
much more cordial with her, almost on the verge of being

friendly. Lexi wasn't sure if that was because they were seeing the real her or because they thought she'd given up on opening her bakery and took this job instead.

Lexi hummed to the song playing from the jukebox as she carried a stack of plates to a corner booth. The breakfast crowd was tapering off, and she'd get a break soon. Her stomach rumbled in anticipation. A giant stack of pancakes had her name written all over it.

"Anything else I can get you this morning, Pastor Jeff?"

"Nope. Don't think so. Thanks, Lex—"

The diner suddenly became silent. No silverware clinked on plates. No talking or laughter came from the few guests left eating their food. Pastor Jeff stared at the door, wide-eyed, then toward Lexi. He swallowed and made the sign of the cross before motioning for her to turn around.

Lexi spun slowly on her heel, fully expecting to see Chaz standing in the doorway. But what she saw instead was a woman about her own age, with a heap of curly blonde hair, tight jeans, and cowboy boots that definitely weren't just for show. The woman glanced around, passing her large purse from one hand to another until her gaze settled on Lexi. Her eyes narrowed as she slowly walked to a stool at the counter. She slid onto it and sat primly on its edge, her arms folded in front of her.

Lexi walked over slowly, taking in the woman's immaculate nails and beautifully done make-up. The contouring made her cheekbones look as sharp as the glare she was currently cutting in Lexi's direction. Her eyes were hazel, green flecked with honey. And Lexi would recognize that color anywhere.

"Chris Anntha, I presume." Lexi leaned onto the opposite side of the counter.

"Lexi." The woman nodded.

"What can I do for you?"

"Straight to the point. I like that." Chris Anntha ran her tongue over her top teeth, taking a moment to tap her nails on the scarred countertop. "You can start off by tellin' me what you did to my brother."

"What I did?" Lexi snapped up straight as if struck by Chris Anntha's words. "What *I* did? Maybe you should ask him what he did."

"Oh, I've tried. And he's closed up tighter than a jar of Meemaw's pickles." She leaned further over the counter, lowering her voice. "Which tells me you either hurt his heart or his pride. Maybe both."

Lexi didn't say anything, still trying to feel out where this conversation was going.

"And that's not something a sister can tolerate," Chris Anntha continued. "So, I hate to intrude on your work, but I need some answers."

"You hate to intrude on my work?" Lexi almost laughed. "Yet you're the one who started a petition to keep me from even opening my bakery."

"That's different." Chris Anntha huffed and flicked a hand.
"How?"

Lexi could feel the eyes of everyone in the diner pointed at them, bouncing back and forth like they were watching a tennis match. Even Chuck unashamedly leaned out the pass-through window to stare.

"*You* were trying to intrude on my work. I had to do something."

"So rather than talk to me, you go around town to turn everyone against me?" Lexi shook her head and took a deep breath. "If you want to know what happened with your brother. It was you. You happened."

"Me?" Chris Anntha slid off her stool and pressed her hand to her chest. "Now, I might not have been fond of you comin' into town and taking my baking business, but I certainly never stood in your way of bein' with my brother."

"That's kind of a package deal, you know. Me and my baking? Your brother knew that from the get-go and still strung me along, the whole time knowing you'd be standing in the way of one of those things."

"And why would me standing in your way of baking have anything to do with you bein' together? That's just business, honey."

"It's not *just business* when he chose your side over mine. It's not *just business* when it's his family. Because he will always choose his family." Lexi tore at the ties on her apron, ripping it off over her head. "It was never *just business*."

Lexi threw her apron on the counter and stormed back to her cubby, where she grabbed her purse. Once she made it out the back door, she turned and headed toward the only place she could think of to clear her head. Her kitchen.

She hoped and prayed to any god that was listening that Chaz wasn't there, because if he was, she knew she'd say some words she shouldn't. But there was no holding it back right now. She either threw this anger into some baking or she threw it in his face. One would result in flaky, delicious croissants. The other might result in an assault charge.

With no white truck parked out front, Lexi sighed as she entered the bakery. She hadn't set foot inside since she'd told Chaz to clear his stuff out. Now she was just thankful for some peace and quiet.

She'd texted Silvia on the walk over that she needed a quick break to clear her head and would be back in about twenty minutes. That was just enough time to beat some butter into sheets for making puff pastry. And beating something, anything really, with a rolling pin sounded like just what she needed.

Lexi pulled a couple of pounds of butter from the fridge and cut it into cubes. Then she spread it out over some plastic wrap and covered it, so it was fully encased. She'd just grabbed her largest rolling pin and raised it over her head when she heard a floorboard creak by the back stairs.

She whirled around, rolling pin still raised and ready to clobber whoever dared trespass in her home.

"You sure are a sight to behold, you know that?"

Chaz leaned against the doorframe, cool as a cucumber, while Lexi sputtered and fumed, finally dropping her arm to her side.

"What are you doing here? I didn't see your truck."

"Ah, so you assumed it was safe to come and beat up the poor, innocent butter because there'd be no witnesses."

"Seriously, Chaz." The rolling pin thunked onto the metal countertop, and Lexi crossed arms. "What are you doing here? You were supposed to be out of here days ago."

"Truck's around back," Chaz tilted his head towards the back door at the bottom of the stairs. "It's a little closer for loading all my tools back up. But, I didn't want to leave a job half-finished. That's very unprofessional."

"You just couldn't stand the idea of someone else coming in here to do it." Lexi wasn't sure whether to smile at the idea or be pissed that he didn't do what she'd said.

"We had a deal."

"Sometimes there are things more important than business deals, Chaz."

Lexi turned her back to him and spread the butter into an even layer. Her fingers worked mindlessly as she listened intently to what was happening behind her. A shuffle of boots, then a sliding of paper onto the counter next to her.

"Upstairs's about done. Hope it's to your likin.' I had to make a few guesses on the finishing touches since you weren't, well, you know."

More shuffling of boots. Then the creak of the back door.

"Chaz, wait." The words rushed from her mouth before she even knew what she wanted him to wait for.

"Yes, Lex?"

The door creaked shut as Lexi finally turned back to face him.

"You didn't have to do that. The upstairs, I mean."

"Course I did."

She knew he was right. He'd never have left it undone, no matter if she'd been here every day harping at him and screaming in his ear to leave. And he'd still have done the job perfectly. That was just the kind of man he was.

"I met your sister today."

"Yeah?" Chaz looked her up and down, twisting to look at her sides and down her arms. "No claw marks? Must not have been too bad then."

"Seriously? She came at me in front of everyone while I was working."

"I will definitely have a talk with her about that. Not sure how much good it'll do. That girl doesn't listen to nobody but herself." Chaz cleared his throat and thrust his hands down into his pockets. "I am sorry, though."

"Yeah. She was spouting off all kinds of ridiculousness about how her coming after my business didn't mean you and I couldn't still be together. And what did I do to you because you're like a pickle jar."

"A pickle jar?"

"Not the important part, Chaz."

"Right. Gotcha." Chaz hesitated a moment in the doorway before entering the kitchen. "I can't excuse, or explain, her choice of delivery. But she's not wrong."

"I'm sorry. What?"

"She's not wrong. Just cause you and her have got some baking battle going on doesn't mean it has to affect us."

"It affects everything, Chaz. How can you not see that?"

"Cause all I see is your beautiful face, and the rest doesn't really matter."

"It matters to me." Lexi pushed her hand into her chest where her heart was beating erratically and slamming into her ribs. "And if I mattered to you, then this would matter, too."

She raised her arms to encompass the kitchen around them. Everything they'd worked on for the past couple of months. Everything they'd built together.

"Like I told Chris Anntha, me and baking are a package deal. You don't get one without the other."

Chaz sighed and rubbed his forehead. "Well, what do you want me to do here, Lex? I'm stuck between the two most stubborn women in my life, and it doesn't matter which way I turn, I hurt someone."

"Then choose me."

Please choose me.

"It's not that simple. It's not just picking sides." Chaz's voice dropped low, pleading. "My family has been through so much this past year. I can't put them through any more. Which, maybe you don't understand."

"Maybe I don't understand? What the hell is that supposed to mean?

"Nothin' Lex, that didn't come out right," Chaz growled low under his breath and threw his hands up. They fell with a loud slap onto his jeans. "I can't do it. I can't cause another divide. I don't know if we'd make it."

He chose them.

"I see." Lexi cleared her throat. "I've got your bill. I'll send you payment in the next twenty-four hours and get all this finalized."

"Lex, come on. There has to be some way we can figure this out."

Lexi looked at Chaz's face. The creases between his eyes, the color like the sands of the desert growing them. Lexi set the butter in the fridge, still unbeaten.

He chose them.

"No. I don't think there is."

Chapter 23

"Morning, Sunshine," Mrs. Miller called out across the B&B's dining room. She had her long, gray hair in two braids that fell down her back. As she spun around the room with a duster, her floral skirt flowed around her ankles.

"Mrs. Miller has anyone ever told you that you belong on the cover of every magazine from the 60s?" Lexi rubbed at her eyes, not wanting to look down at her own sad attire. It'd been far too long since she'd bothered to do laundry and she was scraping the bottom of her suitcase.

"Ah, the good ol' days, full of anti-war protests and the civil rights movement." Mrs. Miller shuddered. "We've still got a way to go, but we've come a long way since then." She tipped her head to the side and smiled, swishing her skirt around her ankles. "I don't mind the fashion, though."

"Touche," Lexi mumbled and pushed through the door to the kitchen. They'd long since moved past asking permission to enter areas usually inaccessible to guests. Did that mean they were more like roommates now?

I always knew grandmas would be the best roomies. They're quiet and always have cookies.

Yep. Lexi was more than okay with this arrangement. For now. She needed to get moved into her apartment above the bakery soon. After paying Chaz's final bill, her bank account was looking pretty sad.

"So, what's the plan today?" Mrs. Miller walked in with a few remaining plates from the breakfast buffet.

"Oh, you know. The usual." Lexi plopped onto one stool at the island and helped herself to the pans of leftovers waiting to be packaged up and put in the fridge.

"And what is your usual these days?"

"Avoid certain people. Help Silvia as much as possible. Try to get more baking orders. And take over the world." Lexi popped a ripe strawberry into her mouth. "You know, the usual."

"Sounds lovely." Mrs. Miller grabbed pans around her and quickly had everything packaged in Tupperware. "Now, could you be a dear and put those in the fridge for me? I need to run a few errands before the weather turns."

"Are we getting rain today?" Lexi shoved the last bite of fruit into her mouth and rinsed her plate in the sink.

"Possibly. Maybe more." Mrs. Miller grabbed her jacket off the hook by the back door. "Just keep an eye on the forecast. You never know this time of year."

"Will do," Lexi called after her as Mrs. Miller hurried out the door. "I didn't take Mississippi folks as the kind who'd be worried about a little weather."

Lexi put all the food away and got the dishwasher running. *Yep. Definitely roommates.*

Did that mean she was also rooming with Chaz? Lexi shook that thought right out of her head. She'd been coming to breakfast later so she could purposefully avoid him, but she missed those quiet, calm, early morning hours. The alternative to both of them being in the same room would have been anything but quiet and calm.

More like a chaotic storm of doom and gloom.

Probably only on her side though. Chaz didn't seem to get fazed by much of anything. Which made Lexi even more agitated.

"Darn calm people," Lexi mumbled as she stepped out onto the front porch, turning back to lock the door behind her.

"What have the calm people done now?"

Lexi turned to Lotus, strolling up the front stairs. She'd traded her short hair for long braids, which she had twisted up on the back of her head. Her pale peach shirt made her dark skin glow.

"Girl. How do you always look so amazing?"

"What? This old thing?" Lotus slowly turned, and Lexi knew that her outfit was not old. They'd bought it together on a quick girls' trip to Jackson the night before. "You're the one who wanted a little retail therapy, and yet, you didn't buy a single thing. Then you come out today wearing this drab number." Lotus picked at the old t-shirt Lexi was wearing over an even older pair of leggings. "This is not très chic, darling."

"Yeah, Yeah." Lexi wasn't sure why she didn't buy anything while they were out, especially when she knew what clean options she had waiting for her to wear. She just hadn't seen the point. "I'm just going to get some prep work done in my kitchen and then head over for a shift at the diner. Not like I need to be dressed to the nines when I'll just end up covered in flour and gravy, anyway."

"Wow. How far the mighty have fallen." Lotus shook her head and slid her arm through Lexi's. "This from the woman I met wearing the most lovely vintage ensemble."

"Vintage inspired," Lexi interjected. "I can't afford real, classy vintage."

"Is this shirt vintage?" Lotus pulled at the sleeve again, pressing her face close. "I can almost see through it."

"Oh, leave it." Lexi laughed and swatted her hand away. "I'll do laundry tonight."

"So, where are we headed?" Lotus stepped down off the porch and looked both ways.

"To the bakery." Lexi leaned a little closer and lowered her voice. "Did you come past there? Did you notice any white trucks lingering?"

"I did come past there and there was no lingering noticed. Can't vouch for the back side though. Darn these eyes for not having x-ray vision."

"I suppose I can let that slide." Lexi sighed.

"You can't avoid him forever, you know. This is Fauna. You can't avoid anyone for long." Lotus patted her arm as they walked down the street. "You're going to have to get used to seeing him. Maybe even talking to him."

"Is that what people do in small towns? Just go around talking to exes all the time? Gross." Lexi shuddered when Lotus nodded. "At least in New York, you could literally never see them again. Like they never existed."

"While that sounds lovely in some instances, being forced to get along and play nice isn't always a bad thing."

"Sure, it is."

"You're impossible." Lotus threw her head back and sighed.

"It's one of the many things that you love about me." Lexi pulled her close.

"There are many things I love about you. Your spirit. Your tenacity. Your independence." Lotus pushed Lexi away. "Your impossible-ness is not one of those things."

"Fine." Lexi groaned. "I'll do my best to be civil."

"And?"

"And..." Lexi pursed her lips, not wanting to agree to the rest, but said it for Lotus's sake, "stop being such a chicken about running into him. Or her. Or them."

"Much better."

The sky was overcast, blocking out the normally blistering sun, but the air was still sticky. Lexi pulled at her t-shirt, thankful it was so light, but still hating that it clung to her dampening skin.

"So, what are you up to today?" Lexi hoped to change the subject. Not that she was avoiding anything, though. Especially not talking more about Chaz, because that was totally delightful. "Any big, newsworthy events?"

"Well, there's a hurricane heading for the coast. That could be big."

"But that's like a hundred miles away."

"And hurricanes can be hundreds of miles wide." Lotus looked at her with a 'duh' expression.

"Seriously?"

"Seriously."

Lexi stopped walking and gripped Lotus's arm tightly. "Are you telling me we're going to be hit by a hurricane?"

"No." Lotus patted her hand. "But I'm not saying we won't either. You never really know with these things where exactly they will go or what they will do. But we're far enough inland that if it does come this way, it shouldn't be too bad."

"Oh, that's good."

"Unless we're on the dirty side."

"The dirty side?"

"Yeah. Don't they teach you Yankees anything about weather?"

"Sure. Like, what is a hurricane? Or, how are hurricanes formed?" Lexi stopped walking again. "Not the actual logistics of living through one or that they have clean and dirty sides."

"No one says 'clean side' of a hurricane."

"Well, then apparently I know nothing." Lexi chewed her bottom lip. "Or at least nothing valuable."

"Don't fret. It's been a long, long time since Fauna has seen any action from a hurricane. We will probably just get a little wind and rain and go about our business."

"Good to know."

"But man! Imagine if we do get more than that?" Lotus whooped, her body vibrating with energy. "That would be newsworthy. My piece could get picked up by the Magnolia in Jackson, and then nationally. The whole country could be reading Lotus Johnson."

"Okay. Let's not get ahead of ourselves here. We don't actually want any of that to happen."

"Of course not. But a girl can dream, right?"

"Only you, Lotus, would dream of your town getting hit by a hurricane."

For the rest of the walk to the bakery, Lexi listened as Lotus told her about her dad and brother fixing some fancy car in their shop. Her mind drifted a little as Lotus got to the specifics about the model and types of upgrades. Lexi didn't know a thing about cars and didn't care to, but with Lotus having two mechanics in the family, she was bound to pick some things up.

A few leaves swirled on the ground as they reached the front porch of the bakery, and a slight breeze blew past. There wasn't anything particularly off, but Lexi could feel something. Whether it was the Walkers or the storm, she couldn't tell, but something was coming.

The crowd at the diner that evening was subdued, missing its usual light chatter and laughter. The television over the counter was turned on high, blaring the latest updates about Hurricane Janene, which had made landfall near Marsh Island in Louisiana and was barreling toward New Orleans. Lexi was doing her best to keep her mind off the weather and just do her best at getting everyone what they needed.

"Oh, Lord. Let's hope this isn't another Katrina," a woman said as Lexi delivered their food to the table.

"Or Camille," said another.

Agreeing hums came from all the surrounding tables.

"Were those bad here?" Lexi asked, starting to feel a little nervous.

"Oh, honey, those were bad all over," the first woman placed her hand on Lexi's and gave it a quick squeeze.

"My family lost everything in Camille," the other woman at the table shook her head at the memory. "Granted, we were living south of Jackson at the time."

"Mm. Katrina wasn't much better," said an older gentleman at the next table. "Lots a folks lost everything."

"You ever been through a hurricane, darlin'?" The woman, still grasping her hand, looked up at her.

"No, ma'am. And I'd rather not go through one tonight."

"Well, that's in the Lord's hands, Suga. All we can do is pray."

Lexi left the table as they started talking about Katrina and Camille again. Listening to horror stories wouldn't help her stay calm. She wiped her hands down the front of her apron, fighting the urge to clench them together like she had as a girl.

"We'll be alright, Cariña," Silvia stood behind the counter, wiping down menus. "No matter what, we will be okay. Fauna is strong. We have deep roots."

Lexi looked out the window into the dark, listening to the rain slap against the glass. "Strong enough to withstand a hurricane?"

"We've done it before." Silvia gave her a tight-lipped smile that gave away her anxiety. "We'll do it again if we have to."

The television blared an alarm, a red line racing across the bottom of the screen. The diner fell silent as a mechanical voice began reading off the latest updates.

"Hurricane Janene has made landfall. Its course has shifted in a northerly direction and is passing over Baton Rouge. This is a fast-moving storm that could produce tornadoes and damaging winds. If you are in its path, please take cover immediately..."

Lexi stopped listening. Baton Rouge was directly south of Fauna. If the hurricane was swinging north, they could be right in its path. Lexi looked around the diner. Everyone looked grim as they watched the rest of the broadcast. No one said a word. No one moved. When the alert stopped abruptly, the only sound was the rain pounding against the aluminum siding.

Then, everyone was moving. It was a flurry of coats and umbrellas. Lexi ran to the cash register as everyone wanted to pay at once. Her eyes flew to Silvia as she counted back dollar bills and swiped cards. The old woman was sliding dirty dishes into the sink to be dealt with later and clearing everything off the tables. Chuck was scrambling to shut down the kitchen and pack all the food away. As the last guest rushed out the door, someone pushed past them inside. They were drenched, water running off them in streams onto the floor. They pulled their hood off their head and shook out their hair.

"Chris Anntha," Silvia rushed over. "What in the world are you doing here? Your parents are going to be worried sick."

"We are all heading into town to help board up the church. They were heading out right behind me."

"And the ranch?" Silvia ushered her inside.

Lexi stood rooted to the spot, torn between glaring at her nemesis and rushing around the diner to help. Since she had no idea how to help or what needed to be done, she decided glaring was her only option.

"The boys got it." Chris Anntha waved off Silvia's concern. "Never have to worry about the Walkers. We've got plenty of hands to get any job done."

"That is true. Come in. Come in." Silvia tugged Chris Anntha towards a booth. "We can still get some dinner together for you."

"Oh, no. That's not why I'm here." Chris Anntha's eyes flicked toward Lexi.

"Ah, I see." Silvia stepped away, looking between the two of them. "We already have one storm outside. I expect peace inside, understood?"

"Yes, ma'am," they both mumbled and bowed their heads, looking at their shoes like scolded schoolgirls.

"What do you want?" Lexi asked once Silvia was in the kitchen and out of earshot.

"I actually... well...ugh," Chris Anntha paced the small aisle in front of the booths. "I had a talk with Chaz. And he brought some things to light. And I just wanted to say..."

Lexi leaned forward, trying to catch the mumbled words. "What?"

"I wanted to say I'm sorry, okay?" Chris Anntha threw her hands up at her sides and huffed. "I mean, geez. This isn't the 50s anymore. Strong women should be supporting each other, not tearing each other down."

"Is that what you talked about with Chaz?" Lexi pressed her lips together to hold back a giggle. "Feminist ideals?"

"As a matter of fact," Chris Anntha tried to hide her smile too, "my brother is a feminist and always supports women in what they want to do."

"Oh, I don't doubt that. I would expect no less from him."

"He told me about the pink, frilly apron you made him wear." Chris Anntha was full-on grinning now.

"And he rocked that pink, frilly apron like a feminist boss." Lexi finally let herself smile back.

"Lexi, we got off on the wrong foot. I really am sorry." Chris Anntha walked over to the cash register and leaned on the counter. "If I'd known what you mean to my brother, well, things would probably have gone down real different. But it is like pulling teeth to get that man to spill his guts, let me tell ya."

"Really?" Lexi was surprised. "I'd never have guessed that."

"If you're getting him to talk about feelings and 'other mushy stuff,' he's further gone than I thought."

"Well, none of that really matters now," Lexi sighed, "but I do appreciate the apology. And... I suppose... I should probably say sorry too." She scuffed her tennis shoes on the floor. "I didn't really give you a fair chance, and I think I let some of my frustration with Chaz cloud my judgment of you."

"Ya think?" Chris Anntha threw her head back and laughed. "I don't even want to know what you thought of me."

"No, probably not."

They both chuckled and fell into a stiff silence. The television blasted another alert, and the wind battered the windows. Lexi looked outside into the night, both glad that she couldn't see anything and also terrified at what she couldn't see. What exactly was happening out there?

"Chuck and I are going to put the shutters out," Silvia came rushing from the kitchen.

"Do you need any help?" Lexi looked around frantically, but not sure what she was looking for.

"No, no. We have them on a system, so it will be quick."

"What should I do?"

"Go home." Silvia looked at them both seriously, her eyes dark. "Both of you."

She rushed out the back with Chuck at her heels. Lexi took a calming breath. If she wanted to be a Southerner, she had to learn to deal with everything life threw at them. And that included hurricanes. This just felt like a very rushed introduction to the lifestyle.

Think you could have eased me in a little, universe? Instead of just throwing me in the deep end?

"I guess I better go see if I can help Mrs. Miller at the B&B," Lexi grabbed her purse, which she'd stashed under the cash register earlier. "Or maybe I should go to the bakery."

"Oh, Chaz said he was heading to Meemaw's... the bakery." Chris Anntha looked up at her as she zipped her coat. "He'll make sure it's taken care of."

Ugh. That man.

It made her both furious that he still treated the bakery like it was his property to protect and thankful because she had no clue what to do.

"Okay, the B&B it is."

Lexi followed Chris Anntha toward the front door. The wind was howling outside, and rain fell in sheets, slapping against the siding and windows. It was so loud Lexi could hardly think, let alone make a plan. She needed a moment to catch her breath. To process. To figure out what to do.

But all those thoughts fled from her mind as a piercing siren split the night. The wailing sound sent shivers of terror down her spine, and her breath caught in her chest.

Chris Anntha and Lexi looked at each other and ran out into the night.

Chapter 24

The wind tore at Lexi's shirt, which was soaked through in an instant. Water ran down her face and into her eyes as she looked around them. Lightning lit up the sky, illuminating the terrible, roiling mass of black clouds above them. All along the square, buildings sat dark and empty. Business owners and customers rushed past them on the sidewalk towards the church.

"Get to the basement," a man shouted at Lexi and Chris Anntha, who both stood frozen on the sidewalk. The man tugged at Lexi's arm, but she pulled away and shook her head.

"I have to check on the bakery," Lexi shouted over the wind. She could see Chaz's truck parked out front, its headlights aiming at the house were the only lights visible on the square.

"I'm coming with you," Chris Anntha nodded, brushing water off her forehead.

This is ok. We're all going to be ok.

Thunder roared down from the sky, followed instantly by a blinding flash of lightning. They ran across the brick street, which ran with water deep enough to soak through Lexi's mesh sneakers. The sirens began again, their low pitch winding up higher and pulling Lexi's concentration away from the road in front of her. Her shoe caught on something, and she stumbled into Chris Anntha. The two clasped onto each other and surged forward, almost to Chaz's truck.

Lexi saw him. On a ladder dragging a metal sheet up to the turret window. He had it clipped into place in seconds and slid down the ladder like Lexi had only seen in those fireman challenge videos. Chaz paused a moment when he saw them running towards him, but only for a second.

His hair was matted to his forehead, and his wet clothes clung to his body. Lexi could see a slightly crazed determination flash in his eyes as he turned and moved the ladder to the other side of the turret. Lexi and Chris Anntha reached the yard, the soaked earth sucking at their feet.

"Get to the church. Both of you," Chaz yelled as lightning ripped across the sky.

"Are you crazy?" Lexi lunged forward, pulling at his shirt, his arms, anything she could get a grasp of. "You're climbing up a giant metal lightning rod in the middle of a hurricane."

"Three more windows, that's all," Chaz grabbed the metal shutter and sprinted up the ladder.

"He's going to get himself killed," Lexi looked back at Chris Anntha.

He could slip. Fall. Get fried.

"He won't stop," Chris Anntha yelled, running back towards Chaz's truck.

"Of course he won't," Lexi yelled, mostly to herself. She batted the wet curls out of her eyes and looked up at Chaz in the weak light from his truck.

More thunder rumbled, and the lightning was almost constant, making the sky flicker between an ominous black to white. Lexi had never been so terrified of the weather in her life. She'd been through tornado drills and sirens before, but nothing like this. Hurricane Janene was nasty, terrifying, and coming at Fauna like a mad woman hellbent on revenge.

Chaz's boots thudded onto the ground. Lexi made the split-second decision that if she couldn't stop him, at least she could help him finish faster.

"You get the ladder," she yelled, "I'll get the shutters."

"I've got this Lexi," Chaz barely spared her a glance as he repositioned the ladder down the side of the house at the next window. Lexi followed. "You and Chris Anntha need to get out of here."

"And leave you to get yourself killed? On my property?" Lexi squared her shoulders and grabbed the next shutter off the pile. "I don't think so, mister. I'm not having that on my conscience or my insurance record."

"Dear God," Chaz muttered, barely audible over the wind. "Come on, then."

Lexi handed him the sheet of metal, and he ran up the rungs. She grasped the ladder's legs, using all her weight to keep it in place.

The wind could blow him over. Lightning could strike. He could slip on the wet metal.

Lexi's mind started spiraling through all the things that could go wrong. Her chest tightened. She huffed the water off her lips, which did no good because more replaced it. The sky boiled above them, and the ground below them streamed with rainwater. She'd never understood how a mudslide could happen until that very moment as she glanced down and saw the soil beneath her feet washing away. The ladder leaned as one side sank into the over-saturated earth. Lexi shoved her shoulder into the ladder, pushing it into place, and glanced up at Chaz, who was finishing with the shutter.

He's like a flippin' ladder ballerina.

Lexi knew he wouldn't appreciate that comparison and realized her mind was getting a little loopy with fear. She took a few deep breaths between the booming thunder and stepped away just in time for Chaz to slide down with a splash.

"Last one," he yelled, shaking his head to get his hair out of his eyes. "You got this?"

He really looked at her for the first time, his eyes a dark shade of walnut Lexi hadn't seen before. She reached out and quickly placed a hand on his chest, feeling the thudding of his heart matching her own.

"Do you got this?" he asked again, slower this time.

"Yeah. Yeah." Lexi pulled her hand back and swallowed hard. "Go."

Chaz didn't hesitate and grabbed the ladder. He ran down the side of the house with it as she ran to grab the last shutter. Her feet slipped as she skidded to a halt. She glanced at Chaz's truck, where Chris Anntha was wildly digging through his tool bin in the back. Lexi wasn't sure what she was looking for, and she didn't care.

I can help. I can keep him safe.

That was all that mattered. As the screech of the siren split the air again, Lexi grabbed the final shutter and took off around the corner of the house. Chaz had set the ladder and was starting up as she slid up next to his legs. She hefted the heavy metal into his waiting hand. Again, she pressed her weight into the ladder, holding it steady. The tree branches thrashed overhead, and the trunks groaned. Lexi would never forget the sound of the earth around her battling for survival, just as she was doing with Chaz.

Oh Lord. Survival.

The word slammed into her. Hard. They were fighting for survival. Of their town. Of their homes and businesses. Of themselves.

Snap.

Something crashed above her, and she dove to the side of the ladder, refusing to let go. A tree limb thudded to the ground in a flurry of branches and leaves. Lexi felt a pain slice down her shin but didn't bother to look. A scrape she could handle. A crushed or fried Chaz, she could not.

He slid down next to her, stepping down into the pile of leaves at the bottom. Lexi stared for a moment at the limb, wondering how long it had been part of that tree. Sixty years? A hundred? It'd probably seen countless storms, but this one brought it down.

"Lexi. Lexi." Chaz grabbed her shoulders. "Are you okay?"

"Yeah, yeah." She blinked, tearing her eyes from the ground to look at him. "Fine."

"You're bleeding." He gestured to her leg.

"It's nothing. Let's go."

"Grab the end of the ladder." Chaz turned to lower it down from the side of the house.

"Just leave it." Lexi didn't understand why they weren't running for cover.

"Can't. It'd just be more debris. Could cause more damage."

Lexi grunted and grabbed the end as Chaz lowered it to her. Together, they slid it back down to its compact size and ran around to the front of the house.

"There."

Chaz steered them toward the front porch where Chris Anntha was weaving straps into the railings and tying things down. The porch swing was on the floor, along with the table and chairs, all strapped to the spindles. Lexi couldn't even stop to wonder how such a tiny thing like Chris Anntha got that swing down from the ceiling by herself. They raced up the stairs and pushed the ladder into the pile. Chris Anntha was ready and tossed a strap to Chaz. As they wound it through the rungs and tightened it to the railing, Lexi looked out at the square.

Under the porch roof, she finally didn't have rain pelting her face. She could see the trees whipping in the wind, bending to unimaginable angles. Water ran down the roads, washing out the lawns and green spaces. Anything not bolted or strapped down was toppled over or blowing down the streets.

For the fourth time, the sirens wailed.

Lexi's eyes whipped to Chaz. He pushed Chris Anntha in front of him and grabbed Lexi's arm as they ran down the front steps.

"We have to get to the church basement," Chris Anntha yelled. Lightning lit up her golden hair and pale skin, giving her an almost ghostly appearance.

Lexi let herself be dragged down the walkway. As the icy rain pelted her skin again, her mind froze. Fear seized her body, and her feet stumbled beneath her, unsteady in the rushing water.

Chaz gripped her tighter, almost carrying her into the street. The siren continued to blare, and in her haze, Lexi thought that was odd. It had been shorter the last couple of times, hadn't it? The lightning was a strobe light, buildings flashing in front of them. In and out. Light and dark.

"Mama and Daddy were coming right behind me," Chris Anntha hollered back at them. "They should be there already."

They sloshed through the street, stepping up onto the sidewalk in front of the diner. Light flashed off the metal shutters covering its windows. Silvia had been right; their system was quick. The lights were all off, and it looked deserted. Lexi hoped Silvia and Chuck had made it somewhere safe.

Cars were parked haphazardly outside the church. Some blocking others in. Some in the grass of the square across the street. It was like all the apocalypse movies Lexi'd seen; the roads impassable with cars parked in a desperate rush.

They reached the stairs leading up to the door but stopped. Chaz scanned the scene in front of them, looking for something.

"I don't see their car," he yelled.

"They have to be here." Chris Anntha stepped onto the stairs next to them.

Lexi was vaguely aware of Chaz's hand tightening around her waist. His fingers wrapped into the soaked fabric of her shirt. She looked out over the parking lot, not knowing what they were looking for, but desperate to help.

"They said they'd be out right behind me." Chris Anntha's voice was a mixture of determination and pleading.

"They aren't here," Chaz said finally. "I have to go find them."

"What?" Lexi and Chris Anntha both yelled.

"I can't go in there knowing they might be out here somewhere."

"Chaz," Chris Anntha said at the same time Lexi pulled out of his grasp.

"You can't be serious." She stepped in front of him, studying his face. "You can't go out in this."

"I have to."

"No. No, you don't." Lexi stamped her foot, not caring if she looked like a child.

"Lexi." Chaz gripped her shoulders, looking into her eyes. "I do."

He pushed her towards Chris Anntha and stepped down onto the sidewalk. "Get inside and stay there. Don't come out until this is over. You hear me?"

Chris Anntha nodded and looped her arm through Lexi's, giving her a quick squeeze. Lexi twisted in her grasp to stare at Chaz. Was he really leaving them? Leaving her?

"Chaz..." her voice was whisked away in the wind.

Chaz rested a hand on her cheek; his normally warm palm was cold and slick with rain. "Take care of her." He looked at Chris Anntha, who nodded. "I'll be back. Promise."

Then he turned and ran back the way they'd come. Water splashed up around him as his boots pounded down the street. Lexi couldn't believe what she was watching. He was choosing them again.

She tore at Chris Anntha's grasp, but her arms only tightened more. The sirens continued to blast around them as the trees slashed across the sky. With each bolt of lightning, each step he took away from her, Lexi could feel her heart cracking a little more.

"We have to get inside," Chris Anntha tugged at her arm. "You have to let him go."

"Why should I just let him go?" Lexi spun, lightning fueling the fire in her veins. "Why?"

"Because he'd hate himself if he didn't."

And me for being the reason.

"He'll be back. He promised." Chris Anntha tugged again. "Let's go."

Lexi took one more look over her shoulder. In the flickering light, she could just see his truck pulling out and turning off the square.

He'll be back. He promised.

Lexi nodded to Chris Anntha, and they ran up the steps. As they reached the top, they paused. The siren still wailed. The thunder still rumbled. The lightning still flashed. But the wind suddenly went still. All around, the rain slowed, and an eerie calm settled over them.

Chris Anntha and Lexi spun slowly, looking out over the square from the top of the church steps. Leaves and branches littered the ground, and in the distance, they heard a strange crunching, snapping sound. Then, as lightning lit the sky again, they saw it.

A massive, swirling funnel cloud was heading straight toward them.

Chapter 25

Pastor Jeff ushered Lexi and Chris Anntha to an available spot in the crowded basement community room. The thin stream of light from his flashlight bobbed away as he hurried to help someone else. It was dark and warm. Lexi didn't like the feeling of being underground, surrounded by damp earth, while the world was being ripped apart above them.

Everyone gasped as the church creaked and moaned. Lexi's ears popped as the sound of shattered glass rained down onto the floor above them. People's sobbing could barely be heard over the cacophony of destruction. Breaking. Snapping. Whirling wind. It was like nothing she'd ever heard before. Around her, people clung to one another. Pastor Jeff stood in the center of the room loudly praying, his wavering voice barely audible. Lexi sank down to the floor, pulling her knees up to her chest and covering her ears to block out the deafening sounds.

Just as suddenly as the noise had started, it stopped. Leaving only the pounding of rain above and an eerie silence below. Everyone collectively held their breath, waiting. But no new sounds came. Lexi desperately wanted a hug, a comforting rub on her back, a squeeze of her hand. Anything to ease the tension and terror holding her body rigid.

I wish Chaz were here.

She wanted him to wrap her up in his arms and tell her it would be ok.

Instead, he was out there somewhere. Hopefully safe. But she didn't know. And that was killing her.

Damn you, Chaz Walker.

"I can see that look in your eyes," Chris Anntha sank down next to her with a heavy sigh. "You're cursing him, aren't you?"

"Damning him, actually," Lexi huffed. "But close enough."

"Wouldn't be the first time a woman damned one of my brothers." Chris Anntha stretched out her legs. "And definitely won't be the last. The Walker boys are nothing if not stubborn."

"Just the boys?" Lexi raised her brows.

"Are you comparing little ol' me to my herd of pigheaded brothers?" Chris Anntha put a hand to her chest in mock surprise, appearing oddly at ease in the situation. "Yeah, you're right. I'm probably the captain of that team."

They fell silent and listened to the whistling of the wind above them and the whispering of prayers around them. Lexi shivered as her drenched clothing absorbed the chill of the linoleum floor. Even though the air was warm from the crowd of bodies, Lexi's teeth chattered and her arms shook.

"Here, darlin'." The woman next to them handed Lexi a blanket. "You two are drenched to the bone."

"Th-th-thank y-you," Lexi stammered. "Although I th-th-think this is more nerves th-than c-cold."

"Mm. That adrenaline will get you through it, but then it leaves you to it." The old woman nodded and turned back to her family.

Lexi laid the blanket out across her lap and slowly stretched her legs out too. She held up the extra, and Chris Anntha nodded. They both pulled it up under their chins in silence. Lexi let her head fall back against the wall and closed her eyes, focusing on relaxing her body.

"You know," Chris Anntha's voice wavered, making Lexi realize she wasn't the only one shivering. "We aren't only stubborn."

"Well, I assume, that as a whole, the Walker family must have at least one redeeming quality."

"We have a couple, mind you." Chris Anntha elbowed Lexi under the blanket. "The biggest being that we are loyal to a fault."

Lexi snorted. Chaz might be loyal to his family, but that didn't seem to extend to her. He didn't think twice about running off and leaving her in a hurricane.

But can I really blame him?

Lexi thought about her family. Would she run into a storm to make sure they were safe? After all the years of manipulation and emotional abuse?

As much as she wanted to say she wouldn't, she knew she would.

So why was she holding it against Chaz for doing the same? Especially when he had such a strong, supportive family. Of course, he'd want to make sure they were ok.

But she wanted him here. She wanted him to hold her and make her feel better. She wanted him with her. She wanted to know that he was safe and dry. She wanted him.

I still want him.

Lexi sighed, realizing that it didn't matter what she wanted. "Well, I don't think I could ever compete with the loyalty he has to your family."

He may be what she wanted, but he wasn't what she needed. Right now, all she needed was to get her business running. That was it.

"Are you kidding? I've never seen him act the way he does with you," Chris Anntha turned to face Lexi, still clasping the blanket beneath her chin. "He's in new territory. And he does not handle change well." Chris Anntha blew out a breath. "So, maybe he's made a few mistakes. Don't we all?"

"I mean, sure. I'm not perfect either."

"Humph. I know that." Chris Anntha stopped herself. "Sorry. Old habits."

"It's ok. I probably deserve it." Lexi turned to face Chris Anntha, pulling her legs up underneath her.

She looked at Chaz's sister in the dim light. Her golden hair was plastered against her head, but she still looked beautiful. She was the kind of woman who could never take a bad photo because she would look fabulous wearing a potato sack. Lexi envied that easy appearance, because she was positive she looked like a drowned rat.

"I spent the last two months in Florida helping my aunt recover after a hip replacement, so I haven't seen everything that's been going on since you arrived. But seriously, try to cut Chaz some slack. He's been through a lot this past year, and I think losing you could really send him into a tailspin."

"I'm sorry about your Meemaw," Lexi said. "She sounded like a wonderful lady."

"Oh, she was the best. She's the one who taught me to bake." Chris Anntha gave a distant smile, thinking of some memory long past.

"Well, I might regret saying this." Lexi couldn't believe she was about to admit it. "Your pecan pie is one of the best I've ever had."

"Oh, my goodness," Chris Anntha did a little shimmy. "Thank you so much. That was my Uncle Benny's favorite, so Meemaw had that recipe down to a tee."

"The first time I tried it, I told Silvia I'd like to hire whoever made it," Lexi laughed.

"Seriously?" Chris Anntha's tone shifted immediately. "You'd hire me to work in your bakery? In an actual bakery?"

"Sure. It's hard to find people who understand the value of a well-baked crust."

"Well, I accept."

"Wait," Lexi blinked. "What?"

"I accept. The job." Chris Anntha beamed at Lexi. "I've always wanted to work in a commercial kitchen."

"Um, do you really think that's the best idea?" Lexi stammered. "Us working together?"

"I don't see why not." Chris Anntha shrugged. "You managed to work with my brother. So, working with me should be a piece of cake."

Lexi doubted that immensely.

"Oh, and you have to hire Dandy. She worships you."

Lexi thought of the young girl who'd won the pie contest. They'd talked once since then about careers in pastry, but Lexi hadn't offered her a job. She couldn't afford to pay anyone yet, not even herself. Now, she'd come running into this church to escape a tornado and would walk out with a whole kitchen staff. Life sure was a whirlwind.

"Okay, let's not get ahead of ourselves. I'm not even officially open yet."

"Yeah, well, you can be anytime though, right? Chaz said you had everything in place."

"Except for the display cases. Those were on back order." Was she seriously discussing this with Chris Anntha? Right now? All the while totally ignoring the possibility that there might not even be a bakery left standing. Lexi couldn't let her mind go down that path. "And what about that petition you had people sign?"

"Oh, I'll tear that up and tell them all it was a misunderstanding." Chris Anntha waved it off with ease. "Besides, if we're both working at the same place, there's only one spot for them to come. No more choosing. Ohhh. This is perfect."

"Um, well. Ok then." Lexi shrugged. It could be the adrenaline wearing off that was making her not think straight, but this honestly didn't sound like a bad idea. What Chris Anntha said made some sense. "You're hired."

"So, now that our beef is under the table," Chris Anntha leaned back a little, really taking Lexi in, "is there still an issue with my brother?"

"I don't know, Chris Anntha," Lexi could feel the dread seeping back into her stomach, like a squirt of unripe grapefruit down the throat. "I'm not sure I can be with someone who doesn't put me first. I know that sounds selfish, but my family has put me last my whole life, and I don't want to compromise and spend the rest of my life in last place, too."

"That doesn't sound selfish, but I think you're lookin' at this all wrong. We aren't on opposing sides. We're all on the same team. And sometimes the quarterback, Chaz, needs to make a play with the wide receiver, and sometimes he throws to the running back. But they all still work together in order to win."

"I don't get football," Lexi muttered. She much preferred Silvia's baking analogy. "But I get what you're saying."

"Yeah, like he sold Meemaw's house to you. That's a huge play. Like a 90-yard touchdown run . He did that despite knowing I'd get tackled. Because he knew his next play would probably keep me safe."

"I still don't understand sports references." Lexi shook her head.

"Just run with it; I'm on a roll." Chris Anntha waved away her concerns. "And when he helped you out at the Garden Society tea party?"

"Touchdown?" Lexi guessed.

"Eh. Maybe a big play. And when he went to the fair with you instead of his brothers, which he's literally done every other year of his life?"

"Really? He didn't mention that."

"Touchdown." Chris Anntha waved her arms wildly as she mirrored teams running from one end of the field to another, raising her arms to symbolize a touchdown. "Chaz is a good quarterback. He can handle working with an entire team. The question now is, can you?"

"I don't know if I've ever been part of a team," Lexi realized. Not in her family, surely. Even at work, she was usually the only pastry chef in a kitchen full of savory chefs. She'd always set her own schedule and forged her own path.

"Well, Fauna is like one big team. But the Walkers? We're like our own team too." Chris Anntha tapped her shoulder against Lexi's. "And we're always happy to welcome new players."

Lexi didn't say anything, and Chris Anntha left her to her thoughts. Could she be a team player? She knew she wasn't selfish. She didn't want someone doting on her every move. She wanted a partner, didn't she? Someone she could trust to handle half of whatever life threw at them. Which would probably mean plenty of drama from her family. And Chaz had helped her handle her sister once already. So, couldn't she help him with his family? Couldn't she be a team player and give him the support he needed?

The room was mostly quiet as Lexi let these ideas mull in her mind. Above them, the rain had tapered off to a light patter. Lexi's heart clenched, remembering the terrible screeching and crashing earlier, and she hoped Chaz made it somewhere safe.

If I realize *that I'm going to be a team player for him, and he ends up getting himself offed by a tornado, I'm going to be pissed.*

Lexi rested her head back against the wall but couldn't relax. Not knowing where Chaz was or what they'd walk out to when this was over kept her body tight and her mind tense. Between the tornado and her heart, she wasn't sure what tomorrow would bring.

It took five people pushing, but they could finally open the door at the end of the hallway. Early morning light shone through the hole where the church entryway should have stood. Lexi's chest tightened as everyone shuffled out of the dark basement. She could hear the gasps and sobs of the people ahead of her and tried to steel herself against what she'd find when she walked through that door.

But as her eyes adjusted to the light, nothing could have prepared her for what she saw.

They stood on the church's foundation with nothing but sky above them. Glass crunched under her sneakers as she took in the devastation. Wood and drywall littered the ground. Large slabs of the roof lay on top of the few remaining pews. A woman next to Lexi collapsed to the ground, wailing to God for help.

Chris Anntha rushed to her side, comforting her and offering reassurance.

How could it all be gone? I just walked through here last night.

With a tornado right on her heels.

Lexi picked her way over to where the front door had stood only the night before, but now all that remained was the snapped-off framing bolted to the concrete below. Lexi clutched her chest as she got her first view of the square.

"No. No." The word rushed from her lips, over and over, as if saying it could erase the nightmare before her. "No. This can't be."

Slowly, she made her way down the steps, picking her way through the soaked debris. Her hands pressed tightly together, trying to ease the heartache. All around her, people were emerging from basements and shelters, looking bewildered and lost.

The rows of magnolia trees were all gone. Uprooted or snapped in half, some lying on the ground, some totally gone. Their dark green leaves littered the sidewalk among shingles and insulation. The courthouse in the center was missing half its roof, exposing the trusses to the sky, like the ribs of a picked-over carcass.

"Silvia," Lexi gasped and ran to the old woman's side at the front door of the diner.

The shiny aluminum building was buried in debris, and its metal shutters were bent and rippled. Silvia grabbed onto Lexi with one hand, squeezing tightly as she put the key into the lock with the other. Rivulets of water ran out over their feet as they pushed their way inside. A tree branch, or maybe the whole tree by its size, rested at an awkward angle, jutting through a window where it had punched right through the metal shutter. Water dripped somewhere further inside, but they couldn't get past the limbs.

"Oh, Silvia," Lexi wrapped the woman in a fierce hug, and they held on to each other desperately. "I was so worried when I didn't see you at the church."

"Chuck and I stayed here in the diner's cellar. I came out the back door to see the damage."

Lexi could barely breathe. Could barely think. All around her, everyone's lives were in ruins. These people she'd come to love and cherish, and now everything was gone. This dream town was nothing but piles of broken dreams.

"You're ok?" Silvia pulled away, wiping her eyes. She patted down Lexi's arms, looking her over, tutting over the gash on her shin. "You and Chris Anntha?"

"Yeah. We're fine. It's just a scratch."

"Good. Good." Silva swallowed hard. "And Chaz?"

"I... I don't know."

Even though it felt impossible, her heart squeezed even tighter. Lexi stumbled, bracing herself on the door frame behind them.

"Hey. Hey." Silvia grabbed her face with both hands, forcing Lexi to focus on her. "He will be fine. You hear me?"

"Yes."

"We're all going to be fine." Silvia's shoulders curled in, those words being the only strength she had left. "As long as our people are okay, Fauna will be okay."

Lexi pulled out her cell phone for the hundredth time, praying for enough signal to send the few text messages she'd typed. But they still sat on her screen.

"Towers are down," she mumbled.

"Oh, yeah. Probably will be for a few days at least." Silvia had turned away, pawing through the leaves to get a better view of the rest of the diner. "How's your bakery?"

"Not sure." Lexi wet her lips and stood up straight. "I haven't had the heart to look yet."

"Oh, Cariña." Silvia turned back and placed a shaking hand on Lexi's arm. "Do you want me to go with you?"

"No. No. You've got enough to deal with here." Lexi placed her hand on top of Silvia's. "I had to make sure you were alright first."

"Go. I'm fine. Here's Chuck now."

Lexi passed Chuck in the doorway with a tight-lipped smile. Leaving Silvia in capable hands made her feel a little better.

Outside, the only human sounds were the low hum of hushed talking punctuated with sobs and groans. Sunshine filtered through a lightly overcast sky in total contrast to the sorrowful mood. Papers flapped in a slight breeze, and leaves rustled from the ground instead of their normally majestic placement at the tops of ancient trees.

She didn't want to turn the corner towards the bakery. It was easier to pretend it was completely unscathed than to face the reality that all her dreams and life plans had been wiped out in one night.

"Hey." Chris Anntha appeared at her side, arms wrapped around her middle, hugging herself tightly.

"Hey."

"Silvia okay?"

"Yeah, I think so." Lexi looked down at a picture frame by her feet. A smiling family looked up at her through shattered glass. "This is..." She wasn't even sure how to describe the devastation around them, so she didn't even try.

"Yeah." Chris Anntha pulled in a shaky breath. "It sure is."

"Are you okay?" Lexi knew if this was bad for her, it must be worse for someone who'd called Fauna home their whole life. "I mean, as okay as you can be, I suppose?"

"I'll be alright." Chris Anntha looked over with a small smile. "Let's go see what we're dealing with at Meemaw... your bakery."

Lexi could feel her chest tightening again, like chocolate seizing in water. There was only one Walker sibling she wanted here with her, and this was not the right one.

Why'd you have to leave? Why didn't you stay?

"Any word on Chaz? Or the rest of your family?"

"No. Not yet."

"I'm sure you'll hear soon."

"I'm sure *we* will."

Lexi wouldn't allow herself to go down the mental path of Chaz not being alright. Every time that thought even tried to pop up, she punched it down like bread dough. She'd always been a worrywart. Anxiety had kept her from totally falling apart most of her life, so pretending it wasn't there was not easy. But she knew the alternative was being a nervous wreck and taking attention away from what was more important.

"Well, are you ready?" Chris Anntha held her hand out to Lexi.

"Not at all." Lexi took the offered hand in her own, thankful she wasn't doing this on her own for once. Even if it wasn't Chaz.

Lexi took a moment to be thankful for at least one thing that had changed last night. Chris Anntha was going to keep her on her toes, but at least they were on the same side now.

Lexi took a deep breath, and together they made their way to the bakery.

Chapter 26

T he house was in worse shape than Lexi had hoped, but not leveled to the ground like the church. It looked like the tornado cut a path straight through the center of town. The buildings on her side of the square were the least affected, even though they all still had significant damage.

"Oh, thank the Lord. She's still standin'," Chris Anntha hurried up the front walk, dodging a pile of white picket fence posts scattered across the small front yard. "We can work with this."

Lexi didn't feel quite so optimistic. The entire turret was gone. Her dream reading nook evaporated into thin air. Or, more than likely, was laying a block over in someone's bushes. The shutters that had covered the bay window hung from their bottom hooks, swinging in the breeze. The rest of the roof over the living area was peeled back, exposing the rafters. Most of the shingles were gone. And the beautiful veranda, with Chaz's hand-carved spindles, was nothing more than a heap of sharp wood and siding.

Lexi stared up at the damage for a long time, wondering how the little money she had left was going to fix all this. And she would need money to live on for months while the work was being done. And who was she going to hire to do the work?

Who am I kidding? It's going to be Chaz.

Where was he? Was he safe? Was he lying in a ditch somewhere? She pulled out her phone to check again. She had texts waiting to go through for both Chaz and Lotus, but both still said unsent. Lexi wasn't typically one for praying, but in that moment she asked the universe for a couple of things.

Please, please let Chaz and Lotus be ok. And please help me figure out a way to fix this. Without this dream, I have nothing. I'll never ask for anything again if you can help me out here. Please. I am begging...

"Can't get in the front." Chris Anntha was picking her way back down the front walkway. "Let's go check the back."

Lexi nodded and followed. Around the back, they could see more roof damage and through to the neighbor's backyard, which explained where all the fence posts had come from.T he windows in the backdoor were shattered, but the shutters had protected the rest.

Thanks to Chaz.

Lexi pulled her key out of her pocket and stepped onto the first stair. The wood underneath her foot creaked, and the small staircase leaned away from the house.

"Oh, geez," Lexi slid over until she was up against the wall, and the porch leaned back. "Be careful. This is going to need to be replaced."

The door opened easily, pushing broken glass out of its path. Lexi bit down on her lip hard as she looked up the stairs to her apartment. Once the roof was gone, the rain had poured in. It still trickled down the stairs, puddling at her feet.

"The kitchen!" Lexi rushed through the doorway and sighed once she saw that all her equipment was still there. The walls were still standing. There just happened to be a couple of inches of water standing on the floor.

"Could be worse." Chris Anntha sauntered up behind her, putting her hands on her hips and looking around the room with narrowed eyes. "I loved my Meemaw's kitchen. But," she paused, giving the room a second sweep, "I like what you've done here."

"Really? I thought you'd hate it, like your brother."

"Well, obviously you needed to make some changes. It's not like you could run a full bakery out of a residential kitchen. I know because I've tried." Chris Anntha leaned back against the counter, as nonchalant as her brother always was. "He really gave you a hard time, huh?"

"Oh, my gosh. Such a hard time." Lexi was so glad someone finally understood her point of view. "That man did not want to change a single thing."

"That's Chaz for ya. We always call him a stick in the mud because he wants everything to stay the same."

"Yeah, what's up with that?"

"He's the oldest of a herd of siblings." Chris Anntha shrugged and pushed off the counter with her boot. "Someone's got to keep things sane, or it would just be chaos all the time."

"Hum." Lexi took a deep breath, ready to face the worst of the damage. "Want to see your Meemaw's kitchen in its new home? Assuming it isn't crushed or washed away."

"Definitely."

They made their way slowly up the stairs, careful not to slip on the slick wood and testing each step to make sure it was secure. She hadn't set foot up here since Chaz had said it was almost complete, and now she wished she'd taken the time to see it. But maybe it was better this way. Now, she wouldn't have some glossy finished picture in her mind to compare it to.

"Oh. Oh no." Her hands flew to her mouth as she saw the damage.

Everything was soaked with dirty water, which was still puddled across most of the floor. The new walls Chaz had put up for her bedroom and bathroom were crushed under a large section of roof. Branches, shingles, and bricks lay scattered across the floor. The turret was the worst, missing parts of the walls and all the windows, as well as the entire roof. Lexi walked over, testing the floor as she went.

"Be careful," Chris Anntha warned. "We don't know what kind of structural damage there might be."

"I just need to see." Lexi felt drawn to the reading nook, or what remained of it. Water still dripped slowly onto the floor from the branches overhead. A couple of trees on the side of the house made it through the storm, but, without the roof there, their branches sagged into the room. Lexi could see straight up to the sky and across the whole town square. The path of the tornado was easy to see. It'd left a trail of destruction from one side of Fauna to the other. A deep wound that would undoubtedly leave a lasting scar.

The clouds were clearing and letting bright sunshine through for the first time. Lexi closed her eyes and turned her head to the sun's warmth. Even with the view of devastation behind her, she suddenly felt that it would be ok. The sunlight burned away some of her anxiety and fear and left behind a determination that surged through her with an intensity she hadn't expected or felt before. She finally had something worth fighting for, and she wasn't going to stand aside and let it go to waste.

Lexi opened her eyes and took in the space around her. She could see what Chaz had finished, even though it was now destroyed. He'd painted her bedroom a soft lavender and the bathroom buttery yellow. Normally, she went for bolder colors. But the softness felt right here and went so well with the sage green in the kitchen.

How could he possibly know what I wanted? I didn't even know what I wanted.

She clenched her hands at her sides, needing to feel the pressure of her nails on her skin. Anything to distract her from the need to see him. To feel him. To know that he was okay. And once she found that out, she was going to chew him up one side and down the other for doing this to her.

With a huff, she walked over to Chris Anntha, who was staring at the kitchen. At least the roof had stayed intact in this corner, so the only issue was the water on the floor getting to the bottom of the cabinets.

"It's just like Meemaw's." Chris Anntha ran a finger along the counter, a tear trickling down her cheek.

"It's beautiful. I couldn't stand to see it go." Lexi smiled softly. "It belongs in this house."

"Thank you." Chris Anntha spun and wrapped Lexi in a hug. "I forgot how much this kitchen meant to me."

"Thank your brother. He's the one who dragged all those cabinets up here." Lexi laughed. "Now, I have a couple of brooms around here. What do you say we get to cleaning?"

"Now you're talkin' my language." Chris Anntha wiped at her eyes. "Let's get to work."

Together, they made a plan to start on the top floor and work their way to the main floor. Soon, they were sweeping water down the stairs and out the back door. Once everything had dried, they could fully assess the damage. It wasn't the best cleaning job, but it was all they could do for now. Lexi hoped it was enough.

By late afternoon, Lexi and Chris Anntha were sweating, exhausted, and covered in grime. They'd taken a break earlier, trying to find a ride out to the Walker ranch. But they were told the road was impassable because of downed trees and power lines. So, all they could do was wait. And clean. And wait some more.

Sweeping and scrubbing were the only things keeping Lexi's mind off Chaz, so she dove into it headfirst, cleaning every crevice she could get to. Silvia had passed out sandwiches to everyone hours ago for lunch, but Lexi had worked up an appetite again.

"Ugh. I would kill for a cheeseburger," Lexi leaned her ruined broom against the kitchen wall and hopped up onto the counter. They'd finished upstairs and were focusing most of their energy on the commercial kitchen. The rest of the rooms on the first floor were still pretty much empty.

"Or a big, rare steak," Chris Anntha sighed and slid up next to her. "With a baked potato and crispy fried onions."

Lexi's stomach growled so loud that they both started laughing.

"Hello?" The back door creaked open.

"Hello?" Lexi leaned forward to see who it was.

"Sorry for barging in." The insurance inspector, Harlan, stepped into the kitchen. "Oh, Chris Anntha. Hey."

"Hey Harlan," Chris Anntha said. "You doing alright? How's your family?"

"Good. Good." He slipped off his baseball cap and wrung it in his hands. "Chaz here?"

"No. You haven't seen him?" Lexi slid off the counter and rushed over, grabbing his hands in hers. "I've been hoping all day that he'd show up."

"They just cleared the road." Harlan's cheeks turned a shade of red almost as deep as his hair. "You two want a ride out?"

"Yes." Chris Anntha jumped off the counter and threw her arms around Harlan from the side. "Thank you. I can't even tell you what this means to me. I've been worried sick all day."

"Course." Harlan ducked his head and took a step back, his face impossibly redder. "I'll be outside."

"Is he always so chatty?" Lexi whispered.

"Always." Chris Anntha looked at her with a 'you know it' kind of expression. "Let's go."

They rushed out the door, leaving the soggy brooms on the back porch to dry, and hopped into Harlan's waiting truck. Chris Anntha sat in the middle, and Lexi took the window seat. It was a tight squeeze for three very dirty, extremely smelly bodies. But it didn't matter.

They were going to find Chaz.

The sun was setting as they turned down a gravel road, its shades of peach and pink melding into dark purples that bled right into the very earth itself. Its beauty was lost on Lexi, though. The only thing that mattered was getting to Chaz.

She needed to apologize. She needed to tell him she was sorry for not letting him explain himself about Chris Anntha. For going back on their agreement. For expecting more from him than she'd even given herself. For not even trying to understand his needs and why his family was so important to him. There were so many things she wanted to say.

And after I apologize, I'm going to kick his butt.

Just as much as she wanted to apologize, she wanted to tell him off. How dare he not tell her about his sister, who was turning out to be quite wonderful. How dare he not take her side on the petition. And the big one: how dare he leave her during a hurricane.

She could write off the other issues as miscommunication or misunderstanding, but there was no confusing his running away from her on the church steps. That image was seared into her brain. She hoped that wasn't the last image she had of him because it was tainted with so many bad feelings.

"Well, I'll be." Harlon leaned over the steering wheel and slowly pulled over to the side of the road.

Lexi and Chris Anntha squinted out the windshield as a pair of headlights came into view. A white truck was barreling toward them, kicking up a dust cloud to rival Hurricane Janene.

Is that...?? Could that be him?

The white truck screeched to a halt next to them, and out of the driver's seat sprang Chaz, with all his limbs intact and looking unhurt, from what they could see.

"Oh, my God." Lexi fumbled with the door handle, trying to get out of the truck. Her hands shook as she finally got it open and tumbled out into the warm arms waiting for her.

"I was so worried." She wrapped her arms around him, soaking in his warmth. Savoring the strong arms around her waist.

"I'm so sorry." He entwined his fingers in her hair. "So sorry. I never should have left."

"No. I understand." Lexi pulled back, looking at him through the tears in her eyes. "I get it. The quarterback needed to make a play with the kicker."

"What?"

"Yeah, that's my fault," Chris Anntha said sheepishly and patted Lexi on the back. "We really need to teach you about football."

Lexi stepped back, and Chaz pulled Chris Anntha into a long hug.

"I shouldn't have left you either," he said when they stepped apart. He walked over to Harlan, who'd been leaning against the hood of the truck, and gave him a huge slap on the back. "I can always count on you. Thanks, man. I owe you one."

Harlan grunted and gave Chaz a nod.

"Is the ranch okay?" Chris Anntha rushed forward again. "What about Mama and Daddy? The boys? What about Sherbert?"

Lexi stayed where she was, off to the side, watching the three of them and unsure whether she belonged in the conversation. She twisted her foot into the dirt. Chaz glanced at her and waved her over.

"Ranch is alright," Chaz said as he slid his arm around Lexi's shoulders and pulled her in tight. "We've got some pretty bad tree damage, but nothing a day or two of work won't clear up. Mama and Daddy are shaken up, but they'll be okay. The boys are... well, the boys. And Sherbert has been missin' you something fierce. Gave me a nasty bite this mornin', mind you."

"Okay," Chris Anntha nodded along, the tension draining from her shoulders. "And I'm sure you did nothing to deserve it, either. Don't think I don't know you're always pickin' on each other."

"Pick on? What? Me?" Chaz scoffed. "I would never."

"Right."

Lexi wasn't sure who or what Sherbert was, but knowing Chaz, he probably deserved what he got.

"Now, I don't want to sound mean here or anything, cause I don't know what you've been dealing with all day." Chaz held his hands up and took a small step away from the rest of them. "But y'all are filthy. And you kind of stink."

"Hey," Lexi and Chris Anntha said together.

"Not tryin' to be mean. Just callin' it like I see it. What do you say we head back and get y'all cleaned up?"

"Do you have hot water? Because I would kill for a steamy shower." Lexi groaned at the thought. "Maybe not kill, but I'd do some shady stuff right about now to get this funk off me."

"No shady stuff necessary." Chaz laughed. "The ranch has a generator and solar power. Can't rely on the electrical lines all the way out here."

"Hallelujah. Praise the Lord." Chris Anntha raised her hands to the sky. "Let's go."

Lexi turned back to climb into Harlon's truck, but Chaz snagged her wrist.

"Where do you think you're goin'?" He said as he pulled her towards his truck.

"Didn't think you'd want my stench in your truck."

"Well, I don't really," he glanced at her out of the corner of his eye with a smirk on his lips, "but I would like a few minutes with you to myself before my whole family descends on you. If that's alright."

Descends? Lexi gulped. She hadn't thought this through. Meeting the whole family? Was she ready for that?

"Um, yeah, sure."

Chaz opened the passenger door, and Lexi climbed inside. She looked down at herself while she waited for Chaz to get in. He wasn't lying when he said they were covered in filth. Her legs were caked with dirt. The gash on her shin was going to need a serious scrub and some hearty antibiotic ointment. She reached up to pat her hair and picked out a leaf.

"I can't meet your family like this," she turned to Chaz in panic as soon as he opened his door.

"Don't worry. I'll sneak you in the back. You can use the shower in my room while I go scrounge up some clean clothes for you." Then his voice softened, and he reached out to place his hand over hers as he turned the truck around. "You don't have to meet anyone until you're good and ready."

Hot water ran down her body as she watched the grime from the day wash down the drain. Until the water hit her shoulders, she hadn't realized how sore she was. She could stand there forever, just letting her muscles relax in the steam, but Chaz told her to make it snappy. The water heater didn't work as quickly on the generator, especially with three people showering at the same time.

She quickly scrubbed some shampoo and conditioner into her curls and got as much of the dirt off her skin as she could. The cut on her shin and her nails would need more work, but that could be done without wasting all the water in the shower.

"Hey, Lex," Chaz's voice came from the bedroom next door, "I've got some clothes on the bed here for you. They're my mom's, so sorry."

"Thank you," Lexi called out nervously. Having Chaz close enough to talk to while she was in the shower was unfamiliarly intimate. "They can't be worse than what I had on earlier."

"You might want to save that judgment until you see 'em." He paused for a moment. "We'll be in the kitchen. Right down the hall. Come on out when you're ready. We're makin' dinner."

Lexi's stomach rumbled at the very mention of food. She grabbed a towel and was out of the shower in thirty seconds flat. The door squeaked slowly as she cracked it open to peek into the bedroom, which was blessedly empty.

On the bed sat a combination of patterns that should never be paired together. Lexi pulled on a pair of red, fuzzy pajama pants covered in cacti saying 'Can't Touch This.'

Is his mom trying to send a message here?

She picked up the shirt, a flannel abomination of mint green and peach with pearl buttons up the front.

"I don't think anyone would want to touch me in this any-way," she cringed, feeling certain that Mrs. Walker was sending a message loud and clear.

Lexi pulled it on, but the buttons didn't quite cover her curvier areas without gaping inappropriately. Giving the Walkers a peep show was not on her list of most anticipated activities for their first meeting.

"Ugh," she groaned, looking over at the pile of filthy clothes she'd dropped when getting into the shower. She'd intended to throw them all in the trash, not put them back on. Then she saw another pile of clothes on the dresser. She picked-up a t-shirt that looked to be just her size. "Hope you don't mind, Chaz."

She pulled it over her head, relishing the woodsy smell that she'd come to associate with only one man. After a quick scrunching of her curls in the mirror, she walked out into the hall. The walls were covered with old family photos that Lexi stopped to study. So many smiling faces looked back at her. Different themed photos started with just one kid, obviously Chaz, and continued down the hallway, adding more kids and years as she walked.

Seven kids. I cannot even imagine.

Lexi's stomach grumbled again as the smell of garlic and marinara hit her nose. She could hear voices and laughter at the end of the hallway.

Well, it's now or never.

She stepped around the corner, and everyone turned in her direction. Her mouth went dry. There were so many of them.

"Um, hello. I'm Lexi."

"Lexi, honey, come in, come in," a woman she assumed was Chaz's mother ushered her over to the large island everyone was huddled around. "You must be starving. Let me get you a plate."

"I got it, Mama," Chaz stood up and offered his stool to Lexi, who slid onto it with a small smile.

"Oh, well. Ok then," his mom waved her hands like she was backing off.

Chaz returned a second later with a heaping plate of spaghetti and meatballs.

"Everyone, this is Lex." Chaz waved his hand around the circle. "Lex, this is everyone."

Chapter 27

"So, you're telling me that people pay $4000 a month for an itty-bitty apartment?"

Lexi laughed. Chaz's younger brothers were peppering her with questions about life in New York City. They seemed fascinated by practically anything she told them.

"Well, that would get you a fairly decent one, maybe without rats. Or mold. But not both. You could never get both."

"That's disgusting. Why do people live like that?" Chaz's youngest brother, Winston, asked.

Or at least Lexi thought it was Winston. His twin brother, Gavin, was sitting right next to him, and she couldn't quite keep them straight.

"Ok. Ok. That's enough." Chaz put his hands up to stop them from asking anything else. "I think we've all had a long day, and the next couple are only going to be longer. How about we get some sleep? You'll have plenty of time to assault Lexi with your questions tomorrow."

"Alright, *Dad*," one of the twins said while the other rolled his eyes. They both pushed back from the kitchen island, all lanky legs and long arms, and disappeared down the hallway calling out behind them, "Night, Lexi."

"Good night." Lexi gave Chaz a huge grin. "I don't mind, really."

"I do. I'm about to drop. This old man needs some sleep."

"Alright, *Old Man,*" Chaz's mom, Calla, mimicked the boys as she walked over. She put her arm on Chaz's shoulders and kissed the top of his head. "Go get some sleep. We've got a town meeting first thing in the morning."

"Oh, are the phones back up?" Lexi grabbed hers, anxious to hear back from Lotus or Mrs. Miller.

"No, they probably won't be up for a couple of days. We have an old CB radio that Hank got working this evening and spoke with Davis, er Mayor Bennett, a little while ago."

Lexi liked Hank and Calla Walker immediately. They had an ease about them that made it impossible not to be comfortable. And she could tell, just by watching them for this short time, that they really loved each other and all their kids. In the midst of this tragedy, there was still so much love here.

"Any word about Lotus? Or Mrs. Miller?"

"No, honey, but we'll ask in the morning."

"Okay, thanks." Lexi tried to put on a good face, but her stomach tied into a knot.

"Now, I expect Chaz will give you his room, and he'll be bunking with Harlon in the lofts?" She turned a stern eye on her son.

"Yes, ma'am. That was the plan." Chaz nodded instantly.

"Good." She patted his shoulder and turned down the hallway after the twins. "Get some sleep; we have an early morning."

"Thanks, Mrs. Walker," Lexi called out after her.

"Well, I'll get you all settled and be on my merry way then." Chaz stood up and offered Lexi his elbow. "Shall we?"

"We shall."

They made it back to the bedroom and stopped just outside. Chaz leaned against the doorframe while Lexi fought the urge to clench her hands at her sides, feeling oddly nervous. Seeing Chaz in his home territory felt different. Meeting his family had been wonderful, but she couldn't help but feel that it added more pressure.

"So, they weren't too overwhelming, were they?"

"No. Not at all. Your family is wonderful. I get now why you cherish them so much."

"They are a special bunch, that's for sure." Chaz chuckled.

"Um, did you need to come in to grab anything?"

"I'd better not. My mama would be over here in an instant if she thought I was being anything less than a gentleman."

"Oh." A blush spread over her cheeks. "That isn't what I meant."

"You sure about that?"

Lexi swatted his chest, and he caught her hand. He held it there, flattening her palm over his heart.

"I will see you bright and early." He pushed off the wall, slowly letting her hand go, and turned down the hall. "Night, Lex."

"Night, Chaz."

Lexi walked into the bedroom, closing the door gently behind her. She could barely think as she collapsed onto the bed. She drifted off, surrounded by the woodsy smell she'd grown to love so much. If the next couple of days were going to be harder than this one, she wasn't sure how she'd get through them.

It was still dark when the whole Walker family, plus Lexi, piled into several vehicles to drive into town. They drove under a large sign at the end of the driveway that Lexi hadn't even noticed on the way there. She twisted in her seat to read it.

"Walker Ranch. Established 1884." Lexi gave a low whistle as she turned back around. "That is a long time."

"Yep. Walker blood runs deep." Chaz smiled as he turned onto the gravel road.

"How big is your ranch? And what exactly do you... ranch?" Lexi picked at her nails as she looked out the window. A pastry chef should never have dirt under their nails, and it was driving her insane.

"We used to have over a thousand acres, but there were some rough times, and we lost some land a few generations back. We still got almost 400 acres now. And we *raise* cattle and sheep."

"Ahhh, so that's why you got so feisty about cattle rustling."

"Who's rustling?" Chris Anntha leaned forward and looked between them with fire in her eyes.

"The hunks in Lexi's romance novels," Chaz snickered.

Lexi jabbed her elbow into his side, cutting off his laughter with a grunt.

"Oh, yeah." Chris Anntha sat back in the passenger seat. "Those are good ones."

"What?" Chaz's head snapped to his sister, who just shrugged.

The drive into town was quick and quiet. Everyone seemed tired but on edge. As soon as they entered the square, Chaz's body stiffened. Lexi rested a hand on his shoulder, knowing how it felt to see the damage for the first time. Even with all the work done yesterday, the destruction was overwhelming.

Chaz pulled into the driveway behind the bakery. Chris Anntha slid out, but Lexi didn't move. Chaz's knuckles were white as he gripped the steering wheel.

"You ok?" she asked softly.

"Nope."

Lexi had never heard so much emotion in his voice. That single word carried the weight of the world. For a man who didn't like anything to change, this was going to be an extremely difficult day. Words would never be enough to ease this kind of heartache, so Lexi just sat with him in silence, rubbing her hand over his tense shoulders. Slowly, they relaxed, and his hands fell from the wheel.

"I didn't know it was this bad," he finally said.

"Fauna is strong. We'll figure this out."

"No." Chaz shook his head and looked at her. "How could I have left you in this? How could you ever forgive me for letting you deal with this by yourself?"

"Well, I was planning to kick your butt, but figured I'd wait until we got through today," Lexi squeezed his arm. "And I wasn't alone. I had Chris Anntha with me."

"Good." Chaz nodded slowly. "You two seem to be gettin' along now."

"Yeah. She's pretty great, actually. Somehow, I ended up hiring her for a job I didn't know I had available."

"Well, shoot. That's great, Lex." Chaz's face lit up. "Two of my favorite ladies in one place."

Lexi liked the idea of being one of his favorite ladies. It made her stomach feel warm, like she'd just taken a bite of a gooey brownie just out of the oven.

Judge, Chaz's middle brother, knocked on the driver's window, motioning them to get a move on. The rest of the family waited at the end of the driveway. When Chaz and Lexi joined them, they all started toward the city hall in the center of the square. Every available parking space was full, with cars parked out onto all the side streets. It looked like all of Fauna had shown up.

"Attention. Attention." The gavel banged down on the podium. "Can I get everyone's attention, please?"

The crowd hushed around them as Mayor Bennett raised his hands to silence them. He'd left off his linen suits in exchange for jeans, work boots, and a long-sleeved shirt. Lexi kind of missed his dapper look, but this seemed much more appropriate for moving debris. She was glad to be in a town where the leaders didn't just talk the talk but walked the walk.

"I know that Hurricane Janene has dealt us a heavy blow. The question we face now is what are we going to do about it?" Mayor Bennett paused. "Fauna wasn't the only town hit yesterday. Hurricane Janene left a trail of devastation in her wake, from Marsh Island all the way to our doorstep. I talked to Austin at Pine Belt Insurance this morning. He said they are going to see what they can do for everyone, but with the extensive damage to so many of our homes and businesses, they might not be able to fulfill everyone's claims."

The crowd around Lexi surged forward, and people began yelling questions. She could see the fear and anger on their faces. Again, Mayor Bennett held up his hands for silence.

"Quiet. Quiet please." He waited a moment. "Let me finish. We have other pathways, as always. FEMA is already on its way to the area. Since we were in a declared state of emergency, we will be eligible for federal aid. That being said, we are looking at a long road to recovery."

The crowd surged again, people talking, jostling for attention to ask questions. Lexi felt the press of bodies around her in the crowded auditorium. Chaz was at her side, but this many people always made her nervous.

"What are we supposed to do until we get funding?" someone hollered from the crowd.

"Why are we even paying insurance if they don't help us when we need it?"

"How long do we have to wait for help?"

Lexi could practically taste the fear and desperation in the air around her. She could feel her heartbeat slowly rising, faster and faster. They were expecting her to sit around and wait? Let more damage continue to happen to her home as it sat there without repairs?

No, *thank you. Not today.*

"All good questions," Mayor Bennett said. "I don't have all the answers yet, but I'll let you all know as soon as I hear."

"I'm sorry," Lexi couldn't hold it in any longer. All eyes turned to stare at her as she interrupted the mayor. "Are you actually suggesting we sit and do nothing, just waiting for federal funding?"

"Well," Mayor Bennett puffed out his chest. "Miss Caehill, you might not have gone through a hurricane before, but many of us have. This is how things work down here."

"I don't accept that." Lexi took a step forward.

"Well then, what do you propose? Are you willing to fund the rebuilding of this town?"

"I don't have that kind of money." Lexi pushed Chaz's hand off her hip, where his grip had tightened.

"What are you doing?" he hissed.

"None of us do," someone shouted, and everyone started turning back to the front of the room.

"I may not have that kind of money." Lexi raised her voice. "But I'll tell you what I do have. Two arms for cleaning and moving debris. Two legs to walk from one site to another. If we can get electricity, I have a commercial kitchen that can feed a lot of people. And I've got a heart that I gave to the town of Fauna that I'm not willing to let go of."

"That's all lovely sentiment." Mayor Bennett shook his head.

Lexi pushed her way to the front, standing beside the mayor. A fire of determination burned through her veins, overpowering her nerves. She wasn't going down without a fight this time.

"I came here with nothing more than a dream. And you know what I found? A place where people love each other and look out for one another. This was all foreign to me. No one gives you a second glance in New York City. But here? I've been told time and time again that this is what sets Fauna apart. This love and care for one another are what make this place so wonderful. And now, in Fauna's greatest hour of need, you want to just forget all that? No, I don't think so. I didn't sign up for that. I signed up for the small-town dream."

In front of her, people began to nod. The mood in the room slowly shifted from despair to a smidgen of hope.

"Now, I might not be able to do everything, but I know that if we all pitch in, we could really do something amazing here."

"And how do you plan to fund all this?" Mayor Bennett asked again.

Lexi's mind spun for a moment. Ideas popped and sparkled like fireworks. One made her gasp and left her feeling breathless.

"This will take some refining, but I do have an idea."

Mayor Bennett moved aside and motioned for her to take the podium. She thought he might be upset, but his face was eager, as were the faces of those in the crowd. They wanted Fauna to flourish just as much as she did.

"What if we all work together and focus on getting the businesses up and running again so we can start bringing income back to the town? Then we could all focus on common spaces and residences if insurance isn't able to help."

"We never get that much business. That would never work," someone hollered.

"Not unless we become the regional hub for a very lucrative industry." Lexi pursed her lips, thinking for a moment. This was the crux of her whole idea.

"And what industry would that be?" Mayor Bennett rubbed his fingers together in excitement.

"Weddings."

The crowd erupted again. Chaz took that moment to step up to the front next to Lexi.

"I'm not totally sure what you're doing, but keep goin'," he whispered. "You're losin' 'em."

"Think about it. Fauna is a beautiful town. And we have almost everything we need to make this Wedding Central for the entire Gulf Coast. In New York, people would pay top dollar for a Southern vibe at their wedding. And you have that here in bucket loads. With the right marketing, we could draw in some big clientele."

Lexi had never felt so confident about an idea in her life. They could make this work. If they all worked together.

"Chris Anntha and I have cakes covered. There's the beautiful plantation home or the church, once it's rebuilt, for venues. We have a jeweler, a salon, and a florist." Lexi pointed to the business owners in the crowd. "Fauna could be a one-stop shop for everything a couple needs."

"I'd be happy to offer deals at my dress shop," a short woman in the front raised her hand.

"And at my stationery store," another called out.

"I've always wanted to offer catering." Tia Silvia beamed at Lexi.

"I'd pitch in wherever construction is needed." Chaz stepped forward and clasped Lexi's hand with a grin.

"Well, that's a very interesting idea," Mayor Bennett stepped back up to the podium, moving Lexi to the side. "I think it's one that we should all give a lot of thought."

"Fauna is the first place that ever felt like home," Lexi smiled at everyone. "This is the first place I've felt like I've found a family." She glanced at Chaz. "Some people here might take that for granted, but it's something others look for their whole lives. And if we could offer people a taste of that, of just how special Fauna is, that would be such a gift. And I know if we all come together and bring a little of that Fauna magic, we can do this."

"Lexi's right," Chaz nodded next to her. "Now, I know we aren't all fans of changin' things around here, me included, but this could push Fauna to be greater and better than ever. And isn't that what we should always be strivin' for?"

Chaz reached down and twined his fingers through hers, right there in front of everyone. Several women's gazes shot down to their hands, and Lexi assumed this was as good as a formal declaration about where they stood. For a moment, all ideas about Fauna and rebuilding flew from her mind, and all she could think about was the man standing next to her.

Take that, ladies of Fauna.

"Fauna is a truly special place." Chaz glanced at her with a smile, his eyes flashing gold. "Lexi's idea would not only remind all of us of that, but allow us to share a little of it with others."

Lexi didn't even hear what Mayor Bennett said after that. She felt lighter than a Pavlova with Chaz at her side. And he'd stepped up for her, supported her in front of the town.

Maybe town meetings aren't so bad after all.

Lexi leaned into Chaz, taking a moment to collect her scattered thoughts. She looked out over the sea of faces, some of which she'd never seen before, but a good majority were people she was coming to know.

Then her eyes settled on a familiar head of curly dark hair, not unlike her own, and she felt chills run down her body. Acid filled her throat as her sister, Mia, waved at her from the back of the room. Her mom and dad stared at her with thinly veiled contempt.

"Oh God, no." Lexi's legs felt weak as she turned to Chaz.

"What? What's wrong?" He put his hands under her elbows to support her as she teetered.

One storm in Fauna wasn't enough? Now, her world was really going to be turned upside down.

"My family is here."

Chapter 28

"Lexi, you were amazing," Lotus gushed as she ran up to her after the town meeting and threw her arms around her shoulders. "This is going to be a big article. I can see it now. 'New Resident Rallies Town.' Oh! Or 'Recent NYC Transplant Reminds Residents of Fauna Magic.'"

"Lotus." Lexi's back was ramrod straight as she stared at her parents.

"Oh, or what about this one?"

"Lotus," Lexi said through her teeth this time.

"What?" Lotus stepped back, her eyes going wide at Lexi's stance. "What's wrong? If you don't like those, I can come up with something better."

"No, those were great. I'm sure you'll do amazing," Lexi softened momentarily, shifting her gaze to her friend and then back to her parents. "Lotus, meet my family."

Lotus's eyes widened, and she slowly turned on her heel, mouthing 'what?' as she spun. By the time she was facing them, she had a somewhat pleasant smile on her face.

"Well, sure is a pleasure to make your acquaintance," she said in a slightly higher pitch than normal.

"I'm sure it is," her mother said blandly. "Now if you'll excuse us, we need to speak with our daughter. Privately."

"Ok, then." Lotus turned back to Lexi and gave her a quick hug, whispering, "I'm here if you need me. I've got a nasty right hook and an even nastier vocabulary."

Lexi closed her eyes for a moment and took a deep breath. Knowing she had friends here who had her back was a new and glorious experience.

"Thank you. I've been trying to text and check on you. I'm so glad you're alright." Lexi squeezed her tightly before letting go. "Is your house ok? You dad and brother?"

"Missing part of the shop roof and some flooding, but over-all, we're alright," Lotus said, hushed and rushed. "Where's Chaz?"

"He's talking to the mayor about moving some debris, or something."

Lexi didn't quite remember what Chaz had whispered in her ear after the mayor wrapped up the meeting. Something about giving her some time with her folks and talking to Mayor Bennett. She did distinctly remember the last thing he said, though.

"I'm right here. And I'll be watchin'. If they step out of line, you let me know."

Lexi's heart swelled at the thought. She darted a quick glance his way, and he was indeed watching. His arms were crossed over his chest as he talked to the mayor. He wasn't being obvious about it, but Lexi caught his quick wink when he saw her look his way.

"Well, if this little powwow is about over, we have some things to discuss." Her mother tapped her foot impatiently on the floor.

"Yeah, then we can get out of this dump." Mia shuddered, lips curled in disgust.

"I'll come find you later, ok?" Lotus gave her hand a squeeze and walked over to join Chaz, where she mimicked his stance and squinted at her family in what Lexi guessed was supposed to be a menacing way, but just looked like she needed glasses. Regardless, Lexi appreciated her effort.

"Well, that was a lovely speech you gave."

Lexi turned back to her mother, who couldn't look more bored. Or impatient. Which was a hard look to pull off, but her mother had perfected it.

"Especially the last part about finally finding a family." Her mother looked down at her nails. "Very touching."

"Yeah, totally touching." Mia rolled her eyes, more like someone who was twelve instead of twenty-four.

"What are you guys doing here?" Lexi asked, fighting the urge to cross her own arms too, but she'd learned over the years it was better to look calm. If they knew they were getting to her, it would just be worse.

"What? Are parents not allowed to visit their children?" Her mother pouted. "You haven't even told your father hello."

Her dad was a mousy man with no real interests or concerns of his own. His whole existence was being her mother's shadow. When she was little, if he was away from her mother, he actually wasn't too bad. A little fun even. But it was hard to respect someone who let their partner treat their children the way her mother did.

"Hey, Dad," Lexi walked over and gave him a one-armed side squeeze.

"And your sister," her mother demanded.

"Hey, Mia," Lexi sighed and gave her the same awkward embrace.

"And me."

Lexi approached her mother and gave her two air kisses, one for each cheek. That was the greeting her mother preferred— no actual contact, but still appeared loving. Lexi thought it looked snooty and ostentatious. Which were two words that also described her mother.

Lexi also knew this was all for show. If there were no people around, her mother would have breezed right in and gotten straight to business. But one must always keep up appearances.

"Now, why don't we go back to your place and talk a bit?" Her mother clasped her hands together, one hand primly over the other.

"Or we could just talk here and then you can get on your way," Lexi said a little over sweetly. "Wouldn't want to keep you."

"Don't be ridiculous, Alexandra." Her mother turned herself towards the door, ending any discussion and waiting to be shown the way.

"Sure thing, Mother." Lexi barely contained her eye roll. "Let me go tell my friends where I'll be."

"No, thank you. As you said, we're in a bit of a rush. So, let's get going."

Shame and anger simmered beneath Lexi's skin. She was a grown woman, living her own life, and her mother still treated her like a small child with no autonomy or control. Why did she think she could come in here and treat her like this?

Because you've always let her before.

Lexi pulled out the bakery keys, still on their poppy keychain, and dangled them for Chaz and Lotus to see. She knew they'd understand. Her mother had positioned herself in front of the door, so Lexi had to slide around her in order to lead the way out.

"Really, Alexandra. What *are* you wearing?" Her mother huffed as they walked out the door onto the town square.

Lexi looked down at her borrowed clothes. She'd had to go with a skirt because Chris Anntha was quite a bit shorter and none of her pants would fit Lexi's long legs. But a long, flowy skirt that hit her at shin length worked just fine for her needs. And she'd paired that with another of Chaz's T-shirts. This one was from FaFoFe, or Triple F as she'd dubbed it, a few years ago.

"If you haven't looked around, we're in the middle of a disaster here." Lexi started across the lawn, stepping over debris, and not bothering to look back to see if her family was following or not. "My clothes are the least of my concerns right now."

When she reached the street and started across, her mother huffed again.

"Are you expecting us to walk there?"

"Yep."

Lexi made it across the street and stopped in front of the bakery. It brought her slight enjoyment watching her mother and sister tiptoe across the still soggy ground in their sandals. Her father offered them each an arm, and they both swatted him away.

Lexi walked toward the corner and around to the driveway at the back of the house. The Walkers' cars were all still there.

"Alexandra, you know that I have a bad ankle. The doctor said—"

"We're here."

"Oh," her mother stopped complaining and craned her neck back to take in the house. "Well, isn't this... charming."

"It was, before yesterday." Lexi hesitated. Did she really want them inside her new home? As torn up as it was, it was still *her* space. But they were here. And her mother would throw a holy fit if Lexi made her talk in the driveway. With a sigh, she pressed herself against the wall and up the leaning back steps. "Stick close to the house. These stairs need to be replaced."

Inside, it was dank and warm. Even though they got most of the water off the floors yesterday, the slight fragrance of mildew tainted the air.

"Might want to leave the door open." Lexi called out to her family as they inched their way up the steps.

They all walked in, clustering together in the center of the commercial kitchen. Lexi had no intention of showing them any other part of the house.

"Well, this is..." her mother waved a hand to encompass the whole room, "... -anyway. I'm sure you know why we're here."

"Actually, I have no idea." Lexi slid up onto the counter and swung her legs. She wasn't going to make this easy for them. "So, you'll have to spell it out for me."

Her mother's eyes narrowed into slits. "Very well. We're here for our part of the inheritance from my dear mother, rest her soul."

"You'd have to talk to her attorney about that." Lexi knew this was coming, and yet it still always shocked her at their outright entitlement.

"We already have. He said he gave it to you." Her mother sniffed. "Now, you can just write us a check, and we'll be on our way."

"I don't have your money." Lexi slid off the counter to brace herself on the floor. She needed something solid beneath her to give her strength. "As I was told, Grandma didn't leave anything for you. The money I was given was expressly for me and me alone."

"That's not at all true, Alexandra," her mother gasped. "Now, stop being greedy and hand over our money."

Stop being greedy? Seriously?

"There is no more money. It's all gone."

"What?" all three of them parroted at the same time.

"It's all gone," she said slowly.

"How could you do that to us?" Her mother pressed her hand to her chest, and Mia copied her. "After all we've done for you."

"All you've done for me?" Lexi almost laughed.

"How could you spend so much in such a short time?" Mia asked.

Just like you used to spend all my paychecks.

"Look around you. It takes a lot to open a business."

"You spent it all... on this?" her mother sputtered, tapping the big dent in the mixer. "This broken old junk?"

Just as Lexi was about to defend her choices, a knock came at the back door. Before Lexi could make it across the room, Chaz was walking in. Her heart skipped a beat looking at his strong face, set in a stern scowl.

"Excuse me. You can't just barge in here like that." Her mother clutched her necklace in an attempt to look frightened. Her father slid in front of her to be protective, but her mother shooed him away. "Who do you think you are?"

"Mom, Dad, Mia," Lexi stepped up next to Chaz, thankful for the warmth coming off him, even in the sticky air of the house, "this is Chaz."

"Ok. That tells us nothing. Who are you, Chaz?" Her mother spat out his name like the pit from a rotten cherry.

"Well, ma'am, I'm the previous owner of this home and a," he glanced at Lexi with a question in his eyes, "friend of Lexi's. I'm also the contractor working on turning this into your daughter's dream bakery."

"Oh, really?"

"Yes, ma'am. Your daughter is quite talented, and we sure are lucky to have her here in Fauna."

"Yes, well," her mother brushed off the compliments like a piece of lint on her 'borrowed' designer jacket, "we're in the middle of a private conversation. We don't need *the help* interrupting, thank you."

"Don't." Lexi's voice was barely above a coarse whisper.

"I'm sorry, what?" her mother leaned an ear in her direction, challenging her to say it again.

"I said don't." Lexi swallowed the lump in her throat. "Don't talk to him like that."

"How exactly should I talk to the hired help then?"

"With respect and decency. Like you should talk to everyone." Lexi threw her hands in the air.

"Respect is earned. And from what I see looking around this house, a contractor of this level of work shouldn't garner much respect at all."

Lexi grasped Chaz's arm, where she could feel his muscles and veins straining. She looked up at him briefly, with a quick nod, to let him know she could handle it.

And she could. Whether it was his presence lending her strength, or if Fauna had fundamentally changed her, or maybe a combination of everything, she was finally ready to put her foot down.

"We just went through a devastating hurricane. And you think this is the time to show up demanding money that isn't even yours? And on top of that, you insult the man I love, who happens to be one of the most talented people I've ever met." Lexi's voice rose with each sentence. She stepped away from Chaz, facing down her family on her own. "How dare you?"

"What has gotten into you, Alexandra?" Her mother stepped up to meet her. "You don't talk to your parents with such disrespect."

"Respect is earned. And from what I've seen, parents of your level shouldn't garner much respect at all." Lexi used her own words against her.

"Alexandra, you apologize this instant."

"I will not. And I'm going to ask you to leave. And not come back until you've learned some manners and decency."

"We aren't leaving without our money," Mia pushed herself up next to their mother.

"You get no money. Grandma pointedly wrote in her will that you three are to get nothing. Not a dime. Want to know why?" Lexi looked into their heated gazes, not caring what the fallout would be anymore. "Because none of you have ever done anything to better yourselves or anyone around you. You just use people until you can't anymore, and then you move on to the next schmuck you can manipulate and do it all over again. Well, I have been a schmuck for far too long, and that time is over. I would highly suggest you move on because I have nothing for you anymore."

"I don't know what this town has done to you, but this is not the Alexandra that we raised."

"This town has shown me what it's like to be accepted for who I am, not what I can offer. It's shown me that people really can care about others without expecting anything in return. And most importantly, it's shown me what family really should be."

Lexi's mother pursed her lips, looking Lexi up and down before realizing she'd lost this battle. With a flourish, she pulled her large purse onto her shoulder and lifted her chin.

"You'll be hearing from our lawyer, Alexandra. Come on, Mia, let's get out of this cesspool."

The three of them marched out the back door, the sound of her mother and sister's sandals slapping the damp wood floors as they went. That sound was followed by a low groan and a shriek as the back porch leaned out and they all fell into the grass and mud. Lexi looked at Chaz, and they both burst out laughing.

"Damn, girl. I am so proud of you right now." Chaz rushed at her, grabbing her by the waist and swinging her around. When he finally set her down, they were both dizzy and giggling. "I never truly understood what you meant about your family, but I get it now. And what you just did took some serious guts."

"Thank you." Lexi whooped, running high on adrenaline. "That felt so good. Like, why didn't I do that sooner?"

"Well, I'm glad you didn't. Because then I wouldn't have been able to see it."

Lexi paced the room, shaking her hands at her sides. She felt like she could move a mountain, or lift a tree off a school bus, or do any of those massive feats people say are possible when the right hormones were flying through their systems.

"Thank you for coming." Lexi grinned. "I think having you here pushed my confidence over the edge and allowed me to do that."

"Nah, I think you would have gotten there all on your own." Chaz grabbed both sides of her face, looking deep into her eyes. "You've had that fire in you the whole time. You just needed to let it breathe so it could grow."

Lexi's breath was coming in rasps, and having Chaz so close was doing weird things to her head. She rested her palms on his chest. Her eyes drifted down to his lips and then back up to his eyes, the golden color practically charged and glowing.

"So, I feel like maybe we should clear up a few things." Lexi was going to ride this high for all it was worth and wasn't backing down from anything.

"Yeah, there was a little something you said in there that I had a few questions about myself."

Lexi thought back to what she'd said to her family. *And on top of* that, *you insult the man I love, who happens to be one of the most talented people I've ever met.* Lexi grinned. Of course, he wouldn't miss that part.

"Hello? We saw some city folk leaving in a huff. Is it safe to come in?"

Lexi couldn't believe Lotus's timing. Again. That woman was a walking romance wrecking ball.

Chaz pressed a quick peck to the very tip of Lexi's nose and took a step back with a smile.

"Yeah," Lexi sighed deeply, "come on in."

Lotus scampered inside, with Mrs. Miller right at her heels. Lexi squealed and ran over to wrap Mrs. Miller in a hug. All three of them spun in a hopping, screeching mass for far too long before stepping apart.

"Mrs. Miller, I am so glad you're okay." Lexi clasped her hand between both of hers. "I was so worried."

"Oh, you don't have to worry about an old bird like me. I've been through it before. I know the drill."

"Is the B&B okay?"

"Lost the front porch to a tree, and the carriage house is a complete disaster." She reached her free hand out to Chaz, who stepped over to take it. "Sorry dear. Anything you had in there has probably blown to Alabama by now."

"That's all right, Mrs. M. It was just clothes. Nothing that can't be replaced." Chaz let go and stepped back to lean on the fridge. "Sure am glad you're okay though."

"Y'all are too sweet."

"So, what happened with your family?" Lotus pushed her way in and waggled her eyebrows. "Concerned friends need to know."

"You should have seen her, y'all." Chaz whistled. "She was really somethin', tearing them up one side and down the other. I'm surprised they could still walk out of here after the whoopin' Lex gave 'em."

"You go, girl!" Lotus gave Lexi a high five. "I knew you could do it."

"No, you didn't." Mrs. Miller laughed. "You were worried about her and talking about it the whole way over here."

"Geez, Lo, thanks for having my back." Lexi pretended to pout, then smiled. "Just kidding. I didn't know I had it in me either. Until it was spilling out of my mouth."

"Sometimes that's the best way." Mrs. Miller nodded. "If you think about things too much, they just get muddled. But things that fly out are usually the most genuine."

"Amen to that." Lotus raised her hands to the roof.

"Hopefully, we won't be hearing from them for a while." Lexi crossed her fingers. "So, now that one fiasco is over, what are we doing about the other?"

"You're just moving from one train wreck to another. And with so much grace, I might add." Lotus tossed her arms around Lexi's shoulders and turned her towards the stairs.

Lexi reached back for Chaz's hand, and they walked into the clean outdoor air. The back stairs hadn't fallen completely off the side of the building, and with a little finagling, Chaz got them temporarily reattached.

"So, what now?" Lexi asked when they all had two feet squarely on the ground.

"Well, we could go back to Town Hall. People are still straggling in from the outskirts. Some are hanging around, helping move debris." Chaz pointed to the groups working around them.

"I was so impressed with your idea this morning, Lexi," Mrs. Miller said. "But I know some people are still pretty unsure about focusing all our efforts in one direction. Maybe if we stayed here today, talking to people about it, we could convince more of them over to our side."

"That's a fabulous idea," Lotus quipped. "I'll get right on it."

And off she marched to the nearest group of people hauling bags of crumbled drywall out of the flower shop down the road. Mrs. Miller was right on her heels, waving back at Lexi and Chaz as she trotted down the road.

Lexi chewed her lip. The rush of dealing with her parents was wearing off, and the thought of trying to win people over all day sounded daunting at best, hellish at worst.

"What do you say, boss? Ready to go lead these people to the light?" Chaz wrapped his arm around her shoulders and took a long breath.

"Do you think it's a good idea?" Lexi asked nervously. "Like, really?"

"I had some concerns at first," Chaz cleared his throat and looked up, like he was trying to think of the right words. "But after givin' it some thought, and talkin' to some folks, well, I think it's great. It really brings the heart of Fauna to the forefront."

"You wouldn't mind people coming in from out of town all the time? Maybe more," Lexi lowered her voice to a whisper, "big city folk?"

"Not if they're coming here to enjoy everything Fauna has to offer. Kinda like this one big city gal I know." Chaz offered her his elbow, and they began to walk down the street, arm in arm. "She came here with these big notions of bringin' the big city to Fauna. But now, she's got the right idea of bringin' the small town to the city folks. Only problem I see is..."

"Oh, Lord. What?" Lexi let her head fall onto his shoulder.

"They might not want to leave."

Lexi laughed, thinking about this onslaught of city slickers moving to Fauna, with their fancy cars on the dirt roads and their designer clothes in the humidity and heat.

"So, what now? We just have to convince everyone else?" Lexi continued nibbling her lip, looking at the small clusters of people around them.

"Want to start easy or get the hardest out of the way first?"

"Ugh. Who's going to be the hardest to convince? Let's talk to them while I still have a smidge of energy."

Chaz walked her back inside the Town Hall. With the sun fully up and no electricity for air conditioning, it was getting pretty toasty inside. Outside wasn't much better, but at least the air was moving. Inside, the air was stagnant and ripe with the aroma of the many unwashed bodies still crowded in the room.

"There ya go," Chaz pointed to one corner of the room. "If you can convince him, you can convince anyone."

Lexi looked where he was pointing and groaned again.

Hank Walker stood in the corner looking like he was about to blow steam out of his ears.

"Of course it has to be your dad."

Chapter 29

Lexi rolled out of bed, her bones aching and a headache throbbing in her temples. All night, she'd tossed and turned, wondering what she needed to do to convince people that Fauna would be the perfect Southern wedding destination.

Yesterday had been a slog, between dealing with her family and then trying to convince Chaz's dad her plan would work. Hank was a man who knew his mind, and changing it wasn't an easy feat. Lexi still wasn't sure whose side he was on. And he held a lot of sway with the other farmers, ranchers, and blue-collar families throughout the whole region.

Lexi scrubbed her face and threw her hair in a ponytail. One of the benefits of being in town yesterday was getting her suitcase from the B&B. Mrs. Miller wasn't allowing guests because of the damage being an insurance issue, so Lexi ended up back in Chaz's room at the ranch.

Not that I'm complaining.

She really enjoyed spending time with the Walkers, especially all of Chaz's brothers. She could even tell them all apart now. Winston and Gavin were the youngest twins, distinguishable only because Gavin was slightly taller, and Winston was vastly goofier. Then came Judge, who looked most like Chaz, but was painfully shy and seemed like he'd rather be surfing the dark web than doing anything else. Then came Rhys, Mr. Orderly. Then Chris Anntha, who could rough and tumble with the best of them. Lexi enjoyed watching her with the herd of boys. She didn't take any guff and could probably out sass them all. Then came the mysterious Mason. All she knew was that he'd moved away after their MeeMaw passed. The only clue about him that Lexi got was when Mrs. Walker, Calla, said she was glad he and Chaz spoke on the phone when Lexi bought MeeMaw's house. That made Lexi think Mason might have been part of why Chaz was so upset about selling, but also maybe about his abrupt change after the paperwork was signed. But that was all just an assumption and could be as far off the mark as serving overstuffed creampuffs at a formal dinner party.

The feeling of wearing her own clothes again wiped away some of her dread about the day. She pulled on her oldest pair of jeans that slid on like butter, and her rattiest, thinnest, comfiest t-shirt.

"Now that's more like it," she sighed.

It was no use getting prettied up when the only things on the agenda today were hauling debris and scrubbing walls.

She sighed again, thinking about the bakery. Her bank account was depleted. She'd be lucky if she had enough to live on for the next couple of months, let alone cover any repairs the insurance couldn't cover. Why was money always such a factor? Life would be so much easier if they could go back to a barter system.

Hey, can you fix my roof? Cool, you get cupcakes for life.

This had been one of the things keeping her up most of the night, and she had a plan in place if it came down to it. As she walked down the hall toward the smell of coffee and bacon, she knew she had to tell Chaz over breakfast. It could change all their plans moving forward, and she didn't want to start any work on the bakery today if they were just going to have to backtrack down the road.

"Good morning, Lexi," Calla called out from in front of her monster eight-burner cooktop, which she managed with ease.

"Morning, Calla. Can I help with anything?" Lexi rubbed at her eyes and yawned.

"I've got this down to a science after all these years. Why don't you pull out some juice and cups? Then everything should be ready when they all decide to come down."

"I don't know how you can be so chipper this early." Lexi leaned into the fridge and pulled out an assortment of juice jugs. "I'm used to being up early, but I'm never very happy about it."

"This is my favorite part of the day," Calla plated up a mountain of bacon and turned back to the stove. "The house is still quiet, the birds are singing, and the sunrises off the back porch are just breathtaking. You should go have a look."

"I think I will." Lexi grabbed a steaming mug of coffee and padded over to the screen door.

Outside, the Walkers had a massive, covered patio. One end had a recessed firepit with bench seating all around. The other end had a fireplace with several couches. In the center was an outdoor kitchen to rival any grill master. The whole setup was like something off HGTV.

She walked past it all towards a solitary bench set at the edge of the well-kept lawn. Beyond the fence was all grass-land, which reminded her of the always-moving waves of the ocean. The constant low mooing from the barns set her tumbling mind at ease. She snuggled down, gripping her warm mug in both hands and focused on being present in the moment. Soaking in the sounds and sensations before heading into a hectic day. The sun crested the horizon in an amazing show of hot pink piercing the velvety sky.

"Mind if I join you?" Chaz's drawl dragged out his words even more than usual in the mornings.

"Sure."

He slid in next to her, and they watched the sky change into brilliant gold and orange. Eventually, she lifted her head off the back of the bench, and he slid his arm around her. She rested her head back down on his shoulder, wiggling in with a sigh.

Is this really my life?

The morning mist burned away, and birds began to sing and swoop. The full sun was visible now, but Lexi still didn't want it to end. She wanted that moment to last. Not just because it was beautiful, but because she was dreading what she needed to tell Chaz.

"So, I'm glad we have a little time alone." Lexi cleared her throat and sat up, instantly regretting losing contact with Chaz.

"Yeah, what'd you have in mind, pretty lady?" Chaz wiggled his eyebrows.

"You are incorrigible, Chaz Walker."

"Only with you, Lexi Caehill."

Her heart fluttered, and she could feel heat rising into her cheeks. Why did he have to go and say things like that when she was trying to have a serious conversation?

She took a deep breath. "Ok. We need to talk."

"Uh oh." Chaz scooted uncomfortably on the bench. "That's never good."

"No, No." Lexi waved her hand between them. "It's nothing to do with us. Although we do need to discuss that at some point. This is about the bakery."

"Oh." He sagged with relief. "Okay, shoot."

"I don't know if you heard what I told my parents yesterday."

"I heard a lot, but I'm not sure what part you're thinkin' about."

"The part where I have no more money." Lexi looked at her lap, where her hands were clasped tightly together, her mug abandoned on the ground next to the bench.

Chaz placed his hand on top of hers, pulling one apart to twine their fingers together. He didn't say anything, just offered his steady strength.

"If the insurance can't cover all the repairs on the bakery, I won't be able to afford to fix the damage." Lexi swallowed hard, ready for the part she didn't want to say. "If it comes down to it, I'm planning to sign the house back over to you. I know what it means to your family, and I can't stand to be the person who would let it fall into disrepair."

She pulled her hand away and covered her face as tears pricked the corners of her eyes. Her shoulders shook as shame tore sobs from her throat. She'd promised she'd take care of the house, and here she was a few months down the road, not even open for business yet, and she couldn't hold up her end of the deal.

"Hey. Hey, now." Chaz pulled her to him and wrapped her in his arms. "What's all this about? Lexi Girl, you are the biggest worrywart I've ever met, and Lord help me if it isn't one of the things I love about ya."

"Huh?"

"I'm going to need you to come with me." Chaz stood and offered her his hand.

"What?" Lexi wiped at her eyes, confused.

"Come on. I need to show you something.'"

Lexi snatched up her coffee mug and took his hand. He pulled her into the kitchen. Lexi had just enough time to set her mug on the counter as he pulled her past.

"Lex and I are heading out early," Chaz called to his family. "We'll see y'all later."

A chorus of farewells followed them out the front door. Lexi barely had to for a quick wave before the door shut and Chaz was shoving her into his truck. He jogged to the driver's side and jumped in with a smile.

"Where in the world are we going?"

"You'll see."

Chaz pulled the truck into the driveway behind the bakery. Lexi looked around, but nothing had changed since yesterday. The neighbor's fence was still torn out. Her back steps were still leaning. The bakery roof was still missing in places.

Chaz opened her door and held out his hand. As she slid off the seat, she heard the banging of hammers and the buzz of a saw. Chaz grinned at her and pulled her onto the sidewalk.

"Chaz, will you tell me what's going—" Lexi stopped dead in her tracks as they rounded the corner.

The entire front of the bakery had been cleaned up. The collapsed porch was gone. All the stuff that had been strapped to the railings sat in a pile to the side, proving that Chris Anntha's plan had worked. A temporary staircase had been pushed up underneath the front door, and people were teeming in and out, some carrying lumber in, others hauling broken bits out.

"What? What's happening?" Lexi could barely believe what she was seeing.

"Ah, here's the woman of the hour," Mayor Bennett hustled over, wearing a pair of worn-in overalls. "Lexi, we're so glad you're here. We wanted your permission before we took out the damaged walls upstairs."

"I'm... I'm confused." Lexi looked between the mayor and Chaz, who was still just grinning at her.

"You didn't tell her?" Mayor Bennett swatted Chaz's chest. "You rapscallion." He ushered Lexi forward. "We had a quick city council meeting last night over the CB radios. Interesting process. Not one I'd like to repeat, but it got the job done."

"Okayyy." Lexi was starting to get an idea of where this was going, and her palms began to sweat.

"We still need to work out a few kinks, but we all love your idea and we're moving forward. As a token of our appreciation for metaphorically kicking us in the hiney when we needed it most, we're starting with your bakery."

"Mayor Bennett!" Lexi was almost speechless as she watched more people arrive wearing work gloves and bringing loads of lumber. "I don't even know what to say."

"You don't need to say anything, my dear. And please call me Davis. We're past formalities now." He patted her shoulder. "It took a big-city girl to remind us all how special Fauna is." He tilted his head, considering what he'd said. "Former outsider. You're officially one of us now. Mayor's orders."

Lexi's lips trembled as the mayor hurried over to help unload a trailer of two-by-fours. Her vision blurred as she looked at the bakery. Through her tears, she could almost see the house how it was before the storm. And how it would be again.

"You knew about this?" Lexi turned to Chaz.

"I stayed up with my dad, trying to do some late-night convincing. Then, Davis came over the CB, and my dad heard how excited everyone else was at the idea. I think he knew he was the only holdout, so he defected to our side."

Lexi didn't like that Hank still had reservations about her idea, but she knew that over time he'd come around. Especially once he saw all the good it was doing for Fauna.

"So, they're really fixing up the bakery?"

"Well, not all of it." Chaz pulled her towards the stairs. "Right now, we are in preservation mode. The main goal is to get all our buildings cleaned up enough that mold doesn't set in, and to make sure the structures are stable until we can come back and fully fix the damage. There will be a lot of roofs covered with tarps, but that's better than roofs letting all the elements in."

"That's ok." Lexi followed him up the stairs, shaking hands with everyone she passed. "As long as no more damage is being done, we can all deal with some temporary repairs."

"Exactly." Chaz waved her through the kitchen and up the back stairs, which was a squeeze as people were carrying down bags of debris for the dumpster sitting out front.

Lexi's heart still hurt seeing how much work would need to be done in her living space, but knowing it would be safe from further damage took a lot of the weight off her chest. She walked over to her reading nook again and looked out over the square. More and more cars were parking along the roads, and people were streaming into the buildings on all sides. A chorus of construction sounded all around them, punctuated with laughter and happy hollering. It was the sound of hard work, but also of joy.

It'd been a long day, and Lexi wanted to end it where it had started. The sky was just darkening, and everyone was heading home for a dinner that they more than earned with all their hard work.

Lexi stood in her reading nook, looking out over a totally different town square than she had that morning. A family she hadn't met before offered her their large fishing boat cover to use as a tarp for her roof, but it wouldn't arrive until tomorrow. Luckily, there was nothing but clear skies in the forecast.

"Pretty amazing what can be accomplished when everyone works together, huh?" She heard the stairs creak behind her, knowing only one person who'd be joining her up here.

"Sure is amazing when one little spark becomes a flame." Chaz's boots thudded across the floor until he stopped next to her.

They both stood and enjoyed the view until the sky turned black and the first stars twinkled in the sky. Lexi liked that they could be together like this. Not having to fill the space with words or activities. Just being.

Chaz's hand slid out of his pocket and wrapped around hers. The shadows etched Chaz's face in sharp angles as he looked down at her.

"You know, I've told you a lot of memories I have in this house."

"Um hum."

Their faces were so close now that his breath tickled her cheek. He reached up and tucked a rogue curl behind her ear.

"But I don't think I've told you my favorite one."

"And what would that be?" Lexi felt breathless as he leaned closer.

"This one. Right here with you."

His lips brushed hers ever so softly. Lexi saw sparks of her own as she leaned into his arms. And those sparks ignited another flame as their lips met again.

Something clicked inside her, sending a rush of joy through her entire body. Lexi had finally found her place and her person.

She was finally home.

Epilogue

Two Months Later

"We're going to need more butter."

"No, we'll be fine. I promise."

"If you say so, boss." Chris Anntha threw another pound into the mixer. "I have never seen so much buttercream in all my life."

"Welcome to the bakery biz," Lexi laughed and brushed away a stray curl with the back of her hand.

She swirled a piping bag over another dozen cupcakes before the timer went off. Lexi set it down, rushing over to pull multiple trays of croissants out of the oven and slide them onto the speed rack to cool.

"How are we looking on all those sack lunches?" She hollered to Chris Anntha, who'd moved out to the dining room turned staging area.

"Good. Just need one more box of apples to finish them off."

"There should be more by the front door. I think Frank dropped off another delivery this morning. I haven't had a chance to get to it."

"On it, boss."

"Stop calling me that." Lexi huffed.

"Why? It's what you are."

"Feels too formal," Lexi muttered to herself, getting back to the piping bag.

Footsteps thundered down the stairs, and Lexi looked up just as a freshly washed and shaven Chaz hopped off the bottom step. Butterflies erupted in her stomach, a feeling she hoped would never go away.

"Good morning, Chef," Chaz wrapped his arms around her waist and kissed her cheek. "What's on the agenda today?"

"We are just finishing up the lunches to take over to the crew." Lexi turned to him and held up a finger covered in icing.

Chaz eyed her finger, then popped it into his mouth. Lexi couldn't help but giggle. Aside from blueberry pie, Chaz also had an intense weakness for frosting.

"Ew. Gross." Chris Anntha gagged as she walked in with a half-empty box of apples. "Get a room."

"Already have one, thanks." Chaz grabbed the box and spun toward the fridge.

They both knew it was a little crazy moving in together so quickly, but with the carriage house at Mrs. Miller's destroyed, Chaz needed somewhere to stay in town. Mrs. Walker wasn't initially a fan of the idea, but after she saw how happy they were, and how much more they could help with rebuilding being in the center of it all, she finally hopped on board and even knitted Lexi a beautiful blanket for their bedroom.

"Let's get these lunches loaded up so we can get over to the plantation." Chaz snatched an apple before setting the box in the fridge and took a massive bite. "You know Lady Carmichael won't be thrilled if we're late."

"Double ew." Chris Anntha pushed at him as they both tried to squeeze through the double door. "Don't talk with your mouth full."

Lexi chuckled. It seemed siblings never grew out of annoying each other.

"I'll be right out," Lexi called when her phone rang from her pocket. "Who in the world would be calling this early? Hello?"

"Miss Caehill?" a crackly voice asked from the other end of the line.

"Speaking. Who's this?"

"This is Phil Norbert, your grandmother's lawyer. Did I catch you at a good time?"

"Sure. How can I help you, Phil?"

"Oh good. I knew pastry chefs kept early morning hours, so I wanted to catch you before you got too into things."

"Thank you. That was really thoughtful."

"I just wanted to let you know that your parents have been contacting multiple lawyers trying to file a suit against your grandmother's will."

"Oh geez. I'm so sorry if they are causing you any hassle."

"No need to worry, Miss Caehill. This is fairly common when someone as wealthy as your grandmother passes."

"That's awfully sad."

"It really is." He paused. "I wanted to let you know that your grandmother's will is ironclad. And that she had express instructions not to give your parents or your sister a dime. You haven't given them any of your inheritance, have you?"

"No sir. They tried, but I remember what you said."

"Good. Good. Your grandmother had a second addendum to her will that I didn't share with you the last time we spoke. Do you have a moment to go over it?"

"Um, sure."

Chaz walked into the kitchen, and when he saw Lexi on the phone, he cast her a concerned glance. She held up a finger and turned to lean on the counter so she could focus.

"Your grandmother knew that this would happen and wanted to have something in place to encourage you on your journey. To help foster your independence, if you will."

"Ok, Phil. I'm not really sure what that means."

"It means that if you can prove where all the money has gone from the sum I previously gave you, and if none of it went to your family, you will get another sum of equal amount. Not as a reward, but your grandmother wanted to assist you in getting out from under your parents' thumb."

"What?" Lexi stood bolt upright. "Are you serious?"

"Terribly so."

"Phil. Mr. Norbert," Lexi sputtered. "I don't know what to say."

"No need to say anything. Just get copies of those bank transactions sent over to me as soon as possible."

"Of course. Thank you."

Lexi got off the phone and turned to Chaz with a squeal.

"What's all the commotion?" Chris Anntha poked her head in.

Lexi told them the whole conversation, stopping to fill in the backstory as necessary. Which was quite a bit, since her family was so messy. By the time she got to the part about the second inheritance, they were pulling into the back parking lot at Lady Carmichael's home.

"Lexi, that's amazing." Chaz squeezed her hand.

"I know, right? Imagine all the good that can do around Fauna."

"You can't give it all away." Chris Anntha looked at her like she'd grown a third head. "You have to keep some for yourself."

"Why? This town has given me so much; there's nothing I really need."

"What about your future? You never know." Chris Anntha shrugged, with a smug look on her face as she slid out of the truck. "Maybe for a new car, or a bakery van, or maybe a wedding."

The door closing did nothing to cover up her laughter. Lexi and Chaz looked at each other for a moment and then shook their heads. They may have moved in together quickly, but that was due more to practicality. They were in no rush in their relationship. That was the Southern way of things after all, slow and easy.

Another white truck pulled up next to them. Both Lexi and Chaz waved at Harlan as they got out. Chaz went to get a box of lunches out of the back end, but Lexi grabbed his elbow, stopping him.

"Hey, hold on a minute." Lexi ran over to Harlan and whispered to him quickly, then back to Chaz. "Ok. Cover your eyes."

"What's going on?"

"Well, I've been meeting with your best friend behind your back for about a month now."

"What?" Chaz's hand fell from his eyes as he gaped at them.

"Close your eyes," Lexi insisted. "As I was saying. We've been meeting in order to make this."

Lexi held her hands out with a "Ta-Da" as Harlan pulled something large from the back of his truck.

"Lexi." Chaz's eyes darted from one detail to the next. "This is amazing."

Harlan, known throughout the region for his amazing woodworking talent, had hand-carved a sign to hang on the bakery's porch.

"Poppy's Patisserie." Lexi read the name in a bold flowing font, surrounded by bunches of the flowers themselves.

"Poppy's what now?" Chaz stumbled over the word, trying to read it.

"Told ya so," Harlan muttered.

"It's French for pastry shop." Lexi rolled her eyes. "But I suppose we can just call it Poppy's Place for short."

"Poppy's Place. I love that." His eyes turned to Harlan. "How'd you keep this secret?"

"She threatened me." He pointed at Lexi and took a step further away.

"Lexi, you can't go around threatening a man's best friend. Even if it is for a wonderful, heartfelt surprise."

"Wha—? I didn't threaten him with bodily harm or anything, geez. He's like twice my size." Lexi put her hands on her hips. "All I did was threaten not to let him eat any of the cupcakes from the bakery."

"That's even worse," Chaz exclaimed. "You did the right thing, buddy."

"You two are ridiculous." Lexi shook her head and grabbed a box of food out of the back of Chaz's truck. "Now, put that away. This food shouldn't be sitting out in the heat."

"Yes, ma'am," they both quipped and hopped to work.

Lexi carried the box into the kitchen, where a whole crew of people were already unpacking and filling the massive refrigerator. The rebuilding efforts had moved from the town square to Lady Carmichael's sprawling estate. Most of the work here would be on the grounds. So many of the ancient, Spanish moss-covered oaks had fallen during Janene.

"Morning, Miss Lexi," Dandy, the winner of the pie contest, grabbed the box out of her hands.

"Good morning, Dandy. We're still going to see you bright and early on Monday for your first day, right?"

"I wouldn't miss it for the world, Miss Lexi." The teen beamed at her.

"Great. We're so excited to have you join us."

Lexi made her way further into the kitchen, pitching in wherever she could. As soon as the food was packed up, everyone made their way outside. It was Lexi's first time seeing the backyard, if you could even call it that. It looked like acres of hedge mazes and rose gardens, with multiple gazebos and fountains.

"You can close your mouth now, dear," Lady Carmichael stopped next to Lexi. She tapped her walking cane against the brick patio, overseeing the work being done to her property.

"This is gorgeous."

"Well, it was."

"Oh, I assure you it still is."

"Well, some of us uphold higher standards."

Lexi sighed. It appeared Lady Carmichael hadn't changed a bit. Except that she'd agreed to open her home up to weddings in the future. Lexi was pretty sure it was just so she could brag, but whatever the reason was, Lexi didn't care. This was an integral part of the plan to turn Fauna into the wedding hub of the Gulf shores.

"Did you hear the news?" Lotus popped up at Lexi's shoulder.

"Why don't you tell me what news you're talking about, and then I'll let you know if I've heard it or not."

"Ugh, you're no fun," Lotus lowered her voice and looked around, but there was no one within earshot. She still whispered, "Mayor Bennett has decided not to run for reelection."

"What? Why? He's so good."

"He said he wants to retire and spend time with his grandkids."

"Well, I mean, you can't really blame him for that." Lexi shrugged. "He is getting up there in years."

"Don't tell anyone. This is my scoop, and I won't have time to write the article until we're done here today."

"My lips are sealed."

Lexi didn't think it mattered. Fauna was a small town, and everybody knew everything by the end of the day. It was both infuriating and comforting knowing that everyone had a vested interest in everyone else.

Especially now that they were all working towards the same goal. They'd made huge strides and would make more changes and additions to the town over the next year or so.

She looked out over the vast yard in front of her. Mrs. Miller was trimming hedges with her church group. Lotus had pulled on waders and was knee deep in the largest fountain, pulling out piles of dripping leaves. Chris Anntha was barking orders at a group of men who looked like deer in the headlights. Chaz and Harlan were both running chainsaws to cut up the massive branches that had fallen.

And Lexi?

Lexi was perfectly, blissfully happy.

Thank you for joining me in Fauna with Lexi and Chaz!

Simply Sweet is my debut romance novel, and I loved every minute of writing it. I hope you enjoyed it and will come back for more fun in the Flora & Fauna series as we follow the Walker siblings falling in love and seeing what makes Fauna such a magical place.

Elaina Kellogg

Simply Sweet was nominated for a Swoony Award!

Celebrating the best in clean, secular romance

Chris Anntha can lead the
town's rebuild, but can she
follow her heart to love?

Join us back in Fauna for

Brightly Shining

By Elaina Kellogg

About The Author

Elaina Kellogg loves love. As a child, she fell in love with anything fluffy. In college, she fell in love with her husband. When her son was born, she fell head over heels in love. Now, she writes sweet, cozy stories of made-up people falling in love. She also loves witty banter. And pie. She's also one of those people who starts listening to Christmas music in September because it makes her feel lovely.

Facebook: @elainakelloggwrites
Instagram: @elainakelloggwrites
TikTok: @elaina_kellogg_author

Also by Elaina Kellogg

as part of the Kaleidoscope Author Co-Op

Away from the roads and city lights, the glow of lanterns shines bright, but the glimmer of desire burns brighter in this excerpt from 'Summers at the Lake.'

Summers at the Lake

By Elaina Kellogg

A large package sat on the stoop, oddly misshapen, like an old teddy bear, mashed and abused, but lovingly smooshed back into a semblance of its original shape. Its corners were mushed in, the address smudged, and the name completely washed away by what looked like raindrops, if the dark circular stains told Gwen anything. There was no telling how long it'd been sitting there, with no protection from the elements.

Gwen sighed, mentally adding 'porch awning' to the growing list of renovations she'd need to finish before putting the cabin on the market. She shuffled the travel bags in both her hands to pull the key from her pocket. The white paper tag dangling from a piece of twine wrapped around the single key resembled the package at her feet, creased and crinkled from being stuffed in her pocket for the long drive.

She pushed the box aside with her foot so she could reach the knob without extending her arm too far with her heavy bag. The floor hadn't been swept in ages, and the thought of dirt, dead leaves, and whatever else was crunching under her heels getting onto her Louis Vuitton luggage made her lip curl. After doing a few acrobatic stretching moves to angle the key correctly while reaching around the box, she finally slid the key into place and the door clicked open.

Gwen pushed the box further inside with the side of her foot, leaving it to hold the door. Sunlight streamed in behind her, shining off all the dust floating through the air, making it look like raindrops falling. A sudden memory flittered across her mind, leaving a smile on her face. Laughter, splashing, a hand sliding down her arm to wrap around her fingers and pull her into deeper water.

"Sweet summer love," she chuckled and shook her head. "If only you knew what was going on out in that lake, Nana. You would have killed me."

Gwen's heart pinched at the thought of her grandmother. Nana passed so suddenly that Gwen didn't have a chance to be there with her, even though she'd desperately wanted to hold her hand and let her know how loved she was. It had been some time since she'd last visited. That high-paying job at a firm in Chicago had seemed like such a great idea. Gwen had every intention of looking for an assisted living place closer to her new apartment, but with the demands of the new job, months slipped by, and now it was too late.

All she had left from her Nana was a deep regret, and this cabin she thought had been sold decades ago. Gwen looked around, expecting the worst, but was pleasantly surprised. It wasn't the run-down, abandoned, rotting mess she had imagined. In fact, the décor had been updated since the last time she'd visited the summer after her senior year of high school. Gwen took a quick peek into the kitchen, two bedrooms, bathroom, and then around the living room she stood in. It wasn't a big space, but it was well laid out. Everything looked clean but slightly dated. After a few quick updates, it should sell quickly. The cabins on Johnson's Lake were always in high demand.

"How'd you hold on to this all these years?" Gwen shook her head and sank down onto the wood-framed sofa. "And how did I not know?"

She slid off her heels with a sigh and stretched out, reaching her arms above her. She'd left straight from work and driven here through the night. Her boss only gave her three days off to get everything sorted, so, including the weekend, she had five days to whip this place into shape. She would spend the first day cleaning and getting ready for the contractor's crew coming tomorrow. Even though she hadn't slept and tiredness was seeping into her bones, she didn't have time to relax.

Gwen shoved herself off the couch and lugged her bags into the smaller bedroom. It wouldn't feel right sleeping in Nana's room, even if it was bigger. The back room had always been hers, anyway. Her heart melted when she saw the old yellow quilt on the little twin bed tucked into the corner of the room. Her collection of bears sat on the shelf under the window, their colors bleached by years of sunshine. She carefully hung her clothes in the small closet and slipped out of her wrinkled pantsuit. The fabric of the t-shirt and pair of old jean shorts she pulled on was so worn it felt buttery on her skin.

"That's better." She rubbed her hands down her sides as she walked back to the living room. "Now, where do I start?"

Her eyes fell on the package still propping open the door. The tape on top was no longer holding the flaps closed and easily came off. Gwen ran a finger over the address, only making out the first three numbers and 'Camelia Lane'.

"Let's see what you've got, Nana."

She peeled back the top flaps and picked a few leaves out. Inside sat a large rectangular metal tin, closed with a simple clasp. Gwen pulled it out, expecting it to be a toolbox of some kind, or, being at the lake, more likely a tackle box. She set it on the coffee table with a thud.

"Thank goodness you're waterproof or you'd be in a similar state to *that* box," Gwen motioned to the cardboard box, which had now collapsed in on itself. Gwen chewed her bottom lip, debating whether to open it. "Well, I can't know who you belong to if I don't know what you are."

With a quick flip of the clasp, Gwen opened the metal box and knelt to inspect the contents. It wasn't lures and bobbers or a ratchet set. Inside the box were hundreds of handwritten letters, tied into bundles with colored ribbon. Gwen's eyebrows pulled together as she flipped through the stacks and stacks of envelopes. The bundles on top were yellowed with age, whereas the ones toward the bottom were crisp and white. Little tags were slipped under each ribbon, with nothing more than a simple year written on them.

Gwen gingerly picked up the top stack, reading the tag. '1943' was written in thin, slanted font. Her mind churned with ideas about what these letters could be. The past fifty years had left the paper feeling feeling light as she untied the deep red ribbon. It slid to the floor as she lifted the first envelope.

Inside was a single sheet of paper. It felt thin in her fingers. She unfolded it to find a letter, the creases and edges worn from use.

September 1943

My dearest Daisy,

I rode aboard the Queen Mary, a magnificent vessel, with thousands of other worried souls, but we made it here safely. Where 'here' is, I can't say. Not because I can't, but because I don't know.

What I can say is that I'm thankful to the universe, or God (whomever you choose to credit) for this last summer at the lake house. Meeting you has given me a reason to come home, which many of my brothers here lack.

But I will, dear Daisy, come home to you. I will...

A car door slammed, jarring Gwen back to the present. Her hand had made its way to her chest, covering her beating heart. Whoever had written this letter had been going through... something big. She set the letter down on top of the 1943bundle, walked to the porch window, and pulled the curtain aside.

An old, rusted Chevy pickup now sat next to her Mercedes in the neighbor's adjacent driveway. It looked even more ancient next to her brand-new car, which had been her first big purchase after getting the new job. And she'd only been able to afford it because they were pushing out the '97 models to make way for the new '98s. But with all its bells and whistles, it had never brought her as much joy as that old truck had. The blue paint on the pick-up was more faded than the last time she'd seen it, which she hadn't thought would have been possible, but there it was.

"No way."

Gwen felt herself pulled to the door, walking out onto the porch. She shielded her eyes from the sun as she made her way over the gravel drive. Her fingers slid over the hot metal of the hood and stopped on the drivers-side handle. Inside, the cracked leather seats looked the same. She could feel the rough, ripped edges on the back of her thighs as they'd bounced down the dirt roads. The warm hand in hers, even though it should have been on the wheel. The hard, rushed mouth crashing onto hers, nipping and eager.

"Excuse me, could you kindly remove your hand from my truck?"

Gwen jumped back slightly, her hand falling from her warm lips, at the voice directly behind her.

"It's got an expensive paint job; wouldn't want to scratch it."

Gwen smiled at the twang in his voice, goosebumps rising on her arms. She spun slowly on her heel and wished she hadn't just come off an all-night car ride.

With her long hair cascading around her face, she looked up at him through her lashes, not quite ready to meet his eyes. He was just as she remembered. The dark blonde hair that waved over his ears. The deep turquoise eyes that still, all these years later, haunted her dreams. But his boyish charm was gone. He wasn't a lanky kid anymore. He was tall, lean, and his thin shirt stretched over his broad shoulders. Gwen's fingers twitched at her side, itching to slide up and over those shoulders like she had so many times that summer so long ago.

"Well now, I might be willing to make an exception." He smiled at her, revealing the dimple in his left cheek she knew would be there. "This truck might look a little rough, but it can still give a good ride."

"Still using the same ol' line, I see." Gwen shook her head and chuckled, then fully met his gaze.

The smile fell from his face, and he took a small step back. Gwen wasn't sure if it was from surprise or wanting to get away from her. Her own smile faltered at his reaction. She'd wistfully thought about this moment so many times over the past fifteen years, but in none of those dreams did it end up with him looking like he just ate a sour lemon.

To see what happens with Gwen and Lance, check out 'Summers by the Lake' in the Kaleidoscope Author Co-Op's anthology, *Light and Longing*. Available anywhere books are sold.

ALSO BY KALEIDOSCOPE AUTHOR CO-OP

SONGS of SEAS and STARS

Madeline Dau   R.A. Krueger
Chelsea M. Brown   Katharine Bost

warmth in Winter

KATHARINE BOST ❋ CHELSEA M. BROWN
ELAINA KELLOGG ❋ MADELINE DAU

AVILABLE ANYWHERE
BOOKS ARE SOLD

Christmas
IN
Reverence Ridge

By Elaina Kellogg

**Available anywhere
books are sold**

Everleigh

By Elaina Kellogg

M onday December 20

Everleigh brushed a final layer of glitter across her eyelids and stood back to admire her reflection. It was a special day, so she'd busted out all her favorites. Her dusky eyeshadow, with its layer of silver glitter, contrasted nicely with her cherry red lipstick. Her eyebrows were plucked and filled to perfection, both cheekbones popped with a golden bronzer, and her nose was contoured to adorableness.

Everleigh grabbed her phone and turned the volume to the max. As Chuck Berry's wicked guitar riffs and upbeat lyrics blasted from the small speaker, she bebopped from her bathroom to the bedroom. The outfit she had picked out last night waited for her on the sunny paisley chair next to her bed. As Chuck encouraged Rudolph to run, Everleigh pulled on her warmest pair of long underwear. Not the most fashionable, but necessary in her line of work. Over that, she pulled on a pair of flowy black pants and an extra chunky red sweater.

She squealed a little when she slid her necklace of golden sleigh bells over her head and large wreath earrings into each ear. To complete the look, she tied each braided pigtail with red tinsel garland. Her heavy-duty black boots waited next to the front door, ready to get her through one of the busiest mail delivery days of the year. Before opening the door, she paused for a moment, wondering if there was any way to make her look more festive. Then she remembered her elf-shoe boot covers.

"You're slippin', girl." She shook her head and grabbed the boot covers, her purse, and a special gift she'd spent far too long wrapping. Before walking outside into the silent, early morning, she paused her phone in the middle of one of T. Swift's upbeat holiday tunes.

It was still dark enough to see the stars from her small porch, but just a hint of sunrise was showing over the mountaintops. The air was cold, crisp, and invigorating. At least it felt dry, and it hadn't snowed overnight, so there was no need to scrape the windshield. She pulled at the door of her well-loved Fiesta. The groans as it begrudgingly inched open felt obscenely loud in the still morning. Cringing, she thought for the hundredth time that picking a car based solely on its name wasn't the best philosophy. But shouldn't a car called Fiesta be a lot more fun than this poor rust bucket? It was irony at its finest.

As soon as she was inside and the engine finally agreed to turn over, the radio clicked on to the local morning show. Her heart pattered a little faster as a deep, sultry voice filled her car.

"We have a local time of 6:10 on this lovely Tuesday morning. Current temps at about thirty-eight. So, bundle up folks it's a chilly one. It should be nice and sunny until later tonight when we have a chance of snow. Stay tuned after these messages for our favorite part of the morning show, *Everleigh* Tells *Everything*."

As she pulled out of her driveway and crept down the road, she had her phone at the ready. She chewed her lip, waiting impatiently for it to ring. Even though she was expecting it, she still jumped slightly when her phone chirped. She answered it on speaker, the phone resting in her lap as she kept both hands on the wheel.

"Good morning, Buck."

"How's my favorite lady this morning?"

"I'm great," she responded. "How are you?"

"Better now that you're on the line."

"Oh, Buck." She could feel her cheeks heating as she rounded the corner onto Main Street. Today had to be the day he finally asked her out. It just had to be. They'd been having these morning calls every weekday for months.

"Alright, our commercial is up in ten, hold on."

The line went silent briefly as he clicked back on air. Everleigh tapped her fingers on the wheel and glanced around at the dark houses. Soon, the lights would come on and the town would be bustling with holiday shoppers and tourists, but right now it was just hers.

"We're back on the air with Everleigh, our favorite morning know-it-all." Buck's voice felt overly loud after the silence.

"Correction, Buck." Everleigh pulled the phone up to her ear. "I tell it all. I would never claim to know it all."

"Pardon me, folks. I stand corrected." Papers rustled in the background. "We had someone write in a question for you, Ev."

"Really?" She wasn't surprised. People always wanted to know something. "Do tell."

"Dear Ms. Tells Everything," Buck read. "Oh, very formal."

"I like it. Continue."

"I don't know what to get my girlfriend for Christmas this year. We've been together long enough that it needs to be something nice, but not long enough that it needs to be something extra nice, if you catch my drift. Help. Signed Clueless at Christmas."

"Well, Clueless, thanks for the abundance of details." Everleigh sighed and shook her head. "But seriously, gift giving is itself kind of a gift. Did you know, Buck, that gifts are actually one of the five love languages?"

"Um, love languages? No, I can confidently say that I did not know that."

"Yeah, so, for some people, giving gifts is the way they show love. For some people, the way they want to be shown love is by receiving gifts. So, if Clueless's girlfriend is the type whose love language is receiving gifts, he'll really need to put some thought into it."

"Come on, seriously? There are so many better ways to show love than buying people stuff. That's just materialistic."

"Well, Buck, you obviously have a different love language. But don't scoff at other people's preferred ways of showing or receiving love."

"Ok, sorry folks. I'm still learning here." Buck chuckled. "So, Ev, what's your love language?"

"Well, very fitting for this conversation, my main way of expressing love is through gifts. I put a lot of thought into presents, probably too much time actually. I always remember little things people say about what they need or want."

"And what about receiving love?"

"Wouldn't you like to know?"

To see what happens with Everleigh and Buck, check out *Christmas in Reverence Ridge* by Elaina Kellogg.
Available anywhere books are sold.

Book Two in the Reverence Ridge series,

12 Days
IN
Reverence Ridge

Releasing November, 2026